D1346140

R.J. Ellory is the author of seventeen novels published by Orion UK, and his work has been translated into twenty-six languages. He has won the Quebec Booksellers' Prize, the Livre De Poche Award, the Strand Magazine Novel of the Year, the Mystery Booksellers of America Award, the Inaugural Nouvel Observateur Prize, the Quebec Laureat, the Prix Du Roman Noir, the Plume d'Or for Thriller Internationale 2016, the Theakston's Crime Novel of the Year, both the St. Maur and Villeneuve Readers' Prizes, the Balai d'Or 2016, and has twice won the Grand Prix des Lecteurs. He has been shortlisted for two Barrys, the 813 Trophy, the Europeen Du Point, and two Crime Writers' Association UK awards.

Among other projects, he is the guitarist and vocalist of The Whiskey Poets, and has recently completed the band's third album. His musical compositions have been featured in films and television programs in more than forty countries. He has two television series and two films in pre-production, and has recently premiered his first short film, 'The Road to Gehenna'.

THE DARKEST SEASON

R.J. ELLORY

ORION

First published in Great Britain in 2022 by Orion Fiction,
an imprint of The Orion Publishing Group Ltd.,
Carmelite House, 50 Victoria Embankment
London EC4Y ODZ

An Hachette UK company

1 3 5 7 9 10 8 6 4 2

A CIP catalogue record for this book is
available from the British Library.

ISBN (Hardback) 978 1 4091 9860 4
ISBN (Trade Paperback) 978 1 3987 0814 3
ISBN (eBook) 978 1 4091 9862 8

Typeset at The Spartan Press Ltd,
Lymington, Hants

Printed and bound in Great Britain by Clays Ltd,
Elcograf S.p.A.

www.orionbooks.co.uk

Acknowledgements

As is always the case, there are a number of people without whose input and assistance this book would never have been written.

To Marie Misandeau at Sonatine Editions, for her inspired suggestion that I choose this location.

To Emad and Celia at Orion, not only for their utterly invaluable editorial advice, but also their ceaseless support and encouragement.

To Michael D., for his endless willingness to answer questions concerning geography, flora, fauna and climate.

To my wife, Victoria, for thirty-two years of patience and love.

Finally, to my remarkably devoted and generous readers, without whom none of this would matter.

I

Each and every one of us is broken, though not in the same places.

The thought occurred to Jack Devereaux as he stood in the black and waterlogged ruin of yet another burned-out building. For nearly twenty years he'd been doing this – trawling through the smouldering debris of extinguished lives, trying to answer questions that were rarely asked, trying to make sense of things that would never be understood.

This time there was a little boy, too. The father strung out on God only knew what, the child – no more than four or five – screaming from the top of his smoke-filled lungs, then finally conceding defeat. The boy had lain down beside his unconscious father, and they'd died in one another's arms. The bodies had been taken away less than an hour ago.

Jack waved at his colleague, Ludovick Caron.

'Ludo,' he said. 'It's here.'

Ludo made his way through the charred remnants of furniture, careful to avoid the incessantly dripping skeleton of beams above them. He crouched to look at the place Jack was indicating. The tell-tale emanation point, the scorching pattern, the faint swirls of colour in the floor from melted wires. These things echoed a story that was already told.

'Space heater,' Jack said.

Ludo nodded. 'Looks that way.'

'Can you mark it up? I'll get the camera.'

'Sure thing,' Ludo said.

Jack's cellphone rang. He stepped away, took it from his pocket. 'Yes?'

Minutes later, Jack stood quietly on what little remained of the front porch. He breathed slowly, purposefully, as if to quell some inner turmoil. In the bitter cold, his breath obscured the details of his face. It was dusk. The streets were empty. Somewhere in the far distance a siren wailed. Perhaps another fire. Perhaps another life extinguished.

Down on the sidewalk, the crews were rolling hoses. Men with black hands and black faces, their eyes burdened with so many things a man shouldn't see. They said little, they went through the motions, they prepared to leave.

Jack Devereaux wondered if some people were consigned to wrestle with darkness for ever.

At the other end of the line a stranger had asked if he was Jacques Devereaux.

It was the name on his birth certificate, but the French in him belonged to a history he wished was not his own. A different name from a different life.

'Yes, this is Devereaux,' Jack said. 'Who is this?'

'My name is Bastien Nadeau. I am calling about your brother, Calvis.'

'What about him?'

'I'm with the police in Jasperville.'

With those words it had all come back. The Torngat Mountains, the far-distant forests. The smell of wood fires, scorched metal, wet oilskin jackets hanging in the hallway. Damp garments frozen as brittle as slate in the morning. Crazed ice patterns – layer upon layer – on windows and walls. The bleak horizontal emptiness of the past; nothing to see but distance.

'Monsieur Devereaux, you are there?'

'Yes. Yes, I'm here. What about my brother?'

'We are holding him here in the police station, Monsieur Devereaux.'

'Holding him? Why?'

'I don't know how to tell you this. He's like a man possessed by something. Like a wild animal. He attacked a man. He tried to kill him. We don't know if the man will live.'

Jack Devereaux closed his eyes and breathed deeply.

There were few details shared over the phone. Nadeau, a sergeant with the Sûreté du Québec, had been unwilling to divulge the name of Calvis's intended victim.

Jack had listened, and when the sergeant was done talking there was silence.

Eventually Nadeau had said, 'You don't have any questions, Monsieur Devereaux? Or perhaps you have some explanation for what has happened to your brother?'

Jack hadn't replied.

'Are you coming to help him?'

'Does he need my help?'

'From what I have learned, your father—'

'I haven't seen my father in a long time.'

'Then you know that your brother is alone in this,' Nadeau had said.

'Yes.'

Again, a tense silence that spanned the seven hundred miles between them.

Jack hadn't voiced the words in his mind.

'And ... and he says these terrible things, monsieur. The most terrible things about—'

'Yes,' Jack had replied, cutting the man off before he could say anything further.

'So, you will come to help your brother?'

3

'Yes,' Jack had said abruptly, knowing that his concession was inevitable. Never a question of *if* he would return, but when. Perhaps also the reason for going back.

'I will come as soon as I can,' Jack had said, and ended the call.

The abiding memories of Jack's childhood were hurt and hunger. Sometimes the hurt was born out of hunger. Other times, the hurt was a thing all its own.

For him, even now, they were strong words. Evocative words. Words that could be folded and twisted and manipulated in so many ways.

Beyond the purely physical, the hurt was sadness, longing, a profound sense of loneliness. The hunger was just a yearning for freedom.

As a child, Jack had known all these things – with the same familiarity as the contours of his face – and yet, despite their once-seeming permanence and inevitability, he'd also known that one day he would escape. And escape he had.

But Calvis had stayed. More accurately, Jack had left Calvis behind.

Calvo. Cal. Pipsqueak, Dwarf, Kiddo, Junior, Little Man, Peanut, Shortie.

And then there was Juliette. Big Sis, Jules, Julep, Juju, Etta, Ettie. Dead for all these years.

The simple truth was that bad things happened to good people. And the past was a country with its own language, a language so very many people learned to forget. The words of that language were like songs once known by heart. Reminded, they returned, and the melody was as familiar and haunting as it had ever been.

Jasperville. A million miles from nowhere. A million miles too close.

Jack looked back at Ludo working away in the guts of the house. Ludo had the camera. Sudden flashes illuminated everything for a fraction of a second. Jack was aware of the cold on his face and hands, so much so that it stretched his skin taut. He guessed it was minus eight, maybe minus ten. Summer compared to Jasperville. He wanted to smoke, but had been quit for three years. Still he hankered for the burn in his throat, the taste in his mouth. He'd heard the first forty years were the worst.

He buried his hands in his pockets, and headed towards his friend.

No matter the road taken, it would always lead him home. Jack knew this, but didn't want to believe it.

And now, at last, the time had come. Get all the way out to Sept-Ilês, ten hours of ice roads and heart-slowing cold, then a twelve-hour train journey with no stops. Or fly out of Montréal to Wabush, take the last hundred or so miles by bus. Be there in a quarter of the time. But that would be a quarter of the time to try to understand things that still made no sense.

No, he would not fly. He would drive. He would take the train. He would be there in two, maybe three days.

And then he would find out why it had taken so long for Calvis to lose his mind.

2

The Devereauxs had once been a family. A father, a mother, three siblings, a grandfather in tow because there was no other place to send him. The history of that family was broken and wrecked, scattered in pieces and parts to the four corners of nowhere. The last one, Jacques – the boy once known as Jackrabbit – was now a man in hiding from that history.

Blood so often binds those who should never have been bound. Blood is a trail, a thread of shared experience, and – like wool unravelling from a skein – it forever attaches you to the place of origin.

And that place was Jasperville.

The name was an irony in itself. *J'espère-ville.* Bastardized over years by immigrant workers, non-French speakers. Now called Jasperville, and had been that way for as long as anyone could remember. Town of hope, and yet a more hopeless place it would have been hard to find.

Quebec. Three times the size of France. Indigenous Innu, Inuit and Métis peoples in communities and villages, hunting and trapping and wrenching survival out of a land that should never have been settled. The immigrants came for the iron ore, raping the land, paying no heed to what the aboriginals had to say.

By the mid-1960s, the population of Jasperville neared five thousand. There was a main street with saloons and general stores and a place for saddles, harnesses and hitches. Behind it was a small farrier's workshop. The farrier was second generation, as good as his father ever was, though known as a drunkard and a liar. There was a veterinarian, a schoolhouse, lodgings for visiting surveyors and other transients, a medical centre for fractures, severed fingers, burns and stitches. Anything more serious and you were in the hands of God, his sole representative a minister of uncertain denomination with three fingers missing on his right hand. The church tilted awkwardly to the left, but remained standing through one winter after another. There was a baker, a butcher, a pawn shop, a repair shop for electrical and hydraulic equipment, a post office that got letters to the train every ten days or so. Weather permitting, it was the same train that carried the quitters, the unemployables and the widows back to Sept-Ilês, then onward to whatever fate awaited them. Finally, there was the police station. A one-storey brick-built affair with a basement for the crazy-drunk, the sleeping-it-off drunk, the brawler, the thief, the adulterer who needed sanctuary while the cuckold simmered down and thought twice about murder. There was one officer of the Sûreté du Québec, and the SQ had the good sense to rotate him every two years.

The people who died in Jasperville died of natural causes and Nature herself. There was hypothermia, pneumonia, frostbite that became gangrene; there were heart attacks, livers that failed, tetanus, septicaemia, severed limbs and arteries that bled out before anyone had a chance. Sometimes there were folks buried alive beneath tons of earth, and Canada Iron, the mighty colossus that it was, would deign to compensate the widow and orphans with enough to get them out of Jasperville and never to return.

Jasperville was founded on exposed igneous rock. The winter was eight months long and bone-chillingly cold. Weeks could pass without sight of the sun. Summer saw a plague of flies and mosquitoes, and then the sun would never set. Little more than five miles from the Labrador Peninsula, it was not accessible by main road. By any road, for that matter. A half-mile out of town was a narrow airstrip, now weathered and cracked. Times past, Canada Iron had flown in geologists, metallurgists and rail engineers from the city, but once the mines, manufacturing and means of transportation had been established, there was little reason to maintain it.

To the east, the Torngat Mountains formed a peninsula that separated Ungava Bay from the Atlantic Ocean. Torngat was an Inuktitut word. It meant *place of evil spirits*. A child – a child just like Jacques Devereaux – looking out through frozen ice-crazed glass towards those vast hulks of shadow, where billion-year-old coal seams wound their way through the oldest rocks on earth, could so easily believe that such a place was the perfect home for dark and twisted things.

The Devereaux family didn't have a history in Jasperville. Jacques' father, Henri, was Montréal-born and raised, and his paternal grandparents – Cédric and Clodine – were first-generation French who'd imagined a better future across the ocean. Disappointment killed Clodine before the outbreak of the Second World War. Cédric, meanwhile, hated the notion of being a father so much that he drank himself to death to avoid it. It took more than ten years of cheap, hard liquor. Henri was an only child, and by the age of fifteen he was also an orphan.

Through the subsequent six years, Henri Devereaux worked the kind of jobs that were reserved for those who didn't read and write. He'd sworn against drink, but perhaps a slug every once in a while might have smoothed off the edges of his awkward personality. He was all kinds of mad at most everything, and seemingly afraid of no one. Irrespective of height or girth, if Henri believed a man had eyed him any way that displeased, he would unpack his fists and let loose. By the time he reached

8

nineteen, Henri had twice broken his nose, busted a half dozen ribs, cracked a clavicle, shattered some knuckles, even suffered a fractured skull.

Henri believed that the only time violence didn't solve things was when you didn't use enough. Only a woman would be capable of taming and corralling such a whirlwind. Fortunately for Henri, such a woman existed. Her name was Elizabeth Swann. The daughter of a banker who'd fled London in the midst of an embezzlement scandal, Elizabeth taught English at a school in Montréal and tried not to think about the future.

In the winter of 1956, when the temperature went south, the pipes cracked in the school basement. A man was sent for, and that man happened to be Henri Devereaux. Elizabeth volunteered to wait on. If the pipes were not repaired, then the school wouldn't open the following day.

Elizabeth's first impression of Henri Devereaux was tempered by the fact that Henri, despite his aggressive nature, was intimidated by women. The prettier they were, the more intimidated he was, and Elizabeth – though perhaps not beautiful in a classic sense – possessed an elegance that was so unlike the women with whom Henri was familiar.

'Pipes,' Henri said. His accent was laboured, his voice gruff, and – for just a moment – she was confused. It was as if he'd said *Papes*.

'I beg your pardon,' she said. 'Your name is Papes?'

Henri looked at her, frowned for just a moment, and then he started laughing.

Elizabeth didn't understand, but laughed with him.

'I am here to fix the papes,' Henri said.

Elizabeth, realizing her misunderstanding, laughed even harder.

Once in the basement, Henri produced wrenches and grips

from a canvas holdall. Elizabeth watched him work for a few minutes, and then said, 'I will leave you to it, Monsieur Papes.'

Henri was still howling with laughter as she reached the top of the basement stairs.

An hour later, Henri appeared in Elizabeth's classroom.

'It is good,' he said.

'That is really wonderful,' she said. 'Monsieur—'

'Devereaux.'

'I'm so pleased you could repair it, Monsieur Devereaux.'

'It was not a big problem.'

'If you give me your name and address, I can arrange for the bursar to send your payment.'

Elizabeth produced a pen and paper, and set it down on the desk.

'Please,' she said.

Henri looked momentarily flustered. 'I will tell you,' he said.

'It would be better if you would just write it for me,' she replied. 'And that way we can be sure of no mistake.'

Henri didn't move. His expression didn't change.

'It's okay,' he said. 'No payment.'

Elizabeth paused, and then she understood. 'You can't write, can you?' she said.

Henri looked at Elizabeth as if she'd laid bare the fragile core of his soul.

'Can you read, Monsieur Devereaux?'

Henri said nothing.

'Do you read French?'

'I didn't finish my school,' he said. 'My father died and I had to work.'

'And your mother?'

'My mother has been dead for a long time.'

'I lost my mother, too,' Elizabeth said. 'In England. But I came here to Canada with my father.'

The teacher seemed like a nice lady, but still Henri wanted to leave.

'But you speak English,' Elizabeth said. She could see that she was making the man uncomfortable, but she had a curious nature and had decided to dig.

'To work you need English,' Henri said. He smiled and shrugged. 'Enough English to say papes, anyway.'

'But you cannot read a newspaper, nor a book. And you cannot write a letter.'

'A little in French, yes, but it's not necessary for me to know these things to do the work I do.'

'Do you want to learn, Monsieur Devereaux? I could teach you to read and write.'

'I have no money for this. I cannot pay you.'

'I have an idea,' Elizabeth said. 'Could you return here at five o'clock tomorrow?'

Henri paused, wondering perhaps what feminine wile was being deployed. 'I could, yes.'

'Then please do that, Monsieur Devereaux, and I may perhaps have an arrangement that would suit us both.'

Henri touched the peak of his cap. He smiled.

'Au revoir, madame,' he said.

'Au revoir, monsieur,' Elizabeth replied.

Henri returned the following day. The arrangement was simple. The school would give Elizabeth a fee for teaching Monsieur Devereaux in her own time. Monsieur Devereaux wouldn't pay for his lessons, but he would maintain the boiler, the pipes, and other matters relating to the general upkeep of the school building. The demand on his time wouldn't be great, nor the demand on hers. Everybody won.

The lessons commenced and continued twice-weekly. Elizabeth found Henri both challenging and charming. Henri found good manners and diligence he didn't know he possessed. It was not so long before the relationship moved beyond teacher and pupil.

Elizabeth Swann – uncomplicated, trusting, fiercely intelligent yet emotionally naïve, and Henri Devereaux – tough, dependable, a man's man, awkward and unschooled in so many human matters, were married in September of 1957. William Swann, drawing on some of the money he'd embezzled, paid for the wedding. He didn't much care for Henri Devereaux. Possessed of only one daughter, he wouldn't have cared for any man save a younger version of himself. The fact that he was a widower, a fugitive from the law, a man of weak will and narrow spine, was quite beside the point. As was the case with most people, he viewed himself in a light that others couldn't see.

Within three weeks of the marriage, Elizabeth was pregnant. Juliette was born prematurely in May of 1958. Frail beyond description, there was a chance she wouldn't survive. Nevertheless, whatever she lacked in physical strength was more than ably compensated for by her spirit. It was that resolve, seemingly present from her first breath, which kept her alive for a great many more years than seemed possible. Had Juliette Devereaux known the kind of future that lay ahead of her, she might very well have given up the ghost in the crib.

In October of 1964, Elizabeth – already conscious of the degree to which her husband's moods and manners were changing – became pregnant once again.

Life had already brought pressure to bear on her. She suspected that Juliette's temperament – skittish and perpetually withdrawn – was attributable not only to the girl's basic nature, but also the overbearing way in which her father spoke to her. Juliette was afraid. That was the only way to say it. Afraid of speaking, of making mistakes, of reprimand, of loud noises, of animals, of other children. Of life. Coaxing Juliette Devereaux to engage, socialize and participate was like coaxing a sleeping tortoise from the shell.

And then there was Elizabeth's father, William, now living alone in the house he'd rented when they'd arrived in the city. The speed with which his psychological condition had deteriorated was matched only by the extent of the deterioration. It was as if parts of his mind had fallen away and been left behind. Elizabeth's concern for her father's well-being grew ever more intense, and finally – just a month before the second baby was due – she convinced her husband that it would be best for all concerned if William came to live with them. Henri didn't want the man, but was reconciled to it when Elizabeth suggested that Henri manage William's finances. Perhaps only William himself would know the full amount he'd stolen from his previous employers. Even as he took up residence in the attic room, he was still a man of considerable wealth, and Henri willingly assumed control of the numerous bank accounts William had established.

Henri and Elizabeth Devereaux's second child, Jacques, was born in June of 1965. He was neither premature nor frail. There was a visible sea-change in Henri's manner and attitude. He had the son he'd always wanted. Even William seemed to surface from the darkness. He became a doting grandfather, and by the time the boy was six months old, both Henri and Elizabeth were content to leave Juliette and Jacques in William's care. Henri, drawing on William's considerable financial reserves, spent more and more time with his family, less and less time working, and – at least for a while – life assumed an aspect that satisfied them all.

By the time Jacques was three – long since used to *Little Jack*,

Jacky-boy and *Jackrabbit* – the tide turned once more and took the Devereaux family in a very different direction.

The money had run out, near as dammit, and when Henri started pawning things to pay the rent, Elizabeth sensed that their troubles had only just begun.

She loved her husband. There was no doubt about it. However, she'd fallen in love not only with Henri as he was, but also the man she'd believed he would become. Problems arose when it became clear this belief would never be realized.

Elizabeth was filled with anxiety and trepidation. She thought about how things had been, about how things could be, but most of all she thought about how things were.

'This is not how I imagined our life together,' she said.

'What do you want me to do about it?' Henri replied.

'You need to find work.'

'There's no work. Times are hard for everyone.'

'But we can only go on like this for so long. I would teach again, but I have Jules and Rabbit and my father to look after.'

Perhaps another man would have lost himself in drink. Not Henri. He was determined not to follow the same path as his own father. There was also a streak of pride, something akin to a sense of duty when it came to the welfare of his family.

Opportunity knocked in early 1969.

'Canada Iron,' Henri told Elizabeth. 'They're mining in a place called Jasperville. They will give us a house, a good wage. There's a school, a hospital, everything. It will be a change from here.'

'Where is this place?'

'In the north-east,' Henri said. 'A long way, but perhaps a long way is what we need.'

Henri showed her a map. She looked closely, wondering what kind of life she could make for herself and her children in such a wilderness. She looked at her husband, her father, and then to cupboards that hadn't been well stocked for a long time.

'Very well,' she said. 'I came all the way from England for a new life. Perhaps I just need to go a little further to find it.'

3

Ludo Caron looked at Jack Devereaux and frowned. 'I didn't know you had a brother.'

'You know now,' Jack replied matter-of-factly.

'How long have we known one another?'

'The fact that you didn't know I had a brother isn't any reason to question the nature of our friendship.'

'Guess that depends on how you define friendship.'

Jack set down the gas cans and leaned against the back of his truck. 'I guess it does.'

'In fact, it's probably fair to say that I know almost nothing about your life before we started working together.'

'What do you wanna know, Ludo?'

'Do you have any other brothers?'

'No.'

'Sisters?'

'One,' Jack said.

'Older, younger? Name? Where is she?'

'Older. Juliette. She's been dead for thirty years. My mother's been dead for over twenty-five. My father...'

Jack paused. His shoulders ached. His eyes hurt. He wanted a drink, a smoke, a reason not to go.

Ludo didn't say anything.

'Anything else you want to know?' Jack asked.

Ludo shook his head.

'I guess some people don't talk about the past because they're ashamed or traumatized or ... hell, I don't know. People have their reasons, right?'

'What's your reason?' Ludo asked.

'I ain't figured that out yet,' Jack said. He picked up the gas cans and put them in the bed of the truck.

'What did Caroline say?'

'I haven't told her. She's due over at my place tonight.'

'It's strange, man.'

'What's strange?'

'All of it,' Ludo said. 'I'm helping you load your truck for some godforsaken horror of a trip up north because you've got a brother I didn't know about who's in jail someplace I never heard of. You also got a dead mother—'

'Your mother's dead, too.'

'Sure she is, but you met her, didn't you? You had dinner with my family a whole bunch of times. You even came to her funeral, for Christ's sake. I guess what's really strange is that it's only now that I appreciate how little I know about you.'

'It's not so important,' Jack said.

'I know it's not so important, but it's kind of important.'

'What can I say? Some questions don't have a good answer, just like some stories don't have a good end.'

'Fuck it,' Ludo said, and smiled. 'It doesn't matter. We are who we are, right?'

'Help me finish packing,' Jack said. 'Then we can get drunk.'

Seated in a booth at the back of a bar downtown, Jack was already three sheets to the wind when Ludo started asking more questions.

They'd been acquaintances, then work colleagues, then friends. That history alone ate up the better part of twenty years. Fire insurance investigation was where they'd met, both new to the profession, both stumbling out of one thing into a new thing like the new thing would be easier. It wasn't. It was a lot of study, and what they achieved at the end was an awkward no man's land of a job. Neither cop nor forensics nor straight insurance agent, it was a cousin of all three. The remit covered everything from failed businessmen torching properties to attempted murder. One case involved a woman dousing her adulterous husband in a litre of aged small-batch whiskey and setting him on fire; yet another a pair of siblings working on a life insurance angle that required the deaths of both parents and an aunt. Theirs was a job that required stout boots, a strong stomach, and a dispassionate view of all people, no matter how they appeared to be. In time, Jack Devereaux was good, as was Ludo Caron. Cases had seen them assigned as a team, and out of that had grown the kind of friendship realized in unplanned circumstance or necessity. Jack was the more laconic of the two, a reticence that many translated as unfriendliness. That was not the case. He was just of a mind to say only those things that needed saying. Ludo was married, a father of two girls, caught up in a whirlwind of school runs, grocery shopping, ferrying one to dance classes, another to piano. His life engendered conversation about routine and responsibility. Jack listened attentively when no one else would. It was a life that Jack believed his own parents might have had if things hadn't gone awry.

'So,' Ludo started it. 'This younger brother of yours. You say his name is Calvis?'

'Calvis, yes.'

'How much younger?'

'Seven years.'

'So you left this place ... where was it?'

'Way up in the north-east. August '84. Calvis had just turned twelve.'

'And you've not seen him since.'

'No.'

'Was there some—'

'It was an escape, Ludo. I hung in there as long as I could, and then I got away.'

'Got away from what?'

Jack smiled, but there was no humour in the expression. 'Everything,' he said.

'So this cop. He says that your brother beat the shit out of someone, yeah?'

'Enough questions. Give me a cigarette.'

'No. You quit.'

'Then get me another drink.'

Ludo headed for the bar.

Jack leaned back and closed his eyes. He merely had to think of Jasperville and it tightened the knots within. For someone who didn't know the place, it would be hard to understand how so much horizon could become such a prison.

Ludo made his way back to the table, inelegantly balancing two glasses of beer and four shots on a small tray.

'So how's Florence?' Jack asked.

'My wife is the same as always,' Ludo slurred. 'My ruin and my salvation.' He raised his glass. 'To Florence.'

Jack raised his glass, too. 'To Florence.'

'Hey, you gonna marry Caroline?'

'Marry? No, I will never marry. I told you already.'

'Marriage is a good thing. If you don't want to marry Caroline, then you should marry someone else.'

'You're too drunk to give me advice about anything.'

Ludo turned to Jack as if any movement of his head was a challenge. 'You're gonna be okay?'

'Fuck knows. I always knew I'd have to go back. Maybe when

my father died, you know? Now this has happened, it kind of feels inevitable.'

'Inevitable that your brother would do whatever he's done?'

'Sure,' Jack said. 'I'm surprised it's taken so long.'

'Man, everything you say makes me feel like ... Christ, I don't know, like you have this fucking nightmare of a past that no one knew anything about. You could have talked to me about it.'

'To what end, Ludo? It's the past. Digging around and sharing it out serves no purpose.'

'Whatever, man. I was just saying, you know?'

Ludo reached for his glass. He knocked it, and beer spilled across his hand.

'Come on,' Jack said. 'We've both had enough. Let's walk you home.'

'I ain't leaving drinks I paid for,' Ludo said.

'Then spill some more so you don't drink so much.'

They tumbled out of there a half hour later, skidding like novice skaters on the icy sidewalk. Half a block away, Ludo fell into someone's trashcans. Jack hauled him up, and they went slowly up the hill to Ludo's house.

The noise they made as they crashed along the veranda was sufficient to bring Florence out.

She glared at Jack. 'Tu es une mauvaise influence,' she said.

'Me?' he said defensively. 'Your husband is the bad influence.'

'Go,' she said. 'Get out of here before you wake the girls.'

'Je suis vraiment désolée, Florence,' Jack said.

'Don't talk French,' she said. 'Especially when you're this drunk.'

'Au revoir, Ludo,' Jack said, and clapped him on the shoulder.

'Safe journey, my friend,' Ludo said. 'Whoever your brother fucked up, I hope they deserved it.'

Jack reached the end of the road and looked back at Ludo's

house. Lights burned. Children were asleep. Ludo would be explaining himself to Florence. A real life. Real people.

Jack thought of Caroline. She would hate him when he told her he was going away. He could hear her words already, like nails being hammered into something hard and unforgiving.

4

The Devereauxs arrived in Jasperville in April of 1969.

Eisenhower was dead, Bobby Kennedy's killer was bound for the gas chamber, and the death toll in Vietnam had exceeded that of Korea. The wider world, however, couldn't have been more distant and unknown for the Devereauxs.

Alighting from the train after an arduous twelve-hour journey on the Quebec North Shore and Labrador line, Henri, his wife Elizabeth, their two children, Juliette and Jacques, and William, now sixty-two years old, stood on the platform and took stock of the decision they'd made.

There was no doubt that Jasperville was a town, but the sole reason for its existence was iron ore. Established in 1954, it had then taken seven thousand people three years to lay the rail track from Sept-Ilês. With the mines so came the workers, and the town had grown and grown again throughout the subsequent decade and a half. With a population now exceeding five thousand, the houses were like scattered building blocks between southern boreal forests and the tundras of the northern Canadian Shield. There were treeless ridges, forested valleys, numerous lakes, and in the three or four months of summer the ground was carpeted with a sea of moss and lichen.

At the station, the Devereauxs were met by a representative of the company.

'Name's Wilson Gaines,' he said. 'Housing Supervisor for

Canada Iron.' Heavy-set, jowls like a bulldog, his entire bulk wrapped in a thick hide coat, he grinned at them as if they were long-lost relatives.

Gaines indicated a young man who stood by a car ahead of the station. 'That there's my boy, Robert. He'll help us ferry everything over to your place.'

Robert was rake-thin, his hair fine and sandy-coloured. He said nothing at all, merely nodded in acknowledgement of his father's introduction.

The house had been built as one room alone, and then more rooms added haphazard and unplanned. The sense within was of a maze of odd-angled corners and irregular walls. Between landing and bedroom, the floor dropped six inches, the rooms themselves like stacked orange crates, perhaps a box intended for shoes, another for blankets, the collection all hammered together yet held more by gravity and tension than bolts and screws.

The interior – defying dimensional logic – seemed of greater size than the exterior. The kitchen was substantial. Centring it was a long and wide wooden table with benches either side, on the left a cooking range, a sink with running water, cupboards to the right, a dresser, an alcove for hats and coats and boots. The floor was stone, the wooden walls possessed of a sheen that came from years of wood resin bleeding from the grain. It had solidified, and thus gave an amber hue to the interior. Beyond the kitchen was a parlour with a fireplace, to the left of it a bookshelf, ceiling-high, shelves loaded and sagging. Many of the volumes were in French, but there were others in Portuguese and Spanish, a good few in English, too. Atlases, picture books of faraway places, half an alphabet of encyclopaedias, almanacs, recipe books, a biography of Captain Cook with hand-engraved plates of sailing ships, distant shores, unknown peoples. Holding three-year-old Jacques on her hip, the ten-year-old Juliette traced her finger along the battered spines. It was a wonder that so many books could exist.

'Juliette, please don't touch,' her mother said.

'Oh, those have accumulated over years,' Wilson Gaines said. 'You sort of inherit them with the house. However, if you've no use for them I can arrange to have them all taken away.'

'No,' both Juliette and her mother chimed in unison.

'We would be happy to take care of them,' Elizabeth said. 'Thank you kindly, Mr Gaines.'

The top of the stairs gave onto a wide landing with four doors. There were three substantial bedrooms, a fourth room too narrow for a bed but ample for storage and the like.

The house appeared unstable, but later, as winter broke down all barriers between inside and out, when the wind howled and screeched, when blizzards were keen enough to strip the shingles right off and spin one Devereaux after another into the howling weather, that strange house held, and held firm. No matter the fury of the storm, the headcount was always the same come morning.

'And that's all there is to it,' Gaines said. 'Simple but sturdy. Please furnish as you see fit, and don't hesitate to let me know if there's any issues arising with water or electric. Robert here is very skilled with his hands. He can make and mend anything he sets his mind to.'

Robert looked awkward for a moment, as if embarrassed by his father's compliment.

'The boiler and tank?' Henri asked.

'Out beyond the kitchen,' Gaines said. 'Looks like it was built before Noah was a babe, but it's as dependable as you'll get. Get that going and the place'll be plenty warm enough. Oil is supplied by Canada Iron. Never a shortage, so don't be concerned about that.'

'That'll do just fine,' Henri said.

'Good. Tomorrow morning you report up to the administration office. No later than nine o'clock. They'll have prepared your documents, your work detail, your training programme and all that.'

Gaines extended his hand. Henri took it and they shook.

'Welcome to Jasperville,' Gaines said. 'Welcome to the Canada Iron family. We're glad to have you, and we hope you'll be truly happy here.'

William held out his hand.

Gaines seemed momentarily uncertain, and then reached out and took it. 'And welcome to you too, sir,' he said.

With that, Wilson Gaines put his hat back on his head, corralled his son, and left the Devereauxs to unpack their belongings.

'What do you think?' Henri asked his wife.

Elizabeth smiled, took her husband's hand. 'A building makes a house, but people make a home.'

With almost everything still in suitcases and canvas bags, Henri walked on up to the main drag and found the general store. He bought sufficient provisions for two or three days. Upon his return, Elizabeth lit the stove and started preparing dinner.

'How is it?' she asked.

'Busy,' Henri said. 'A lot of people. Mostly French-speaking, but there's aboriginals too. Don't understand a word they're saying.'

'Montagnais-Naskapi,' Elizabeth said. 'I looked it up. They have radio out here, and the company even has its own television station. It all sounds very civilized, considering how remote we are.'

'You think we made a mistake?'

Elizabeth turned and looked at her husband. She was both level-headed and wilful. The past would remain where it was.

Regret was about as much use as a busted watch. Less, perhaps. At least a busted watch gave up the correct time twice daily.

'People spend their whole lives wondering about what might have been, Henri. We made the decision. Now, whatever comes, we make the best of it.'

Henri reached out and took her hand. He kissed it.

'You're like an anchor for me,' he said.

'Well, that would make you a boat, would it not? And we have found this safe harbour together.'

Later, after nightfall, Jacques in his crib, Juliette lay awake. She was unsettled by the strangeness of this new place. Through the small window above her bed, she could see a handful of lights, mere flickers and flashes, like promises of gold in the depth of the riverbed. So unlike the city where she'd been born and spent the first ten years of her life, this place was a wild country, a place for pioneers and outlaws. Who would want to live here, so far from anywhere and anyone? People who wanted a different life, perhaps. Or those who wished to escape some former life.

She wondered which of these best described her father. She loved him, she trusted him, but not in the same way that she loved and trusted her mother. Hard to fathom, it was as if two men resided in the same body. That was the only way she could understand it. Her father and his shadow, no longer separate, but pressed together within the same mortal frame. Perhaps there was a battle between the two, she thought, and then she turned her mind to other things.

Elizabeth also lay awake. She listened to the sound of her husband's breathing. Beyond that there was nothing but the groaning and shudder of the heating pipes, the yawing and creaking of the timber, the ghosts of wind, the far-distant whoop and shrill of unknown birds. They were faraway sounds, unfamiliar, somehow unwelcoming. She was here because of her husband. She was in Canada because of her father. She was no anchor, despite what Henri said. She was the boat – cast adrift, without compass or sail. She had no idea of how the tides would carry her, nor to which horizon. Never one to succumb to superstition, she nevertheless felt a strange sense of disquiet when looking toward the future.

Elizabeth worried little for her father, and not at all for herself. She worried for the children, what this strange new present would hold for them. Most of all she worried for her husband, and the man he might become.

5

Jack had been home less than half an hour when Caroline came through the door.

'Who were you drinking with?' she asked.

'Ludo.'

'Celebrating something without me?'

'No, Caroline. I wasn't celebrating anything.'

Jack sat down at the kitchen table.

'I have to go away,' he said.

'Go away? Go away where?'

'Up north. Something has happened with my brother.'

Caroline's expression was one of concern. 'The brother you never talk about, right?'

'Only one I got.'

'So?'

'A cop called me. They have him locked up. Apparently he beat someone half to death.'

'And after God only knows how many years, you're going to see him?'

'Yes.'

'So take me with you.'

Jack Devereaux looked at the woman with whom he'd maintained some semblance of a relationship for the last two and a half years. Caroline Vallat was thirty-eight years old, the same age as Calvis, seven years Jack's junior. Jack believed he could have loved her, but he didn't really believe in love. She was a strong woman, a fighter. She'd wrenched herself away from a difficult past. She deserved better than Jack, but she didn't know it.

'You don't have a dog in this fight,' Jack said.

Caroline frowned and shook her head. 'Only you would say something like that. What does that even mean?'

'It means it's not your business. More importantly, it's not something I want you to get involved in.'

'If I'm involved with you, then I'm involved in every part of your life.'

'The things I have to work out with my brother don't concern you.'

'How long are you going to be away for?'

'I don't know.'

'Have you spoken to your superintendent?' she asked.

'It won't be a problem. I'll take compassionate leave for a week. If needed, I can use some vacation time. Ludo can cover my existing cases.'

Caroline folded her arms. Her expression was defiant. It was a familiar stance. 'It's not right. This isn't the way a relationship is supposed to be.'

'Okay.'

'What do you mean "Okay"? What the hell does that mean?'

'Doesn't mean anything, Caroline.'

'Well, it should mean something. You should want me to go with you.'

'Why?'

'Just because.'

'That's not a reason,' Jack said. 'There are plenty of reasons for you not to come.'

'You promised me a vacation. If you're going to use vacation days, then you should absolutely let me come.'

'No one goes to Jasperville for a vacation. You think it's cold here? Out there is a wilderness. Winter is eight months. There's times when the sun doesn't rise for days, sometimes weeks on end. Minus twenty, minus thirty. It's just an empty frozen hell, Caroline, and within a day, within hours, you would be begging me to get you back to the city.'

'This isn't how I want things to be.'

'You think I want it to be this way? My brother's in jail.'

'I was talking about us.'

Jack felt the tide of his thoughts slow to a crawl.

'Whatever you're trying to work out, it doesn't concern me,' he said.

'You know, you're just unbearable sometimes. Truly unbearable. Christ almighty, even when I'm here you spend most of the time with your nose in some damned book.'

Jack didn't rise to the bait.

'So what has to happen before something happens?' Caroline asked.

'Depends what you expect.'

'Consistency, reliability, the truth, maybe?'

'The truth about what?'

'About you and me. About what we're doing. About where we're going.'

'I'm going to Jasperville, Caroline. I have to get up real early, so it's probably best if you go home.'

Exasperation emanated from every pore of her. Jack could feel it thickening the air between them.

'You have to be the most stubborn man to ever walk the face of the earth,' she said.

Jack doubted that, but didn't challenge her.

'You're going to call me, right?'

'If the lines are down, then—'

30

'You have a cellphone, Jack. You can call me with your cell-phone.'

'Out there a cellphone is about as much use as a square wheel. Most of the people who live out there haven't even seen one.'

'So correct me if I'm wrong. You're going without me. You have no idea for how long. I'm not going to hear from you, and there's no way to find out when you're coming back.'

Jack shrugged. He was thinking about Calvis. Last time they'd spoken, Calvis was twelve. Just the thought of how things had been, what he'd left behind, everything from which he'd fled, gave him a deep sense of unease. Jasperville represented the sum total of his fears.

'I need to get some sleep,' Jack said. He took a step toward Caroline. He intended to hold her close, perhaps just to remind her that he was real. They had a history together, even though both of them would tell it a very different way.

Caroline's expression spoke of hope, followed swiftly by betrayal.

All you need is patience, he wanted to say. *Give it enough time and everything good goes bad.*

'To hell with you,' she said. 'We're done.' With that she turned. She grabbed at her coat in the hallway. It fell to the floor.

'Fuck,' she said, snatching it up. The door opened. The outside hurtled in with a frigid blast. She slammed the door behind her.

Jack stood there. He was not a gambler, but he knew plenty. They didn't bet to win, but to lose. They didn't stop until every-thing was gone. Then they'd go find more and lose that, too. So maybe he was a gambler after all, but a different kind.

6

It got cold, and then the cold never stopped.

The Devereauxs' first winter was as harsh as any before. Most mornings, with ice packed against the window frames and door-jambs, it seemed unlikely they would escape the house. After Christmas, the weather became so bad that two or more days a week would see the school closed. Even with the boiler running full tilt, it was necessary to keep both the fire and the stove stoked.

Once a teacher always a teacher, Elizabeth sat with Juliette and tutored her: times tables, long division, trigonometry, algebra. Juliette had a tongue for languages, took to English like a native, enjoyed long conversations with her grandfather about this small island where her mother had been born.

Juliette, eleven years old, sharp-minded, hammered away with endless questions.

Where does the Queen live? Did you ever meet her? Why do English people eat so much for breakfast? How did such a small island build such a grand empire?

Together, Juliette and her grandfather read of Captain Cook, and with the large atlas they traced the routes he took, the islands he discovered. They hefted down the encyclopaedias, pored over the history of Abyssinia, the formation of the Alps, the history of the Americas in all their violence and beauty.

From there they learned about Babylon, the Bayeux Tapestry and the Bible.

Jacques, four years old, was an undemanding infant, seemingly content in his own company. He chattered away, often to himself, and Elizabeth would stand in the kitchen and watch her daughter and her son, acknowledging to herself that the children had never been anything other than a blessing.

Yes, the weather was unforgiving, the landscape bleak and formidable, but they were a family, and they were together. Spring would bring longer days, lighter skies, and an improvement in all things. Of this she felt sure.

As if Fate had been tempted, she began to see signs of further and more significant mental deterioration in her father as the weather changed and Juliette's twelfth birthday approached.

Despite the bitter climate growing incrementally warmer, William had taken to wrapping himself up in two or three blankets and sitting out on the porch. For hours he would seem motionless, moving only to take another swig from his flask, but then, without any forewarning, he would launch into a whispered monologue. It seemed that his mind was inhabited by a dozen other people, each of them clamouring to take centre stage.

'There's no time for this ... let me in and I will tell you everything ... but he was scalded and his skin fell clean away ... and then it never stopped raining, and it rained for a month and the trees just drowned ... but when the child lied to his father, they all knew there was no way to undo the damage that had been done ...'

'Who is Papi talking to?' Juliette asked her mother.

'People in his imagination, my dear,' she said. 'Here, come sit with me.'

Juliette took a seat at the kitchen table.

'Sometimes there are illnesses you cannot see,' Elizabeth explained. 'People get older, they forget things, they imagine things that happened to other people are things that happened to themselves.'

'Is he mad?'

'A little, yes. But we don't say that. It's called dementia. It's just a nervous disorder, and there's nothing to be afraid of.'

Elizabeth looked away for a moment. There was a palpable sadness around her.

'Will he get worse?'

'I think that's more likely than improvement.'

'I love him, Maman. I don't want to lose him.'

'We won't lose him, my dear.'

'But the things he says sometimes. They scare me.'

Elizabeth reached out and put her arm around her daughter's shoulders. She wondered how much of her father's dementia was rooted in guilt. The reason they'd fled to Canada weighed on her conscience, but William's burden would be greater. Seeing no other means of evading reality, perhaps people lost their minds and memories as a final means of escape.

'You need to understand that Papi is always there, Juliette. No matter what he says, he's still there. When he says scary things, just pretend it's someone else.'

'Like someone else is controlling his thoughts and his body?' Juliette asked.

'Perhaps, yes,' Elizabeth said. Such a notion chilled her to the bone, for such a thing seemed altogether too possible.

Juliette looked at her for further explanation, for words of consolation. Between them, for those few moments, there was an awkward silence.

'Maybe the person that controls him is not such a good person,' Juliette said.

'Oh, my darling, no ... you cannot think like that. Papi would no more harm a hair on your head than he would take off right now and fly to the sun.'

Juliette looked out towards the blanket-clad shape in the rocker on the porch.

'It's not Papi I'm scared of, but the one who takes over,' she said, and she said it so quietly that Elizabeth was uncertain if she'd heard her daughter correctly.

Elizabeth's attention went to the other side of the room. Jacques was sitting bolt upright on the floor, his expression one of bemusement, as if something was happening for which he had no explanation.

'Jacques,' she said, but the child didn't even blink.

'Jacques!' she repeated, her voice raised a little.

Jacques looked momentarily surprised. His lower lip quivered, his brow creased, and then the tears came. ¡

Elizabeth went to him, picked him up, comforted him. He settled quickly, his attention easily distracted by a toy. All the while Juliette's expression was strangely distant, as if she understood what was happening with greater clarity than anyone else.

'Maybe he saw it,' Juliette said.

'Saw what, dear?'

'The thing inside Papi's body.'

Later Elizabeth told Henri what had happened.

'I'm not surprised your father is going crazy,' he said. 'However hard he tries, a man cannot outrun himself.'

'You wish him dead so you don't have to care for him, don't you?'

Henri looked at his wife as if she were a stranger. 'Is it the case with all women that what they hear and what they think they hear are never the same? All I'm saying is that he's punishing himself for what he did. He ruined people's lives. He left people with nothing.'

'Do you think God is punishing all of us?'

'No,' Henri said. 'Men create their own punishment. God is just someone to blame.'

Elizabeth was unnerved. Children were sensitive and vulnerable. Their perceptions weren't clouded with cynicism. Though attributed to imagination, the things they saw perhaps had nothing to do with imagination at all.

She wondered then if she herself was the cause of these anxieties. Or perhaps it was something else, something real, something tangible. Perhaps it was something that had expected their arrival in this bleak and terrible place.

7

In the cold gloom of early morning, Jack Devereaux drove to Caroline's house. He parked up, then walked down and laid a bunch of flowers outside her door. She would know who they were from. She would know why.

Looking back from the truck, Jack couldn't help but see this small gesture as symbolic, like laying flowers on a grave.

Before Caroline, years before, there had been another girl. She had quit on him too. Something she'd once said really hit home.

Your heart is like an empty building. Anyone who chooses to live there is going to live alone.

At the time, it hadn't made a great deal of sense. Now it seemed to make more sense than almost anything else.

A strong relationship was built on strong foundations – communication, openness, honesty – but when one person possessed no foundations, how could it work?

He knew he was at fault. To have subjected Caroline to so much distance and silence had been cruel and unfair. Perhaps, for both of them, a semblance of something had been better than a reality of nothing. There had been moments of closeness, but few and far between. A man who doesn't know his own feelings will struggle to share them. A man who fears himself will fear what he can do to others. There were so many things he could've tried to explain to Caroline, but he didn't understand them himself.

Whether Caroline would hear him out when he returned – *if* he returned – was one thing. Whether he really wanted her to hear him out was a different matter altogether. For both their sakes, it might be better to let the thing die.

Jack headed out of Montréal. He had sandwiches, a flask of coffee. There was no reason for him to stop. The jerry cans in the truck bed were for the long haul at the end, the last few hundred miles of endless forest, no gas stations, not a living human soul. He would make Sept-Îles by darkness, stay over in a motel, take the train out of there for Jasperville on Sunday evening. Had it been summer, he perhaps would have driven at night, but now, with temperatures dropping into the minus teens, getting stranded was a death sentence. Even inside the vehicle, the heaters wouldn't stop the cold. Hypothermia would set in, poor circulation to the heart, the brain, the limbs. He would last two, maybe three hours at best. He knew of the confusion that set in, the utter disorientation, men with blue faces and blue fingers believing they were on fire and stripping off their clothes and running headlong into the freezing darkness. However his life would end, that wouldn't be it.

As he drove, thoughts of Calvis folded seamlessly into memories of his grandfather, of his mother, of the way Juliette's life had come to such an abrupt and horrific end.

Jasperville was all their history, and a history he'd tried so hard to forget. Little reminders were everywhere – a sound, a smell, a few seconds of a song on the radio that he hadn't heard in years. He'd left just three months after Elizabeth's body was found. Twenty-six years ago. For more than half his life he'd been away from that place, and yet it was right there, within arm's reach, still possessed of all its power.

He remembered Papi William's illness, how it seemed to invade not only his own mind, but everyone else's. Juliette did all she could to persuade both himself and Calvis that their grandfather was not a monster. To them, he seemed like one. As old as the ocean. As old as nightmares. Black eyes; no more life in them than still water. Fists like knots of twisted bone as he gripped the arms of his chair. During those rambling, seemingly incoherent spells, he spoke of dark and disturbing things, things that seemed both terrifying and altogether too real. And then he would change once again, and whatever it was that had stolen his mind just gave it back. He was Papi again. Nothing more, nothing less.

Jack focused his mind on the present. The road was empty but for log haulers, tractor trailers, the bigger pick-ups that could hold to the road through a blizzard. The predominance of vehicles was headed back towards the city. The air was a thick gunmetal grey, the light like a yellow bruise.

Even though he wasn't hungry, he ate a sandwich. He balanced the cup from his flask on the passenger seat and got three or four inches of coffee into it before he lost his nerve. He wanted a cigarette more than he could ever remember.

Jack thought of his father, how the violence crept up on them so slowly, so insidiously. Finally, it seemed as though it had never been any other way. As he remembered these things, he watched the landscape change. The changes were slight, but perceivable nevertheless. It was not so far before the landscape was beyond the reach of Man. Too hard, too cold, too desolate to be tamed. And if the people left the city, the wilderness would swiftly recover the land and leave no trace of them at all.

They never should have gone. That was the truth. His father should never have agreed to work for Canada Iron. They never should have taken William. What else could they have expected but his slow descent into solitary madness? And for himself, Juliette, Calvis, the place itself was an invitation to be afraid – lightless, lonely, nothing but strange sounds in the black of night, the ever-present sense that something dreadful lay beyond their line of sight.

Jack remembered nights he couldn't sleep, standing there on the edge of the bed and peering through the frost-crazed glass. There were things out there in the darkness, holding their breath, biding their time. Their eyes were a dull, gleaming blacklight that didn't give them away. They could hunker all night, low and squat on their haunches, their nostrils twitching to the rhythm of children's hearts. Sensing dawn below the horizon, they would skulk away, covering their tracks as they went, patient enough for a better time to steal the young. Eventually, inevitably, they would find sufficient courage to get inside the house, and they would spirit all of them away – one by one – and devour them.

And then there were the girls from the town. The ones they lost. The ones that were taken. And the stories that Papi told of what had taken them.

As a child, he'd believed in such things with enough certainty to make them real. Perhaps he still believed in them. Perhaps the memory of being that afraid was yet another thing that had kept him away.

He was beginning to understand that the ghosts were within, and no matter the direction he took, they would be waiting for him.

Night fell fast, and it was dark by the time Jack reached the outskirts of Sept-Îles. He was tired. His body was numb from the interminable drive. He'd stopped twice to put gas in the truck. It had been so bitterly cold he could barely breathe. Even the water in his eyes seemed to freeze. His coat was down-filled; beneath that he wore a thick woollen sweater, a shirt and an undershirt, but still the sensation of being stung with a million needles was all over his skin. Some said you could acclimatize, that it took years, but it could be done. Jack didn't believe it, and had no intention of finding out.

With thirty or forty miles to go, he pulled over. It seemed there was still a chance to turn back. It was meaningless, of course. He could just as easily drive back to Montréal in the morning. In theory, nothing would be easier. Had he considered it, he would've said that not even the prospect of Calvis being tried, convicted, shipped out to Donnacona or Port-Cartier Maximum Security, would have been sufficient to take him back to Jasperville. But such questions bore no connection to the emotions that he was experiencing. There was a reservoir. There was a dam. Now he sensed a crack in that dam, and it scared him.

The last time he'd seen Sept-Îles, he'd been heading the other way, all the while convincing himself that there had been no other option. Calvis was twelve years old. Almost a man in Canuck years. He was more than able to take care of himself. Yes, their father was crazy, but not truly dangerous. Calvis needed to complete his schooling, and when he was old enough he would make his own way in the world.

Despite knowing that maintaining the lie took far more work than facing the truth, Jack had kept on lying. The twisted nature of it went right through him and kept him tethered. It wasn't conscience or guilt that held him captive. It was beyond such things. As immutable as gravity, he was forever aware of its weight.

With the heaters up full blast, the feeling returned to the tips of Jack's fingers. He wanted to be somewhere that didn't require half a dozen layers of clothing.

With each mile, he felt more and more certain that whatever had really happened in Jasperville was both inevitable and inescapable. Why had he not challenged Nadeau on the phone, insisted that he explain what had happened?

Who did Calvis attack? And why?

He'd not insisted because he hadn't wanted to know, but – even more than this – because of what he feared. That Calvis – like his father, his grandfather before him – had vanished into a world of twisted delusion. That he'd attacked this man because he'd believed him to be the thing of which Papi William had spoken. The very thing that had taken those girls.

Was it as William had told them time and time again – that there was not only a Jasperville curse, but also a curse for the Devereaux family?

Jack forced himself not to think of the stories. It hadn't been real then and it was not real now. True, he'd left Calvis out there with their father, but how much of it had been that terrible, desperate place?

Jack remembered the morning they'd found out about the first girl. Lisette Roy. She'd been just seventeen years old. Juliette had known her. Everyone had known her. Her parents, Baptiste and Violetta, owned the boarding house. The sergeant at the time, Gustave Levesque, had come to the Devereaux house at first light. He and Henri had shared subdued words. Henri's expression was grave, his eyes dark. He'd left with Levesque, and hadn't returned for hours.

With the memory of that day as real as ever, Jack hefted the truck into gear and started back along the highway.

8

By the winter of 1971, there was no doubt that William had withdrawn to the place he'd spend the rest of his life. Much of the time he was quiet. When he did speak, it was primarily to the children. He told them stories of his years as a sea captain, a jungle explorer, a fire-eater in a travelling circus, a much-feared gunslinger in a western pioneer town. So many flights of fancy, but imaginative and engaging, and though Elizabeth knew they were delusions, it seemed harmless enough. He entertained Juliette and Jacques, regaled them with feats of heroic daring, and there were times she would listen from the kitchen and hear nothing but laughter.

Henri was working long hours. He'd been at the mines for over two and a half years, earning a reputation for consistency, reliability and a solid work ethic. Unlike so many of the men, he didn't drink. For the majority, the cheap whiskey that seemed to flow without end was the only respite from the cold, the monotony, the absence of anything to see but the unchanging landscape. Few had families, and thus Henri – with his pretty wife, his teenage daughter and six-year-old boy – seemed the perfect candidate for the foundry supervisor position. The money would be significantly better, as would the hours, and it was Henri's in-principle verbal approval for the post that precipitated talk of another child.

'If we're to have a third child, I don't want to leave it much longer,' Elizabeth told her husband. 'I'm thirty-four, and a woman... well, you understand well enough, don't you?'

'You're sure?'

'If you are, yes. We need to be sure together.'

'Juliette and Jacques are happy,' Henri said. 'Your father...' He shook his head, his mouth a thin line of uncertainty.

'In his mind, my father is twenty years older than he should be,' Elizabeth said. 'Wherever he is, he'll stay there. Juliette is old enough now to help me with an infant. We're not the same family we were when we arrived here, Henri.'

'Agreed, but there's another way to look at this.'

'How so?'

'Captain Cook,' he said. 'When the tide is with you, lie on your oars.'

Elizabeth laughed. 'You've been reading with the children.'

'We're in this boat together. All of us. If this is what you really want, then that's what we'll do.'

'And you? You have to want another child, too?'

'I do,' Henri said. 'Yes, I do.'

By Christmas, Elizabeth was already a month pregnant. She knew it as well as she knew her own name. She told her father. He said, 'But there are children here already. Are they to leave?'

When she told Juliette and Jacques, their excitement was almost overwhelming. Juliette wanted a little sister, Jacques a little brother. Elizabeth told them there was no way of choosing so they would have to be satisfied whichever way it turned out.

If only in small ways, the new year heralded a new life. Henri spoke of building yet more rooms at the back of the house, and as spring approached there was a sense of calm and orderly well-being. It seemed that leaving Montréal had actually been a good decision, that there was nothing in their future to fear.

The brief sense of contentment was ruptured unexpectedly, violently, not only for the Devereauxs, but for all of Jasperville.

On Monday, 7 February 1972, the body of a seventeen-year-old named Lisette Roy was discovered. She was petite, dark-haired, softly spoken, a little shy. At her parents' boarding house she took names and addresses, filled out registration cards, assisted with the preparation of meals for their guests, attended church without fail, and had never kissed a boy.

She'd been at church that Sunday. That much was known. The minister had even spoken with her, and as Sergeant Levesque of the Sûreté du Québec made his enquiries, it soon became very clear that she'd also been seen by a good number of the congregation.

After church, Lisette had returned to the boarding house and assisted her parents with the meal. There were seven guests in all, three of them known and trusted long-term residents, a middle-aged Polish doctor on his way south to Labrador City, and three newcomers, much as Henri Devereaux had once been, but young, single, eager to work.

Once the meal had been served, Lisette told her mother she would be returning a book to a friend, that she would be no more than an hour. She headed out a little after three in the afternoon. Her father saw her from an upstairs window, making her way carefully down the main drag, doing her best to avoid the deep ruts of frozen mud that bordered either side.

It was dark by five. Baptiste asked his wife about Lisette's errand. What friend? Which book? Violetta didn't know, hadn't thought to ask. The three young guests readily volunteered to accompany Baptiste Roy in the search for his daughter.

By eight that evening, the matter had come to Levesque's attention. Levesque had been in Jasperville for thirteen months, had a further eleven to serve, and then he would be rotated back to Québec City. He was methodical and conscientious, but bitterly resentful of his posting. At forty-one, still unmarried, he knew that time was running out if he was ever to have a family. He was counting the days until his departure.

Lisette Roy's seeming disappearance troubled Levesque from the first moment he heard news of it. The girl knew the environment and she understood the weather. She was sensible by all accounts, and though he didn't know her well, he did know her parents. They were good people, thoughtful and considerate, and he had no doubt that Lisette was much the same. From talking with Violetta, he appreciated that Lisette wouldn't have stayed with her friend without prior arrangement.

'She's never stayed away,' Violetta told Levesque.

'But this friend. You have any idea who this could be?'

'She has three close friends,' Violetta replied. 'Francine, Isabelle and Leonore.'

'Do you know anything else? Their families?'

Violetta was agitated and upset. 'It's hard to think.'

'I understand, Madame Roy, but you must try. Their family names. I need to know their family names.'

'I didn't ask,' Violetta said. 'Perhaps they told me, but I don't remember.'

Levesque waited with Violetta until Baptiste returned. He then went to one of the bars to speak with his friend, Juvence Morin. Morin had been in Jasperville for fifteen years, had owned and run the bar for twelve. There were few people he didn't know.

Behind the bar was a triangular dinner bell. Within moments it had silenced the rowdy herd of drinkers.

'We're looking for girls called Francine, Isabelle and Leonore,' Morin shouted. 'Does anyone here have daughters with these names?'

A man came forward. 'My daughter is called Isabelle.'

'What is your name?'

46

'Gagnon,' he replied. 'Philias Gagnon.'

'Your daughter is friends with Lisette from the boarding house?' Levesque asked him.

'Yes,' he said. 'Baptiste and Violetta's girl. I know her. She was at my house this afternoon.'

'At what time?'

'Perhaps four o'clock.'

'Was she still there when you left your house?'

'I cannot be sure,' Gagnon said.

'We go now,' Levesque said. 'To your house. I need to speak with your daughter.'

'What is this about?' Gagnon asked, evidently unwilling to leave his friends and his whiskey.

'The girl is missing.'

Gagnon's expression changed immediately. He closed his eyes briefly, muttered a few words, and then crossed himself. In the dark and the cold, missing meant as good as dead.

Isabelle had seen Lisette. Yes, Lisette had returned a book. She'd arrived around half past three, had left at quarter past four. By then it was already close to dark, but it was not so far to walk.

Isabelle, a mere fifteen years old, was visibly perturbed. Before the conversation was over, she was tearful and distressed.

'You saw her leave?' Levesque asked.

'Yes. Yes, of course.'

'And she went directly back towards the main road?'

'Yes.'

'And for how long did you watch her?'

Isabelle's eyes widened. 'I didn't watch her,' she said.

'It's okay,' Levesque said.

It was clear from the girl's expression that she would shoulder a burden of guilt for not keeping an eye on her friend.

47

'You've done nothing wrong,' Levesque assured.

Isabelle burst into hysterical tears. The damage was already done.

Back at the bar, Levesque rallied more than a dozen men. Wilson Gaines and his son, Robert, joined the search party. Between them they arranged sufficient torches. Even before they began, they knew it was a futile endeavour. Beyond the properties was nothing but black wilderness, treacherous and hostile. To prevent any man falling into a ravine, they would have to be tied together. But then, if one fell, that man would take down three or four more. There were wolves out there, bears too. If one man was attacked, then half a dozen more would die or be injured in his defence. Hence, they could search only where Lisette Roy had walked, knowing that at any point on this route she would have been close enough to call out for assistance from passers-by. Regardless, they filed out across the main drag and then walked down it from one end to the other, calling the girl's name time and again until it was nothing more than a meaningless sound that echoed into a black and frozen silence. *Lisette! Lisette! Lisette!* They did it out of duty, out of desperation. They did it because it was the only thing they *could* do. They searched sheds, stables, outhouses, looked beneath verandas and porches. They scoured every yard of the route she would have walked from the Gagnon house to her home.

It was close to midnight before they finally gave up.

Levesque went to the boarding house, delivered up the news.

'Nothing,' he said. 'I'm sorry. Perhaps she's safe, nevertheless. Perhaps she fell, twisted her ankle, found somewhere to stay warm until light.'

What he was saying meant nothing, less than nothing. They all knew she was dead. It was now just a matter of finding the body before a predator took it away.

Lisette's body was discovered less than a hundred yards from the Jasperville limits. Something had dragged her out there, and then eaten as much of her as possible before she was irretrievably frozen. Her fingers were gone, her ears, her nose, and deep gashes striated the exposed belly, the thighs, the neck and shoulders. One of her eyes was missing. Levesque suspected a bird, but there was no way to determine anything until the body thawed and a full autopsy was done. That procedure could only take place in Sept-Îles, and would be entirely dependent upon whether the girl's parents consented. There was no obvious indication of foul play. It seemed altogether unrealistic that one person could have dragged a body such a distance. An animal, however – a bear, a timber wolf, perhaps? Yes, such a thing could have happened. By law, nothing but the filing of an accidental death was required.

When the body did thaw, Levesque could clearly see bruising and swelling about the left ankle. Her head and face were too mauled to support his hypothesis, but he believed that Lisette had twisted her ankle and stumbled. As she'd fallen, she'd struck her head and been knocked unconscious. She'd lain there and died of hypothermia. There were few people about, and it took no leap of credibility to appreciate how she could have gone unseen. Folks hurried through the cold and the dark, head down, eyes forward, concentration focused on nothing but their destination.

Perhaps a black bear, but more likely a wolf, had scented her before the search began. Timber wolves were everywhere, as many as ten or twelve in a pack. Sometimes a hundred and fifty pounds in weight, a good six feet long, they could savage musk oxen, deer and caribou. A girl as petite as Lisette would have been no challenge at all. Levesque suspected a mating pair, hunting together, the two of them dragging the girl's body away and eating what they could before being disturbed. The gang of men hollering in the street, the movement of lights as they searched, had spooked the wolves and they'd bolted. If it had been a pack, they wouldn't have fled. If it had been a pack, there would have been nothing left of Lisette but bones and tracks in the bloody snow.

There was no autopsy. What remained of Lisette Roy was not shipped out to Sept-Îles to be dissected, probed and analysed. It was as if her parents saw this as losing her a second time. They were unwilling to authorize Levesque's request. It was an accident. A terrible, heartbreaking accident. Between them, Baptiste and Violetta Roy knew they didn't have enough years to come to terms with what had happened, but anything that served to prolong their agony could only make it worse.

The funeral was a town affair. Juliette went, but Jacques was not permitted. He stayed with Papi. Why that had affected him so much, he didn't know. He was six. He was nearly half the age of Juliette, and yet she was allowed to attend. It had seemed like a blunt refusal to acknowledge him as an equal member of the family.

'No,' his mother had said.

'But—'

'But nothing, Jacques. That is my word, and it's final.'

Papi had tried to explain.

'Her parents will be suffering terribly,' he said. 'It was a dreadful accident, and she was the only child they had.' He hefted Jacques onto his knee and looked at him directly. 'Can you imagine if something like that happened to Juliette? How your mother and father would feel? How terrible it would be?'

Jacques couldn't imagine it, and he didn't try. Now, in hindsight, it seemed like a prophetic omen.

When Juliette, Henri and Elizabeth returned from the

church, they were withdrawn and wordless. Juliette didn't want to play. She wanted to be left alone. Elizabeth said she had a headache. She went to her room and closed the door. Henri, despite the cold and the gathering gloom, went out to the yard and chopped wood for nearly two hours.

Jacques remembered sitting in the kitchen waiting for a meal that never came. Finally, Papi made him a sandwich, gave him a glass of milk, two cookies, and carried him up to bed.

Jacques' last memory had been of his grandfather leaning over him and smiling, that familiar haunt of whiskey, and what he'd said as his eyes began to close and his breathing slowed.

'Whatever took her, it won't take you. Nor your sister. It won't take any of us. Don't be afraid, little Rabbit. Don't be afraid.'

In late March of 1972, Baptiste and Violetta Roy closed up the boarding house and moved to Trois-Rivières. The place remained empty for just a handful of weeks. It was bought by a man called Philippe Bergeron. He arrived with his wife, Marguerite, and two young daughters, Thérèse and Carine. As if dictated by some sort of gravitational force, the Devereauxs and the Bergerons were drawn together. Henri, as newly appointed foundry supervisor, bore responsibility for the temporary berthing of newcomers. Canada Iron had maintained a monthly account with the Roys, and Henri saw no reason not to extend the same facility to the new owners. The boarding house would take as many men as could be roomed and fed; Canada Iron would pay them the going rate. Without that constant supply of work-hungry individuals, there was no way a boarding house would survive in a place such as Jasperville.

Henri and Philippe saw eye to eye. Marguerite was a listener, and as down-to-earth a woman as could be found. Within minutes it seemed, everyone considered her a lifelong friend and confidante. Thérèse was fourteen, and thus was placed in the same school classes as Juliette. Carine was five, and though she and Jacques didn't have more than half a dozen words to say to one another, all four children would walk back from school together. Oftentimes, Juliette and Jacques would stay at the boarding house for a little while, Thérèse and Juliette completing homework assignments together, Jacques and Carine content to sit in the kitchen while Marguerite prepared the evening meal for the boarders.

It was not long before the Devereauxs invited the Bergerons for supper. They accepted on the condition that the gesture would be reciprocated before too long. Elizabeth had entered her third trimester. She was well, and there were no contra-indications of any sort. Nevertheless, Marguerite arrived early and assisted Elizabeth with the final preparations. It was a considerable amount of work, the Devereauxs numbering five, the Bergerons four, and Elizabeth had chosen to prepare an English roast beef dinner accompanied by something called Yorkshire pudding.

There was a table for the adults, another for the younger members of the respective families. Philippe Bergeron brought wine, a very good one, and even though Henri was not a drinker, he took a glass as a courtesy.

The Bergeron girls were the model of politeness and good behaviour, and both Juliette and Jacques – ordinarily prone to little squabbles and cross words – were as mannered as Elizabeth could have wished.

The evening was a resounding success, despite the fact that William – his thirst somewhat quenched by three or four stiff whiskeys before the wine was even opened – had made a crude joke about a Portuguese sailor and a girl named Fanny.

Later – the Bergerons gone, William, Juliette and Jacques in their respective beds – Henri was subdued.

'Where have you gone, dear?' Elizabeth asked him.

Henri hesitated before speaking, and then said, 'I'm troubled still by the death of that girl.'

'The Roy girl?'

'Yes,' Henri replied.

'What is it that troubles you?'

'It was Sunday evening. The bars are full to bursting, people back and forth, lights and noise.' Henri looked up at his wife. 'You've not seen it, but there are so many people ...'

His words trailed away. The silence was palpable.

'What are you saying?' Elizabeth said, already sensing a growing anxiety.

'Wolves.' Henri shook his head. 'They're wild, yes, but they're instinctively wary of humans.'

'You don't think she fell? You don't think she died of the cold?'

'I don't know what happened to her,' Henri replied. 'Perhaps wolves, yes. Even if they were scared away by the search, they would have come back later and there would have been nothing left in the morning.'

'It's just too dreadful to consider,' Elizabeth said.

Henri's expression was intense. 'I could be wrong. I'm no frontiersman. Sometimes they come, the wolves. Just two or three of them. They make it as far as the fences at the edge of the foundry compound. You only have to holler and they run. If you go towards them, they run even faster.'

'But if it wasn't a wolf, then ...'

'Then it was a man.'

'No,' Elizabeth said. 'What you're saying is too frightening for words. That a human being could have done something like that to a young girl.'

Henri raised his eyebrows and looked at her in surprise. 'Human beings are capable of far worse things than this.'

'We've had such a pleasant evening, Henri. Please, enough of this. Why on earth would you bring up something like this?'

'The Bergerons. They're good people. They have daughters, just like Baptiste and Violetta had a daughter. I watched her, the older one. What was her name?'

'Thérèse.'

'Yes, Thérèse. I watched her. Not so different from Juliette. Not so different from Lisette.'

'Henri—'

'All I'm saying, Elizabeth, is that we have a duty to protect them, to make sure no harm comes to them. If it was a wolf, then so be it. If not, then—'

'Then it's the business of Sergeant Levesque.'

Henri shook his head. 'Gustave Levesque is not Juliette's father.'

Elizabeth sighed deeply. 'I'm going to bed, Henri.'

'I'm sorry if I have troubled you,' he said.

Henri looked up at her, extended his hand. Elizabeth took it, then leaned down and kissed his forehead.

'Come to bed,' she said.

'Soon,' Henri replied. 'I will join you soon.'

Elizabeth went upstairs. She paused at the top, waited there in the shadows to see what her husband would do.

Henri got up and crossed the room to the window. He stood there, peering out into the frozen darkness beyond. And then he leaned forward, his face mere inches from the glass, as if convinced that there was something to see.

Henri spoke. Elizabeth felt sure of it. A whisper, a mere handful of words, but she felt sure her husband had spoken. Not English, but French. A prayer. A curse. An oath. Why she felt it was significant, she didn't know. Something was happening in Henri's thoughts – something dark, something that disturbed him – and it was now disturbing her in turn.

Elizabeth closed her eyes. She said a prayer of her own – that the baby would arrive without complications, that her family would be safe, that things would return to normal in Jasperville.

Most of all she prayed that Lisette Roy, sweet, gentle girl that she was, had been taken by a wolf.

The subsequent weeks were without incident. Thérèse and Juliette became inseparable, and thus Jacques found himself spending more and more time at the boarding house. He protested, but he didn't protest too long. Carine, once her initial reticence was overcome, was outgoing and confident, forever dragging Jacques into scrapes and adventures. If they weren't hiding in old barrels in the cellar, they were getting under guests' feet in the dining room. One late afternoon they got it into their heads that building a fort from large pieces of coal was the best idea of all, and the pair of them showed up for supper as black as pitch, their clothes ruined. Jacques' nose ran grey for a week, and Elizabeth had no doubt it was the same for Carine.

As the summer faded and fall reminded her how cold the winter would be, Elizabeth became less and less able to cook and launder. William did his best, but it was Marguerite Bergeron who became the Devereaux children's godmother. For Elizabeth, the woman was a blessing beyond measure, and, on one occasion, Elizabeth commented that if Marguerite decided to have another baby, then she would find her generosity reciprocated.

'That will never be,' Marguerite told Elizabeth. 'Carine's birth was difficult. There will be no more Bergeron children.'

'I am sorry,' Elizabeth said. 'I had no idea—'

'Of course you didn't,' Marguerite said. 'Don't be sorry. I'm fortunate to have two beautiful, remarkable girls.' Marguerite hesitated then, as if she thought to say something that would be better left unsaid. A dark aspect – like the shadow of a cloud – passed over her features.

'What is it?' Elizabeth asked.

'It's nothing.'

'Tell me, Marguerite.'

The light and levity, usually so present in Marguerite's expression, was gone. 'The girl,' she said. 'The daughter of the people who owned the boarding house before us.'

'What about her?'

Marguerite half smiled, as if doubting herself. 'It's a foolish thought...'

Elizabeth sensed what was coming, and she didn't want to hear it. The door, however, had been opened, and there was no closing it.

'Sometimes... sometimes it feels like she's still there. I hear things...'

'You hear things?'

'Crying. I thought it was Carine, but Carine was sound asleep. And the sound was not coming from the girls' room.' Marguerite laughed dismissively. 'It was the wind, I'm sure. Nothing more than a gust of wind.'

'Yes, of course,' Elizabeth replied. 'I have heard some remarkable things, too. And the imagination can play tricks.' She looked toward the window. 'Out here.'

'It's a lonely place,' Marguerite said, 'but Philippe was determined to come.'

'Why *did* you come?' Elizabeth asked.

'Sometimes we need to begin our lives again, don't we? Sometimes the only way to be free of the past is to leave it behind completely.'

For a moment Marguerite was elsewhere, and then she turned, smiling, bright and animated. 'Listen to me,' she said, 'maundering like a spinster.'

Elizabeth reached out and touched Marguerite's shoulder. 'I'm happy that you're here. You've been a godsend to me, to my family. I don't know how I can ever repay you for all you have done to help us.'

'Oh, it's nothing at all. Without you and your wonderful children, I think I would have lost my mind in this soulless place.'

Compelled was the only word that could describe what Elizabeth then felt. She was *compelled* to speak, to ask a question, and there was nothing she could do to stop herself.

'Do you think it's a bad place, Marguerite?'

'A bad place? Can there be such a thing? I mean, people can be bad, of course, but a place?'

'You know the mountains?'

'Yes, of course.'

'Torngat. That's what they're called. It means place of evil spirits.'

'I don't believe in such things,' Marguerite said, almost too quickly. 'I mean, I know I said that thing about the girl, but I also know it was just my imagination. Thérèse and Carine are afraid of the dark, of course. We're all afraid of the dark when we're children, but then we grow up and we realize that there's nothing to be afraid of at all, don't we?'

'Yes, of course,' Elizabeth said. 'There's nothing to be afraid of.'

'Everything will be fine,' Marguerite said. 'You will have a new baby to occupy you very soon, and Philippe says that the winter will be busier for us than any other time of year.'

Elizabeth hesitated for a moment, and then she said, 'Can I ask you something?'

'Of course, my dear.'

'Did something happen? Where you were before? Did something happen that made it necessary for you to leave?'

'Why on earth would you think that, Elizabeth?'

'I don't necessarily mean something bad—'

'Sometimes things happen so other things can happen,' Marguerite said matter-of-factly.

To Elizabeth it sounded like a considered response, a means to avoid any further explanation.

'My father did something bad,' Elizabeth said. 'That's why we had to leave England.'

'All men are capable of wickedness,' Marguerite said. 'Nevertheless, what a man does is often less important than what he does next.'

'Yes, indeed,' Elizabeth said. She wanted Marguerite to open up, to explain what she'd meant, but she knew that now was not the time. She also knew that there might never be a time.

'We make the best of it,' Marguerite said. 'There's nothing as futile as trying to change something that cannot be changed.'

'Then we shall say no more,' Elizabeth said.

'Yes,' Marguerite replied, unable to look at Elizabeth directly. 'It's better that way. Let the past stay right where it is.'

9

Sept-Îles itself was yet another place established by Canada Iron, right there on the north shore of the St. Lawrence between the Sainte-Marguerite and Moisie rivers. Jack found a motel on the bay. It was cheap and functional. The room was warm, as was the shower, and he stood beneath it for a good while.

He dried his hair and got dressed. Out through the window he could see the seven islands that had given the city its name: the Boules, the Basques, Manowin, Corossol and the Îlets Dequen. Nearby were the Uashat and Maliotenam *reserves indiennes*, and First Nations people still trapped and hunted in these territories. The history went way back to before the Commonwealth and the Parliament Acts. Basque fishermen made it here from Europe in the 1500s for whale and cod, but they were not the first to do that. In the grand swathe of history, the city of Sept-Îles was as meaningless as Jasperville. If the iron ore ran out, everyone would disappear.

Jack walked, but not far. Half a dozen blocks from the motel he found a bar and grill. He drank a beer, ordered another with a steak, and then took a seat in a booth near the back. He could feel the exhaustion of the journey in every bone, every muscle, every nerve.

We are ourselves, but with us we carry the ghosts of all the people we might have become.

The thoughts didn't feel like his own. Already his mind was playing games.

What would have happened if he'd stayed?

But he hadn't. He and Calvis had once been inseparable. Seven years apart, but living out of one another's pockets for more than a decade. Though Calvis had pleaded to be taken along, Jack had been resolute. He could hear himself even now, the way he'd refused and refused again.

'Your steak.'

Jack looked up. Exhaustion, alcohol. The room moved. For a moment he'd been elsewhere completely.

The waitress smiled and set the plate down in front of him.

'You need another drink?' she said.

'Most definitely,' he replied.

'Is everything okay?' she asked.

Jack frowned.

'I'm sorry,' she said. 'It's none of my business—'

'Family things,' Jack said. 'Just some family things.'

'Yes,' the girl said, as if she knew exactly what Jack meant. 'I have a brother. God only knows where he is, but I guarantee he's doing something that decent folk wouldn't want to know about.'

Like hurting someone so bad that they might die? Jack thought, but the thought stayed in his head.

'I'll get your drink. Crown Royal, right?'

'Yeah. A double, no ice.'

'You want another Molson, too?'

'Sure. Why the hell not?'

The girl smiled. 'No reason I can think of.'

She walked away. Instinctively, Jack wanted to call her back. He had nothing to say to her, nothing that she would have any wish to know, but the mere presence of another human being, the sound of a voice, the comfort of a meaningless conversation about music or books or anything at all, was needful. He was lost. He knew that much. Caroline hadn't been the first to see it. A man builds a castle to protect himself, and then traps himself inside. Whichever way he goes, the corridors return him to the same place. There's no map for the human mind; trains of thought become so confused that there's no way to find their origin. Everything started with Jasperville. Perhaps everything would end there, too.

The waitress returned with his drinks.

'Thank you,' he said, and, as she turned, he added, 'What's your name?'

'Juliette.'

Jack's reaction was immediate and startling. 'Juliette?' he said.

'No, Violette.'

'I'm sorry. I thought you said Juliette.'

Violette smiled, left him to the rest of his dinner.

Violette, not Juliette. Now he was hearing things. But still, Violette reminded him of Violetta, the mother of Lisette Roy.

And then he was thinking of the second girl to go missing. The second one to die.

With hindsight, as was so often the case, he could see now that the death of Anne-Louise Fournier was the point at which everything had started to unravel.

10

It was 12 August 1972, a Saturday, and Juliette and Jacques were not in school. There was a midwife and a doctor from the medical centre, but Elizabeth wanted Marguerite by her side. Henri was home, but wouldn't be present at the birth itself. He would stay downstairs with William and the children. Philippe would arrive with Thérèse and Carine later in the day.

Elizabeth went into labour a little after ten in the morning. To the children, it sounded as if their mother was being tortured to death at the top of the stairs. William did his best to explain what was happening, but still the wailing and gasping seemed to contradict the very essence of this occasion. A new baby would bring joy and happiness, so why did it manifest such pain?

At two that afternoon there was an indication that the child was breeched. The doctor held his nerve. Marguerite called for Henri, and Henri went up to see her.

When Henri came downstairs, he was pale and agitated. A month earlier, he and Elizabeth had discussed the possibility of taking the train to Sept-Îles. The hospital there was ably staffed and could better deal with any problems. Elizabeth didn't want to leave Jasperville. She wanted to have the baby with her family around her. She was so assured that everything would be all right that Henri hadn't insisted. He wished he had, but he knew his wife better than anyone. She was not a woman whose opinion could easily be swayed.

Sensing that there was some anxiety, Juliette had asked her father if everything was going to be all right.

'Of course, of course, of course,' he replied. He held out his arms and she went to him. Jacques went too, and the pair of them clung to him like a lifeline.

At five that afternoon, news came from Marguerite that the baby was not breeched. All was well. Elizabeth was approaching the final moments. As six o'clock chimed on the small clock above the mantle, they heard the baby's first cries. Henri charged up the stairs, three or four risers at a time, almost losing his footing at the top. He was in the room no more than two or three minutes before he reappeared, saying, 'A boy! It's a boy! You have a little brother!'

If Juliette had been disappointed, that disappointment vanished the instant she saw the infant. He was strong, healthy and oh so noisy. Jacques marvelled at the size of the baby's fingers and toes. Every detail was perfect, but captured in such minuscule proportions.

'Calvis,' Henri announced when everyone was present. 'That's his name. It means "faith".'

'Calvis,' Juliette said. 'It's a beautiful name.'

Jacques went to his mother. She sat upright in the bed, her hair in sweat-drenched tails, her cheeks reddened. She was both exhausted and overjoyed. She held Calvis close, and all that could be seen was his face and one tiny grasping hand.

Jacques reached up tentatively. He wanted to touch his brother's fingers.

'It's all right, sweetheart,' Elizabeth said.

Jacques neared the baby, and then, without even opening his eyes, Calvis gripped Jacques' finger. Jacques took a sudden intake of breath, and then he smiled so wide. There were tears in his eyes, and he looked around for his sister so that she could see what was happening.

Everyone had seen. There was silence in that room. It was a remarkable moment, for it seemed that everything that had happened to bring the Devereaux family to Jasperville was nothing but a ghost of the past, and it held no sway and it possessed no power, and it could no more influence them than the change of seasons or the next fall of snow.

Calvis was here, and everything was going to be good from now on.

Sergeant Gustave Levesque left for Québec City in March of 1973.

The Americans and the Vietnamese were exchanging prisoners. An ever-more paranoid Nixon was fighting for his presidential life as Watergate unfolded.

Levesque's replacement, Maurice Thibault, was barely past his thirtieth birthday, and had somehow convinced himself that a posting to this wild, featureless nothing of a place was a good career move.

Within days there were jokes in the bars about *Petit Maurice*, wagers on how far and fast he could run if a fight broke out, if he'd had to train with weights before he could lift his pistol. The jibes and jests were unwarranted. Sergeant Thibault had been raised in a place called Girardville, north-west of Lake Saint-Jean. He was no stranger to bitter winds, ice storms, rain so hard and cold it felt like a shotgun blast of needles. His father, a tough man with an unquenchable thirst for cheap liquor, had schooled his son to hunt, to butcher, to fish, to bivouac, even a bastardized form of lumberjack fighting that sat somewhere between the Marquess of Queensberry and wild-eyed fury. Thibault's mother, on the other hand, had taught her son manners, courtesy, respect for his elders, and an abiding faith in God's plan for all men.

Had Maurice Thibault been called to break up a barfight,

he would have fared far better than any of the naysayers could have expected. He knew what too much drink and too distant a horizon could do to a man. An idle mind was the Devil's playground.

Within a month, Sergeant Thibault of the Sûreté had made himself known to almost every family in Jasperville. Though many considered him young for the job, he nevertheless impressed with his professionalism and attention to detail. Elizabeth found him intense, a little too serious for someone so young, but also appreciated that he was doing what was required to establish himself in his new position. Two years in Jasperville would make or break him. She suspected the former rather than the latter.

The subsequent eighteen months were reassuringly uneventful. By the fall of 1974, the Devereaux family were as settled as they would ever be in Jasperville. Calvis was two years old. Juliette, a very grown-up sixteen, had assumed a role as secondary mother to the baby. Jacques, just turned nine, had his head forever buried in a book. William – prone to mumbling, flights of fancy, long periods of silence – existed in a world of his own invention. He seemed content there, and though he was close to all the children, he often referred to them with different names. Calvis he just called *baby*. Juliette and Jacques could be Edith and Edward, Katherine and Leonard, Arthur and Guinevere. It didn't matter. The children responded, and they responded with patience and with love.

The Bergeron girls had blossomed. Thérèse, just six months older than Juliette, was half a head taller, slim and elegant. Carine, seven years old, was her opposite. Tomboyish, sporting muddy dungarees and scuffed shoes, she and Jacques were forever in and out of streams and ponds, intent on catching char, grayling and Dolly Varden trout. That they never caught anything bigger than darters and sculpins didn't seem to diminish their enthusiasm or self-belief. Off they would go, clutching bamboo rods and tin buckets, always back before dusk, always filthy, always starving.

Henri proved to be a responsible and able supervisor. He spent time in the bars, but he didn't drink. He took to smoking a foul-smelling pipe shag, its aroma more of burned rubber than tobacco. He'd found a place in the world, and he intended to hold firm to that place. He ran a crew of more than five hundred men. They called him Chief, and when he walked in town with Elizabeth, they would acknowledge him with a nod or a touch to the cap.

Elizabeth didn't think about the years ahead, nor did she wonder what would have happened had she remained a schoolteacher in Montréal. The memory of England and the first two decades of her life was of a different life altogether. It was too long ago to miss, and missing it served no purpose. If there was one thing learned in Jasperville, it was pragmatism. That, and the futility of complaining.

Early November saw an unprecedented drop in temperature. The ground was granite. Digger buckets snapped their metal teeth, picks broke, strong men with shovels couldn't even scar the dirt. Canada Iron sent miners home, kept the foundry running until the stock ore was smelted, and then sent the foundrymen home, too. The last train out of Jasperville reached Emeril Junction where the line crossed the Trans-Labrador highway. There it stayed, the tracks and the wheels no longer running true to one another due to a variance in contraction. Roads closed, footpaths were impassable, and Jasperville was as accessible as the far side of the moon.

By the second week of the month, it was minus thirty at high noon.

Darkness was swift and sudden, and with it there was a further drop of fifteen degrees. People left their homes for wood and food, and that was all. Thibault rounded up a half-dozen hardy volunteers, and they did a single daily run from one end of town to the other. Dressed like Amundsen and Scott, they checked up on the older ones, those with infants, anyone exhibiting signs of pneumonia or frostbite. It was on one of those runs – the late morning of Tuesday the nineteenth – that the disappearance of Anne-Louise Fournier was reported. Anne-Louise was an only child. Four months earlier she'd turned fifteen. Dark-haired and strikingly pretty, she would have spent her life breaking the hearts of men whose names she would never know. Her parents – Étienne and Odile – had been Jasperville people since 1956. Their daughter, much like Lisette Roy, was no stranger to weather. This was her place of birth, her home, and, aside from books and photographs, it was all she knew of the world. The idea of Anne-Louise wandering off alone was inconceivable. She'd gone out to cut wood, just as she did each morning after breakfast. From an upstairs window, Odile had seen someone walking towards the back of the house. She'd assumed it was Lucien Dube, the sixteen-year-old son of their neighbours. Lucien and Anne-Louise had been close since childhood; there was every possibility they would marry. There were two types of children in Jasperville: those who yearned to leave, and those, like Lucien, who had never even considered such a thing.

Had Sergeant Thibault not asked after Anne-Louise, her disappearance might not have been noticed for another half an hour. But he did ask, methodical as he was, wanting to ensure that everyone was accounted for, if only for his own peace of mind.

'Just check through the window,' he asked of Anne-Louise's father.

'She's out there. She's cutting wood.'

'Please, Étienne,' Thibault insisted. 'Just go and look.'

Étienne returned within a minute. 'I cannot see her,' he said.

Thibault stepped past him and went through the lower part of the house to the back door. The door was stiff. Tugging it open, a flurry of snow came in on a bitter breeze.

Étienne pulled on an oilskin, his heavy boots. He followed the sergeant out of the house and into the yard.

The woodpile was disturbed. Logs were scattered here and there. The axe lay on its side, almost buried in the snow. Whatever footprints might have existed were long gone.

'How long was she out here?' Thibault asked.

Odile Fournier appeared at the back door. 'What is happening?' she asked.

'Anne-Louise has gone,' Étienne replied.

'She'll be next door,' Odile said matter-of-factly. 'With Lucien.'

Thibault marched across the yard and up to the back door of the Dube house. He hammered on it with the side of his clenched fist.

Within seconds, Lucien's mother, Josephine, opened up the door to find out what warranted such urgency.

'Madame Dube,' Thibault said. 'We're looking for Anne-Louise. Is she inside with Lucien?'

'With Lucien? No. She's not here. I haven't seen her this morning.'

Odile Fournier, now enrobed in a thick fur and a woollen hat, joined her husband. 'He was outside this morning,' she said. 'I saw him from the window.'

Josephine turned and called her son. 'Lucien! Lucien, come here!'

It was a good thirty seconds before the boy appeared, and it was evident – from his tousled hair, his sleepy expression – that he'd been roused from his bed.

'You were outside this morning,' Odile Fournier said. 'Here, in the yard, talking to Anne-Louise.'

'No, Madame Fournier. I have been sleeping.'

'Have you seen Anne-Louise this morning?' Thibault asked.

'No, sir.'

Thibault looked out toward the barren, white wasteland beyond the yard. He squinted through the flurries of powdery snow for any sign of movement, a dip or rise in the seemingly uninterrupted blanket of white.

'Where is she?' Odile asked, in her voice the beginnings of panic.

'She won't be far,' Étienne said, his voice that of a man trying to convince himself of something he doubted.

'Where is your husband, Madame Dube?' Thibault asked.

'Upstairs,' she said.

'Go and fetch him at once,' Thibault urged, and then to Lucien he said, 'Get dressed. You need to help us look for her.'

Thibault went back to the street and rounded up his volunteers. Within fifteen minutes there were nine of them at the back of the Fournier house.

Before they started out in the direction of the Torngat Mountains, Thibault questioned Odile as to precisely what she'd seen from the upper window. It was as she'd earlier said, a single figure – presumably Lucien – walking toward Anne-Louise.

The search party started out a little before eleven. The drifts were too shallow for snowshoes, but the men carried walking sticks and skiing poles, tentatively probing the ground left and right, alert for the slightest sign of earlier footprints, animal tracks, anything that could help identify the direction Anne-Louise had taken. At first they were three or four yards apart, but Thibault soon had them close ranks a little. He intended to miss nothing, and he most definitely intended to find the Fournier girl. Thibault had heard the story of Lisette Roy, both from his predecessor and from Philippe Bergeron at the boarding house. That wolves had taken her seemed unlikely. An autopsy had never been done. He himself hadn't seen her body. He knew something of the strength and mindset of timber wolves. There were packs of them around Lake Saint-Jean. Hungry, they would brave anything. A few people and a few lights wouldn't dissuade a wolf from the promise of food, especially if there were cubs. The Roy girl could have fallen, succumbed to the cold, been dragged away, but the mere fact that her body was savaged and then abandoned didn't make sense.

Casting pessimistic thoughts from his mind, Thibault urged the men on. It had to be twenty-five below, and already the sun, now grazing the horizon, was on its downward trajectory. They had an hour, perhaps two, and then it would be too dark and cold to go further.

Here and there they found signs of wolves, even a bear. A black scoter, its outstretched wing stiff like a Japanese fan, lay dead on an exposed punctuation of rock.

Close to despair, exhausted and unbearably cold, it was Anne-Louise Fournier's own father who found her body.

Perhaps he no longer possessed the strength to cry, for he simply dropped to his knees, his face wracked with anguish, his arms outstretched as if pleading with someone or something unknown to turn back time and undo this horror.

Anne-Louise's emerald eyes were open, as pale as glass marbles. Her mouth formed an 'O' as if caught in a moment of surprise. She lay on her back, her head tilted slightly toward the right. Her gaze was directed toward her house. Her hair was splayed across the snow, her arms outstretched, and had you seen nothing else you might have believed she was making an angel in the snow. Below that, everything tilted into nightmare. From the base of her ribcage, the meat of her stomach had been torn open. The organs within had been savaged too, some scattered, others trailing left and right. The girl had been ripped open. There was no other way to describe it. Ripped open and emptied out.

Lucien Dube sobbed and retched. His father hurried him back towards town. Two men helped Étienne Fournier to his feet and urged him away from the scene. He wouldn't leave, however, determined that he would accompany his daughter's body back to the medical centre. That was the only place Thibault could think to take her. It was beyond belief that such a violent act against a human being could have been perpetrated by anything other than a wild animal. However, aside from deep gouges in the breasts and thighs, there was nothing to suggest that the girl had been killed as prey. Animals killed for no other reason than food or self-defence. If for food, there would be nothing left of the girl. It made no sense.

From the moment that Thibault had seen the half-naked teenager in the snow, he'd been overcome by a sense of horror. He was a realist, a thoroughly grounded man, but he couldn't deny the intuitive and undeniable feeling of utter dread that clouded his thoughts.

Anne-Louise Fournier hadn't been savaged by a wolf. Or a bear. Or anything else on four legs. She had been savaged by a person, and perhaps that very same person had been the one to kill Lisette Roy less than three years before.

Thibault engineered a makeshift stretcher from his oilskin undercoat. The girl's body was carried back to Jasperville. The blood inside her had frozen. She was as rigid as a board. As they walked, Thibault's gaze was drawn back time and again to the girl's eyes. That pale, ghostly expression, the sense that whatever energy or force had animated her was long gone. Now nothing more than a brittle shell, the life had been torn from her body and that body had been cast aside like a husk.

At the medical centre, Thibault instructed the resident doctor to keep the body there, to let no one see it or examine it. He would return shortly, and after making his preliminary notes and taking some photographs, he would arrange to have the body held at the undertaker's until outside assistance was secured. Though Thibault didn't doubt his own competence in many matters, this was beyond his investigative skills. He was neither coroner nor detective, and he considered that both would be required to understand what had happened.

But first, there were the immediate issues. He would go to the Fournier house, then to the Dubes. He would see if there was any additional information to be gleaned about what might have caused Anne-Louise to leave the yard and head out of town. That was how he would couch the question, even though he didn't believe for a moment that that was what had occurred.

Anne-Louise Fournier had no more walked alone into that desolate wasteland than she'd lain in the snow and disembowelled herself.

Someone had abducted and murdered that poor girl, and Sergeant Thibault didn't believe it was the first time it had happened.

II

Jack was not a habitual drinker. The walk back to the motel seemed twice as long as the trip out. He was unsteady on his feet, but at least he was too drunk to feel the cold.

Once inside the room, he kicked off his shoes and lay on the bed. He couldn't get the thought of Anne-Louise Fournier out of his mind. He'd been just nine at the time, yet he could remember her so clearly; each time he closed his eyes her face was right there. That sweep of dark hair, those startling emerald eyes. He remembered Maurice Thibault – so serious, so intense, almost frightening. Years later, after another sergeant and yet another, there was a rumour that *Petit Maurice* had gone half crazy about that girl. No one came to help him. No one from Sept-Îles or Montréal or Trois Rivières or Québec City. He filed reports, and then he filed more reports, and apparently he'd even gone back to Montréal to request investigators and a forensics analyst. Each time his pleas were rejected. Too few resources. Too little funding. It was wolves. It was bears. These things happen. And the Fourniers themselves, seemingly reconciled to the fact that the truth would never be known, didn't support Thibault's cause. Once again, there was a fatalistic resignation that couldn't be challenged. Lisette was dead. Anne-Louise was dead. Whatever analysis of events might be made, it wouldn't change reality. The girls were gone, and nothing would bring them back. Let us bury our daughters. Let us grieve. And if you can't do that, then just let us be.

Thibault was rotated out in June of 1975, a week or so before Jack's tenth birthday. Jack remembered the party they held at the boarding house. Under the supervision of Marguerite Bergeron, Juliette and Thérèse baked *pets-de-sœurs* and butter tarts. There was sweet lemonade, a wind-up car from the Bergerons, and his father had given him a knife with a tooled leather sheath.

'This is for cutting rope, for whittling, such things as that,' he'd said. 'If you are a responsible young man, as I believe you are, then you will keep it sharp, keep it clean, and keep it safe. Do you understand?'

'Yes, I do,' Jack had said, barely able to control his excitement. That knife was on his belt every moment he wasn't in school. What had happened to it, he couldn't remember. Lost in the drift of time. Perhaps, even now, it was somewhere within that crazy house where he'd spent his childhood. The house he couldn't wait to leave.

Jack got off the bed and made it to the bathroom. He looked in the mirror at the face he deserved.

Denial was in his blood, in his bones, in every part of him. Denial of the past, of his responsibility for his own father, for Calvis, for the slow deterioration of his own state of mind. Perhaps more than all of this, how he'd denied the promise he'd made – and then broken – to take care of Carine Bergeron.

Everything was coming apart at the seams.

What do you do when everything that used to work doesn't work any more? When all the fallback positions and familiars are gone? What then?

Caroline had seen it. Ludo, too. Even Ludo's wife, Florence.

As Jack stared at himself, he recalled another birthday – his fortieth. They had gone to a restaurant in downtown Montréal – Ludo, Florence, himself and another girl. Try as he might, he couldn't recall her name. What he did remember was something Florence had said. It had come out of the blue, completely unexpected. He'd realized that people saw him very differently from how he saw himself.

Returning from the restroom, he'd met Florence in the corridor.

'You know something?' she'd said.

'What, Florence?'

'If you want to make peace with others, you first have to make peace with yourself.'

He'd frowned. 'What the hell is that supposed to mean?'

'You know what it means, Jack.'

'Well, explain it to me, just in case I don't understand.'

'You think you're the only one who carries the weight of the world on your shoulders. Well, you're not. Everyone does. Different things, different reasons, different burdens, but to each of us they weigh the same.'

'You're drunk, Florence.'

'And so are you. And, you know, the only time I ever feel like I might get through that granite façade is when you've got three or four bourbons inside you.'

He'd laughed, but it sounded defensive. 'I don't have a façade.'

'Okay,' she'd said. It was a lie, and they both knew it.

'You don't know anything about me,' he'd said.

'You're right, I don't. And the only reason for that is that you don't want anyone to know anything about you.'

That had hit home. He was hiding everything in plain sight.

Florence had held up her hand in front of his face. 'This,' she'd said, 'whatever *this* is, is bullshit.'

With that, she'd turned and gone back to the table.

Jack had stood there for a moment, and then he'd leaned back against the wall. He'd watched Florence. She'd sat down again, smiling, laughing with her husband, with Jack's girlfriend,

75

and it was as if he was watching a movie. This was his cue. He would walk on set and deliver his lines. Except he had nothing to say.

Jack leaned forward, his hands on the edge of the sink.

'What the living fuck are you doing?' he asked out loud.

In the reflection he could see the child he'd once been, the teenager, even the man he'd hoped to become.

There were some places very few had been. Of themselves, they didn't know what they'd left behind. And, in returning, they didn't know what they'd carried with them.

Not only had the past absorbed and erased his own life, but he was now the person he'd tried everything not to become.

He was returning not only for Calvis, but for Juliette, for Lisette, for Anne-Louise and all the other girls.

It was not true that the dead had escaped. They were all still there, biding their time until he found his way home.

12

Early on the morning of Friday, 11 March 1977, Odile Fournier went out through the back door of the house to collect wood from the lean-to in the yard. It was something she'd done many thousands of times before. Étienne was on his hands and knees in front of the burner in the kitchen, cleaning out ash and fragments of wood from the previous day. Above him on the hotplate was a pan of milk. Once the fire was lit they would make oatmeal, just as they had done every morning for as long as they could recall.

Anne-Louise had been dead for two years. She was buried in a plot behind the church. Each week, right after the service, Étienne and Odile would walk down there and stand over her grave. They said nothing, for what they felt was beyond words. At first they would remain for an hour, sometimes longer, the biting cold making its way through to the bone. As the months had passed, it had seemed less and less necessary to remain. They just needed her to know that she was not forgotten, that she would *never* be forgotten.

Étienne got up off his knees. His bones ached quietly, constantly. He went to the back door and peered through the ice-frosted glass. For a moment he didn't know where to look. He couldn't see Odile. It was no more than four or five yards to the woodpile, and unless she'd gone into the shed or the outhouse, there was no reason for her not to have returned.

Étienne put on his boots and a fur-lined jacket. He donned his hat and gloves, and before he crossed the threshold, he hesitated for no more than ten seconds. In that brief moment, it seemed that his thoughts just vanished. He didn't know how it was possible to think of nothing, to be *able* to think of nothing, but that was what he experienced. When his thoughts returned, the first was *So, this is how it feels to be dead.*

He was troubled before he called Odile's name. His unease and disquiet rapidly escalated as he called her name once more.

'Odile! Odile! Où es-tu?'

Out before him from the back door to the fence at the end of the yard, beyond that to the low carpet of moss and lichen, even as far as the horizon, there was nothing but a wild and breathless silence.

Once again, 'Odile!' The urgency in his voice reached an anxious pitch.

Étienne felt a cold hand grip his heart. His stomach turned. The aching knees seemed too fragile to hold his own weight. He could not see his wife.

He moved slowly, as if willing everything to move with him, back to some earlier place and time when Anne-Louise was still a child, when there were no stories of dark things with twisted thoughts that came to steal the daughters of men. There were many things he couldn't understand, most of all how such a sweet and innocent girl could have wandered alone into an icy wilderness and been torn apart.

Odile lay on her back in the mud between the shed and the outhouse. Her left arm was twisted and trapped beneath her torso. Her eyes were open, and her ragged gasps of breath were so shallow as to barely make a sound.

Étienne was on his knees, his hands beneath his wife's shoulders, freeing the trapped arm and trying to help her up.

'Anne-Louise,' she sighed. It was an exhalation, nothing more, but the words were clear.

Odile tried to move her hand. Her eyes widened. There was some deep and wrenching pain inside her that tortured her expression.

'There,' she gasped, her eyes moving out towards the fence, the low shrubs, the featureless landscape beyond.

Instinctively Étienne turned and looked in that direction. He knew his mind was playing tricks. Nothing but fraught imagination, the fact that he *so* wanted to see something, but, for the briefest of moments, was there not a flicker of movement against the far shadow of low, stunted trees?

Anne-Louise? he said, but it was merely a thought.

He turned back as Odile moved. She looked up at him, her eyes soft and watery, a faint smile on her lips, a sense that somewhere she was letting go of something.

'No,' Étienne said, his voice barely a whisper. 'No, Odile... no...'

But he knew there was nothing he could do. She'd slipped away even as he watched. Even as he grasped her shoulders and brought her up to him, whatever life was inside her was gone.

Étienne Fournier looked up at the bleak and empty sky. Every line and furrow in his face conveyed the reality of an unforgiving life. He now understood that he was truly, heartbreakingly alone.

He knelt there for close to an hour, until his legs ached, his arms too. He knelt there and sobbed in broken gasps and hitches, surrounded by the bitter cold, the unrelenting wilderness. Whatever happiness might have been salvaged after the death of his daughter was obliterated in the single sweep of some brutal, merciless hand. Anne-Louise was gone. Odile was gone. There was nothing left.

Étienne went back to the house and fetched a blanket. Carefully, lovingly, he wrapped it around and beneath his wife.

Once cocooned, there was nothing showing but her face. She seemed at peace. That was all he could think. The hurt and fear and longing that seemed present in every glance had somehow faded. Perhaps, after all, she did see Anne-Louise. Perhaps that was what she was trying to say with her last breath. Anne-Louise is out there. Anne-Louise is waiting for us.

For a while, Étienne lay down beside Odile.

He knew if he lay there long enough, he would just slip into hypothermic shock and die. But it would take time. Too much time. He didn't want to be left behind.

He turned slowly. He reached out and touched his hand to her face, and then he leaned and gently kissed her brow.

When he got up again, it was not without difficulty. Every muscle seemed taut and strained. The hurt within had found its way to every inch of his body.

From a hook on the wall of the shed, he took down a length of stout rope, and then walked back to the house.

Once inside, he took off his coat, his gloves, his hat, his boots. He swept up the last ashes from the grate. He took the pan of milk, poured it down the sink, then washed the pan and set it aside. He took a chair from the kitchen table and carried it upstairs to their bedroom. He placed it in the centre of the room.

Taking care not to slip on the varnished seat in his stockinged feet, Étienne looped the rope over the rafter and secured it with a rolling hitch. With the other end he fashioned a makeshift noose. He didn't know what he was doing, but it would have to suffice.

Looping the rope over his head, Étienne pulled it taut. He looked down at his toes against the lip of the seat.

And then he paused. In such a moment, a prayer would have been appropriate. For much of his life he'd been a God-fearing, churchgoing man, but Anne-Louise's death had changed everything. Now, with the loss of his wife – a woman who had been by his side for thirty-seven years – he knew without doubt that there was no God. At least no God that loved him, cared for him, listened to his prayers. There was something out there, but it was neither beneficent nor charitable. It haunted the shadowed places, the white nowhere, the frozen wasteland that stretched out and for ever beyond the limits of Jasperville.

Like a relentless tide, waves of grief crashed inside Étienne's mind.

Everything had gone, and there was no reason to remain.

'Cette vie n'estrien,' he muttered, and then took a single, decisive step forward.

The chair fell backward. The knot pulled taut and sudden. He started to choke. He hung there gasping for close to a minute and a half, and then he fell unconscious. Aside from the brief shuffling movement of his stockinged feet, there was no movement at all, and after five or six minutes he was dead.

Maurice Thibault's replacement, Sergeant Antoine Tremblay, was called to the scene by the Fourniers' neighbours. He attended the scene, and then called for Dr Pelletier from the medical centre. They examined the bodies together. From all indications, it seemed clear that Odile had suffered a massive and fatal heart attack. There were no tracks in the snow but her own and those of her husband, and the fact that she lay there with both hands clutched to her chest was the clearest sign of all. Étienne's cause of death required no hypothesis at all. The two of them brought him down carefully and laid him on the bed. From the back yard they carried Odile into the house and laid her on the kitchen floor. With the blanket, they covered her completely, and then they sent for the minister.

*

On Saturday, 19 March, the double funeral of Étienne and Odile Fournier was held. Canada Iron paid for the caskets. A wreath had been dispatched from Sept-Îles by some well-meaning company functionary, but the blooms were wilted beyond recovery by the time it arrived.

The church was crowded. Every member of the Devereaux family was there, as were the Bergerons, Sergeant Tremblay, Dr Pelletier, and almost everyone who had known or worked with Étienne. It was a sombre affair, and when the minister encouraged a rousing rendition of 'Onward, Christian Soldiers' the response was lacklustre and dispiriting. The only person in the church who sang as though he meant it was William Swann, standing there beside his daughter and son-in-law, his three grandchildren wan and subdued, Juliette doing her utmost to manage a feisty four-year-old Calvis. Between them, the Devereauxs and the Bergerons numbered ten, and together they all headed back to the boarding house where a spread of *creton*, *tourtière*, meatball ragout with pigs' feet and sugar pie was laid on. Once again, Canada Iron had deigned to fund the buffet. Twenty years of dedicated service from Étienne Fournier warranted a meaningful gesture.

Jacques and Carine crept away at the earliest available opportunity. They sat side by side at the bend in the stairs, a plate of treats between them. Carine, doe-eyed and optimistic that Jacques, her prince-to-be, would grow up and build her a storybook house with a picket fence and a dog and a cat, listened as he frightened her with a story he'd heard from his grandfather. He used a word that she didn't understand, and she was too scared to have him repeat it. It was the first time she'd been to a funeral. All she knew was that something terrible had happened to a girl and her mother – so terrible, in fact, that the girl's father had killed himself to get away from it.

It was this thing – this terror – that Jacques told her about, and the most frightening thing of all was that it was under the earth and all around them, and no matter what you did, you could never get away. At least, that's what Papi William had told Jacques, and Papi William was as old as the earth and he knew things.

And then the wake was over, and the Devereauxs, along with so many others, headed home. A slow procession of downcast people made their way along the main street, and there seemed to be a wordless agreement that what had happened to Lisette Roy and the Fourniers was far beyond the understanding of mere mortals.

Jasperville was a good place, a place of hard work and community, of people striving together to wrestle a living from the earth. It took a special kind of person to survive here, and the only true challenges were the remoteness and the climate.

Though they worked hard to convince themselves of this, they were full of doubt. There was something happening in Jasperville, and William Swann was not the only one who believed it.

13

Much of Saturday night Jack had lain awake. His mind turned over half-forgotten events. He'd dozed, dreamed, woken with a start, and then dozed again. Images of the church, the boarding house, the way the streets would empty as soon as temperatures dropped. Even the light seemed different from any other place he'd known. There were few shadows, but every shadow remained until the air itself was filled with memories of darkness. It stole your strength – both of mind and body – and the longer you stayed, the less there was of you to leave.

On Sunday morning Jack took breakfast, then stayed in his motel room and watched TV. He'd planned to walk around Sept-Îles, to see what he remembered, to see what had changed, but in the light of day it seemed a futile activity.

The train didn't leave until the evening. He would reach Emeril Junction around four on Monday morning. There would be a brief stopover, and he'd make Jasperville around nine. He would find Sergeant Bastien Nadeau, he would see his brother for the first time in twenty-six years, and he would get answers to questions he didn't want to ask.

A little before seven, Jack checked out and took a cab to the terminal. The driver wanted to talk. Jack's non-committal and monosyllabic responses soon dissuaded him.

The cab pulled up. Jack got out, paid the driver, and then watched as the cab headed back the way they'd come. He dropped his bag, put his hands in his overcoat pockets, and he breathed deeply. He felt exactly as he had when he'd stood on the porch after the call from Nadeau.

And... and he says terrible things, monsieur. The most terrible things...

He was no longer even considering the possibility of backing out. By distance, he was two-thirds of the way there. He could feel the pull of it – some dark magnetic force that possessed the power to drive you away but bring you back once more. Was it the same with everyone who left? Was it the same for all of those who could never leave?

Jack picked up his bag and walked down to the station. He could hear the train, that low guttural rumbling, the way it seemed to resonate through the ground beneath his feet. Like something lurking deep beneath the earth. Something that was laughing at his frailty.

Jack presented his ticket for the inspector. He was Inuit, perhaps sixty-five or seventy. He clipped the ticket, indicated the platform with a nod of his head.

Behind the engine was an old Amtrak food service car; next came two coach cars for First Nations people; the last passenger car – the one where Jack took his seat – was a refurbished Southern Railway coach. It boasted new upholstery, an illuminated map of the line – Sept-Îles to Emeril Junction, then on to Jasperville – and heaters between each bank of four seats. Behind the coach ran a chain of eight boxcars, each laden with cargo for unloading at Emeril and Jasperville. There would be tinned and dry provisions, footwear, clothing, electrical appliances, white goods, hardware, tools, sacks of mail, books, magazines, stationery supplies, and pretty much anything else that couldn't be supplied some other way. Some of the cargo would be unloaded and sent west by road to Labrador City and

Wabush, twin towns that had been established by Canada Iron back in the 1960s.

It was pitch dark as the train pulled out and began its eight-hour, slow-motion, snaking journey. They would hit fifty miles per hour and stay there. Contraction on the lines, wedges of ice, odd places where the snow had banked up against the sleepers and caused them to swell, presented a range of hazards. Hit those anomalies at seventy or eighty and the train could derail. Fifty was safe. Fifty was born out of decades of experience.

The coach had five other passengers: an elderly man with a heavy, ankle-length fur coat, a young couple, and a middle-aged woman with a boy of twelve or thirteen, his face a perpetual mask of glum indifference. The young couple were the only ones who talked, but they talked low, whispering to one another, laughing in turn, pouring coffee from a flask into matching plastic cups. Jack guessed they were newlyweds. Perhaps he'd secured a job with Canada Iron and they were headed out for this brave, new life. They had no idea what they were letting themselves in for, and it was none of Jack's business to warn them. Besides, had he said something, he would have been nothing more than some lunatic on the train. The young man looked his way at one point. Jack half-smiled, nodded, and the man reciprocated the acknowledgement.

'Jasperville?' the man asked.

'Yes,' Jack replied. 'You?'

'The same.'

'You have work out there?'

'I do, yes.'

'The mines?' Jack asked.

'Not the mines themselves, but for Canada Iron, yes. Administrative work. Finance and payroll. Stuff like that.'

'First time you've been there?'

'Yes. I mean, I know it's pretty remote an' all that, but it'll be an adventure, right?'

'That'll be the least of it,' Jack said, and knew he should have said nothing.

'Is that where you're from?' the woman asked. She leaned forward. She pulled back the fur-trimmed hood of her coat. Dark-haired, green-eyed, there was something about her that reminded him of Anne-Louise Fournier.

'Originally, yes. Montréal-born, but my parents took me out there when I was three years old. I left again twenty-five or so years ago.'

'And you've not been back since?'

'I haven't, no.'

'I'm Vivienne Girard,' the woman said. 'Vivi. And this is my husband, Paul.'

'Jack Devereaux. Pleasure to meet you.'

Vivi seemed hesitant then. Jack knew what was coming. He willed her to stay silent, but he could see the light of curiosity in her eyes.

'Can I ask you a question?' she said. 'I mean, it's kind of stupid, I know, but I have to ask.'

'Sure,' Jack replied, and even he could hear the reluctance in his tone.

'There seems to be … well, there seem to be hearsay, old wives' tales, I guess, but—'

'Vivi, seriously,' her husband interjected.

'It's not a big deal, Paul.'

'Hearsay about what?' Jack asked.

'About this place we're going to. Jasperville. I heard its name came from *j'espere*, but now everyone calls it Despairville.'

'I've not heard that,' Jack said.

'So, the things about people going mad out there, people being murdered—'

'Vivi, enough,' Paul said. 'I'm really sorry, Jack. My wife has a fertile imagination when it comes to such things.'

'It's okay,' Jack said. 'It's a faraway place, for sure. This is pretty much the only way in and out. There's an airstrip out there, but most of the time it's too cold, too much ice, too strong a wind to bring a plane in. They don't have a runway for the big passenger planes, only the little ones, the two-prop, ten-seaters, and the storms out there would just throw a thing like that to the ground. So yes, it has its challenges, but you're gonna get the same challenges anyplace up in this region. Environment like that brings people close. It's a community. People help each other out.' He smiled reassuringly. 'I'm sure you'll do just fine.'

'But the stories. The thing about the girls who got killed, and there's this Algonquin legend about something called a—'

'No,' Jack interjected. He didn't want to hear it. He knew he would have to, but not now. Not yet. 'Believe me, the only things that kill people out there are weather and time.'

'See,' Paul said. 'I told you. It's just stories. There's no curse and there's no serial killers, and there's certainly no Algonquin cannibals. You have way too much imagination.'

Vivi didn't buy it. She looked at Jack for just a little too long. He looked away, but he knew she was watching him. He could feel her eyes burning right through him. *You know, don't you?* she was saying. *You know there's something out there, and you're afraid.*

Jack wished he hadn't acknowledged them. Perhaps he'd done it subconsciously. Perhaps he'd wanted to be asked. For more than a quarter of a century he'd avoided the subject altogether, and now, here he was, due to arrive with the daylight, and there was a reservoir of words and feelings, thoughts and anxieties that needed to be exorcized.

Yes, he should have said. *Everything you've heard is right, but you've heard so little of the truth. After a month, you'll forget where you are. You'll lose all sense of orientation. Every direction you look, the darkness will be waiting for you, but you won't even know which direction you're looking in. Time collapses. Even the sun hides. After a year you'll feel like you've lost all connection to the outside world. You can't reach it, and it can't reach you. And even if you manage to escape, you'll take so much of the past with you that the past and present will no longer be distinguishable. There'll be no dividing line. So yes, Vivienne, you might think what you've heard is hearsay, old wives' tales, but the truth is worse. I should know, because I was there for most of it and I will carry it with me for the rest of my life.*

Vivi's hood was back up, her face framed in the shadow. She was leaning against her husband's shoulder, looking out through the window as the dark, silent landscape unravelled behind the train.

Jack wanted to sleep, but didn't dare. All he could think of was Thérèse Bergeron, and the very last time he'd seen her alive.

14

Jacques stood at the top of the stairs. He was infuriated. It was his birthday, and he was going to be a teenager. This day – 20 June 1978 – was supposed to be a memorable day, but Calvis was sick with a fever and the party had been postponed.

'We'll make it right,' Elizabeth said. 'As soon as Calvis is better we'll have the party, I promise.'

And then his father's voice boomed from the kitchen. 'You get down here now and eat your breakfast, Jacques. You're a young man now, so you better start behaving like one.'

Jacques thumped down the stairs. He would do as he was told, but resent every second of it.

Papi was sitting at the kitchen table. He looked up and smiled. 'Well, what do we have here? Correct me if I'm wrong, but I do believe this is the rudest boy in the world.'

Jacques glared at him.

'Why, yes indeed. Ladies and gentlemen, we have ourselves a winner. Look at the frown, the sour face. Look at the wickedness and spite in those beady little eyes—'

'Oh, Papi!' Jacques said, and started laughing.

'Come, sit with me,' Papi said. 'Eat your breakfast. I'll walk you to school and tell you a story.'

Jacques ate his breakfast, and Papi did take him to school. He told him a story but left it incomplete. 'I will tell you the rest later,' he said.

After school, Jacques and Carine would walk back to the boarding house, and from there Jacques and Juliette would walk home. Since the beginning of the year, however, Juliette had begun working into the early evening. The boarding house was full. There were beds to make, sheets to launder, and an endless procession of plates and cutlery to wash. Most days Jacques would walk alone, admonished to keep to the pedestrian thoroughfare and never diverge from it. As for Juliette, she and Thérèse were joined at the hip, each often mistaken for the other. Twenty years old, just three months separating them, there was not a young, single man in Jasperville whose dreams didn't feature either or both. For the older, married men the affliction was far worse. Carine, just a month from her eleventh birthday, had replaced the almost obsessive attachment to Jacques with a somewhat diffident nonchalance. She appeared to want him around, went to some extraordinary lengths to ensure this happened, but once he was present, she barely said a word. Jacques really didn't know what had gotten into her. Girls were just different, it seemed. There was no requirement for him to understand them, and thus he didn't try.

Beyond the demands of his school studies, Jacques had developed a passion for reading that surprised even Elizabeth.

He devoured books, one after the other. He'd swept through those in the house like a tidal wave – everything from *Moby Dick* to *Sherlock Holmes*, Jack London to Ernest Hemingway. Elizabeth would sometimes look through the volumes he was reading, and here and there she found slips of paper tucked into the pages. Upon them, Jacques had carefully copied out individual words.

'What are these?' she'd once asked him.

'Words I don't know,' he'd replied. 'I go and look them up in the dictionary at school.'

Elizabeth, still drawn to her life as a teacher, couldn't have been more pleased. Though Jacques didn't find it easy to make friends, those friends he did have were close. He was a thoughtful boy, and even when Carine needled him to the point that Elizabeth was all set to slap her into next Sunday, Jacques didn't rise to the bait. It was clear that Carine was besotted with Jacques. Her teasing and taunting was merely her way of keeping his attention. The notion that Jacques and Carine might make a life together, whether here or in some other far-flung corner of the globe, gave Elizabeth a sense of accomplishment. After all, what was it to be a mother, if not to prepare a child for a life that they could happily live in your absence?

Though she didn't communicate it, Elizabeth was troubled that they wouldn't be celebrating Jacques' birthday. A boy becoming a teenager was significant. In many faiths and cultures, this was seen as the transition between child and man. In some tribes, a thirteen-year-old was expected to hunt alongside his elders, to bring back sufficient food for his siblings. In the Jewish faith, it would be *bar mitzvah*, not only a coming-of-age, but also when the father was no longer held accountable for the sins of the child.

But Calvis had a fever. Neither serious nor of great concern, it was nevertheless irresponsible to have children congregate when one of them was sick. Until the fever broke, Calvis would be contagious. The party would be postponed until Saturday; Elizabeth felt sure Calvis would be more than well enough by then.

That morning – with breakfast done, Calvis still asleep upstairs, Henri and Juliette at work, William having walked Jacques to school – the house was quiet for just the briefest time. Elizabeth couldn't recall the last time there had been this much silence in the Devereaux home. Once the table was cleared and the dishes washed, she stood at the window and looked out toward the Torngat Mountains. They had been here for nine years. She recalled that first day, and how they'd been met at the station by Wilson Gaines, the Housing Administrator. And then there was the son. What was his name? Robert. That was it. Such a pale boy, and so very quiet. For the life of her, she couldn't remember having seen either of them again after that first day.

William returned to interrupt her reverie.

Elizabeth made him some coffee and he took it at the kitchen table.

'Sit with me a moment,' he said.

'I need to check on Calvis...'

'Just for a moment.'

Elizabeth dried her hands and sat down.

William paused before he spoke, and then said, 'Do you ever regret coming here?'

'Why d'you ask that?' she replied.

'Because of the way you sometimes look, my dear.'

'Seems to me people spend their whole lives wishing for something different. Very few get it, and most often realize it's no better than what they had. Then it's too late to undo it.'

'True indeed,' William said. He held her gaze with his rheumy eyes, every moment of his seventy-one years etched in his face.

Elizabeth knew there was something he wanted to say.

'I know what I did.'

'Father—'

William raised his hand. 'Likely I'll never speak of this again, so let me say what I have to say.' He looked away for a second. 'My mind is going. I know that. Sometimes I look at people I've known since we got here, and for the life of me I cannot remember their names.'

'I know, Father, and you manage it far better than I could.'

'That's the thing, you see? You manage it. The irony is that

I can remember the things I regret as clearly as the day I did them.'

'You don't need to talk about it.'

'I *need* to tell you something. And I have to tell you now just in case I don't remember it the next time I summon enough courage.'

'Enough courage? What do you mean?'

There was something in William's expression then, something that Elizabeth had never seen before – not when he was drinking, not when his mind slipped its moorings and he drifted into a reality only he could see and understand. This was something different, and it scared her.

'I fear for you,' William said, his voice hushed, as if anxious not to be overheard.

'You fear for what, Father?'

He leaned in closer, conspiratorial now. There could be others listening.

'This place,' he said. 'This desolate, godforsaken place. The things I hear. The things I see.'

'What?' Elizabeth asked. 'What do you hear? What do you see?' There was anxiety in her voice. She wanted to know it was nothing more than some wild flight of imagination that had somehow cornered his thoughts.

'Henri,' William said.

Elizabeth felt the colour drain from her face.

'I'm afraid that he will be possessed by this place, that he will do something truly terrible—'

'What are you saying?' Elizabeth said. 'Henri is—'

'I am out there,' William interjected, his voice a whisper. 'Out *there*. I can see everything, what happened to those girls. I can hear them in the darkness, Elizabeth, and they tell me that—'

'No,' Elizabeth said. 'No! I don't want to hear it!'

'But you must!' William urged. He reached forward and

gripped her hand. He pulled her with some force. The edge of the table was against her ribs. Her father's gaze was unerring, and there was something so disturbing about the way he just stared.

'You must listen to me!' he said. 'It's about Henri.'

'No!' Elizabeth said. She pulled her hand free, and she got up from the chair.

'I don't know what's going on, Father. I don't know if you've been drinking again or you've had one of your spells, but I won't have you say a word against Henri. I know you've never liked him, and I know you blame him for the fact that we're out here a million miles from anywhere. Do I need to remind you that the only reason I'm in this country in the first place is because of what you did in England?'

'I'm just thinking of you and the children—'

'They're my children, and Henri is their father, and he's done nothing but provide for this family since we got here.'

'But there are things here, Elizabeth ... and they have been here a great deal longer than any of us.'

'That is just about enough,' Elizabeth said. 'This is the non-sense that you've been telling Jacques. Filling his head with all sorts of ghost stories and Lord only knows what. He tells Carine. The poor girl is scared out of her wits. Marguerite tells me that she's taken to sleeping in her sister's bed. Now, I know it's different with boys, and perhaps they're not frightened so easily, but—'

'Jacques understands,' William said. The words were uttered with such calm directness that for a moment Elizabeth didn't know how to respond.

She gathered herself. She stood her ground. Granted, this was her father, but he had no right to disturb the children and insinuate that there was some problem with Henri.

'Jacques is a boy with a mind all his own,' Elizabeth said,

'and I would appreciate it if you would stop trying to fill it with spectres and ghouls and whatnot. As for my husband, he's *my* husband, and just as he's devoted himself to the well-being and welfare of the children, so he's taken it upon himself to ensure that you have a roof over your head—'

'And to help himself to every last penny—'

'Those pennies never being yours in the first place!'

Elizabeth felt the anger rise in her chest. She was having none of it.

'Now, you hear what I have to say, William Swann. No more ghost stories. You mind your manners and your tongue, or I'll throw you out into the cold and... and well... well, you'll damned well freeze to death like those poor girls you seem so keen to talk about!'

Elizabeth turned on her heel and went to the stairs. She glanced back before she went up to Calvis, and the look of defeat and despair in her father's eyes made her immediately sorry for what she'd said. He was an old man, frail of mind and body, and she'd charged at him like an elephant and run him down.

'Father—'

William raised his hand. 'I heard you loud and clear, Elizabeth. Go see to the boy.'

Elizabeth knew he'd raised his defences. She would proffer an apology, but not now. He would wind himself down, and then, more than likely, he would be the one to bring the olive branch. They argued rarely, and it had always resolved itself. She told herself that this time would be no different, but as she stepped quietly through the bedroom door and looked down at Calvis, his eyelids fluttering, his forehead beaded with sweat, there was a palpable sense of anxiety and tension all about her. She started to think about what it was that William had intended to say about Henri. She couldn't go back and ask him. Not yet. But did she want to know? Why had her father raised the subject of both Henri and the dead girls in the same conversation? It was a dark and terrible thought, and she cast it from her mind at once. She drew a chair to the side of Calvis's bed. There was nothing to punctuate the silence but the sound of his breathing, beneath that the rapid beating of her own heart. She was disturbed. There was no denying it. Something about the certainty with which he'd spoken, the flash of fear in his eyes when she refused to hear him out, and now she was listening to her sleeping child and praying that his breathing didn't stop.

Elizabeth checked herself. She was being entirely foolish. She heard the back door open and shut. William would be out there ruminating and muttering with his pipe and his shawl. She would let him be. Calvis would sleep, and she would busy herself preparing for this evening. If there was to be no party, then at the very least they would have a cake and some candles so Jacques could make a wish.

It was a little after seven when the Bergerons arrived. Juliette had made the arrangements, and it was a surprise for everyone. Yes, there would be a party when Calvis was well, but this day couldn't pass without a proper acknowledgement.

Dinner was finished, and Jacques was at the sink washing plates when the kitchen was suddenly filled with noise and cheer.

Philippe and Marguerite made a performance of presenting Jacques with a large parcel. It was wrapped in butcher's paper and tied with baling twine. Thérèse and Carine were so very keen to have him see what was inside. Jacques set it down on the table, took his sheath knife and cut the string. He folded out the paper. The anticipation in the room was palpable.

They'd ordered it from Montréal, and according to the patch inside it was hand-crafted from the finest deerskin, the lining nothing less than shearling, a real honest-to-God trapper's jacket with buckles to cinch the waist, hand-warmer pockets, press studs at the rear vent for when a young man was venturing out on horseback.

Both Henri and Elizabeth were utterly taken aback. Such a thing must have cost a fortune.

Jacques was speechless, but he stumbled through a dozen or more *Thank yous* as he hugged both Marguerite and Philippe.

'It's a special birthday,' Philippe said. 'You are now a young man, Jacques.' He turned to his youngest. 'And Carine here has something to tell you.'

Carine looked awkward and embarrassed, but she stepped forward and said, 'We wanted you to have something really special, Jackrabbit. We all saved up, and I put my pocket money and some money from chores, and we really, really hope you like it.' With that, she stepped forward and kissed Jacques on the cheek. He blushed beet-red, and everyone laughed in good humour, and the love that was present in the Devereaux house seemed sufficient to ward off any ill wind that had a mind to disturb them.

William was right behind Elizabeth. He put his hands on her shoulders and leaned to whisper to her. 'I'm sorry,' he said. 'For speaking out of turn.'

Without turning, she closed her hand over his and squeezed it reassuringly. He'd proffered the olive branch, just as she'd expected he would, and there was nothing to do but graciously accept it.

Elizabeth presented the cake, and the candles were lit. There was wine for the adults and fruit punch for Jacques and Carine, and Jacques wore his coat like he was Daniel Boone all set to blaze the Wilderness Road.

And later, as the Bergerons were readying themselves to leave, Thérèse took Jacques aside. Her cheeks were flushed with the wine and the warmth of the stove, and her eyes were as bright as he'd ever seen them.

'I want you to make me a promise,' she said.

'A promise? About what?'

Thérèse glanced toward her sister, pulling her boots on near the front door, her mother and father still chattering with Henri and Elizabeth.

'About Carine. That you'll take care of her.' She paused, and for the briefest of moments she closed her eyes. 'If something happens.'

'If something happens? What do you mean?'

The bright eyes burned right through him. He could not look away.

'Just promise me,' she said. 'That no matter what happens, you will always take care of Carine.'

'Y-yes,' Jacques said, taken aback by the intensity of her tone. 'Yes, I promise.'

'Good,' she said. And then the determination in her expression was gone, and she smiled with such tenderness.

'Happy birthday, Jackrabbit,' she said, pulling him close and hugging him as if both their lives depended on it.

15

Jack started awake as the train began to shudder. The sounds of the wheels trying to gain traction on the icy rails was shrill and unforgiving. He leaned sideways and looked out of the window. Up ahead he could see the Emeril Junction sidings coming into view through the flurries of snow. He glanced at his watch – 4.40 a.m. They were running late. The first haunt of light had crossed the horizon, but it was cold, bruised and grey. He couldn't recall falling asleep. He knew he'd dreamed, too. There was disturbance in his mind, and his body ached as if he'd been wrestling with something unseen.

In the canteen car, Jack took some coffee and *Pets de Soeurs*. That cinnamon taste reminded him so much of those days with the Bergerons. The more distant his mother and father became, the more he'd felt a sense of belonging to his second family. Nevertheless, when circumstances required that he step up and take responsibility – not only for Calvis, but for Carine – he'd taken the path of least resistance and fled.

He hadn't even returned when Henri was committed in Saguenay in the middle of 1995. He'd convinced himself that he was being resolute. After all, Calvis was nearly twenty-three by that time and was more than able to deal with it. By telephone, Jack had spoken with the officials at the institution. They'd told him that Calvis had dealt with all the paperwork, the interviews, had attended the consultations. Jack had taken that as confirmation that Calvis was in control of his own life. Henri had been certified 'schizophrenic', whatever the hell that meant. Even before he'd left Jasperville in 1984, Henri was talking to himself, to people who weren't there, repeating the same stories Jack had shared with Carine.

It all seemed as real as yesterday. The past never changed, no matter what happened in the present.

As the train came to a halt, Jack waited patiently for the door lock to be released. He didn't make eye contact with anyone. He wanted some time alone outside, the cold air against his face, no expectations to speak, no obligation to be interested in anything but his own thoughts.

The door hissed. The huge metal hinges strained. Suddenly, winter filled the carriage. He pulled his coat around him and stepped down onto the platform. He walked quickly – away from the train, away from people, voices, everything – and he stood silently at the end of the trees that ran a parallel line to the track. He watched his fellow travellers as they shared cigarettes and conversation. He didn't belong. He'd convinced himself that he'd never wanted to belong. But that was a lie. He'd moved town, state, country, buried his mind in work, in endless books, but it counted for nothing. Conscience was an internal country. No matter how much you changed the land-scape, there'd always be something to remind you of the worst you ever did.

Despairville. So fitting, and so utterly true.

Once they resumed the journey, it would be another four hours. He wouldn't sleep, at least not intentionally. He felt wired, as if amphetamine was coursing through his veins. He knew he'd have to have a plan of action, but until he arrived there was no way to formulate one. It was not lack of care that had failed him; it was sheer stupidity. What kind of person travelled the better part of a thousand miles into a situation without asking precisely what had happened, and what would be required of him when he arrived?

The train rumbled. It looked as if people were heading back to the platform. Resentfully, Jack made his way along the tree line in the direction of the carriage. It was only as he neared that he realized that everyone seemed to be waiting for something. One of the conductors started walking down toward them.

Jack didn't move. Paul Girard sauntered over.

'An electrical issue, apparently,' he said.

'Not long,' the conductor explained. 'Maybe half an hour or so. One of the batteries for the carriage heaters needs changing. It's the cold. It happens a lot.'

There was a murmur of frustration. Most of the passengers went up into the carriages. It was too cold to stand outside.

'You heading back?' Paul asked.

'In a little while,' Jack said.

'Hey, I'm sorry about my wife. The questions. That's just the way she is.'

'It's no big deal.'

'Can I ask why you're going back? You said you'd been away for – what? – twenty-five years?'

Jack took a breath. It was inevitable that he'd have to start talking at some point, so why not to a stranger?

'I have a brother out there,' he said. 'He needs some help.'

'Oh,' Paul said, as if this was not the conversation he wanted. 'I hope nothing serious.'

'Serious enough.'

Vivi joined them.

'Jack here is going back to help his brother,' Paul said.

'Didn't you say you hadn't been back for twenty-five years?' she asked.

'I did, yes.'

'You have other family there?'

'Vivi, it's none of our business.' Paul looked at Jack apologetically.

'It's fine,' Jack said. 'There's no other family out there. I left when I was nineteen. He was twelve. My mother died just a couple of months before, and I had to get out of there.'

'So he was with your father?'

'Vivi, really…'

Jack laughed. 'Are you a cop, or what?'

Vivi looked awkward. 'I'm sorry,' she said. 'I'm a writer. I'm just habitually nosey. I want to know everything about everyone.'

'It's true,' Paul said. 'You're not being singled out for special treatment. She's like this with cab drivers, neighbours, people in the coffee shop.'

'I embarrass him,' Vivi said.

'You don't embarrass me, sweetheart. It's just that some people are private, you know? Not everyone is willing to just open up about their lives.'

'I'm sorry if I bothered you, Jack,' Vivi said.

'Not at all.' He dug his hands in his pockets, looked down at his boots. 'Truth be told, the fact that I don't talk to people probably accounts for half of my difficulties.'

'I think that could be said of pretty much everyone,' Vivi replied. 'We have the face we wear for the world, and then we have who we really are.'

Jack looked up at her. He held her gaze until he sensed that she was becoming uncomfortable. In reality, he wasn't really looking at her. She just happened to be right there in his line of sight. He was looking at someone else entirely. Someone who had no face. And the blood was all around, and it made patterns in the snow, and even as he'd seen it, he knew that this was an image that would always be right behind his eyelids.

Thirteen years old, heart hammering out of his chest, and his eyes so filled with tears it seemed that the whole world was drowning.

16

It was July. Much of the snow had melted. The sun was above the horizon twenty-four hours a day, and only in the deepest crevices and depressions was there any sign that winter would return. Temperatures reached as high as 11 or 12 Celsius, and a thin film of green lichen carpeted the exposed rock. There was rain, too – sudden, brief, torrential. It hammered down and turned the pathways between the houses into deep channels of filthy mud. Efforts were made to keep it level; as soon as the temperatures dropped, it would freeze into sharp ridges that were impossible to cross by foot or vehicle. Surrounding Jasperville was an impenetrable fog. It hung low to the ground, drifting like smoke. Visibility was thirty or forty yards at best, and only when the sun was at its zenith. Much of the time, the Torngat Mountains were completely obscured, but when they came into view they seemed to assume the shape of some distant slumbering beast. Though it was warmer, there was something surreal about the effect of that warmth. The air was heavy and moist. Sound didn't travel. Everything seen and heard was subdued and ambiguous.

In a month it would be Calvis's sixth birthday. He'd been attending school for a year. Jacques and Calvis were as inseparable as Juliette and Thérèse. Though Juliette was now twenty years old, she'd never once spoken of leaving Jasperville. In equal parts comforting and puzzling, Elizabeth had yet failed to come to a conclusion about this. Juliette helped with William; she cooked, she cleaned, she did the boys' laundry. She was kind and considerate, of infinite patience, and seemed to want for nothing.

One morning, a week or so after Jacques' thirteenth birthday, Juliette was readying herself to leave for the boarding house.

'Sit with me a moment,' Elizabeth said.

'I need to go,' Juliette said. 'I'll be late.'

'Five minutes, my dear. That's all.'

Juliette sat at the kitchen table.

'I just wanted to talk to you,' Elizabeth said.

'About what?'

'About your future plans. You take care of everyone, and it's time someone took a little care of you.'

'I'm fine, Ma,' Juliette said.

'I know you're fine, Juliette, but you're twenty now. You're an adult. Surely you must have some notion of making your own life, moving away from here, perhaps going back to Montréal, find a husband...'

'Lord, no,' Juliette said. 'A husband?'

'Do you not want to get married? Or perhaps there's a young man you have your eye on here?'

'I'm content with things as they are,' Juliette said. 'I have a job, I have friends, I have our family. Besides, what on earth would you do without me?'

Elizabeth smiled. 'True. Some days I have no idea how I'd manage on my own.'

Juliette got up. 'Don't worry about me,' she said. 'Things are just fine as they are. If I plan on doing anything different, then you'll be the first to know.'

'You're sure now?'

'Ma. Really.'

And with that, she put on her overcoat and left.

Elizabeth was reconciled to the fact that Juliette had a mind of her own, and she was the only one who would change it. She thought nothing more of the matter until a week or so later. It was 4th July. The American employees had a big celebration planned for that evening. It was Tuesday, and the last thing Henri needed was three- or four-dozen hungover miners. Try as he might, he couldn't convince them to postpone their party until the weekend.

In the early afternoon, Marguerite Bergeron came to the house. Even before she spoke, there was something in her manner that was troubling. She seemed ill at ease, polite as always, but the familiarity which defined their friendship seemed absent. She even asked where William was and if he might overhear.

'He's on the porch,' Elizabeth said. 'He doesn't hear much of anything these days, Marguerite.'

Marguerite took a seat at the table. The expression in her eyes said that trouble was on its way.

'What is it, dear?'

'Sit down, Elizabeth,' Marguerite said. 'There's a matter we need to discuss, and I really don't know how to say it apart from just saying it.'

Elizabeth dried her hands on the dish towel. She sat down. They looked at one another in silence.

'Speak,' Elizabeth said.

Marguerite took a deep breath. 'I saw something.'

Elizabeth didn't reply. She tried to relax.

'I saw something that I know I wasn't meant to see, and it's troubling me greatly.'

Marguerite closed her eyes. Whatever it was, it was right there at the forefront of her mind.

'I wish I hadn't seen it, of course, but I did. And now I've seen it, it cannot be avoided or ignored. It's something that concerns both of us, and we're the only ones who can make a decision about what to do.'

'What is it, Marguerite?' Elizabeth asked. 'What on earth are you talking about?'

'Our daughters,' Marguerite said. 'I'm talking about our daughters.'

Elizabeth knew then, but she didn't dare let herself believe it.

'What I saw, Elizabeth ... I don't want to say it ...'

A wave of emotion flooded through Elizabeth. Her chest tightened, as if the air itself had become harder to breathe.

'Marguerite, please.'

'They ... they were together,' Marguerite said, her voice little more than a whisper.

'Together?' Elizabeth said, trying to force herself to rewind time, to go back an hour, a day, a week.

'They were intimate, Elizabeth. With one another. I saw them. The way a man and a woman are intimate—'

Elizabeth felt the colour blanche from her face. 'I understand what the word means, Marguerite.'

Marguerite's eyes filled with tears.

Elizabeth knew then she would have to manage this situation. Marguerite was in no state to make a decision about anything.

'These things happen,' Elizabeth said. 'It's not the first time such a thing has happened, and I'm sure it won't be the last. Young women, and young men as well ... well, they begin to understand that they ...' She paused. She had no idea what she was thinking, let alone what she was saying.

'They were touching one another,' Marguerite said. 'They were kissing and touching one another.'

The walls of Elizabeth's internal world seem to sag and fold inward. She didn't feel disgust or shock. She felt dismay. It was not a matter of what she was being told, but how she would deal with it. She loved her daughter beyond measure, and there was nothing that Juliette could ever say or do that would change that. Her concern was for Henri, for Jacques, for the people they knew, the people they had to see each and every day. She knew there would be those who saw fit to label them shameful.

'What are we going to do?' Marguerite said.

Elizabeth breathed slowly and deeply.

Marguerite opened her mouth to speak.

'A moment, please,' Elizabeth said. She rose from the chair and walked to the window.

'For a little while, they will have to be apart,' Elizabeth said. 'I will speak to Juliette. I will come now and bring her home. I will talk to her. That is what I will do.'

'Don't come to the house,' Marguerite said. 'Let me go back. I'll tell her that I visited with you, and that you sent for her as you needed some help with ... with William.'

'Yes,' Elizabeth said. 'Yes, that's better.'

'Tell me that all will be well, Elizabeth.'

Elizabeth took her friend's hand. 'All will be well, Marguerite,' she said, and even as the words left her lips, they sounded hollow and meaningless.

Juliette arrived within thirty minutes. Elizabeth saw her sharing a few words with William on the porch. Elizabeth knocked on the window and waved her in.

'What's going on?' Juliette said. 'Marguerite said you needed my help with Papi. He seems just fine.'

'I sent for you because I wanted to talk to you.'

'Again?'

'Sit down, Juliette.'

'What's going on, Ma?'

'Juliette, I'm asking you to sit down. Please do as your mother asks.'

Juliette hesitated, and then she took a seat at the kitchen table.

'I need to ask you something, Juliette, and before you answer I want you to know that no matter what you say, I'm your mother, and there's nothing in the world that would ever make me love you less.'

Immediately, Juliette's expression changed. She paled visibly, and when she reached up to tuck back a stray lock of hair it was obvious that her hand was shaking.

'I want you to tell me the truth about your friendship with Thérèse.'

It was as if she'd been slapped across the face. Juliette's eyes widened, and tears welled against her lower lids. Her cheeks reddened, and she started to take short, shallow breaths, as if desperately withholding herself from breaking down.

'Thérèse ... Thérèse is my best friend,' she said, her voice faltering.

'I'm well aware of that fact, sweetheart. You two have been inseparable since they first arrived. I'm asking about the *nature* of your friendship.'

A single fat tear broke free and rolled down Juliette's cheek. 'Wha-what do y-you mean?'

Elizabeth sat down. She reached out and took her daughter's hand. 'The fact that you're already upset about this tells me there's a great deal we need to talk about.'

'There's nothing to talk about.'

'Juliette, please. You need to answer my question. You need to tell me about your relationship with Thérèse.'

'I love her,' Juliette said. 'And she loves me. We love one another.'

'As more than friends. You love her as a woman loves a man ...'

Juliette frowned. 'No,' she said. 'I love her as a woman loves a woman.'

'Okay,' Elizabeth said, and the resignation was clear in her voice. 'I understand.'

'You don't. You can't. It's not something anyone could understand unless they have experienced it themselves.'

'I didn't mean that I understand it in that way. I meant that I understand the situation we're dealing with.'

'It's not a situation,' Juliette said. 'It's a fact. Thérèse and I are in love.'

'And you've been intimate with one another,' Elizabeth said.

'Wha—'

'Marguerite saw you, Juliette. She saw you and she came here to see me.'

'Oh God.'

'That is the situation, my dear. What you feel, what you think you feel, whatever you imagine or believe this to be, is secondary to the reality of who and where we are. This is a small community. Some of the people here are neither liberal-minded nor imaginative. A revelation of this nature would see both of you ostracized, perhaps even hounded in public—'

'Then we'll leave.'

'No, Juliette.'

'Why not? We have money. We have each other. We can go back to Montréal and decide how we live our lives without having to worry about what other people think.'

Elizabeth leaned back and sighed. 'Let's not make any impulsive decisions. Just for now, just for a little while, I think it's better if you don't see one another.'

'No,' Juliette said. Her wilfulness rose in protest.

'Juliette—'

'No, Mother. You can't stop me seeing her. I'm twenty years old.'

'It's not a matter of stopping anyone doing anything, Juliette. It's a matter of stepping back from the brink and really looking at whether or not you want to jump.'

'What, because you think this is a phase? That it's a little schoolgirl crush? Is that what you think? That it's just a little flirtation. Well, it's not. This has been going on for two years. She and I have been *intimate*, as you put it, for over two years. I love her. She is my life. She's everything to me. As far as I'm concerned, unless Thérèse is part of my life, then I might as well not have any life at all.'

'Don't say that, sweetheart.'

'Why not? You asked for the truth. Well, there's the truth. She and I have lain together. Naked. I know everything about her, every inch of her. She and I are lovers in every sense of the word, Mother, and there's nothing you can do about it.'

'Okay, okay,' Elizabeth said, feeling that everything was moving too quickly. 'I need to talk to your father. I need to talk to Marguerite and Philippe. I need to just take this on board and work out how I'm going to best help you be happy. This is not an easy situation, Juliette, and I want you to trust me. I want you to do what I ask, okay?'

'You want me to stop seeing her.'

'I do, yes. Just for a little while. A month, two weeks even …'

Juliette was shaking her head before Elizabeth even finished speaking.

'Then can you give me enough time to talk to your father? Please, if nothing else, just give me that.'

Juliette leaned forward. The colour had returned to her complexion. Her eyes were fierce and bright. Elizabeth saw passion, and she knew there was nothing she could do to change it.

'Speak to him,' Juliette said. 'Tell him however you want to tell him. But know this … I will be with Thérèse whether you approve or not, whether you allow it or not. I have my own life.

I can choose who to love, and I have chosen to love Thérèse.'
Juliette got up. 'I love you too, Mother. You know I do. The last thing in the world I want to do is make you unhappy, but I know that you wouldn't want me to be unhappy either.'

The look in her eyes was nothing but defiant.

Juliette headed for the stairs. She didn't look back.

Elizabeth sat in silence for what seemed like a very long time. She couldn't speak to Henri. Henri was as hard-headed as he'd ever been. Such a notion would be so far beyond Henri's ability to comprehend that he would dismiss it out of hand. What could he possibly do? Have her committed to an asylum? Send her to a convent? Elizabeth didn't want to even think about it.

It was this place. This desolate, lonely wilderness into which they'd dragged their children. They should have stayed in the city. Their existence, their lives, their future, everything that they had become was governed by the cold and the snow and the rain and the mud. She hated her father for being a thief. She hated Henri for being pig-headed and insensitive. She hated herself for agreeing to come here.

Standing at the window, Elizabeth looked out at the dense bank of fog that obscured her view. She thought of just walking into it. Just take a direction and keep moving until she dropped from exhaustion. Let it all go to Hell.

She steeled herself. She was stronger than this. Self-pity was an inevitable route to even greater hardship. She *had* to deal with this. This was her daughter, her family, her life, and if it came to a choice between her own happiness and Juliette's, then she knew the decision she would make. After all, she was a mother, and that's what mothers did.

It was the sense of calm that Juliette exhibited that was the most unnerving of all. The subject was not raised, even when she and Elizabeth were alone in the house. Juliette did exactly as she'd agreed. She didn't go to the boarding house. Thérèse was also nowhere to be seen. Marguerite didn't visit, and though Elizabeth considered heading over to the boarding house to see her, she didn't. For three or four days following the discussion, it was quiet.

Later, it became clear what had happened. As their respective families slept, Juliette and Thérèse had met late at night. So used to the sound of the wind, the rain, the creaking and groaning of the house, not one person was awakened by either of them leaving. They'd taken articles of clothing, even food, and hidden it. They were taking the train out of Jasperville on the morning of Monday the 10th, the day of Carine's eleventh birthday. What they were going to do once they reached Sept-Îles, whether they would stay there or head on to Montréal, seemed utterly irrelevant after the fact.

It was Philippe who hammered on the front door of the Devereaux place. Henri had already left for work, and Jacques was the one to greet him. It was only when Elizabeth understood that Thérèse was not at home that she knew what was going on. Juliette's bed was empty, too. Clothes and shoes were missing. The reality of their elopement was immediate and alarming.

Elizabeth told Jacques to get dressed. She assigned Calvis to William's care. She didn't take the time to explain why Juliette and Thérèse would vanish together, merely that they had, and that they needed to be found. Philippe would go back and fetch Marguerite. Carine would stay at the boarding house, just in case they changed their minds and returned.

The train was not due to leave Jasperville for another hour, and thus there was every possibility that the girls would be found. How she could even begin to explain the truth to Henri was another matter entirely. First things first.

There was no sign of them at the rail terminal. As yet, no

tickets had been purchased. When questioned, the North Shore and Labrador Rail superintendent said he'd spoken to a young woman two or three days before, that she'd asked the cost of two one-way tickets to Sept-Îles. Had he seen her that morning? No, he hadn't.

It was then that Philippe urged everyone to split up.

'There are four of us,' he said. 'We can each go different ways. They can't be far, surely. The train leaves in an hour.'

'But someone should stay here,' Jacques said, still struggling to understand what was happening.

'I'll stay here,' Marguerite said, appreciating that Jacques would be no match for a determined big sister.

The only way out of Jasperville was on that train, and had they all remained exactly where they were then seeing the girls would have been inevitable. However, doing something seemed to be a far better option than doing nothing. It was instinctive. They just wanted to find the girls, to know that they were safe.

It made sense in that light, of course, but it also resulted in a thirteen-year-old boy heading off to find his big sister on his own. Of course, no one could have predicted what he would find. Not in their wildest nightmares could they have imagined the sight that would greet the boy's eyes as he came around the back of the terminal warehouse building.

Juliette was there. She was kneeling on the floor. Her hands were covered in blood, and her skirt was dappled with blood, and there seemed to be more blood on the ground all around her.

Jacques' mind wrestled with the image ahead of him. Instinctive disbelief and denial, a sense that he was hallucinating perhaps, but when Juliette threw her head back and screamed all holy hell, it hit home with all the force of a North Shore freight train.

Thérèse was right there, right beside Juliette. Lying on her side, her head thrown back at an impossible angle, her arms outstretched. The only way Jacques knew it was Thérèse was because of her clothes.

Thérèse's face – what little remained of it – was nothing but a bloody, torn memory of how she'd once looked.

But the thing that would remain with Jacques through one brutal nightmare after another was the image of Juliette. Her eyes wide, her whole body wracked with horror, her fragile form shaking as she held onto the lifeless body of her friend.

For years, Jacques would remember the sound that then erupted from her throat – as if her heart had been torn from within and then cast into the howling wind.

17

From which book Jack couldn't remember, but the words had stayed with him: *If you want to go far, go together. If you want to go quickly, go alone.* It had become his mantra. It had governed every day of his life since leaving Jasperville.

No wife, no kids, a job that challenged only part of his intellect. He didn't socialize with anyone but Ludo. The situation with Caroline was a textbook repetition of every previous girlfriend. He'd been present, but without heart, without spirit, without passion.

The only person with whom he could say he'd shared anything real was Carine, and he'd abandoned her, too. He couldn't undo what had been done. That didn't stop him punishing himself with it.

Once they were back in the carriage, Vivi was her inquisitive self.

'I've tried to research as much as I can,' she said, 'but there just seems to be so little available information. I really have no idea what it's going to be like out there.'

'What do you want to know?' Jack asked.

'Okay... well, how cold does it get?'

'In winter it can drop to minus thirty. Lowest it ever got was the Christmas after I left. That was minus forty. It gets above zero in the spring and summer months, but the downside is that the sun doesn't set during that time.'

'The sun doesn't set?'

'Well, it's low on the horizon, sure, but it doesn't go below.'

'So it's like daylight twenty-four hours a day?'

'No, not really. It's like dusk. And then during the winter it's sometimes the case that the sun doesn't rise for weeks.'

Vivi turned to her husband. 'You hearing this?'

'I am, sweetheart, yes.'

'So I guess there ain't a great deal of trees and flowers and whatever,' she said.

'Moss, lichen, low shrubs. Under the topsoil is permafrost. Hard as rock. Nothing can root, you see. There are trees, but they're a good distance away near the Torngat Mountains.'

'I read about those mountains. It means something, right?'

'If you believe the legend, then it's an Inuktitut word. It means *place of evil spirits*.'

'Yes, that's it.' She pretended to shudder. 'Creepy.'

'It's a good distance from Jasperville. I think it's safe to say that the evil spirits pretty much stay where they are.'

'So, what do I need to know? You can look things up on the internet, but there's no substitute for asking a local.'

'I'm not a local any more,' Jack said.

'But you were there a long time.'

'In summertime the snow melts and it becomes a wetland,' Jack said. 'The flies and mosquitoes are awful. Once you're out there, then this route back to Sept-Îles is pretty much the only escape. Used to be the case that French was the main language, but that changed when the Canada Iron workers started coming in. That was how it was when I was there, and I guess it's still the same.' Jack leaned forward. 'A place like that kind of hangs in time, if you know what I mean. Things get established, and they get established because they work. People live the way they do because of the climate. The climate doesn't change, so habits and routine stay the same. The things that were built out there by Canada Iron go on serving the purpose, and that industry was in decline for years. It's only recently that it's gotten a new lease of life.'

'Which is how Paul got the job,' Vivi said.

'And is that the only reason for going?'

'No, not completely. I mean, if Paul hadn't got the job then we certainly wouldn't be going out there to live. We would've visited, for sure. It's somewhere I've been meaning to go for a long time.'

Jack's surprise was evident. 'What in God's name would you want to go out there for, unless you absolutely had to?'

'Well, believe it or not, I have a family member who used to live there. I mean, a long time ago, back in the fifties and sixties, but their daughter died, as far as I know. I think she got sick and she died. I don't know a great deal. It's one of those things that people either don't know about, or if they do, they don't want to talk about it.'

'And who was the family member?'

'My paternal grandmother's sister. I guess that would be a great aunt.'

'What was her name?'

'The family name was Roy. My aunt's name was Violetta.'

'Lisette,' Jack said matter-of-factly. 'That was the name of the daughter, wasn't it?'

Paul looked up from his newspaper.

'You knew them?' Vivi asked.

'Not really, no. That was in the early seventies. I was just a little kid. I remember that they owned the boarding house.'

'That's right,' Vivi said. 'That's what I was told. And then when the daughter died, they left. As far as I know they went to Trois-Riviérès.'

'I remember very little about them. I have a vague recollection of Lisette. She was maybe three or four years older than my sister.'

'Do you know what happened to her?' Vivi asked.

'No idea,' Jack lied.

'Would your sister remember her? I would so love to find out as much as possible about that side of my family. I don't know why, but I find the whole thing intriguing.'

'I'm sorry,' Jack said. 'My sister wouldn't be able to help. She died over thirty years ago.'

'Oh my God, I'm so sorry,' Vivi said.

'It's okay,' he replied, and then he lied again. 'I've had thirty years to get over it.'

Vivi fell quiet. She reached out and took her husband's hand.

Everyone they were talking about was dead: Baptiste, Violetta, Lisette, Juliette. And now here he was seated across from Lisette Roy's relative. Different generation, different world, but the connections travelled out through time and reached him all the same.

An hour before he'd been reminded of Thérèse, and the memory of that morning had come back to him with as much emotion as the day it had happened. And then there were the stories that William told, the old Indian legend he'd convinced himself was true, and the way those stories seemed to weave their way into everyone's thoughts after what happened that fateful Monday morning back in July of 1978.

The sergeant back then was Landry. He'd been there since the previous October and would stay until Christmas of the following year. And if ever there was a man possessed by the need to know the truth, it was Sergeant Émile Landry.

18

After the death of Thérèse Bergeron, everything changed. Juliette was broken in two. It was only years later that Jacques appreciated the nature of her relationship with Thérèse. At the time, he'd simply understood that Juliette had lost her closest friend. As for Carine, she was utterly devastated. There was nothing anyone could say that provided any comfort. What had happened possessed no reason, no explanation, and there was no context within which to place the killing of this girl.

There was talk in the Devereaux house about the Bergerons leaving Jasperville altogether. Jacques remembered both Philippe and Marguerite being there day after day, as if they couldn't bear to be anywhere that reminded them of their daughter. With them came Carine, and it was during those subsequent weeks that she and Jacques became so very close.

The new sergeant, Émile Landry, wasted no time in initiating as thorough an investigation as he could. Thérèse's body was taken to the medical centre, and even though Landry himself watched as the first examinations were undertaken by Bayard Pelletier, though he took copious notes, numerous photographs, sent telegrams at first to Sept-Îles and then to Montréal, it was as if no one beyond the limits of Jasperville wanted to know the truth of what had happened.

For three or four days after the event, Juliette was admin-istered a mild sedative by Pelletier. When she woke, and she woke often, she would sob and scream hysterically. No matter what Elizabeth did, the hysteria continued. Henri withdrew, as if he couldn't bear to see what was happening to his daughter. He asked Elizabeth if Juliette's mind might be broken beyond repair.

'It is grief, Henri,' Elizabeth said. 'It has power enough to consume everything.'

Henri asked questions that Elizabeth struggled to answer. Where did Juliette think she was going? How did she expect to survive? What was it that she was running away from? Why had Juliette ceased working at the boarding house in the days prior? And then he returned to the depth and seriousness of Juliette's hysteria. He understood that Thérèse and his daughter had been close, but why did Juliette seem even more inconsolable than the Bergerons? Elizabeth could see that none of it made sense to him, and she could say nothing to alleviate his confusion. As far as he was concerned, another girl was dead without explanation, and there was every likelihood his own daughter would never regain her sanity.

It was Friday before Sergeant Landry was able to sit beside Juliette's bed and speak with her. Impressing upon him a wish for discretion, Elizabeth had explained to Landry the nature of the relationship between Juliette and Thérèse. Landry's manner and attitude belied his age. Like Maurice Thibault, he seemed so very much older than his years. He was aware that Henri didn't know the precise details of the situation, and though he made no promise that such a thing would remain undisclosed, he assured her he would deal with it as delicately as possible.

Juliette was propped up in a bed she hadn't left since Monday, still somewhat bleary-eyed from sleep.

'You and she arranged to meet, yes?' Landry asked.

'Yes.'

'And you had planned to leave by train together?'

'Yes. We were leaving for Sept-Îles.'

Landry jotted a few words in his notepad. 'And once you had reached Sept-Îles?'

Juliette looked at Landry, and then she turned to her mother. 'We hadn't decided. We just wanted to get out of this place as quickly as possible.'

Again, Landry made a few notes. 'So you were together, and then you separated.'

'I went to buy the tickets,' Juliette said. 'I was gone for twenty minutes, maybe thirty. The office was not yet open. I went back to tell... to tell Thérèse, and that's when...' Juliette's voice cracked. Her eyes filled with tears.

'You went back to tell Thérèse, and when you got there this terrible thing had already happened.'

Juliette nodded in the affirmative.

'And did you see anything? An animal? A wolf, a bear? Anything at all that might have inflicted such...'

Already Juliette had lifted her head. 'I didn't see anything. She was just there... I just saw her there, and...' She started to sob again. Elizabeth pulled her close and held her.

Landry sat for a while. He needed the body to go to Montréal. He needed a full and thorough forensic examination to be done. He'd seen the reports on the Roy and Fournier girls, and he had a number of unresolved questions in his mind. The injuries sustained, though fatal, were not consistent with a bear attack. Black bears averaged two hundred pounds, and could weigh as much as twice that. One direct blow from a bear and a grown man would be killed outright. However, bears tended to avoid human contact. There were instances of bears aggressively defending their young, but mating season was in June. Cubs were not born until January. The same went for timber wolves. Yes, they could attack in defence of their young, but they were more likely to attack out of sheer starvation. Wolves travelled in packs, and if a pack of wolves had attacked Thérèse Bergeron then there would have been nothing left of her.

The wounds sustained by Thérèse were not consistent with a predatory attack. Pelletier said that the girl appeared to have been beaten to death with a blunt instrument. He also said that he was insufficiently skilled in forensic pathology to give any definitive conclusion. She could have been mauled by something, but if that was the case, why had she then been abandoned?

Landry didn't see one girl, but three. Three girls in six years, each of them of similar age, each of them fatally savaged, each of them then abandoned, and all within line of sight and earshot of the town.

No one heard screaming. No one saw an animal. Certainly in Thérèse's case, there appeared to be no defensive wounds, no indication that she'd tried to escape. Landry couldn't speak for Lisette Roy or Anne-Louise Fournier; the notes were insubstantial and no thorough examination had been undertaken. As Pelletier freely admitted, he was a general medical practitioner, and had merely followed the advice and instructions of Sergeants Levesque and Thibault respectively. Landry intended to contact each of them in turn and see if there was anything of significance they could recall, but he didn't hold out a great deal of hope. Years had passed, memories faded, and most importantly, he didn't believe that either man had viewed the deaths of Lisette Roy and Anne-Louise Fournier as anything other than a terrible accident.

Landry believed – despite the fact there was nothing probative to substantiate it – that Thérèse had been attacked and killed by a human being. This was something he very much hoped to confirm with an autopsy. The Sûreté possessed more than adequate resources and expertise, but Landry knew he would encounter administrative and bureaucratic obstacles. Employees of Canada Iron had been attacked by cougars in years past, and there had been a case of three ice-fishing teenagers being aggressively challenged by a pack of wolves. Only one had suffered serious injury, but the fact that it had happened was on file in Montréal.

If the girl had been killed by an animal, an autopsy wouldn't be warranted. Pelletier possessed authorization to sign the death certificate, and the matter would be closed. The girl would be buried there in Jasperville, or her parents would make arrangements for her to be buried elsewhere. Landry's most promising avenue would be the parents. The Bergerons had every right to demand an autopsy, but thus far there had been no indication from either one that they wished to take that route. They were grief-stricken. They had a younger daughter to take care of, a business to maintain, a funeral to organize. There was more than enough confusion occurring in their lives already, and his suggestion that they initiate a full-blown homicide investigation seemed to have fallen on deaf ears.

The last hurdle was the body itself. Landry was not authorized to leave his post in Jasperville. The body couldn't be transported on the North Shore line to Sept-Îles, then onward to Montréal without an official escort. The only official escort was Landry himself.

This was the conundrum that faced Landry as he thanked Elizabeth Devereaux for her cooperation, as he wished Juliette a speedy recovery from the devastating trauma of all she'd experienced, and made his way back towards the police station.

There on his desk were the files relating to the Roy and Fournier girls. In both cases, the photographs taken were of no great assistance to him. Monochrome, grainy, inadequately exposed, nowhere near close enough to the injuries to make an accurate comparison against the injuries inflicted on Thérèse, they were as good as useless. Had they been professionally taken by an experienced crime-scene photographer, then any observable similarity might have given more weight to his request for assistance.

Landry knew he was alone in his wish to pursue this as a possible murder. No one wanted to hear it – neither in Jasperville, nor in Montréal. This was as remote a station as could be found in Quebec, and the death of Thérèse Bergeron was never going to be news in the city.

But Landry, if nothing else, was not a quitter. If needed, he would circumvent his captain and write to the Chief Inspector. If that failed, he would notify the Director General.

He knew that time and distance were against him. Without the Bergerons' support, he was as good as lost. He needed them to request a full investigation, to keep on insisting until it became a provincial embarrassment to leave it unattended.

That same evening, Landry went to the boarding house. Philippe seemed unwilling to engage in further discussions on the matter, but finally, after some persuasion, he agreed. It was not long before Marguerite joined them in the parlour, silent at first, seated there at the end of the table, much of her in shadow, listening to the exchange between her husband and Landry.

'I'm being direct in this matter because I believe it requires directness,' Landry said. 'If we are to act, then we need to act quickly.'

'We've discussed it,' Philippe replied, 'and we really can't believe that any human being would be capable of doing something like this. We have lost our beautiful daughter. Nothing will bring her back, Sergeant Landry, and I can't see how doing this—'

'I want both of you to consider the possibility that something happened here that may have happened before—'

'You're suggesting there's a murderer in Jasperville,' Marguerite said. 'I don't believe for a second that there could be anyone so cruel as to kill someone like Thérèse.'

'You're trying to find a reason for something that's beyond all reason, Marguerite,' Landry said.

'No, Sergeant. I'm trying to reconcile myself to the fact that less than a week ago I had two daughters, and now I have only one.'

'And I understand that—'

'You do not, Sergeant Landry,' Philippe said. 'We appreciate what you're trying to do, but you cannot begin to understand what we're dealing with. Carine is still a child. The sister she adored was found dead on the morning of her eleventh birthday. That love, that devotion, was reciprocated. No two sisters could have been closer. How can you even begin to explain something like this to a girl of that age?'

It was then that Landry made a calamitous error of judgement. Later, he would reflect on what he'd said, the impulsive nature of his response, and understand that he'd allowed his ego to override his intellect.

'I must ask a question, then,' he said. 'If Thérèse cared for Carine as much as you say, why was Thérèse prepared to abandon her without even so much as a note expressing her reasons—'

'Enough,' Marguerite said. She rose from the chair and looked down at Landry. 'I cannot prevent you from pursuing this along whatever official lines you must, but you're not going to receive any support from me.' She paused only to fix him with a cold glare. 'Or from my husband.'

'Marguerite, I'm sorry,' Landry began, already furiously calculating how he might extricate himself from the hole he'd dug. He could sense the walls of that hole falling in on him, and there was no way out.

'I would like you to leave now, Sergeant Landry,' Philippe said.

'Philippe, Marguerite, I beg you to—'

'Please, Sergeant Landry. We need time to grieve for our daughter, and this means that we have no more time for you.'

Landry stood up. He didn't want to think about the indelicacy he'd demonstrated. The Bergerons wouldn't ally themselves to his crusade. Now it would be a matter of fighting this all the way to Montréal. At the mere thought of it, Landry's heart sank.

Good to the promise he made to himself, Landry did everything he could to overcome the bureaucratic challenges he faced. Regardless, he failed. Inadequate funding, lack of resources, administrative cutbacks, insufficient evidence to suggest foul play, and on it went. Time overtook him. The Bergerons demanded that their daughter's body be released to them for burial. Pelletier signed the death certificate. A service was held. Thérèse was buried behind the church, and it seemed that the entirety of Jasperville turned out to pay their respects. Sergeant Émile Landry, still insisting that outside agencies be engaged, was not invited.

Landry stayed until the following December. Though unconfirmed, rumour had it that he remained in the Sûreté for less than a year, and then he resigned. The photographs that were taken of Thérèse Bergeron's savage wounds were archived, and wouldn't be looked at again until many years later. By that time, the Bergerons would be part of Jasperville's history, as would William Swann, Elizabeth Devereaux and Thérèse's lover, Juliette.

It seemed that history would have the last word, but then history always did.

19

It was in the last leg of the journey that a real sense of foreboding invaded Jack's every thought and emotion. It was daylight, and through the fogged windows of the train, the landscape revealed itself. He'd felt unsettled since leaving Montréal, but with each significant stage of the journey, the sense of impending disquiet escalated. Even though he wanted to fight it, there was no purpose in doing so. Reconciliation was the only option.

The years that unfolded between the death of Thérèse Bergeron and his own departure from Jasperville had seemed to vanish in no time at all, and yet through those years Jack experienced the greatest upheaval. Perhaps, in part, it was exaggerated by the mental and emotional changes he himself had experienced. Between the ages of thirteen and nineteen he'd discovered how much he cared for Carine. After Thérèse's death, Carine was truly alone, and for a long time she seemed almost unreachable. Jack remembered his own mother impressing upon him a sense of duty to help her. He'd done as he was asked out of obligation, but in no time at all that obligation had become a sense of real purpose. Their common ground, Jack discovered, was books. She read as voraciously as he did, and together they were elevated beyond the confines of Jasperville by Jules Verne, Conan Doyle, Tolkien and du Maurier. Carine discovered that the medical centre received a box of retired books each quarter from the Sept-Îles Provincial Library. In a way, it was all the more exciting to have no predictability regarding what would be received. With Dr Pelletier's permission, they borrowed half a dozen at a time, swapping back and forth until everything was read. They talked, they disagreed, even kept a journal of every title they'd shared, and it was not long before books were not the sole motivation for sharing one another's company.

In Carine, Jack found a fellow prisoner. Through walls built from cold and isolation, they had connected. During that time, Carine discovered in herself the woman she would become. Jack, in his own way, was a catalyst for that, providing an empathetic ear, a supportive friendship.

Hindsight, in this instance, served no purpose. Looking back, Jack didn't see how he could have averted any of the things that happened. Perhaps Thérèse's death was the augur of what was to come. From that point, even though years separated events of significance, it was as if everyone had reconciled themselves to the inevitability of what was to happen. It was like trying to turn back the tide. It was nothing so insubstantial and meaningless as bad luck. Luck was a myth. Luck was nothing more than a self-created faith in uncontrollable factors.

Beneath and around him, the sound of the train consumed Jack's thoughts. He closed his eyes and willed himself to sleep, but sleep would not come. He knew that Jasperville would never be anything but home. The hurt and the hunger would still be there, waiting with infinite patience for the day of his return.

20

The winter of 1979 would later be remembered for many reasons, primary amongst them the paralysing cold, but also an event that would be later referred to as 'The Second Collapse'.

In early 1960, Canada Iron, beginning to appreciate just how much potential wealth lay beneath the earth in north-eastern Quebec, relentlessly encouraged engineers and technicians to find faster and cheaper means of filling the cargo hoppers on the Sept-Îles train. The company's enthusiasm led to overworked teams, exhausted men, precariously deep digs, insufficient shoring, and, on one fateful Friday afternoon, a bank of earth and rock that towered a good thirty feet surrendered to gravity. A heavy storm had ravaged Jasperville, and the bank had reached such a degree of saturation that it became a shifting sea of mud and scree. The speed with which hundreds of tons moved down toward the working crews was far greater than any man could run. Those who escaped were simply in a position too elevated for the mud to reach them. The men in the ore valley didn't stand a chance. In all, nine lives were lost. After days of work, bodies were brought up one by one. The last one, a twenty-six-year-old Welshman named Osian Parry, was eleven feet down.

Subsequently, Canada Iron instigated a series of precautionary safety measures to prevent such a catastrophe from ever happening again. Dig limits, bank heights, double ranks of shoring when an excavation exceeded fifteen feet at its deepest point, and on it went. As was the case with all such safety measures, it slowed and inhibited production, and workers' bonuses were entirely dependent upon quotas being met. Over time, the safety measures were relaxed, and after a decade it was as if no measures had ever existed.

Henri Devereaux, by this time a ten-year veteran of the mines, was considered a fair man. However, he was necessarily unforgiving when those same teams came up short on tonnage. A furnace running with an insufficient load was expensive and wasteful. Shutting them down was out of the question; getting them running again was twice the cost of maintaining them. They roared like fury day and night, and the miners were pressed into service to keep them fed.

Who it was that made the decision to run a double crew on the night of Thursday, 15th November was never fully clarified. As each crew began and ended a shift, so the shift supervisor was supposed to log the name of every man, when he'd last completed a shift, and how many shifts he'd completed in the last seven days. Those dockets were rarely filed, and until an incident occurred that required the inspection of said dockets, the fact that they went undone was not noticed. So it was that Thursday.

A crew of twelve had agreed to run a double shift – eight hours, an hour's break, and then a second eight. Strictly speaking, a double shift required a four-hour break, but that could be overridden by the shift supervisor. A form had to be completed giving the precise reason why the four-hour break was being waived, and each crew member had to initial it. Devereaux had been supervisor on the first shift. The sole reason Devereaux kept his job was that he'd handed over responsibility to a different supervisor for the second. Regardless, it didn't stop him from shouldering the tremendous sense of guilt over what took place. That he considered himself indirectly responsible for the death of nine men accelerated his own slow-motion landslide into personal ruin.

Investigation revealed that the excavation had been significantly tougher than most. Strata of igneous rock had hampered progress, and thus it had required more drilling, more dynamite, more hoppers of waste. That waste had been predominantly rock, and thus the weight of the banks were far greater than usual. One too many charges detonated simultaneously, the ground shuddered, and those in the well of the excavation knew something was wrong when the shudder didn't stop. It was estimated that more than a hundred tons of blasted and shattered debris came down on them, and due to the darkness, there was no way to determine from which direction the slide had originated. The overhead floodlights illuminated the trenches themselves, not the surrounding landscape. Knowing that something awesomely destructive was on its way, a handful of men ran right into it. The three who escaped – two Polish brothers and a one-time oilworker from Austin, Texas – had God on their side. That was all that anyone could say. There was no credible explanation for their survival save that the wave of rolling rocks found its way under them and carried them upward and out, as opposed to burying them wholesale.

The Texan left for Texas. The Polish brothers remained in Jasperville, but, when questioned, never spoke of that night.

Devereaux's shift replacement – eighteen years of service to Canada Iron behind him – left for Sept-Îles, never to be heard of again. The nine widows, their children in tow – impressed upon to never speak of what had occurred to outside agencies – were compensated and then spirited away within a matter of weeks. Canada Iron managed to bury it as thoroughly as the men who had died. Bodies were finally retrieved. Plain pine boxes awaited them, followed by a swift and unceremonious interment. Within two months, at least for the majority of Jasperville's populace, it was as if nothing had ever happened. Henri Devereaux, however, was haunted by the experience, and by February of the following year he was drinking on a routine basis.

Elizabeth saw what was happening, and yet couldn't tell how the catastrophe would present itself. All she knew was that something inevitable and unalterable was on its way towards them.

The first real sense of trouble arrived in the spring of 1980. Just as the winter had been bone-chillingly cold, so the spring heralded a breathless and humid summer with unrelenting clouds of flies and mosquitoes. There was something truly claustrophobic about those few months. The sun sat close to the horizon, never rising, never setting, and the air was heavy and yellow and difficult to breathe.

Since Christmas, Jacques was spending more and more time with Carine. Unlike Baptiste and Violetta Roy, the Bergerons didn't leave Jasperville after the death of their daughter. Some said it was because they were determined not to be beaten by their own grief. Others said it was because there was nowhere else for them to go.

In Jacques, Philippe Bergeron found a young man who possessed not only a strong work ethic, but also a desire to learn worthwhile skills. With the management of the boarding house, so came such necessary duties as basic electrical and plumbing repairs, maintenance of the boiler and heating pipes, the re-covering of furniture, the odd instance of joinery and glazing. Wilson Gaines' son, Robert, now in his mid-twenties, was sometimes employed for any major work. If more manpower was required, a second man of Robert's age, Jean-Paul Lefebvre, would pitch in. He was altogether more outgoing and confident than Robert, but he lacked the necessary conscientiousness. Philippe, having no son of his own, was all too eager to tutor

Jacques in these maintenance tasks. Jacques, keen to see as much of Carine as possible, was all too eager to learn.

Jacques' absence in the Devereaux house weighed heavily on Elizabeth. Since the death of Thérèse, there seemed to be nothing that would draw Juliette out of the well of grief into which she'd fallen. She would be twenty-two in May, and it certainly appeared that marriage and a family played no part in her view of the future. Calvis was seven, and so engaged with his schoolwork and his friends that he seemed forever in a world of his own. Henri worked and Henri drank. He was neither mean nor aggressive, but he was out of touch. If he drank enough, he became belligerent and argumentative, but never once did Elizabeth feel she was in danger. As for William, he had slipped into some sort of muttering dotage, roused infrequently – again by the drink – into disturbing monologues about ghouls and spectres that lurked in the darkness near the Torngat Mountains.

More and more often, there seemed to be no one to whom Elizabeth could turn for comfort and friendship. Marguerite was so distant that Elizabeth doubted she would ever return. On the heels of having to contend with her daughter's intimate relationship with Juliette, she'd then had to contend with her death. The nature of that death remained a mystery to all of them. Unanswered questions were a vacuum into which attention was drawn. Closure was not possible. No matter the efforts made to embrace the present, the past dragged like a whirlpool and would never relinquish its grip.

Where once the Devereaux house had been filled with voices and laughter, it now seemed that an unforgiving cloud of despair hung over everything. Where Juliette had once manifested outbursts of grief, even rage, now there was nothing but a deep emotional fatigue, as if she'd experienced everything it was possible to experience and nothing of herself remained.

In June, Jacques was fifteen. Elizabeth made an effort to

celebrate his birthday, but it seemed no one but Carine was interested. In July, Carine turned thirteen, and once again it appeared that the notion of festivities was about as welcome as influenza. Whatever spirit had existed was gone. The bond between the Devereauxs and the Bergerons was held together by the two youngest, and they seemed content solely in one another's company.

It was in the same month – July of 1980 – that Juliette seemed to change. She resumed attendance at church, even began studying her bible. She took a number of meetings with the minister, seeming to once again become the young woman she'd been before the death of Thérèse. Elizabeth didn't question what was happening. She was merely heartened to see Juliette engaging with the family, helping out with Calvis and William, even talking to her father about his work. Reconciliation was the word that came to mind when Elizabeth thought about that change in mood and temperament. Two years had passed since Thérèse's death, and though no one was any the wiser as to what had happened that morning, the event had been absorbed into the collective history of Jasperville. No one spoke of it, and no one wanted to.

On the morning of Saturday, 2nd August, Juliette seemed less troubled and more talkative than Elizabeth could remember. After breakfast, Jacques departed for the boarding house. Calvis went to the TV for cartoons. William sat on the porch in his rocker, his pipe stoked, a flask of whiskey with which to augment his coffee. Henri sat reading a three-day old newspaper.

'I'm going on up to the church,' Juliette said. 'Prayer books and hymnals need repairing, and I said I would help.'

'Of course, yes,' Elizabeth replied. 'Will you come back for lunch?'

'Yes,' Juliette said.

She donned her coat and boots, and then she hesitated in the open doorway.

'Shut the door, my dear,' Henri said. 'Trying to keep some warmth in here.'

'I really do love you all very much,' Juliette said, and then she did as her father had asked.

Only later, after Juliette's body was found, did Elizabeth understand those parting words. Juliette was telling them that she didn't blame them for what had happened. Life had dealt her a cruel hand, and it had taken two years for her to decide that the only way to escape the repercussions of that hand was to escape from life altogether. Perhaps there was another life, and in that life she could be with Thérèse. That was all she wanted. That was all she'd ever wanted. If this was the way to make it happen, then so be it.

After telling her mother and father how much she loved them, Juliette Devereaux walked half a mile into the wetlands.

The glacial run-offs were deep before the earth began its long incline towards the foot of the Torngat Mountains.

Had it been winter, Juliette would have frozen to death out there.

It was summer, and thus she drowned.

21

Jack stood on the platform at Jasperville and waited until every passenger had disembarked and headed off towards the exit. Even Paul and Vivienne Girard, keen to engage with him, perhaps in need of help as they oriented themselves to their new surroundings, sensed that he wished to be alone. They remarked on the cold, asked for directions toward Canada Iron's administrative offices, and then, just as when the Devereauxs had first arrived, a Canada Iron representative appeared and greeted them enthusiastically. Listening to him deliver his welcome speech, Jack imagined how his own parents must have felt. He'd been three years old, Juliette just ten. How exciting it must have seemed, how much of an adventure.

'I hope everything goes well with your brother,' Vivi said, as she and Paul headed off towards the other end of the platform.

Jack closed his eyes and breathed. He needed to find somewhere to stay, and unless anything had significantly changed, he guessed it would be the boarding house. He knew the way. He could have walked it in his sleep. He made a start, urging himself forward with the knowledge that the only way he would ever see the other side of this was to go right through it. There was no sidestepping reality.

The saloons, the general store, the saddler, the farrier, behind him the church, still leaning to the left. The veterinary surgery, the school, the medical centre where he and Carine had gone time and time again to borrow books. The baker's, the butcher's, the pawn shop, the post office. Right in the middle of them sat the boarding house. Though there were different doors, different windows and signage, it was as if nothing had really changed for a quarter of a century.

From where Jack stood, he could see the police station at the end of the drag. He wanted to find a room, get some breakfast and gather his thoughts together before he spoke to Nadeau, before he discovered what it was that Calvis had done to bring him here.

Through the boarding house door and into the reception area he found everything so much smaller than he remembered. It was the same dark wood, the same panelling, the same stairway leading up to the first-floor balcony, two hallways running from there, four rooms off each hallway, and then another floor above that with a further six rooms.

Behind the reception desk was a teenager, no more than fifteen or sixteen. He looked up as Jack entered, noted the bag, the weariness attendant to all those who travelled as far as Jasperville.

'You want a room?'

'I wanted to ask if this was still the only boarding house,' Jack said.

The teenager frowned. 'What? You only just got here and you already don't like it?' He didn't wait for a reply. 'It's the only place I know of, and we only got one room available. If you want it, you better take it now.'

'Yes, sure,' Jack said. 'I'll take it.'

'How long you staying?'

'Uncertain.'

'You want the rate for a week?'

'That'll be fine,' Jack said.

'Breakfast and dinner?'

'Yes.'

The teenager hauled a ledger out from beneath the desk. 'Name?'

'Devereaux. Jack Devereaux. What's your name?'

'Martin.'

'So, who owns this place now?'

'My ma. You got a home address?'

'Yes, in Montréal.' Jack gave it.

'You pay for a week now,' Martin said. 'Room's up top, third on the left.'

'I know the one,' Jack said.

Martin eyed him quizzically. 'You from here?'

'Long time ago.'

'Well, you know how much it sucks then, right? Like the frozen asshole of Hell.'

'As good a description as any.'

Jack paid up, took the key. He started up the stairs, conscious then of how so many of these old wooden buildings would never pass a fire examination.

'Hey, Mister Devereaux?'

Jack looked back.

'My ma says to tell every guest that the room is for one person. That's what you're paying for. If you got company, you keep it elsewhere.'

'I won't be having any company, Martin.'

From the window of his room, a room he'd cleaned so many times, a room he remembered painting, Jack looked along the street and out beyond the town limits to the mountains in the distance. *Place of evil spirits.* That was the first thought that came to mind, and then, close on its heels, was the memory of Juliette's funeral, the way he'd avoided his own parents, how he'd spent more and more time with Carine, with Philippe and Marguerite, almost as if he was trying to create some other family independent of his own. Calvis tagged along. Jack had felt so very responsible for him. Ironic now, considering he'd ultimately abandoned him.

He presumed Calvis was in the police station basement. Jack couldn't postpone his meeting with Bastien Nadeau for long. He would have to see his younger brother, listen to the terrible things he was saying, find out why he'd attacked someone with such brutality.

In his heart, Jack knew the answer to that question. He'd known it from the phone call. He knew those same words had been uttered ever more frequently by William in the last months of his life. After Juliette's death, everything fell apart with such speed. He'd watched it, not only incapable of doing anything to delay or avert it, but convinced that if he didn't leave then, the same fate would sweep him up and devour him. He had thought solely of himself, for Carine had been included in that abandonment. Where she was now, what had happened to her, was something he would possibly never know. Yes, he'd made attempts to locate her, but they had been half-hearted. And finally, a letter had arrived in Montréal that discouraged him from pursuing her any further.

In the small bathroom down the hallway, Jack turned on the shower. He undressed and stepped beneath the water. Every inch of his body welcomed the warmth. At least he'd arrived. And now, moment by moment, memory by memory, everything that had driven him away would have to be faced. This was home, whether he wished it or not.

22

It wasn't the drinking that killed William Swann, but his heart. By the time Calvis was ten in August of 1982, it was evident that Papi wouldn't see Christmas.

As much as possible, Jacques and Calvis spent time with their grandfather. That Jacques and Carine were so very rarely apart meant that the three of them fetched and carried, helped him to bed, brought his meals, an extra blanket, anything else that might improve his comfort.

The fatigue and dizziness William experienced was merely the consequence of less blood reaching the brain and the limbs. Yes, he could be given medication to ease his discomfort, aspirin to thin the blood. Neither of these things would change the fact that he was dying.

William was aware of what was happening, irrespective of his senility. There were moments of bright and startling lucidity when he remembered precisely who he was, where he'd come from, and, most tellingly, that the life he'd lived was reaching its end.

Jacques listened to his grandfather, watched as his gaze moved from himself to Calvis to Carine, and then out into the middle distance as if he was seeing things that weren't there. Perhaps waiting for something he expected to arrive.

Jacques thought of death, of knowing that your life was reaching its conclusion. He thought about Lisette, about

Anne-Louise and Thérèse and Juliette. Where were they? What had happened to them? Were they nothing more than blood and bones and teeth and hair, swallowed into the ground, existing nowhere but in photographs and fading memories? He didn't want to believe that, to think of his sister as nothing, a hollow space, a vacuum. He wanted to believe that the body died, but that there was something beyond all of this, outside of the realm we could see and hear and touch. The human spirit. The soul. Ghosts, spectres, phantoms, reincarnated identities that took on new bodies. He'd read about this kind of thing. The Egyptians, the Buddhists, even the Christians who spoke of Heaven and Hell as if these places really existed. Jacques didn't know what to believe, but he wanted to believe in something. For Juliette, of course, but now for Papi.

'What happens when someone dies?' Calvis asked him one late afternoon. It was October, and although they didn't know it, Papi would be gone just six weeks later.

'What do you mean, what happens?' Jacques asked in return.

'Well, do they go up in the sky and float around, or do they disappear, or do they go to Heaven like they say in church?'

It was hard to answer a question for which he had no answer himself.

'I don't think anyone really knows, Calvis,' Jacques said. 'Different people have different ideas. No one's ever died and come back to tell us.'

Calvis was pensive for some moments, and then he said something that surprised Jacques.

'Maybe everyone has different ideas because everyone goes to different places.'

'Places? What kind of places?' Jacques asked.

'The places they deserve.'

*

In the early hours of 19 November, Elizabeth knew. She woke Henri, who then woke Jacques and Calvis in turn. They each sat around the bed in Papi's room, listening to his breathing as it slowed and faltered.

William tried to speak, but he possessed neither the strength nor the concentration to make himself understood.

Elizabeth prayed. Calvis cried softly, and he held Jacques' hand like a lifeline. Henri was stoic in appearance, but perhaps his conscience found him. Here was his father-in-law, a man from whom he'd taken every cent, and yet he'd treated him as an unwelcome houseguest.

Just after noon, Papi drew his final breath. The silence in the room was palpable. Calvis stopped crying. Henri stood up, said a few words to himself, then walked around the side of the bed and drew the blanket up over William's face.

They all remained for a while. No one wanted to be the first to leave. Henri finally directed Jacques and Calvis out of the room. He wanted a little time with Elizabeth.

Jacques stood at the top of the stairs. As soon as the door closed, he heard his mother start to sob. Why she hadn't cried while they were there, he didn't know. Perhaps there was a grief she experienced that she didn't want to share.

After an hour or so, both Henri and Elizabeth came down. Henri took his coat and hat. He told Calvis to get dressed. They would go to the medical centre and then see the minister together. Jacques asked why he wasn't going.

'I need you to stay with me,' his mother said, and from the expression on her face Jacques could see that she meant it.

Once Henri and Calvis had left, Elizabeth told Jacques to come and sit with her at the kitchen table.

'Are you sad?' she asked him.

'Yes,' he replied. 'Of course. Really sad.'

'And how is Calvis?'

'He's ten years old. He asks me things and I try to answer them in a way he will understand.'

'What did you tell him about Juliette?'

Jacques looked at his mother. He wondered if it was a trick question.

'Did you tell him that she killed herself?'

'No, Maman. I didn't say that.'

'Good.'

Elizabeth looked toward the window. Outside, the snow was already coming down. Word had it that a bitter winter was on the way.

'Are you afraid?' Elizabeth asked.

'Of what?'

'Of the things that Papi spoke about? The stories he told you.'

'They're just stories.'

'Did Juliette ever speak of them?'

'What do you mean?'

'After what happened to Thérèse, did she ever speak of these things?'

'Not to me,' Jacques replied. 'It's superstition. It's stuff to scare children.' He paused. 'Isn't it?'

For a moment she glanced away, and there was a flash of something in her eyes – something that Jacques had never seen before.

'Maman?'

She looked back, smiled. 'Yes,' she said. 'Of course. Things to scare children.'

'Do you believe in these stories?'

Elizabeth sighed deeply. When she looked up there were tears. 'I lost my daughter and now my father. What happened to Thérèse. What happened to Lisette and Anne-Louise. I can barely say three words to Marguerite before she looks at me like I'm somehow to blame for everything—'

Jacques reached out and took her hand. 'Of course you're not to blame,' he said. 'No one is to blame.'

Elizabeth withdrew her hand from his. 'Of course someone is to blame. These were not accidents.'

'You know what I mean,' Jacques replied. 'No one in our family, no one that we know.'

'But how can you say that when you don't know who's responsible? Of course it could be someone we know.' Her eyes were bright with fear. 'It could be someone we know very well, someone we see every day. Did you not think of that?'

'No,' Jacques said. 'I didn't think of that, and I don't want to think of that.'

'Well, you must,' Elizabeth said. 'You have to think of it. You have to watch everyone. You have to be suspicious of everyone.'

'No, I won't do that. And you mustn't think like that, either. That will drive you crazy.'

'I know,' Elizabeth replied. 'I know I shouldn't think like that, but I do. I have even ... even wondered ...' Her voice trailed away.

'What? Wondered what?'

'If it could have been Papi. If he found out about Thérèse and Juliette, and he wanted to scare her, but he got angry, and she challenged him and he lost his temper—'

'Maman! Enough!'

Elizabeth looked at her son. He seemed so strong, so confident.

'Enough,' Jacques repeated. 'Papi didn't do these things, and I don't see how it could've been anyone we know. You need to stop thinking like this. You need to think about the future, about what is best for Calvis. He needs you.'

'And you don't?'

146

Jacques laughed, but it sounded anxious. 'Of course I need you, Maman. We all need you.'

'You're a young man now,' she said, reaching out to take his hand. 'My Jackrabbit. Seventeen years old. So tall and handsome, so clever. I never see you without a book. And I never see you without Carine.'

Jacques felt the colour rise in his cheeks.

'She's just fifteen years old . . .'

'I know how old she is.'

'She's a very pretty girl.'

'Maman—'

'And she thinks the world of you. You know that, don't you?'

'We're just good friends.'

'You must take care of her. Promise me, Jacques, that no matter what happens you'll take care of her.'

Jacques felt the emotion welling in his chest. He could see Thérèse's face, the intensity in her eyes. He recalled the promise he'd made. More than anything he remembered the love and warmth that was all around them that night. And now it was all broken. Now it was all painful memories and heartbreak of such depth it was impossible to fathom.

'Why are you saying this?' he asked. He could hear the way his words fell over one another, the difficulty he was having in even dealing with this moment. 'Why are you asking me to take care of her, no matter what happens? What is going to happen? Do you know that something is going to happen?'

'Hasn't enough happened already?' Elizabeth asked. 'Don't you feel it? Don't you sense something bad in this house, something bad all around us?'

'Stop it. This is crazy talk. Like Papi, but worse. Papi was old and he was losing his mind.'

'Maybe that's what will happen to all of us,' Elizabeth replied. She hesitated then, and for a moment her attention seemed so far beyond the walls of the kitchen, as if her body was right there but she'd left altogether. And then she shook her head and smiled. 'You're right,' she said. 'You're absolutely right. It's just nonsense. Children's stories. I'm just upset. I knew Papi was going to die, but that doesn't make it any easier.'

'It's going to be okay. We're here. Me and Calvis will take care of you, and I promise I will look after Carine.'

'And you should leave.'

'What?'

'You should leave here. When she's old enough, you should take her and go back to Montréal. Go someplace else. Anywhere.'

'I can't,' Jacques said. 'What about Calvis, and what about you? I wouldn't leave you here.'

'I have my own life,' Elizabeth said. 'I made my choices. I have to live with them, but you don't.'

'I'm not leaving. Not for a long time. This is just as much my home as it is yours.'

'You'll change your mind in time,' Elizabeth said. 'This is no place for a young man with a new wife.'

'What is this idea you've gotten into your mind? I'm not marrying Carine, Maman. She's crazy too, you know? Drives me mad with her questions...'

'I know you love her, Jacques. And I know she loves you. You have different ways of showing it, and perhaps you don't see it for what it is, but you were meant to be together.'

Jacques didn't reply. His mother had a way of stating opinions as if they were fact, but there was something about the certainty with which she spoke of his relationship with Carine that hit home. She was fifteen, and yet there was something so very wise and old about her. There was no other way to describe it. The love that he felt, at first fraternal, had evolved into something else, something that he couldn't really think about because she was only fifteen. Just two years between them, but those two years represented a gulf that couldn't be crossed by any other means than time and patience. He would wait for her, of course. He would wait five years, ten, a lifetime. He'd never loved anyone the way he loved Carine, and he knew he never would.

23

It was a little before noon when Jack left the boarding house and headed in the direction of the police station. Snow was coming down, and the ground was already frozen into hard ridges and channels. The coat he'd brought was insubstantial. This was already far below anything he'd become accustomed to in Montréal.

With every step, memories returned. The bleak, featureless nothing of the winter. The sun that didn't rise, the interminable darkness, the sensation that the cold came from inside your own body and would never leave. And then the humidity of the summer, the wetlands, the plague of flies and mosquitoes. There was the smell of Papi's tobacco as he sat in his rocker on the porch; the sound of the front door as his father came in, the thud of boots, the smell of wet oilskins; his mother's voice as she called them down for dinner. It was all there, every second, every heartbeat, and yet he'd somehow managed to shut it all into little boxes in his mind, arranging them in such a way as he'd only ever have to open them one at a time.

Pausing at the top of the steps of the general store, he looked back the way he'd come. The house was down there. His childhood, his teenage years, and everything that had happened here in Jasperville. He knew precisely how long it would take to walk there, but he was not ready. Not yet.

Inside the store it was warm. He took off his gloves, stood

right there in the middle of the room and looked around. The shelves climbed ceiling-high on four walls. Canned goods, flour, sugar, tea, coffee, preserved vegetables, smoked meat, dried meat, cereals, powdered egg, powdered milk, oil, beer, wine, whiskey, cigarettes, cigars and tobacco. And then there were work clothes, boots, socks, blankets, bedding, gloves, hats, basic medicinal provisions such as plasters, bandages, ointments, antiseptic, cough and cold remedies and mosquito repellent. At the back of the store were books, magazines, newspapers, stationery, confectionery, a soda machine, a wide refrigerator and a little area with a machine for cutting keys and repairing shoes.

Twenty-six years had passed since Jack had stood in this room. He'd been nineteen. He recalled exactly why he'd gone there – to buy a holdall within which he'd packed everything he wanted to take with him. Just one bag. No more, no less.

How much of a fool had he been? How naïve? How delusional? Everything he'd wanted to leave behind had just followed him right out of Jasperville.

'Can I help you?'

Jack turned.

A young man stood behind the counter to his right.

'Yes,' Jack said. 'Some cigarettes. Any brand will do. And matches.'

Once outside again, he lit the first cigarette he'd smoked for three years. He stood to the side of the steps and he inhaled. He felt that bite in the back of his throat, the sensation in his lungs. Immediately there was a feeling of nausea, a faint dizziness, but he took another drag and it calmed. Why he needed to smoke and how he imagined it might help, he didn't know. It was just something he had to do.

People walked by, their faces obscured by hoods and scarves. He was a ghost. He went unnoticed. He was more than happy for it to remain that way.

Jack wondered if there was anyone who would remember him. He doubted it. Not after twenty-six years. The world had moved on yet Jasperville was locked in time. It possessed the same atmosphere, the same sense of isolation.

Jack turned right and walked down to the police station. He stood on the opposite side of the street for a good five minutes. He could see someone seated at a desk at the back of the ground floor. Was that Nadeau, or had Sûreté du Québec finally seen sense to have more than one officer out here? He wondered where Nadeau's predecessors were – Levesque, Thibault, Tremblay, Landry, even Arnaud Colin, the sergeant posted here when Jack had left back in 1984. Were any of them still haunted by the inexplicable and unsolved killings that had taken place? And had the killings stopped? That was the question that he wanted an answer to. Had those killings stopped after he'd left, or had there been more?

Jack couldn't prevaricate any longer. He'd come all the way out here for his brother, and now was the moment of truth.

Reaching the door of the station, Jack took a deep breath. If he'd been a man of faith, he perhaps would have said a prayer, but faith was something he'd abandoned many years before.

The warmth surrounded him, even in the vestibule between the outer and inner doors. He kicked the snow off his boots and opened the second door.

The seated man rose. He had on the SQ uniform, the sergeant's stripes on his sleeve. He was the same height as Jack, but younger, perhaps in his late thirties. There was something about him that spoke of Indian blood, perhaps Inuit, perhaps even Algonquin lineage.

'You are Bastien Nadeau?' Jack asked.

'I am,' Nadeau said. 'And you're Jacques Devereaux. The physical resemblance to your brother is strong.'

'Tell me what happened? Who did my brother attack? And where is he?'

Nadeau didn't reply for a few seconds, and then he said, 'Will you have a seat? I'm going to take some coffee. Would you like some, too?'

Jack nodded and removed his gloves. He took a seat at the desk.

Nadeau filled two mugs from a jug on a hotplate in the corner.

The coffee was hot and strong. Jack felt it radiate out through his throat and chest.

'You were here for the killings of Lisette Roy, Anne-Louise Fournier and Thérèse Bergeron, no?'

Jack flinched. Aside from his brief conversation with Vivi Girard on the train, he hadn't heard those names since he'd left.

'Yes,' he said. 'I was here.'

'You arrived as a child and left when you were—'

'We came here in '69. I left in '84.'

'And you've not been back since?'

Jack shook his head.

'And when you left, your grandfather, your mother and your sister were already dead. Your brother was only twelve.'

'Are you asking me or telling me?'

'I'm sorry,' Nadeau said. 'Perhaps I sound accusatory. I'm not interrogating you. I'm just ...' He waved his hand as if he didn't know the words he needed. 'There are many things I'm trying to understand, but I think you can help me.'

'I can help you? How? I've not been here for twenty-six years.'

'And I have been here only five months, Monsieur Devereaux.'

'You're here alone?'

'Yes, of course.'

'Two years, right?'

'We're told two years. Sometimes it's more.'

'And you've already started looking into historical killings?'

'Not out of choice.'

'Out of what, then?'

'Necessity.'

'Because of the things my brother has been saying?'

Nadeau paused as if deliberating whether he should share his thoughts.

'Because of something else?' Jack asked.

Nadeau leaned forward, elbows on the desk, hands clasped together.

'I'm from a place like this,' he said. 'West of here. I grew up there. My father's people go all the way back to the Algonquin. My mother was Québécois. I know this territory, this climate. I know how isolation and cold can send people crazy. I know all of this, and yet the things that have happened here ...' Nadeau looked out toward the street. 'The things your brother spoke of—'

'I have a good idea what he's been saying,' Jack interjected. 'The stories our grandfather used to tell us. About the wendigo.'

'Well, you know that this legend is from my father's people.'

'I do, yes.'

'And you believe it's a legend?'

'You're asking me if I think that these stories are true? My grandfather used to tell us these things to scare us.'

'Do they still scare you?'

'Seriously?'

'They do, don't they? You think of these things and they still make you feel uneasy.'

Jack didn't reply.

'They scare me, Monsieur Devereaux. And they very definitely scared your brother.'

'You're telling me that the man he attacked—'

'You know the story of Jack Fiddler, the Cree Indian?'

154

'Yes,' Jack said. 'The hunter, right?'

'Yes, the hunter. That was more than a hundred years ago, but these stories have been passed down through the generations for centuries.'

'I'm sorry,' Jack said. 'Where the hell are we going with this?'

'This is what your brother's telling me, Monsieur Devereaux. That he's a hunter. That he's been hunting this wendigo for years. He says there are many of them out there in the forests below the Torngat Mountains. He speaks with such conviction, such urgency... and he tells me that if I don't let him go then more people will die.'

Jack felt his mind stretching to absorb the significance and import of what he was being told.

'He tells me there have been more girls. Not only here, but in Menihek, Fermont, even Wabush. He tells me that there have been killings that no one has ever connected to what has happened here.'

'You're saying that my brother attacked a man because he believed he was a wendigo?'

'Exactly, Monsieur Devereaux. He says he hunts these things, just like Jack Fiddler. He says he's known about these things ever since he was a child.'

The walls of the world closed in on Jack. He stood up, breathed deeply, tried to focus, tried to find any point of reference for what he was hearing.

'Monsieur Devereaux?'

Jack looked at Nadeau. The man's face was a blur.

'I need some air,' Jack said. 'I need to get out of here.' With that, he turned and headed for the door.

Nadeau called after him, but Jack's mind was nothing but a roiling ocean of images, sounds, memories, unwanted thoughts. He could see Papi's face. He could remember how much he'd frightened them with those stories of the wendigo. To think that this was now the reason for his return was beyond anything he could have imagined.

Once outside, the snow, like tiny shards of ice, cut into his face. Jack pulled on his gloves, tugged his coat around him, and just started walking.

Jasperville had killed his grandfather, his sister and his mother. It had sent his father spiralling into some irretrievable depth of madness, and now it had done the same to Calvis.

24

It was only after Papi's funeral, as Henri grew even more distant and uncommunicative, as Elizabeth spent more and more hours locked in her room, that Jacques knew that his mother had been right. He would have to leave. That was what his heart dictated. But his head erred toward what was right for Calvis. Just ten years old, Jacques knew that he could neither leave him nor take him along. And then there was Carine. He knew he loved her, but perhaps what he felt was even greater than love. When he thought of her, all other thoughts became secondary.

But he had to get out of Jasperville. Caught between the Devil and the deep blue sea, his mind turned over the problem relentlessly. He said nothing to Carine or Calvis, and did everything to withhold his feelings from his mother. Nevertheless, she could see right through him. There were days he felt that she was watching him, waiting for him to broach the subject, to do something that would lay bare his intentions.

'I know,' she said to him one day. It came out of the blue. 'I know what you're thinking, but I cannot bear the thought of being here without you.'

Afraid to telegraph his thoughts, Jacques turned away.

'Look at me,' she said. 'Jacques. Look at me.'

He turned back.

'You think I don't know what happened to Thérèse?'

'Maman, no,' Jacques said.

'Yes. You must.'

'You know it's nothing more than stupid stories,' he snapped, suddenly angry.

'Believed for hundreds of years by thousands, perhaps millions of people. You can't see God, Jacques, but people believe in Him. It's the same with the Devil.'

'The Devil didn't kill Thérèse!'

'Perhaps not himself, but he climbed inside the mind of a man, and the man did the killing.'

'You're telling me that you believe these things, the things that Papi told us to scare us?'

'I have seen them,' Elizabeth said, and there was an expression in her eyes that Jacques had never seen before.

'Seen what, Maman? What have you seen?'

'I have seen it. The thing that hungers for blood.'

Jacques lowered his head. He felt a sense of defeat.

Eventually he looked up. His mother seemed calm and assured, as if by uttering the words she'd somehow exorcized something from within.

'I lost Juliette,' Jacques said, 'and now I have lost Papi. I don't know what to say to my father any more. He's like a stranger. Please don't tell me that I'm going to lose you, too.'

Elizabeth shook her head. 'I think it's too late,' she replied. 'From the moment we got off that train we were all lost.'

It was less than a week later that the very subject of which he was most afraid was presented in a way that Jacques couldn't avoid.

The teacher's name was Francois Lapointe. He took the History classes, and it was in one such class that the folklore of the Cree and the Algonquin were the topic under discussion.

Lapointe couldn't have looked less like a teacher. He wore heavy tweed jackets with waxed cotton trousers, his calves and feet encased in fur-lined boots, on his head a hat that seemed to have been stitched together from parts of other hats. He smoked a pipe, the tobacco giving off a thick smoke redolent of tar and smouldering wood.

'They were here before any of us foreigners,' Lapointe said. 'To the Indians, we're just outsiders, visitors, tourists. They're waiting for us to finally understand that we can't deal with the climate, and then we'll be gone.'

Lapointe crossed the room and sat on a chair beside his desk.

'They have some interesting legends,' he went on. 'One of which fascinates me greatly, and may be similarly fascinating to those of you who are partial to ghost stories and other scary stuff.'

Jack sensed it then. How, he didn't know, but he knew what was coming.

'Today, ladies and gentlemen, we're going to talk about a creature called the wendigo.'

It was almost a child's word, and yet the horror that it conferred was beyond anything Jacques had felt before. Beyond even that of a girl found dead in the snow.

'Yes, indeed. It's a disturbing story, but I want to assure you that it's nothing but a legend. Let's not be having any nightmares, eh?'

Lapointe smiled as if he knew that nightmares were exactly what his pupils would be having.

'It goes back a long, long time. Centuries, perhaps. There was a tribe of people called the Anasazi, descendants of people who came all the way from Utah, and their entire culture disappeared more than six hundred years ago. This has been attributed to the wendigo.'

Lapointe leaned back in his chair.

'The Algonquin describe the wendigo as very tall and slender. They're emaciated, their skin taut like dry yellow parchment, their eyes sunk back into their heads. They're found in places like this, where it's easy for people to get lost, where it's too cold for a human being to survive without shelter and warmth. They wait for people who are alone, who are starving, and then they possess them. A cannibalistic spirit. That is how it's seen. That is what they believe – that the wendigo turns a man into a cannibal. Not only that, the wendigo spirit can drive a man to murder, to acts of insatiable greed.'

A girl at the back of the class raised her hand.

'Yes, Anne-Marie?'

'What is ... in-saysh—'

'Insatiable,' Lapointe repeated. 'It means that it can never be satisfied.'

Jacques felt his heart in his chest. Like a frightened bird.

'They're believed to exist in Nova Scotia, the Great Lakes region, in the United States as well. This legend has passed down through generations of Ojibwe, Eastern Cree, Westmain Swampy Cree, Naskap, Innu, Assiniboine. Some say the wendigo is many times the size of a human. A giant, almost. Some say that it's surrounded by a sickly stench of death and decay. Others believe that the wendigo grows in size proportional to the flesh it has just eaten.'

The boy two desks across from Jacques piped up. 'And people really believe that these things exist?'

'Enough to have rituals to perform during times of famine and disease,' Lapointe said. 'Enough to believe that the only way to kill one is with silver, steel or iron. Some say that the creature has a heart made of ice which must be shattered with a silver stake, and then the body must be hacked to pieces with a silver axe.' Lapointe leaned forward. 'Cultures, each and every one, have their demons – the vampire, the werewolf, reptilian creatures that lurk in swamps. Each one is perhaps an attempt to explain the evilness of Man. For a man to commit heinous crimes, for a man to eat another man, to torture, to murder children, then he must have been possessed by something, for no man could be that cruel without some external, diabolic motivation.'

Lapointe smiled. 'Any questions?'

The class sat silent and enthralled.

'Okay, so now I will tell you about a man called Jack Fiddler. This is from nearly a hundred years ago. He was a Cree shaman. Does anyone not know what a shaman is?'

No hands were raised.

'So, according to Cree history, Mr Fiddler could conjure animals from the air. He protected his people against evil spells from other tribes, he assured the growth of crops, and he also had what was known as "spirit sight". He could see into the plane of demons and those possessed. He could see when someone had been taken over by the wendigo. He and his brother, Joseph, were trusted implicitly by the Cree people, and during their lives they killed fifteen, maybe twenty wendigo. That is what is on record. Perhaps they killed a great many more. In about 1905, 1910, somewhere around that time, both of them were arrested and charged with fourteen killings. There was a great protest. People demanded they be freed. The North-West Mounted Police investigated this case. They were the ones who arrested the brothers at Sucker Camp near Deer Lake. The first charge that was filed was for the murder of Joseph's daughter, Wahsakapeequay. The police were working to establish Canadian law across these regions, and they saw this as a way to prove that the rule of law should be enforced. They presented this as devil worship and outright murder, and everything was done to stop the Cree protesting about these arrests. Jack Fiddler was eighty-seven at the time. He managed to escape, and he hung himself. Joseph went on to trial, however. Many people came forward in his defence. These people were not aware of Canadian law, and they argued that they had a right to conduct their affairs according to tribal lore that had been established over hundreds of years. According to one testimony, Wahsakapeequay was killed when she was in terrible pain and dying of an incurable sickness. Many Cree said that Jack and Joseph Fiddler were the ones called upon to kill the very old and very sick, as was the custom in their tribe. Nevertheless, Joseph was found guilty and sentenced to life in prison. There were a number of appeals, and he was finally granted a pardon. However, before he even received news of the pardon, he died in jail.'

Lapointe stood up.

'The most important issue here is that these people *believed* in the existence of the wendigo. There were even white Canadian and European missionaries, and they rallied on the side of the Cree and demanded that these people be allowed to practise their beliefs. They said that the Devil appeared in many forms, and a man committed to destroying the Devil, in whatever incarnation, was still doing God's work.'

Jacques wanted to get out of the class. His forehead was varnished with sweat, his mouth dry. He closed his eyes for a moment, and when he opened them Lapointe was looking right at him.

The class ended. Jacques put his book in his bag and got up to leave.

'Monsieur Devereaux,' Lapointe said. 'A word, please.'

The remainder of the class filed out. Jacques stood by his desk. He couldn't make eye contact with Lapointe.

'Are you unwell, Jacques?' Lapointe asked.

Jacques shook his head. 'No, monsieur.'

'This subject is disturbing to you, perhaps?'

'My grandfather has told me about it.'

'And it frightens you?'

Jacques looked up. 'My grandfather says that this thing is ... He says that this creature is responsible for what happened to the girls.'

Lapointe's surprise couldn't be masked. Even as he attempted to withhold himself, he couldn't prevent himself from laughing.

'Oh, my word,' he said. 'What an imagination your grandfather must have.'

'You don't think it's true?'

'The terrible things that have happened here were done by a man, Jacques. A crazy man, a possessed man perhaps, but a man all the same.' Lapointe looked away for a moment, and when he looked back he seemed so very tired, as if just the thought of such things was exhausting. 'I believe in a man's belief. I believe in faith. I believe that a man can think himself possessed, but in reality he's plagued by some terrible mental sickness or psychosis. I don't believe there's such a thing as a wendigo, and if there were, and if it had killed these girls, then the wendigo, true to its nature, would have eaten them, no?'

Jacques nodded.

'So no, I do not think there's a seven-foot-tall, living corpse in our midst. I don't think that there's something out there that is craven and desperate and possessed with the insatiable urge to devour human flesh. What I do believe, however, is that Man is capable of great evil. Whether that comes from the individual himself, or it's directed by some other spiritual or demonic intelligence, is not the business of an old schoolteacher.'

'I think my mother believes it's real.'

Lapointe nodded sympathetically. 'I think a woman burdened with loss and grief must be suffering terribly, and grief and stress can play havoc with the mind and emotions.'

Lapointe placed his hand reassuringly on Jacques' shoulder.

'Just as Stoker's *Dracula* was based on the legend of a real man, so, I believe, is our wendigo. The creature in our midst is most definitely a man of this realm and thus can be stopped by the same things that would stop any other human being.'

25

It was past four o'clock and dark as pitch when Jack Devereaux returned to the station. The lights were burning inside, and he could see Nadeau seated at his desk.

Upon opening the outer door, Nadeau looked up. He just watched without a word as Jack came through the inner door and crossed the room towards him.

Jack sat down. 'I'm sorry, Sergeant Nadeau…'

'I understand,' Nadeau said. 'Believe me, I do.'

'I looked at those records,' Nadeau said. 'Of the killings. The murders. Whatever you want to call them. I went back and looked at the photographs, the notes that were made by Levesque, Thibault, Landry, all of those who were here at the time. And you know there were more, of course.'

Jack looked up.

'More killings,' Nadeau said. 'Not just here. I listened to what your brother said. I looked into it, contacted my contemporaries. There have been other unexplained deaths of young women. A girl in Menihek, another in Fermont, yet another in Wabush. Whether they're all murders, I do not know. Perhaps some of them were animal attacks. My concern is your brother seems to know a great deal more about these things than I do, and a great deal more than the officers I spoke to.'

'Meaning what?'

Nadeau looked away for a moment. He shrugged his

shoulders. 'Meaning that he knows a lot more about these things than anyone else.'

'You suspect that he's involved.'

'I didn't say that.'

'But that is what you're implying.'

Nadeau smiled. 'I get the impression that you're not a man who talks a great deal, Monsieur Devereaux, but what you say is very much what you mean.'

'Perhaps so, yes.'

'Then we're alike. If I suspected your brother of complicity in these killings, then I would say so. The killings that happened when you were here, your brother was just a child. I have also thought about your father, but there have been killings since he was committed in 1995. I have only just begun my investigation, and I'm investigating only one thing right now.'

'This attack that Calvis made on someone.'

'Yes.'

'Who did he attack?'

'A man called Jean-Paul Lefebvre.'

'Lefebvre?'

'Yes. He's an engineer. He works for Canada Iron. He's been working for them for many years.'

'I remember this name. Didn't he used to do some work at the boarding house?'

'If he did, it was before my time.'

'And where is he now?'

'In the medical centre. He's critical but stable. He needs a hospital, but we cannot get him out. There's no way by road, and they won't send a plane from Sept-Îles. If he dies, then your brother will be charged with homicide.'

'When did this attack happen?' Jack asked.

'On the Sunday before I reached you. The 10th of this month.'

'And you waited four days to telephone me?' Jack asked.

'If you had been easier to find, I would have contacted you much sooner.'

'And this man has family here?'

'He had a wife. They arrived here together. However, it appears that she moved to Fort Mackenzie with another man five or six years ago. Aside from that, he has a brother here in Jasperville, but I don't think they're close. I have spoken to him, but he acts like he doesn't even understand what has happened, let alone why. Nevertheless, he's visited his brother in the medical centre every day after work.'

'And where is Calvis now?'

Nadeau indicated the back of the office with a nod of his head. Jack knew that the rear door led down to the basement. There were four cells, each no more than eight by ten, a single iron bedframe bolted to the wall, a metal chair. Nothing but bars and bare stone walls. If nothing had changed, and Jack doubted that it had, then a handful of hours down there made most men regretful and apologetic.

'He's been down there for eight days?' Jack asked.

'I have nowhere else to put him, Monsieur Devereaux. I cannot send him to Sept-Îles without an escort, and I'm the only one who can escort him.'

'You're going to ask me to take him?'

'Absolutely not. That wouldn't be possible. He can only be transported under the jurisdiction of the Sûreté.'

'So . . . what?'

Nadeau shook his head. 'That is the question. As it stands, he's been charged with grievous assault. This could be attempted homicide if the prosecution office decides. But if Monsieur Lefebvre dies, then we're dealing with first-degree murder.'

'And what happens in the meantime? You leave him down there to rot?'

'You're here to help me,' Nadeau said.

'Help you? How can I help you?'

'He doesn't talk to me. He won't answer my questions. He rages, he screams. He tells me that he will paint the walls with the colour inside of me. He says that as soon as he gets to hell, he will tell them that I'm responsible for the next murders that happen.' Nadeau exhaled resignedly. He seemed overwhelmed. 'We've had to sedate him. That's all we've been able to do. My only hope is that someone will come from Sept-Îles to collect him, and he can be dealt with correctly. I don't have the facilities or the manpower to investigate a single attack like this, let alone a series of murders that goes back nearly thirty years.'

'He's sedated now?' Jack asked.

'Yes.'

'And for how long will he be out?'

'From past experience, I don't think he will wake until morning.'

'Is he eating?'

'Yes,' Nadeau said. 'There doesn't seem to be anything wrong with his appetite. In fact, he says that the rest and the food will help him. He says he needs his strength to continue his work.'

'Where has he been living?'

'In the same house where he grew up. The house where you lived.'

'How can that be? Those houses are owned by Canada Iron. Surely they took it back when my father went to Saguenay?'

'Back in 1990 the houses were made available for sale as the ore production decreased. Your father bought the property. It's owned by your family now.'

'I didn't know,' Jack said.

'Well, you've been away for twenty-six years, Monsieur Devereaux, and without a word to your father or your brother.'

Jack didn't respond.

'What happened here?' Nadeau asked. 'Why did you leave,

and why haven't you communicated with your family in all these years?'

'Why is it necessary for you to know these things?'

Nadeau shrugged. He didn't seem offended by Jack's rebuttal. 'It's not necessary for me to know. I'm a policeman. I'm interested in everyone's business, even when it's none of my business.' He looked at Jack, perhaps expecting Jack to now be forthcoming.

Jack didn't say a word.

'So, you have somewhere to stay?' Nadeau asked.

'At the boarding house.'

'Where the Roy girl lived, yes? And then the Bergeron girl who was killed.'

'Yes.'

'And you want to go and see your family house?' Nadeau opened the drawer of his desk and took out a bunch of keys. He placed them in the centre of the desk.

'Your brother's keys,' he said. 'He won't be needing them for a while. I guess there's no reason you shouldn't actually stay there. Save yourself the cost of a room at the boarding house.'

'No,' Jack said reflexively. There was nothing more unappealing to him. He'd hoped never to see the place again. The idea of actually staying there was anathema to him. It produced an almost palpable feeling of nausea.

'Take the keys,' Nadeau said. 'You should go and see what your brother has...' He shook his head. 'Go see for yourself, Monsieur Devereaux.'

Jack took the keys, more to stop the conversation than a commitment to do as Nadeau suggested.

'Come back in the morning. Your brother will be awake, at least. All we can hope is that he talks to you. We need to find out what really happened. Was he provoked? Did he act in self-defence? Does what he say about Jean-Paul Lefebvre have any connection to reality, and if it does, how do we prove it?'

'You think my brother is truly dangerous, Sergeant Nadeau?'

Again, Nadeau smiled in such a way as to suggest that he knew a great deal more than he would ever say.

'If what he says is true, that this Lefebvre is a killer, then who is more dangerous? The killer, or the one who tries to kill him?'

Half an hour later, hands buried in his pockets, face aching from the bitter wind, Jack stood across the street from the Devereaux house. Bought and paid for, occupied by a crazy man, and before him there was another crazy man who was now locked up in Saguenay and talking to people who weren't there.

He couldn't go inside. Just seeing it was enough. Those last months he'd spent here came back at him relentlessly. He felt the tears well in his eyes and freeze before he had a chance to cry.

His mother. His own mother. Elizabeth. She came all the way from England to this unending nightmare of a place. And it was here that she'd died in a way that had haunted him ever since.

26

The spring of 1984 was late. The winter had hunkered down, it seemed, and the warmer weather wished to stay wherever it was.

It wasn't until the tail-end of April that the spears of ice that hung from the eaves began to melt. They would freeze again each night, but with each passing day, as the sun crept over the horizon and her cautious rays aimed westward, the icicles grew shorter. Far into the distance, out near the foot of the Torngat Mountains, the thick banks of fog rose from the earth and obscured the low shadow of trees.

Since Christmas, Henri had been drinking heavily. It was no secret, and he made no attempt to hide it. Whether his decline was born out of grief for the loss of his daughter wasn't clear, but Elizabeth was too weak to fight it. He didn't drink at work, but as soon as he'd shed his oilcloth and woollens, he was there ahead of the kitchen stove, a bottle in one hand, a cracked coffee cup in the other. When he didn't speak, he was morose. When he spoke, he slow-boiled into a furious rage that was directed at both everything and nothing.

Henri Devereaux was not violent. Perhaps Elizabeth wished he had been, for then she would have shown the signs of intimidation. As it was, there was nothing to evidence her husband's abuse. The bullying was psychological, and in some way that seemed even worse. A cut lip or a swollen eye can heal. The wounds inflicted by vicious words would never scar.

Marguerite Bergeron knew all too well what was happening, for she'd heard Henri's raised voice on more than enough occasions. Jacques, now eighteen, spent as much time away from the house as he could. More often than not, he was with Carine, and Carine – now turning seventeen in July – was most of the woman she would ever be. There was no doubt in the minds of either Elizabeth or Marguerite that the relationship between their respective son and daughter was far beyond platonic. Sadly, with Jacques finding sanctuary at the boarding house, it left Calvis alone. Marguerite routinely asked Jacques to bring Calvis along. Elizabeth urged Jacques to take him, not only to relieve Calvis's loneliness, but also to keep him out of Henri's line of fire. However, the kind of talk that Jacques and Carine shared was not for the ears of an eleven-year-old.

Calvis was there when Henri returned from work. Calvis suffered the same degree of intimidation and harassment as his mother. Nothing was right, everything was wrong. The world was against Henri Devereaux. His wife and offspring were in league with whoever had set out to ruin him, and they needed to be constantly reminded of this fact.

There was a time when Jacques stood up to him, and – as was the case with all bullies – Henri found a way to twist the circumstances around and make Jacques feel ashamed for having challenged his father. That gave Jacques a greater incentive to avoid him, and thus he did.

Between the end of January and the beginning of May, it seemed the only time that Henri and Jacques were under the same roof was when they were sleeping.

Calvis clung to his mother. He wet his bed, he suffered nightmares, and he seemed to somehow regress in age. He was prone to tantrums, he refused to eat, his skin became inflamed with eczema. There were days when he seemed never to surface from a vague, trance-like weariness. Elizabeth spoke to Bayard

Pelletier at the medical centre. Pelletier prescribed iron tonics and a programme of exercises to revive the boy's heart rate and pulse.

'It's not a physical malady,' Pelletier told Elizabeth. 'It's a malady of the mind. He has a weak mind. I have seen it before in a child. He will grow out of it, of course, but the sooner he grows out of it, the better.'

Pelletier asked about school, about the boy's home life, about anything that might be contributing to the boy's seeming stress.

'I'm not aware of anything,' Elizabeth lied. She was too ashamed to speak ill of her husband, for to speak ill of him was to admit that she'd failed as both a wife and a mother.

As the first week of May came to an end, Elizabeth took Jacques aside. It seemed that they shared an equal burden of guilt, written clear and bold in their awkward silences.

Elizabeth swallowed what little pride remained, and told Jacques that she was deeply concerned for both her husband and her younger son.

Jacques, expecting another disconcerting monologue on things that lurked in the woods, all of them waiting breathlessly to steal Jasperville's young, was struck by the seeming calmness and lucidity of his mother.

'My fears are warranted,' she explained. 'Your father is drinking, almost daily now, and though he doesn't drink a great deal, it's still sufficient to turn his mind against us. You're not here, Jacques, but he says terrible things about you, about Calvis, and about me, of course.'

'So what do you want me to do?'

Elizabeth smiled understandingly. 'I don't want you to do anything other than be here. You're big enough to be a deterrent to him. You do understand that, don't you?'

'But I don't want to be here for that very reason,' he replied.

'So very often we must do what is best, irrespective of whether or not it pleases us.'

'It wouldn't be so bad if Carine was here with me, but she's terrified of him.'

'Well, there we have the conundrum,' Elizabeth said. 'If you were here, then I have no doubt that his temper would be subdued, and then he wouldn't be so terrifying to Carine.'

'But she needs to work at the boarding house—'

'Jacques,' Elizabeth interjected. 'You're not hearing me.'

'I'm hearing you.'

'Very well, you are hearing me, but failing to understand what I'm saying.'

Jacques could feel the anger boiling in his chest.

'Your father works hard,' Elizabeth said. 'He has a job up there which carries a tremendous responsibility. His job gives us a roof over our heads, food on the table, the clothes we wear—'

'I know about his job. I know how difficult it can be, but that doesn't explain why he's started drinking.'

'Your father is under a great deal more stress than any of us, Jacques, and he's suffered terribly with the loss of your sister.'

Elizabeth paused. She was doing all she could to quell the rising tide of grief that assaulted her. Of all of them she had lost the most, and yet had a duty to bear it in silence.

'All I'm asking is that you spend some time here with me and your brother ... in the evening, you understand, when your father is home from work.'

'Do I have a choice?' Jacques asked, his tone petulant.

'Do you have any notion of how inconsiderate you sound, young man?' Elizabeth asked. 'I understand that you want to spend time with Carine. I really do. Nevertheless, you have a loyalty and an obligation to this family, to me, to do as I ask.'

'I don't know that I have any obligation.'

Elizabeth raised her hand as if to smack him. Fury flashed in her eyes. Her immediate reaction withheld, she glared at Jacques until he lowered his head.

'I'm sorry,' Jacques said. 'That was selfish.'

Elizabeth lowered her hand. Her expression softened. 'We'll say nothing more of it.'

'I'll be here,' Jacques said. 'And if Papa is a little less noisy, then maybe Carine can come over too.'

'You know she's always welcome in this house, Jacques. And yet, we do this for Calvis. You know how much he looks up to you. He's a lonely boy, Jacques. He's also astute enough to understand that he's not exactly welcome at the boarding house.'

'That's not true,' Jacques said. 'Carine's parents dote on him. They actually spoil him terribly, if you must know.'

'I'm not talking about Philippe and Marguerite,' Elizabeth said. 'I'm talking about the young couple that spend their time courting over there.'

The colour rose in Jacques' cheeks. 'We're not courting, Maman.'

Elizabeth reached out and touched her son's hand. 'If the pair of you are not courting, then I have absolutely no understanding of the word.'

Jacques didn't reply.

'So, this is settled. If Carine wishes to be here, then she's welcome, but I would like it if you would include Calvis in your conversations. Perhaps you could help him a little with his schoolwork. I want you to keep an eye on him, look after him. It's not a lot to ask, and I know it would mean the world to him.'

If Elizabeth's guilt lay in failing to control her husband, in failing to understand the emotional predicament that Juliette had suffered, then Jacques' guilt lay in the neglect of his younger brother and the family as a whole. Elizabeth's request didn't come as a surprise, nor was it received as an unjustified criticism.

Jacques knew well enough his own failings, and the conversation merely highlighted everything he'd chosen to leave in the shadows.

Jacques was going to be good to his word. That there was an ulterior motive behind his mother's request never occurred to him, and only later did he truly comprehend the agony and torment she must have been suffering. The week following their conversation he saw almost nothing of Carine, and almost everything of his father. Carine understood, for Jacques took time to explain the situation to her.

'It won't be for long,' he said.

'How can you say that?' Carine asked. 'Do you know something I don't?'

'No, I don't know anything else.'

'Well, if your mother wants you to be there to help look after Calvis and to see that your father doesn't become too rowdy, then how can you have any idea how long it will go on for?'

'Because we're leaving,' Jacques said.

Carine laughed. 'You've been talking about leaving for as long as I've known you.'

'And the more I talk about it, the more determined I am to do it.'

'And I'm to come with you? Leave here, leave my parents behind, and come with you to where?'

'I don't know,' Jacques said. 'Anywhere. Sept-Îles, Montréal, even further perhaps.'

'And how are we to live? How are we to survive? You are eighteen—'

'Nineteen in June.'

'Nineteen in June, then,' Carine said. 'And I will be seventeen in July, and if I'm correct in my calculations then I have all of nine dollars and fifty cents to my name.'

'I'll work,' Jacques said. 'We'll both work. We can do it. My parents did it, didn't they? Your parents, too. That's what happens. You find someone you want to spend the rest of your life with, and then you get busy making that life happen.'

'You're a wonderful person and I love you dearly,' Carine said, 'but I think you're a dreamer with no idea of what it would take to survive in a big city. We're teenagers, Jacques, and I don't think there are very many jobs available for teenagers in either Sept-Îles or Montréal.'

'I'll make it happen,' Jacques said defiantly. 'I'll go ahead. I'll find work. I'll find us a place to live, and then I'll come back and get you.'

'Okay, Mr Dreamer. That's what will happen. You will escape from Jasperville and go out into the big, wide world and you'll find us a magical castle to live in and then you will come and rescue me.'

Jacques took her hand. 'If there's one thing that's worth anything in this godforsaken wilderness, it's my word. I want you to come with me as soon as you turn eighteen, and if you don't then I promise that I'll come back and get you.'

Carine reached up and touched Jacques' cheek with the tips of her fingers. She leaned forward. Her lips brushed against his. Then she put her hand on his shoulder and pulled him forward so she could whisper in his ear.

'You've made an oath now,' she said, 'and I expect you to keep it.'

It was only later that Jacques understood why his mother wanted him to look after Calvis.

It was the day Juliette would have turned twenty-six. Henri was gone by five that morning. Elizabeth woke both Jacques and Calvis at seven. She'd prepared buttermilk pancakes for them both. She asked Jacques if he would be so kind as to walk Calvis to school and then take some money to pay the butcher's bill.

'I'll do that and then head over to the boarding house,' he said. 'Philippe wants some help. There was a leak in one of the rooms and the ceiling is a mess.'

'Of course,' Elizabeth said. 'If you could walk back with Calvis this afternoon and see if he needs help with his homework, that would be really appreciated.'

'When is Papa coming home?'

'I don't think he'll be back until suppertime,' Elizabeth replied.

'I'll more than likely bring Carine back then,' Jacques said.

'As you wish, dear.'

Jacques had left as agreed. He walked Calvis to school, headed back to the butcher's and settled up. He was at the boarding house by eight-thirty. He and Philippe sat for a little while in the kitchen. They drank coffee while Carine folded towels and sheets in the laundry room. Watching her, Jacques' heart swelled. He loved her so very much. It seemed nothing less than destiny that they'd been drawn together, some profound and indefinable force pulling them from different parts of the world to this desolate, unforgiving place. Perhaps there was such a thing as luck, but the right kind struck hard only once. The true difference between good fortune and bad was in the recognition of which was which. In so many of the novels he'd read, Jacques had learned of men who believed they were being betrayed when it was merely Fate's way of revealing a different and unfamiliar path.

The work was hard that day, but Jacques and Philippe accomplished what they'd set out to do before Calvis was ready to be collected from school.

Once he'd washed up, Jacques found Carine in the parlour. She was reticent about going home with him, not only because she was afraid of Henri's temper, but she'd also promised her mother that she would help clean Mason jars for preserves.

'I'll try and come back later,' Jacques told her. 'Maybe after dinner, okay?'

'If you can, yes,' she said, 'but I know you need to spend time with Calvis, too.'

Jacques left. He met Calvis outside the school and they walked home together. It was past four by the time they arrived. Darkness had fallen like a shroud.

The house was empty. Ordinarily, Elizabeth would be busying herself in the kitchen with dinner preparations.

Jacques didn't sense that something was awry. Later, he would wonder why. Even he couldn't believe that he'd predicted what would happen, but there was something about the simple absence of his mother that seemed fateful. It was Juliette's birthday, after all. Perhaps she was in the church. Perhaps she'd entered into conversation with the minister and time had run away with her. Any moment now she'd fly through the door, flustered and apologetic.

But the moments came and went, one after the other. Soon there were too many moments for Jacques to assume anything but the worst.

Insisting that Calvis stay home, Jacques assured him that all was well. Their mother would be perturbed if she returned and the house was empty, so he needed to remain just in case. Their father was not due home for at least another hour.

Jacques hurried to the boarding house. Philippe said he would help in the search. They would go to the church, to the general store, anywhere there were people Elizabeth knew, and if they still couldn't find her, they would go on up to the foundry and fetch Henri.

Very quickly, it became evident that no one had seen or heard from Elizabeth since the previous day. She hadn't visited the church, nor any stores. She hadn't socialized with any of the women with whom she was acquainted. Ultimately, it was not necessary for Jacques and Philippe Bergeron to go on up to the foundry. Henri came down the main drag just as they were heading back to the Devereaux place.

At first, Henri seemed angry that whatever plans he'd made for that evening – drinking, and then further drinking if previous evenings were anything to go by – were being capsized. And then the anger, rapidly passing, was replaced with a profound sense of disorientation, as if everything he knew as certain had been swept away.

'She has to be home,' he insisted time and again. The three of them returned, found Calvis alone, and after Henri had gone up to the room where he and Elizabeth slept, had looked behind the house, in the narrow pathway that ran alongside the building, and when he returned through the front and entered the kitchen, it was as if the reality of her absence had finally dawned on him.

Henri Devereaux looked at each of his sons, and then he folded into a chair at the kitchen table. He put his head in his hands. What little remained of his world collapsed on him like a falling house.

That night no one but Calvis slept, and then only from sheer exhaustion. Marguerite arrived with Carine, and they made food that no one ate. Henri drank. He muttered. He cried at one point, but quickly gathered himself and resumed a stony silence. It was Jacques and Philippe who ventured out at first sign of light and reported Elizabeth's disappearance at the police station.

Within an hour, a team of a dozen volunteers began a fraught and unenviable task that had occurred more times than any of them wished to remember – that of establishing and maintaining an ever-widening search to the limits of Jasperville and beyond.

It took no more than three hours to find her. Dressed head to foot in black, Elizabeth Devereaux had followed the route her daughter had taken a little less than four years before.

The water in which she'd lain was no more than two or three feet deep. Her skirts had billowed out beneath her and frozen. It was as if she was somehow supported on a dark motionless cloud; in one hand a straight razor, in the other a picture of Juliette that could still be discerned.

Elizabeth had cut her forearms deeply from elbow to wrist, and the blood, spooling out in slow motion, had frozen in curves and arabesques. Nothing but her face and the toes of her shoes were above the level of the ice, and the expression she wore was one of reconciliation and peace.

The scene, both terrifying and surreal, was unlike anything any of them had seen before. Elizabeth Devereaux was buried in a drift of frozen scarlet, and the cold and the silence and the unreachable horizon contributed to the awful tableau before them.

The men built fires all around. It was a further two hours before they could lift Elizabeth's body from the crimson water and carry her back to town.

In their own way, the events of Thursday, 10 May 1984 would touch each remaining member of the Devereaux family differently.

With hindsight, as ever, there were things that could perhaps have been done or said. Like the post-mortem that revealed a preventable death, such considerations, by their very nature, were always too late.

Calvis would turn the tragedy upon himself, asking whether he'd somehow precipitated the event. Henri would see in it yet another confirmation that all was lost, that there was no respite from whatever curse had befallen his family. His mind would collapse in on itself, and he would begin to manifest the very deepest neuroses and paranoia. Jacques, appreciating that he was now alone in caring for Calvis, sought solace and comfort in his relationship with Carine, but she herself was too grief-stricken to provide it.

In Jasperville, right into the very heart of this desolate, wind-swept, ice-ravaged nowhere, an emotional abyss was created, and into it fell not only the Devereauxs and the Bergerons, but all those who had known Elizabeth for the generous, patient soul that she was.

In losing her, everyone who knew her seemed somehow to lose a part of themselves. Their failure to understand her true motivation made it all the worse. Had it taken place immediately after Juliette's death, then perhaps it could have been under-stood. Had she perhaps waited until Calvis was sixteen, it would have been interpreted as maternal instinct staying her hand just long enough to ensure Calvis would be able to navigate the crude highway of loss that would stretch before him.

But no, she did neither. She chose to take a hard road out of a hard life.

Kind as she was, it seemed that Jasperville was a place where no good deed went unpunished.

27

Back inside the boarding house, Jack waited for Martin so as to retrieve his room key.

It was then, standing there alone, that he noticed his bag on the floor beside the foot of the stairs. He'd left it in his room. Of that he was certain.

He called out. 'Martin? Martin?'

Martin appeared within a few moments. 'Monsieur Devereaux,' he said, 'I'm afraid there has been a misunderstanding.'

'A misunderstanding?'

'Yes. I'm sorry, but the room I gave you was already reserved for someone.'

'Then I'll take another room,' Jack said.

'There are no other rooms, monsieur.'

'What?'

'There are no other rooms available,' Martin repeated.

'What's the deal here?' Jack asked. 'I mean, the truth. What's actually going on here?'

'Just as I said. The room was reserved for someone arriving later, and we're already full up with guests.'

'I don't believe that for a minute,' Jack said. 'Your mother owns this place, right? Where is she?'

'She's not here.'

'Then go get her.'

'She's not available.'

'You just said she wasn't here. Is she not here, or is she here but unavailable?'

Martin's expression didn't change.

'So?' Jack prompted.

'You're the brother of Calvis Devereaux,' Martin said.

Jack was unable to hide his surprise. 'Yes. Yes, Calvis is my brother. What about it?'

'You have your own house. You can stay there.'

'I don't want to stay there,' Jack said. He was irritated by the situation now. He could feel the anger rising in his chest.

'Okay,' Martin said again.

'This is—'

'This is your own fault.'

Jack turned at the sound of a voice behind him.

Though he didn't move, he felt as if he'd taken several steps back.

'Like my son said, the room is taken. But even if it wasn't, you're not welcome here.'

'Carine?'

Carine Bergeron stood at the bend in the stairwell. She looked down at him. Her expression was cold and dispassionate.

'Your bag is there,' she said. 'I assume that Sergeant Nadeau can give you the keys to your house. I appreciate that you might not wish to stay there, but that's not my problem.'

'Carine,' Jack said again.

From the corners of his mind tumbled a thousand bittersweet memories, and with them came guilt and fear and so many unwanted emotions.

'It's time for you to go,' Carine said.

'But—' Jack started.

'Martin. Give Monsieur Devereaux his bag and show him to the door.'

With that, Carine turned. She walked back up the stairs, and along the hallway to the left.

Jack didn't move, barely able to breathe, his heart thundering in his chest, a cold sweat varnishing his entire body. A deep, needling pain, centred somewhere in the middle of his forehead, drilled right through him. He experienced a wave of disorientating nausea, and for a second – just a split second – he saw blood in scattered patterns across deep virgin snow.

He tried to breathe, but his chest was tight. He turned to see Martin walking towards him, in his hand the bag, and he took a reflexive step away.

'You need to go,' Martin said. 'You're not welcome here.'

Jack didn't move.

'Go, or I'll call Nadeau.'

Jack snatched his bag from Martin's hand. Before he could even think about moving his body, he felt the cold blast of air through the doorway and he was standing in the street looking back at the front of the boarding house.

28

In the weeks before his departure, Jacques found it more and more impossible to spend time around his younger brother. What he was planning to do really hit home when he turned nineteen in June. Both Calvis and Carine had wanted to make something special of it, but such a consideration was out of the question for Jacques. Henri had become as far from paternal as it was possible to be. When he wasn't at work, he was a belligerent drunk, seemingly oblivious to the fact that his wife had committed suicide. Despite the fact that she wasn't there, he expected food on the table when he returned from work. If not, there would be hollering and hell to pay. He would usually lash out at Calvis. Jacques was the same height as his father, if anything a little stockier, and Henri Devereaux was a bully. If Henri started making fists, Jacques stood between them. Henri would back down in a hurricane of expletives and threats. On the rare occasion that Jacques wasn't there, Calvis came away bruised and tearful.

As July unfolded, the tension became almost unbearable. Why Jacques had decided upon August, he didn't know. Aside from the weather, there was no special significance to the month. If he left it later, he wouldn't be able to travel until the spring. He also knew that if he didn't make a specific plan, he would find one reason after another to stay yet one more day, one more week, one more month. The little that he'd been paid by Philippe Bergeron was supplemented by the dollars and coins he'd taken from his father's pockets when he was too drunk to remember how much he'd spent. Over time, Jacques had accumulated enough for rent and food for a month. If he didn't find work within that time, he'd have to come back. That alone would be sufficient incentive to overcome any obstacles he might encounter.

Jacques' emotions were torn and divided. On one hand, he felt both an obligation and responsibility to Calvis. That was born out of a deep fraternal bond, a sense of duty, a promise he'd made both to himself and to his mother. The prospect of leaving Carine behind was emotional torture. That was not born out of anything but love. Yes, he'd promised Thérèse that he would look after her, but his devotion had nothing to do with any oath he'd made. He needed Carine as much, if not more, than she needed him. He found solace in the notion that it was a binary universe, that for every human being there was both an equal and an opposite. In Carine, he knew he'd found everything he could've hoped for, and yet there was no way she could leave her family behind. Without Jacques, Philippe would struggle to keep on top of the general maintenance and upkeep of the boarding house. If Carine left too, the place would fall apart. Love her though he did, the pull from beyond the limits of Jasperville was stronger than any loyalty he possessed. It was this that he'd reconciled within himself. In the end, self-preservation had won out.

In the last week of July, Jacques made the decision to leave on Tuesday 7th August. He bought a ticket that would take him through Sept-Îles with a connection to Montréal. The train left early, and once on board there were no stops before the Gulf of St. Lawrence. It would be twelve hours or more before he had a chance to reconsider what he'd done, and that was how he wished it to be.

Jacques knew that there'd be no way to make things right with his father, and, in truth, he had no wish to. Calvis was another matter, and on the Sunday night he sat with his younger brother and told him that he was going.

'I know,' Calvis said. 'You've been saying that for a long time.'

'On Tuesday,' Jacques said. From his pocket he produced the train ticket.

Calvis closed his eyes. It was a futile effort to stem the tears. When he opened them again the tears just brimmed over his lids and rolled down his cheeks.

'If you're not here, he will kill me,' Calvis said quietly.

'He won't kill you,' Jacques said, aware of the uncertainty in his voice.

'When you're not here, he—'

'When I'm not here, all you need to do is be unafraid. If he comes at you, just stand up straight, look him in the eye, tell him that if he lays a finger on you then you'll kill him in his sleep.'

Calvis smiled weakly, and then he started to cry.

Jacques put his arm around his brother's shoulder and pulled him close.

'Everyone has gone now,' Calvis said. 'Papi, Juliette, Maman, and now you.' He looked up at his brother. 'You could at least wait until after my birthday,' he said.

Jacques had forgotten. How could he have forgotten? The twelfth of August. Calvis would be twelve. He thought back to his thirteenth birthday, the gift he'd received from the Bergerons. He got up from the bed, and from beneath the frame he dragged out a wooden box that had once contained tins of corned beef. Inside, now three or four sizes too small, was the deerskin and shearling trapper's jacket. He unfolded it, and laid it on the bed.

'For you,' he said to Calvis. 'For your birthday.'

The excitement of receiving the jacket masked the emotions they were both feeling, but only for a few minutes. The fact that

Calvis put the jacket on, and then sat there – Jacques feeling as though he was looking back at his younger self – merely served to heighten the intensity of what was really happening.

'I don't want you to go,' Calvis said.

'I know you don't,' Jacques replied. 'I don't want to go either, but I must. One of us has to escape. Once I have a place to live, I can send for you. I can even find you a new school.'

The words were hollow, and they both knew it. Calvis loved his older brother enough to let the lie be truth.

'Yes,' Calvis said. 'Somewhere to live. A new school.' He wiped the tears from his face with the back of his hand. He pulled his jacket tight. He breathed deeply.

'Bad things happen here,' Calvis said.

'Bad things happen everywhere,' Jacques replied.

'Perhaps bad things happen so we don't forget that the Devil is real.'

'Now you sound like Papi.'

'Maybe Papi was right. That thing he used to say from Shakespeare. Remember that?'

Jacques nodded. He remembered it very well.

'Hell is empty,' Calvis said, 'and all the devils are here.'

Jacques didn't tell Carine until the following day. They were at the boarding house, Carine going through the routine of chores as she always did – stripping beds, remaking beds, pressing shirts and starching collars for those guests who'd paid for the laundry service, and then on to the kitchen where she scrubbed pans, washed and dried crockery, polished silverware, swept and mopped the floors.

Jacques had repaired a cupboard door that had warped and wouldn't close. He was standing at the top of the stairs when Carine came out into the hallway below. He called to her. She looked up. He indicated that she should come up and speak with him.

'Later,' she said. 'I'm not finished.'

'I need to talk to you now,' Jacques said.

There must have been something in his tone, some element of finality, because the air between them seemed to shift and cool. Carine's expression changed. Perhaps she understood the import of the moment in Jacques' body language, because she set down the basket of towels she was carrying and started up the stairs towards him.

As Carine neared the top of the flight, Jacques turned and entered one of the rooms. She followed him, closing the door gently behind her. He told her to sit on the bed.

She shook her head. 'You think sitting down is going to make it easier for me to hear this?'

'You know what I'm going to say?'

'That you're leaving. That it's time.'

Jacques' silence was all the affirmation she needed.

'When?' she asked.

'Tomorrow. I'm leaving tomorrow morning.'

Carine sighed deeply.

'In eleven months, I will be eighteen,' she said.

'I know.'

'You've been here sixteen years. You can wait another eleven months.'

'Carine, the only reason I've stayed here as long as I have is because of you.'

'So that should be reason enough to stay a little longer.'

'I need time to get things ready.'

'But if we left together then we could do it together.'

'It doesn't work that way.'

'Why not?' she asked. She looked up at Jacques. Her eyes flashed with hurt.

'Don't be mad,' he said.

'Too late for that.'

'You always knew I would go ahead of you.'

'For yourself, yes. Not for us.'

'I'm doing this for us,' Jacques said.

'No, Jacques. You're doing it for yourself, and I'm just a second thought.'

He was genuinely surprised by her response. 'How can you say that? How could you ever consider yourself a second thought?'

'Because if you thought of me first you would wait for me.'

Jacques sat down beside her, put his arm around her shoulders and pulled her close.

'You'll disappear,' she said. 'I'll never see you again.'

'That's just crazy,' he said.

'And what about your brother? He's eleven years old.'

'Twelve on Sunday.'

'That makes it even worse.' She looked at Jacques with disbelief. 'You're not even staying for his birthday?'

'I can't.'

'Can't and won't are very different.'

'I can't,' Jacques repeated. 'I have to get out of here. The only thing that could make me stay is you, but I know you'll be all right. And as soon as I have a job and somewhere to live then I'll let you know.' He took her hand. 'Maybe it would have been easier if I'd just gone.' He looked at her. 'Written you a letter and then just gone.'

'I love you,' Carine said, 'but I think I hate you more.'

'I don't think you could hate me more than I hate myself.'

'Then stay, even if you move out of your house. I'll speak to my parents. Maybe we could work out how you could stay here with us until I turn eighteen.'

'You can't say a word to your parents.'

'What do you mean? Of course I can.'

'You think they want you to leave? They'll do everything they can to stop you. Don't you see that? You're the only reason that this place keeps on going, Carine. You have to keep this secret, and when you leave you can't tell them that you're going.'

'That's just more crazy talk,' she said. 'I wouldn't just vanish without explaining to them what was happening.'

'If you do that, then I guarantee they'll convince you to stay.'

'So, what are you saying? That the only way we can have a life together is if I let you go now, and then I just abandon my parents? Do you have any idea what that will do to them? They've lost Thérèse already, and you want me to put them through something like that?'

'You write to them. You tell them that you've left to be with me.'

'If your mother was still alive, would you have done that to her?'

It was a slap in the face. He would never have done such a thing, and it was obvious from his reaction that Carine knew this.

'Whatever has happened with your father is your own business,' she said. 'And if you feel that you can leave Calvis behind, then so be it. We're not the same, Jacques. I couldn't do that to my family.'

'I'm sorry,' he said. 'I just want us to be together, *really* together, as soon as possible.'

Carine folded her arms, lowered her head, and she remained silent for a good ten seconds.

Finally, when Jacques was on the verge of saying something – anything – to bring her back, she turned and smiled.

'If you don't come back and get me then I will find you and … and I will be madder than you can ever imagine,' she said.

'I don't doubt that for a second.'

For just a moment more she held his gaze, and then she stood up, walked to the door, and turned the key in the lock.

When she turned back, she was already undoing the buttons on her blouse.

'I'm guessing you know as much about this as me,' she said.

Jacques felt the colour rise in his cheeks. 'I don't know anything,' he said. 'Not really.'

'Well, there we are then,' Carine replied. 'Just about as much as me.'

'And ... and what if ... if you get ...'

'Pregnant?' she asked.

Jacques nodded.

'Then you'll have to come back for two of us, won't you?'

29

Carine Bergeron. She'd changed, of course. She was now – how old? Forty-three. Just two years younger than himself. And Martin? Where was his father? Was she married? What was she doing here in Jasperville? Had she never left, or did she make her own escape only to find herself pulled back here?

What Jack had heard in her words was hate. Hatred that he'd failed to keep the promise to go back and rescue her. Twenty-six years behind them. Twenty-six years for her to feel resentment and betrayal growing like a virus, weaving its way through every memory she possessed of their time together.

He'd left because he was afraid. He'd left because he didn't want to die like Lisette Roy, Anne-Louise Fournier, like Thérèse and Juliette and his mother. Because he didn't want to lose his mind like Papi or his father. And he hadn't come back in all these years because he didn't want to face Calvis or Carine or anyone that could remind him of his failing.

And did she know about the letter from Philippe?

Jack closed his eyes. He inhaled, exhaled, inhaled again. The cold filled his lungs. His heart still raced in his chest, and he willed it to slow down. After a few minutes, he turned and hurried back the way he'd come. He was relieved to see that Nadeau was still in the station.

'Sergeant Nadeau,' he said as he came through the door.

'Monsieur Devereaux. There is a problem?'

'Not a problem. I just wanted to ask about Carine Bergeron.'

'Yes?'

Jack crossed the room to Nadeau's desk.

Nadeau frowned. 'Are you okay? You look very pale, monsieur.'

'How long has she owned the boarding house?'

'I don't know exactly,' Nadeau said. 'She was here when I arrived in May. I think she's been here perhaps three or four years. Her parents used to run it.'

'I knew them,' Jack said. 'They were here at the same time as me.'

'I think perhaps that the mother, maybe the father, I don't know … anyway, one of them became sick. I think the cancer. They moved away. I think Madame Bergeron came with her husband and her son to sell the place. I heard there was some difficulty with the husband. I'm not sure of the details.' He paused. 'Why do you ask?'

'No reason,' Jack lied.

'You took a room there?'

'I did, but there was a misunderstanding. The room is no longer available.'

'Then you will stay in your own house?'

Jack looked at him. That was a detail he'd failed to take into consideration.

'It looks like I have no choice,' Jack said.

'It's not a crime scene, Monsieur Devereaux, but as much as possible I would ask you to maintain things as they are. There are papers, maps, books, photographs …' Nadeau paused. 'You will see for yourself.'

'Okay,' Jack said. 'I guess that's where I'll have to go, then.'

Twenty minutes later, Jack Devereaux stood in front of the house.

He fought against so many images of Juliette, of Thérèse, of Papi in his coffin, how he'd looked like someone else entirely.

And then there was his mother. He'd seen her body at the undertaker's. Her expression had been one of calm reconciliation, so very different from the fraught anxiety she so often displayed. She'd escaped, and her relief was indescribable. That was the way it had seemed to him then.

Jack stepped forward with the key in his hand. This was something he'd never envisioned. He hadn't conceived of the possibility that the house would still be occupied by a Devereaux. That Calvis had stayed here after their father had gone to Saguenay seemed so far-fetched and improbable, yet that was exactly what he'd done.

The key turned. The tongue of the lock snapped back from the striker plate. Jack hesitated. He knew he had to go inside. He knew there was no choice.

He withdrew the key and pushed the door. It swung open into darkness. Reaching through, Jack felt for the switch. The lights came on, and he was there, just as he'd been for so many years, each and every day walking into a house that held more of his past than any place he'd ever lived.

For a moment, it was as if he'd never left. Papi would be there on the porch, winking at him through a cloud of pipe smoke, asking him about school, about what he'd learned, about books he was reading. And then later, as his mind started to unravel, saying things that made no sense, warning him of things only Papi could see.

Jack crossed the threshold and set down his bag. He closed the door behind him. It shut with a strange finality, so much so that he instinctively turned and checked that he wasn't now trapped inside. He felt like the frightened child he'd once been. Perhaps he still was – some small part of him preserved for ever, as easily disturbed now as he'd ever been.

The kitchen. The long table still centring the room. Over to the right the stove, the sink, the hooks on the wall where his mother had hung utensils and pans. He walked through to the sitting room, and there was the fireplace, the bookshelves, those same old atlases, the biography of Captain Cook with the hand-engraved plates of sailing ships and distant shores. In the corner, as if to bring everything crashing down on him, sat Papi's rocker, over the back of it the same faded shawl he'd worn over his shoulders.

Hadn't anything changed? Of course it had. It had to have done. Twenty-six years. It was almost impossible to reconcile how long he'd been away with the intensity and clarity of his recollections.

Jack fired up the boiler. He heard the familiar shudder and groan as the pipes began to warm. Beside the stove was a basket of kindling. He built a fire both there and in the fireplace. It was not long before the house began to warm. He filled the kettle. He found coffee, a clean cup, and he made a drink for himself.

Jack sat down at the kitchen table. He lit a cigarette. The habit had returned like his past, as if it had never been any other way.

Closing his eyes, he wished himself elsewhere. He wondered about Calvis, if he was sleeping, if Nadeau had told him that Jack was coming, what his response had been. He wondered if he was as lost as Papi, as lost as their father, or if there was still some vague semblance of rationality and reason lurking there amongst the wild ramblings and outlandish hypotheses.

Jack thought that Calvis was the only one he'd have to deal with, but now there was Carine. Carine who hated him, and justifiably so. He could even remember what he'd said that day.

If there's one thing that's worth anything in this godforsaken wilderness, it's my word.

And then he'd promised that if she didn't leave with him, he would come back and get her. Rescue her. That had been *her* word: *rescue*. He hadn't come back, and he hadn't rescued her.

He'd justified it, of course. And with Philippe's letter, he'd found a reason to give up altogether.

Stay away, it had said in so many words. *My daughter has a new life, and she doesn't need to be reminded of the past.* How Philippe had found his Montréal address, he didn't know, and he didn't try to find out. The message was clear enough, but it also gave him a means to deny any further responsibility.

He'd left them all to their own fates, and only now – after a quarter of a century of forgetting and rationalizing and somehow trying to make it right in his own mind – he'd returned to confront his fears, his failings, his demons.

And if he didn't? If he just took the train back to Sept-Îles, on to Montréal, back to Caroline and Ludo and his job? He could be back before he knew it, safe in his own house, where the cold and the desolation, the unforgiving horizon, the shadow of the Torngat Mountains, the absence of light and the sun that never rose, and the endless, endless snow couldn't find him.

What would happen if he pretended that all of this had been nothing but another bad dream, a nightmare from which he'd eventually wake?

But it wasn't a dream. These things had found him. And no matter how far he ran, he knew they always would.

Had it been a blessing or a curse that it had taken this long? The simple truth was that he'd spent twenty-six years living no life at all for fear of living his own.

This was his life. This was his family. What he was feeling was the consequence of his decision. And that included Carine, the only girl he'd ever really loved, the only girl he believed had ever loved him. Every girl since had seen nothing but some disconnected façade, a mask, a character.

Carine needed to understand how and why he'd broken his word. Whether she would forgive him was another matter entirely. And Calvis? Calvis needed to be rescued from whatever world of fear and paranoia he'd created from his own experiences.

It all came back to the day he left, to the things he'd said to his brother, to the very last time he'd seen Carine.

Right there in the kitchen, a place he'd believed he'd never see again, the memories tore right through him like a brutal Canadian storm.

The lies he'd built were fragile. The truth was so very much stronger than anything he'd told others, and everything he'd told himself.

He'd escaped from one prison, only to find himself in yet another, and that was a prison he would live inside no matter where he went, no matter how far he travelled.

To truly escape, and to be free of this place for ever, he had to face all of it – every single action, every failing, every betrayal, every broken promise, every lie.

And if he didn't, he would go to Hell. Perhaps not in the biblical sense, but certainly a hell of his own creation.

And then a memory of his father returned. This table. Seated right here. A moment when both he and Calvis had believed that Henri Devereaux governed not only their lives, but possessed the power to dictate their eternity.

30

Jacques' cheeks coloured up. A cold sweat broke out on the back of his neck and across his scalp. He was fourteen years old, and yet he felt like a terrified little boy.

He glanced to his left. Calvis was as white as chalk.

All six of them – Papi, Henri, Elizabeth, Juliette, Jacques and Calvis – stared at the chocolate wrapper in silence. The only sound was the dull *tick tick tick* of the clock on the wall above the sink.

Henri picked up the wrapper, looked it over, and said, 'Neilson's Jersey Milk Chocolate.'

He smiled as if there was some private joke.

'It seems someone behaved so well they earned a reward.'

No one said a word.

'Is that right, Elizabeth?'

'Sadly not,' Elizabeth replied.

Henri looked at Juliette, at Jacques, at Calvis. It was like being tracked by a searchlight.

'Does anyone want to give me an explanation?'

Juliette glanced at her mother. Elizabeth reached out and touched her hand reassuringly.

'I'm thinking one of you boys needs to speak up,' Henri said.

The silence continued.

'I'm sure there's a perfectly good explanation,' Papi volunteered.

'Father,' Elizabeth said, and William fell quiet.

Henri sighed and leaned back in his chair. He set the wrapper down.

'Maybe, like Papi says, there's a perfectly good explanation,' Henri said. 'If so, I would be very happy to hear it.'

'Father...' Jacques started.

Henri leaned forward suddenly. His eyes were wide, his brow furrowed, and when he spoke his voice was both measured and threatening.

'If a single untrue word leaves your lips, Jacques, so help me God.'

'We took it,' Calvis said. 'We took the chocolate from the general store.' Immediately tears escaped his lids and rolled down his cheeks.

'Up,' Henri said. 'Both of you.'

Jacques hesitated.

'Now. Right now this minute. Both of you, up!'

The boys got up. Calvis started sobbing. Jacques' face was white with fear.

'Henri, please,' Elizabeth said. 'They are children.'

'I'm going to show them something,' he said. 'That is all.'

Henri told the boys to put on their boots and coats. Elizabeth asked where he was taking them, but he wouldn't say.

Henri Devereaux marched his sons out of the house and up towards Main Street. They knew that any word would be futile, so they kept their mouths shut.

Calvis reached out and took Jacques' hand. Jacques looked sideways, and the expression on his younger brother's face was heartbreaking. In that moment, could he have turned back time, he would have made an immediate confession, shouldered all the blame, insisted that Calvis knew nothing of the theft.

But it was too late. Too late to change anything.

It was bitterly cold, but they moved quickly, as if afraid to lose their head start on something stronger and faster.

Through the northern outskirts of Jasperville they hurried, barely a soul around, and then the dark hulking mass of the smelting foundry came into view. Even on a Saturday, the foundry didn't shut down. Three shifts of men kept that place running twenty-four hours a day. The sound was like some great beast huffing and snarling beneath the earth, a beast made of fire and molten rock, a living volcano.

Jacques glanced back at his father. Henri was resolute, unflinching, his gaze directed forward.

Twenty yards from the first outbuilding, he stopped them with a single word.

He went ahead then, directed the way, and both Jacques and Calvis felt the heat growing ever more fierce as they neared the furnaces.

For the last ten yards he held them roughly by their coat collars. He hurried them toward the vast thundering maw of roiling flame and smoke.

Calvis was screaming, believing perhaps that he was going to be hurled headlong into the fire. Jacques' eyes were filled with stinging, bitter smoke. Tears made it hard to see, and all the while his father urged them closer and again closer.

The heat became unbearable, impossible to conceive of in this icy wasteland, but they were mere feet from it now, and Henri was down on his knees between them, still holding them firm, his voice clear and strident over the roar of the furnace.

'The Lord detests lying lips, but he delights in men who are truthful. Look at it, boys. Look at the fire. Feel it. Can you feel the fire? This is Hell. This is where your souls will burn for eternity if you ever, *ever*, lie or steal or cheat. Do you understand? Do you understand what I'm telling you?'

Calvis screamed. He tried to wrench himself away from his father's grip.

Henri pushed him closer. Calvis felt the unforgiving heat pouring through him, scorching his eyebrows, his eyelashes. Jacques tried to back away, but Henri held them immobile.

'Tell me you understand, boys.'

'Yes! Yes!' they screamed in unison.

'Make me believe that you understand!'

'Yes! Yes! Yes!'

Henri pulled them back then – gasping, retching, their throats stinging, tears streaming down ash-blackened faces, eyes red and wild and terrified.

They ran home, leaving their father behind them as they fled.

It was a lesson learned, one of many, and one that their mother never questioned. She took them in, washed their faces, their hands, made them change into their nightclothes. They went to their beds and stayed there, shivering beneath blankets, not only with the cold, but with the true and certain conviction that their souls were bound for Hell.

31

Jack had forgotten about the dark, or perhaps convinced himself not to remember. It came down so fast, so black, so complete. In a city there were always lights – no matter how small, no matter how distant. Not here. Out here there was nothing. The darkness buried everything, and then, finally, inevitably, it seemed as though it was inside you.

He'd lain down on the couch in the parlour, still fully clothed, and fallen into a deep and unbroken sleep. Upon waking, the things he'd remembered the night before were fresh in his mind, and he had the unsettling perception that the divisions between past and present were slowly fading.

Standing at the sink as he filled the kettle, conscious that the light had barely changed with daybreak, he looked out towards the main drag, the flat, unbroken sky, the shape of the mountains on the horizon, and he could have been readying himself for the walk to school.

It was as if he'd left some version of himself behind, and that version was now working so very hard to occupy his skin. He could resist it or he could fight it. Whichever he chose to do, he didn't think he would win.

Jasperville would always and for ever own part of his mind, his life, his very existence. There were no memories he possessed that were not overshadowed by this place. Who he was and what he'd become had all originated here.

Yes, he'd left that August morning.

He had broken Calvis's heart, Carine's too, and he couldn't even begin to imagine what his own father had said about him once it became clear that he was gone.

Jack's first impulse was to go back to the boarding house and insist on speaking with Carine. Whether she would hear him out was unknown, but if he didn't give it his best efforts then he would be twice the coward he already was. His first thought should have been for Calvis, but there was something altogether terrifying about the prospect of seeing his brother in the grip of some profound delusional psychosis. Of course, there was no avoiding it. That was what he'd come here for. The fact that Carine was here was something he could never have predicted.

Calvis needed help. Calvis needed his older brother to step up and do the right thing. The only question in Jack's mind as he readied himself to leave for the police station was how much of his younger brother still remained.

Being unfamiliar with such a place as Jasperville, it would be hard to comprehend how ill-equipped the office of the Sûreté du Québec actually was when considering any crime beyond drunk and disorderly or unlawful trapping.

The simple matter of rotating the sergeant every two years or so meant that any investigation that might have been instigated could never have been maintained with any consistency. If anyone had ever concluded that the deaths of Lisette Roy, Anne-Louise Fournier and Thérèse Bergeron had been perpetrated by the same man, then the fact that they spanned six and a half years made the threads that connected them not only fragile and tenuous, but more than likely invisible. No crime scene, no official photographer, no forensics, no database into which information could be stored and recalled as needed, and the one constant that could have been preserved – the investigating officer – was routinely dispatched to another part of the country altogether.

Just as he'd done the previous day, Jack stood out in the street for a few minutes before entering the station. He'd slept, that much at least, but he had no appetite for breakfast. He was doing what he could to separate himself out from the past, to divorce himself from any preconceptions he might have about what would transpire. It was difficult – far more difficult than he'd thought it would be – for everywhere he turned, there was a clear and succinct reminder of the sixteen years he'd spent in this place. Its isolation alone guaranteed that it wouldn't change. People didn't come here to build a life, but merely to work. Some thought they'd make a fortune and move away. Others came here as a last resort when there was no employment elsewhere. It looked the same, but more importantly, it possessed the same static atmosphere, the sense that once you'd arrived, there were very few ways to escape. How many times had he asked himself what would have happened had he stayed that extra year? He didn't remember. Many times, a hundred, a thousand perhaps. And how many times had he wondered about Carine? The way they'd awkwardly made love the day before he left had been an unspoken consummation, not only of their love for one another, but his pledge to return. Her reaction to his eventual return was not surprising – her refusal to use his first name, to even allow him to stay at the boarding house. The last time they'd seen one another they'd shared the most intimate and important moment of their young lives, and then nothing – not a single word – for over twenty-five years.

Jack knew it would be easy to be apologetic, to beg forgiveness, but it was meaningless. Words cost nothing. And even if she did forgive him, what then?

Nevertheless, there had been something. He couldn't deny it. In the few moments he'd seen her, the anger and defiance in her expression, the unwillingness to even make eye contact, he recognized the young woman he'd so desperately loved. Did he love her still? Was it possible to un-love someone, no matter what might have happened to drive you apart? Martin was far too young to be his son, but there was always the possibility, however unrealistic, that she'd had another child. If so, wouldn't she have made every effort to let him know? Perhaps her parents had convinced her that he should only know if he returned to take responsibility for the life he'd promised her. If that was the case, then why had Philippe written the letter, telling him in the strongest terms to stay away?

In that moment, it was if Jack stepped outside his own body and viewed himself objectively.

His thoughts were spinning out of control. He was hypothesizing in multiple directions about things that bore no immediate relevance to why he was there. He'd come to help Calvis. He was there to try and understand what Calvis had done, and why. He wasn't there to unravel the myriad emotions that came into play when he thought of Carine and his broken pledge.

Jack crossed the street and entered the police station.

'I saw you out there,' Nadeau said. 'Over the street. You ready for this?'

'He's awake?' Jack asked.

'He is, yes.'

Jack shrugged. 'How is he?'

'Lucid, calm.'

Jack's expression was one of relief. 'Which is good, right?'

Nadeau leaned back in his chair. 'I don't know what's better, to be honest. To have him screaming blue murder at the top of his lungs, or to be calm and quiet and looking at me like he knows when I'm going to die and how dreadful it will be.'

Jack wanted to go outside and smoke another cigarette, but he knew he was merely delaying the inevitable.

'You really have had no contact since you left?' Nadeau asked.

'Last time I saw him was August of 1984. Eleven years old. A few days from his twelfth birthday.' He leaned forward. 'And you wanna know something else?'

Nadeau raised his eyebrows.

'Carine Bergeron. That was the girl I promised to come back and rescue. I didn't. Broke my promise. Broke her heart, I'm sure.'

'And that's why, all of a sudden, there was no room for you at the boarding house.'

'Right.'

'You have something to deal with there?'

'God only knows what I have to deal with,' Jack said. 'Feels like everything I've ignored for the past twenty-six years has been waiting here to get revenge.'

'One way of looking at it, I guess.'

'Is there another way?'

'No idea. Not my life.'

'That's one thing to be grateful for.'

'You slept at the house?' Nadeau asked.

'I did, yes.'

'Did you see all the papers and the photos?'

'I didn't see anything like that downstairs. I didn't go up into the bedrooms.'

'Well, when you've spoken to your brother, maybe you and I should go over there together and take a look at what he's been doing while you've been away.'

Jack stood up. 'Shall we?'

Nadeau led the way. Jack followed on, his heart in his mouth.

32

Had Jack seen Calvis in the street, he wouldn't have recognized him.

Crazy though it was, Jack had not considered the fact that his brother would age twenty-six years, just as he had. Beyond that, the years hadn't treated him well. Calvis looked to be the older of them. His hair was long and thick, matted in places, and his beard was similarly unkempt and dirty.

The cell in which he was secured was just as Jack remembered. The walls were a different colour perhaps, but beyond that this was yet another moment of intense *déja vu*.

The immediate emotion he experienced was one of pity. Then, as he'd anticipated, he felt the terrible wrench of guilt.

Calvis was seated on the edge of the bed, itself nothing more than a wrought-iron frame, one edge bolted to the wall, the other to the floor, the thin mattress supported by cross-hatched wire. He was wearing what appeared to be a dark tan one-piece, with press studs from the waist to the neck, beneath that a stained white T-shirt, on his feet heavy boots with no laces. His hands were stained, as was the case with all those who'd spent years in the dirt for Canada Iron. An hour with soap and Lysol, and they would look no cleaner.

'Calvis,' Nadeau said.

Calvis didn't respond. He looked up towards the high narrow

window near the ceiling. The light from the bare bulb bleached the shadows from his face.

Jack's sudden intake of breath was audible. It was then that he saw him – his kid brother. The years dropped away. Jack felt a surge of grief fill his chest. Without knowing it, he took a step backward and reached out for the wall to steady himself.

'You okay?' Nadeau asked. 'Do you want to sit down, Monsieur Devereaux?'

Jack shook his head. He stayed where he was, his hand against the wall, his knees weak, his pulse pounding in his ears. Still Calvis didn't turn and look at either one of them.

'Calvis,' Nadeau repeated. 'Your brother is here to see you.'

Calvis didn't flinch.

Nadeau walked to the bars and stood silently. He seemed untroubled by Calvis's lack of response. Perhaps this was how Calvis always behaved.

Nadeau indicated that Jack should approach.

Jack was reticent. He was both afraid to be known and unknown to his brother.

He took two or three steps. Some powerful force was holding his feet to the ground: fear, guilt, the burden of conscience, the weight of all the years he'd convinced himself that his actions had been right. They hadn't. He had always known it. How much of what had happened to Calvis would have been prevented if he'd stayed? Would this man – this Jean-Paul Lefebvre – be lying in the medical centre in a critical condition, fighting for his very life, if Jack had stayed?

'Calvis … your brother …'

'I have no brother, Sergeant,' Calvis said quietly. He didn't turn. He didn't move at all.

'Jacques,' Nadeau said. 'Jacques is here to see you. To help you.'

Calvis closed his eyes. He sighed deeply. 'Did he die yet?'

Nadeau didn't reply for a moment, as if trying to understand what he was being asked. Realization dawned.

'Lefebvre? No, he's not dead.'

Calvis lowered his head. The gesture was one of defeat and disappointment.

'We will come back later,' Nadeau said. 'You think about whether you want to talk to your brother, okay?'

Nadeau backed up, turned, motioned for Jack to follow him. They went out through the door and up the stairs to the office.

'He will be different later,' Nadeau said. 'Sometimes he behaves like he has no idea where he is or why he's been locked up. Other times he seems...' Nadeau shook his head. 'To be honest with you, Monsieur Devereaux, sometimes it's like having five or six different people down there.'

Jack was too unsettled to speak. What he'd expected he didn't know, but he hadn't expected this.

'Let's go to the house,' Nadeau said. 'You need to see the world your brother created for himself.'

Both the previous night and that morning, Jack had been oblivious to so many aspects of the house. Returning to it with Nadeau, the entire gamut of emotions he'd somehow kept at bay for so very long were there to assault him, exaggerated now as a result of having seen Calvis. It was unmitigated and relentless. There were mementoes of Papi, of Juliette, of his mother. The rug on the floor, pictures on the walls, a walking cane, a pair of boots, a scarf hung on a nail, an ornament, a dent in the lowest newel of the banister – every one of these things a reminder of why he'd never been able to free himself from the past.

His parents' room. The room that he and Juliette shared when they first arrived. The beds, the dresser, the low cupboard, even the curtains seemed not to have been changed in all these years. It wasn't possible, but he saw what he saw. He felt as if he'd soon be asked to cut wood, to clean his father's boots, to help Calvis with some insurmountable mathematical problem that not one person in the house understood.

'Your brother slept in there,' Nadeau said, indicating the room on the right. 'And he worked, if you can call it that, in here.'

Nadeau reached for the door handle of Papi's room.

Instinctively, Jack wanted to run. He didn't want to see the world that Calvis had created, living out here, desperately alone in the middle of this godforsaken frozen wilderness, his mind tortured by some mad delusion about wendigos that hid in the darkness and stole children from their beds and drove men to murder. It was a myth, a legend, a ghost story, and though it was as old as the first man to have ever settled here, it was still nothing but fantasy. There was no such thing as a wendigo. There was no creature lurking in cold forests, waiting for men to starve, seducing them into a craven hunger for human flesh.

Nadeau turned the handle. The door swung open.

Immediately, the impression was of a box lined with news-paper. Nadeau crossed the threshold. Jack went after him, slower, tentatively, and he surveyed the walls. Articles, clippings, handwritten notes, here and there actual photographs of young women, sections of maps, scraps of paper with names, dates, places. There were receipts, diner menus, bus and train tickets, movie theatre stubs, even beer mats. Everything was arranged in a seemingly random but very orderly fashion, and it was only after studying some of the articles and handwritten scrawls that Jack realized that the sequence was dated left to right. The trail, for that was what it seemed to be, started on the wall behind the door. It traversed the room and went around to the other side of the door. In the corner furthest from the door, the exact place where Papi's bed used to be, sat a low table. On it was a stack of journals. Nadeau picked one up and opened it. He showed it to Jack. Calvis's penmanship was meticulous and clear. There were names, dates, times of day, lists of questions, notations of other pages in other journals that bore some connection to whatever it was that he was writing about.

If VF went missing on the 15th, then why was her disappearance not reported until the 16th? Did Marie know that VF had left early?

Jack flicked through a number of pages and stopped again.

Absent on the 9th, but according to the shift rota, he was back in J on the 10th. Did he change that himself, or is there someone covering for him? If so, does this person know why he was really away from work?

'I haven't studied all of it,' Nadeau said, 'but from what I have, it seems your brother has been working on this for about fifteen years.'

'After my father was committed. Once he was completely alone.'

'Perhaps.'

'Your brother convinced himself that Lefebvre was the man responsible not only for the deaths here in Jasperville, but others, too,' Nadeau said. 'One in Menihek, another in Fermont, a third in Wabush. That was why he attacked him, it seems. I have records of Calvis reporting his suspicions about this man to three or four previous sergeants. Finally, about a year ago, after Lefebvre had been questioned yet again and absolutely nothing to tie him to these murders had been found, he secured an injunction against your brother. How official it was, I don't know, but in amongst all these papers you will find a document on Sûreté letterhead telling Calvis that he's not to approach Lefebvre for any reason.'

'And then a year later Calvis attacks him.'

'Yes.'

'And you've spoken with the family?'

'He has no family to speak of. Just his brother, Guy, and they're not close.'

'And Lefebvre's an engineer for Canada Iron.'

'Yes,' Nadeau said.

'How old is he?'

'Fifty-seven. He was born in Montréal in 1953.'

'And he was here in 1972 when Lisette Roy was killed?'

'He arrived here about six months before that.'

'So she died when Lefebvre was eighteen.'

'Nineteen,' Nadeau said. 'His birthday is in January. Her body was found in February.'

'And was there any connections between Lefebvre and Lisette Roy?'

'You would perhaps be more able to answer that question, Monsieur Devereaux. You were here.'

'I was six years old.'

'And I was a little more than one year old and several hundred miles away.'

'I know the name, but I can't remember why,' Jack said. 'But then, thousands of people have worked for Canada Iron over the years.'

'They have,' Nadeau said. 'But your brother got it into his mind that this man was responsible for what happened.'

'And is there anything at all, even circumstantial, that supports this?'

'Well, your brother would tell you there was a great deal to support it. However, much of it is circumstantial, and there are coincidences that can be read one way or another way, depending upon your viewpoint.'

'And all this ... this research is in here?'

'As far as I know, yes,' Nadeau said.

Jack was silent for a time. He looked at the walls, the journals on the table, and then he turned to Nadeau.

'You want me to go through all of this, don't you?' Jack asked.

'I don't want you to do anything, Monsieur Devereaux. It's

your decision alone. However, if I were you, and if I wanted to help my brother, then I would certainly want to better understand why he arrived at this conclusion. After all, he was certain enough in his belief to try and kill this man.'

33

Nadeau had been gone for nearly an hour. Jack sat in the silence of the kitchen. He smoked a cigarette, felt nauseous, but smoked a second. Finally he went back upstairs.

With great care, he began by removing the newspaper articles that were pinned to the wall. Maintaining their date sequence, he laid them out across the kitchen table. He then took down the photographs, noted the names, dates of birth and death on the back of each one. Lisette was there, as were Anne-Louise Fournier and Thérèse Bergeron. The rest were unknown to him, but their names – Estelle Poirier, Virginie Fortin, Génèvieve Beaulieu, Madeleine Desjardins, Fleur Dillard – struck home. These were real people, as real as himself, as Calvis, as Nadeau, and if Calvis was right, they had been killed. Perhaps murdered, perhaps attacked by animals, but there was already an element of coincidence that couldn't be contradicted. They were all young – anywhere from early teens to early twenties – and they were all undeniably pretty. Where a newspaper article detailed the disappearance of one of the girls, Jack put the photograph with the clipping. There were some pictures that stood alone, as if their death had not been sufficiently important to warrant even a few lines in the paper. At once, Jack wondered how Calvis had obtained the photos. Had he gone to see the grieving family, perhaps pretended to be Sûreté, a private investigator?

Once he was done with all the articles and photos, Jack

started to look through the other seemingly random notes. Here and there he found indecipherable scrawls, people's names and addresses, dates of public holidays, saint's days, a pocket calendar from 1989 with half a dozen dates circled in bold red ink, even notations of moon phases. The journals were altogether more unsettling. Calvis, by all appearances, had kept a daily record of his thoughts, sometimes numerous paragraphs, other times a few words, but page after endless page seemed to evidence the slow deterioration of his mind. Disordered, Jack took the time to put them in the correct sequence. There were fifteen of them, the first from August of 1995, just a couple of months after their father had been despatched to Saguenay. This was what loneliness could do. This was the effect that a place like Jasperville could have on a human being. Calvis had merely followed in the well-worn path laid down by Papi, then Elizabeth, and finally Henri.

In one of the piles of newspapers and magazines, Jack found a logbook of Canada Iron employees. Marked *CONFIDENTIAL* and *FOR OFFICE USE ONLY*, it gave the name, date of birth, employment commencement and termination dates, in some cases the date of death of a particular employee. Published in 2005, it went back twenty years. The names were alphabetized, and thus it was not difficult to find both his father and Calvis in the registry. Henri's employment commencement date was listed as Wednesday, 16 April 1969. He was *Retired on medical grounds* on Tuesday, 13 June 1995. Calvis had started working for Canada Iron on Monday, 3 September 1990, just three weeks after his eighteenth birthday.

Jack assumed that Henri would have been granted a pension after his twenty-six years of service. It was a long time; the same number of years that Jack had been away. That, in itself, despite the location, would have been enough to drive any man crazy. Open-cast mining in the bitter cold; a brutal, thankless task.

Where was that pension money going? Did Calvis have control of it, or was it sent on to Saguenay to afford their father some additional comforts? Saguenay was a state-owned and managed institution for the mentally incompetent. It housed psychotics, neurotics, those requiring twenty-four-hour supervision due to numerous suicide attempts, even those suffering advanced dementia. It was not a place for the criminally insane or those with homicidal tendencies. These were people who were either incapable of looking after themselves, or, left to their own devices, would be dead by their own efforts in a matter of hours. Jack knew all about the place. He'd taken the time to research it when he knew his father would be committed. And even then, knowing what Calvis would have been going through, he'd still made no effort to get involved, to help, to support, to even communicate. What kind of person had he become? And for how long could he go on blaming his past, his personal experiences, his childhood for how he treated others?

Jack took the Canada Iron logbook downstairs and put it with the rest of the documents and pictures from Papi's room.

He stood there, his hands in his pockets, and he surveyed the physical proof of Calvis's paranoia. Was that what it was? Is that how it would be classified? A fixation, perhaps? An obsession? Calvis had convinced himself that not only had these girls been murdered, but that Lefebvre was the perpetrator. Failing to gain the support of the law, he'd taken the law into his own hands. Jack went back to the logbook. Jean-Paul Lefebvre was there. His employment date was Monday, 11 October 1971, just as Nadeau had said. It was then that the name came back to him. Lefebvre had been one of the young men that Philippe had employed at the boarding house.

The first death that Jack knew of was Lisette Roy in February of 1972. Then came the Fournier girl and Thérèse. Juliette and Elizabeth had committed suicide. And then there was Étienne

Fournier who hanged himself in March of 1977. Factually, this place was a cemetery, possessed of some inexplicable capacity to steal both the life and the sanity of its inhabitants. He'd not been wrong to leave, nor had he been right.

If Lefebvre died, Nadeau would have no choice but to get Calvis to Sept-Îles or Montréal for trial. However, if Nadeau's description of Calvis's mental state was accurate, there was a good chance he would be declared unfit to stand. He would be destined to a life of inedible food and anti-psychotics in a featureless common room with heavy grilles on the windows.

If Lefebvre survived, it would be a grievous assault charge, perhaps attempted murder. Someone else would make a decision as to whether or not Calvis had been fully aware of the consequences of his actions, and, if so, it would be a lifetime in prison.

This was it. This was now Jack's choice, and he knew there was no other way to go. He'd abandoned his brother before. If he abandoned him again, there would be no future for himself. His own company would be unbearable. He'd wrestled with the decision he'd made for twenty-six years. His entire life had been governed by that one action, and it had been a nothing life. No wife, no family, no real sense of connection or engagement with anything. The past could never be left behind. The past travelled with you, no matter how far you went or how quickly you moved.

Jack sat down. He picked up the very first of Calvis's journals, and he held it to his chest.

He felt the tidal wave of emotion coming at him and there was nothing he could do to avoid it. For the first time in a quarter of a century he cried, and he cried for all of them.

An hour later, wrapped up as best he could with the clothes he'd brought along, he headed back to the general store. He bought provisions for at least a week, a carton of cigarettes, two bottles of Canadian Club, a heavy fleece-lined oilskin coat, a pair of fur-lined boots with deep treads, a sheepskin trapper's hat and gloves. He would have to contact Ludo and tell him that he was staying. He had to keep his mind focused on the decision he'd made. Not only was he the best in the world at making promises, he was also the best at breaking them. This time it would have to be different.

Back at the house, Jack heated some soup on the stove. With it, he ate half a loaf of bread. He'd had no idea he was that hungry. He made coffee, added a good inch of whiskey, and sat at the table with the journals.

Calvis had started keeping these when he was a week from his twenty-third birthday. Henri had been gone for less than two months, and yet Calvis – at least in the beginning – didn't mention him. At first, there was every indication that he was merely occupying himself with day-to-day matters. He spoke of work, of a leak in the roof above the parlour, of having to help someone replace the alternator in a vehicle. But, as Jack read on, there were breaks in the flow of his thoughts, and those breaks were filled with seemingly random sentences.

Most people spend their lives searching for something they don't understand and wouldn't recognize anyway. The rest just run from something that's inside of them.

Over the page, halfway down, it read, *A man is never late for a date with fate.*

Three pages later, circled again and again, was something that really hit home for Jack.

If you're not willing to make sacrifices for what you want, then what you want becomes the thing you sacrifice.

He paused, looked up from the pages. He felt that simple, hard truth worm its way under his skin and right inside him.

So many things had been sacrificed, every single one of them because he himself was not prepared to make any sacrifices.

The account of Calvis's life went on, and it was around the middle of the following year – the late spring and early summer of 1996 – that the first real indications of where his mind was going became evident.

Calvis had cut a small article from a local newspaper. It was dated Friday, 16 November 1979. It detailed the death of a seventeen-year-old called Fleur Dillard in Wabush. Just as was the case with Jasperville, Labrador City was founded by Canada Iron. The population was greater than Jasperville, and Wabush, its neighbour, became its twin city. The two of them were just referred to as Labrador West, but Wabush natives, in the main, resented their loss of identity. Tell a Wabush he was from Labrador and you were likely to get something more than a mouthful of expletives.

The article gave very few details. The girl had been found no more than two hundred yards from her house. Cause of death was uncertain, and reading between the lines, Jack knew this was because her body hadn't yet thawed when the piece was written. Same scenario as the Jasperville girls. Jack went through the pictures that had been stuck to the wall upstairs. There were five that hadn't been pinned up with a related article. Their names were on the back. Fleur Dillard was amongst them. She looked young for her age, but then there was no indication when the picture had been taken. She was in uniform, and from the pose and lighting – a somewhat forced smile and the absence of shadow – Jack guessed it was a school picture. Fourteen, maybe fifteen years old, Fleur looked back at him with her entire life ahead of her, completely oblivious of the fact that it was almost over.

Back in the journal, Jack turned the page, and there, across the top, printed in capital letters, it read: *PERHAPS SOME THINGS HAPPEN SO WE DON'T FORGET THAT THE*

DEVIL IS REAL. It was written in red felt pen. The ink had spread through the weave of the page.

Calvis had said the very same thing to him just a day or so before he'd left.

What if this Fleur Dillard had been murdered? What if her killing had been linked to that of Lisette and the other two in Jasperville? There was always the possibility that Calvis might have been pulling on a thread that tied all these things together. If that was the case, then he was the only one who'd made a connection to reality, and the reality he'd found was far darker and more horrific than anyone had imagined.

Jack paced around the table. He looked down at the collection of notes and pictures, the stack of journals, the maps and bus tickets and everything else that his brother had accumulated in this fifteen-year search. He'd travelled to Labrador City, Wabush, Menihek, Fermont, Fire Lake, even up north to Kawawachikamach and Fort Mackenzie. Either the connections were real, or Calvis's obsession had seen connections where none existed.

Jack knew he'd have to find the gaps in Calvis's train of thought. Objectively, uninfluenced by the endless months and years of isolation, if he could just see how Calvis had approached this, then perhaps he could understand why he'd assaulted this man so violently. What was it that had convinced him that Jean-Paul Lefebvre was a serial killer? If Calvis had spoken to Nadeau about this, Nadeau would've mentioned it. He'd spoken to previous sergeants – men like Nadeau, men with good intentions – but those men were alone, just as everyone else was in this bleak wilderness. Accomplishing anything effective was beset by an inordinate number of obstacles and challenges.

Jack thought of those who'd been posted when he was here, some by sight, some merely by name. Levesque, Thibault, Tremblay, Landry, beyond them the last two in the five years before he left. They could not be faulted. They wouldn't have even known where to begin. Nadeau was now in a similarly impossible situation. Even if Lefebvre died, there seemed to be no way to get Calvis out of Jasperville until the seasons changed. However, a crazed would-be murderer couldn't be left in a holding tank indefinitely.

Jack needed to plot these events in a sequence he could understand, and only then could he make a decision about which direction to take.

34

Beginning with the death of Lisette Roy in February of 1972, Jack sketched out a timeline of names and dates. Anne-Louise Fournier was second, Thérèse was third, and then Fleur Dillard appeared to be the fourth in sequence. The next Jasperville girl found dead was Virginie Fortin in August of 1983, but according to Calvis's notes she was preceded by Estelle Poirier, the daughter of a teacher at Menihek High School. Estelle was fifteen years old, and on Friday, 6 June 1981, she left school along the only road that ran between the school and her home. The Menihek sergeant, Franck Lasalle, was quoted as saying, '*This was a route that Estelle took every school day. It was half a mile. She would not have wandered. She knew better than that. She was abducted by someone, or she voluntarily got into a car with someone she trusted.*'

The statement was an assumption, of course, because it seemed that no one knew precisely what had happened to Estelle. Her body was found that same evening in a densely wooded area no more than three hundred yards from her own back yard. Her clothes had been torn, and physical evidence suggested that whoever had abducted her had intended to sexually assault her. Perhaps scared off, perhaps unable to follow through with the intention, Estelle had not been raped. She'd been strangled, however, and the back of her head had been repeatedly struck against the bole of a tree. She suffered multiple fractures. Beyond the scant details in the newspaper, all additional information was in Calvis's handwriting. There was a section he'd underlined twice for emphasis, and here he'd noted, *Stomach ripped open. Is this part of the ritual, or is this an attempt to attribute the attack to an animal? It must be the ritual. Animals don't rape and strangle people.*

The ritual? Jack wondered why Calvis had chosen that word.

The August 1983 discovery of Virginie Fortin's mutilated body gave greater credence to Calvis's margin note – *Escalation of fury*. Virginie, seventeen years old, was one of three daughters. Her father, Bertrand, had been brought in by Canada Iron as a furnace maintenance engineer, and her mother, Esther, seemed to have worked in some capacity at the Jasperville Junior School. There was a great deal more information in Calvis's journal than in the brief newspaper report, but the circumstances of Virginie's murder were much the same. This time, the girl had not been walking alone somewhere, but appeared to have been spirited away from the church. She volunteered there: cleaning, repairing the well-worn hymnals and prayer books, laundering the minister's vestments, much as Juliette had done. It was from here that she never made it home. Her body was found first thing on Saturday morning in the cemetery behind the church. She was kneeling, doubled-up, her face in the dirt, her arms stretched out before her. The sergeant at the time was Arnaud Colin, the last sergeant before Jack's departure in August of 1984. Jack remembered his arrival in the spring of '83. There was nothing to say when he'd left – presumably somewhere around the middle of '85 – but it appeared that Calvis had travelled somewhere to see him in the early part of '97.

He knows nothing, Calvis had written, *or he knows something and he cannot bring himself to talk of it. I went over some of the information, that I believed some of these killings were connected, that there were common denominators, but he did everything he could to find holes in my reasoning. I feel sorry for him. Fear of the truth has made his mind and his heart weak. It's a mystery to me how someone can lie to themselves for so long.*

Jack sat back in the chair. He exhaled slowly.

It's a mystery to me how someone can lie to themselves for so long.

It was not such a mystery. It was easier than Calvis thought. There were days, sometimes weeks, when Jack had been so engaged with work that he'd barely thought of his family. There were times when he'd drowned his memories in liquor. Like anything, if you worked hard at it, it became easier.

And so, Arnaud Colin, thirteen years after the fact, had been approached by an unknown man in his early twenties and pressed for details about the killing of a girl that had happened more than a decade before. Jack remembered sitting in the bar with Ludo just four days earlier, how difficult it had been to say anything of his own past. People remembered what they wanted to remember, and when forced to recall things that were traumatic or laden with guilt, they just changed their own perception of what had happened. Self-defence? An inherent survival mechanism? The human mind was perhaps a great deal simpler than anyone had ever imagined, and that's what made it appear so complex.

Jack remembered a line he'd read somewhere. Maybe Papi had said it. An idea could bring down a citadel far more easily than a sword. Calvis had an idea. He'd let it take hold of him. Either he was right, or he'd translated everything he'd discovered as confirmation of his primary theory. It was easily done. Jack had seen it in his own line of work. Investigators, poorly trained or with limited experience, had recognized a fire pattern, perhaps the trademark of a particular accelerant, and from that they'd jumped from one assumption to another and arrived at an entirely incorrect conclusion. Was that what had happened here?

From what he could remember, Lisette's death had been

considered accidental. She'd fallen, knocked herself unconscious, and then something had dragged her out into the snow. He had not attended the funeral, though he remembered it happening. He'd stayed with Papi. He did remember going to the grave with Juliette, but that was a good while afterwards.

Anne-Louise Fournier had been a different story. Jack was nine by then. He remembered hearing his parents speak of it. *Torn apart*, was the phrase his father had used. *The poor girl looked like she'd been torn apart.*

Jack was not sure, but he expected, once again, that there had been no autopsy.

This was Jasperville, after all. Things that happened here stayed right here. It was too distant, too unreachable, too far from the woof and warp of humanity for anyone else to be involved. Okay, so some girl got killed. It was a bear, a timber wolf. This was the nature of things. The logistics of mounting an investigation from Montréal, even Sept-Îles, was so far beyond the bounds of practicality that Jack could easily understand some captain of the Sûreté deciding to do nothing.

And then there was Thérèse. Of this, he knew a great deal more. After Juliette herself, kneeling there, her hands and skirt covered in blood, he'd been the first to see what had happened to Thérèse, the torn and bloody mess that had once been her face.

He remembered Émile Landry, the efforts he'd made to convince Philippe and Marguerite Bergeron to agree to an autopsy. An autopsy had never taken place. He remembered the funeral, the burial behind the church, and that had been the end of it. The consequences were far-reaching and tragic. Juliette's heart and mind were broken under the weight of her grief. Two years later, Juliette committed suicide, and four years after that their mother did the same. If these were murders, and murders committed by the same man, then the deaths of Étienne Fournier and two of the Devereauxs were also on his hands.

Jack stood up from the table. He needed some respite from the horror that surrounded him, now pervading every thought, every memory. He would walk a while, take a route along the main drag, back over towards the church and then down to the rail line. From there he would be able to see the foundry, and back across the entire town to the Torngat Mountains in the distance. Place of evil spirits. That's what it meant. Even as he thought of that, he remembered how Papi would lean close and tell them to be wary of the shadows, to always walk in pairs, to never let go of the other's hand.

There are things out there in the darkness, he would say. *They can hold their breath for ever, and their nostrils twitch to the rhythm of your frightened little hearts.*

The wendigo. That was what he'd spoken of, and that was the seed that had been planted in Calvis's fragile, fertile mind.

35

It was not yet three o'clock, and already like a Montréal night.

Standing beneath the low roof of the church doorway and looking back down the main drag, Jack made a promise to himself: if he walked away from this, then he would change everything. If Calvis went to prison for murder, then he would visit him. If he was committed to some institution, he would do the same. If Calvis refused to see him, then he would keep on trying until perseverance won through. Even if it meant losing his job, he would stay here until this situation came to a conclusion. And he would find a way to speak to Carine, if only to get her to understand how truly sorry he was for betraying her.

Jack was well aware of his failings. If he'd been better equipped to express his emotions, he perhaps would have broken down there and then. Jasperville, Calvis and Carine, even the fact his father was locked up in Saguenay, represented not only everything he'd once been, but everything he'd failed to become. Having broken every promise he'd made to others, he'd then broken every promise he'd made to himself.

Jack lowered his head. He breathed deeply. He tried to centre himself, to focus on what was required of him, and then he left the front of the church and walked on to the cemetery. He needed to see what was there, simply because he knew there would be things he didn't wish to see.

*

The graves were close together. Lisette, Anne-Louise, Virginie Fortin, Madeleine Desjardins, and finally Thérèse. Her plot was simple, unadorned with anything but a collection of plastic flowers, their colours muted with a layer of frost. There were plastic flowers elsewhere, too, serving to remind anyone who visited that nothing could grow here. Nothing that was living could even be brought here. Like a vacuum, a black hole, Jasperville sucked the life out of everyone and everything.

Despairville.

Jack knelt down in front of Thérèse's headstone. He traced his finger along the dates: 2 February 1958 to 10 July 1978. Twenty years old. Waiting out there by the rail terminal for Juliette to return with tickets that would spirit them away to the life they would create together. Juliette had left Thérèse alone for thirty minutes. The consequence of what took place in that brief span meant that Juliette would be alone for ever. It took no time at all to take a life, but the repercussions lasted for eternity. Jack had seen it in his work – the cases of arson that had claimed lives, both intentionally and unintentionally.

Jack's fingers were beginning to stiffen. He put his gloves back on. Standing once more, he lit a cigarette. He closed his eyes and inhaled the smoke deep into his lungs. He felt the frozen air inside his mouth, his throat, his chest. In such a place, the cold was as inescapable as the truth.

Both Papi and his mother had spoken of a curse. Was it possible that there were forces beyond the bounds of ordinary human perception that could influence human experience? Magnetism was invisible, as was gravity, *déjà vu*, even memory save anywhere but the mind's eye. Never having been drawn to faith or religion, Jack could still conceive of Man as a spiritual identity. The body was temporal, subject to age and decay and all aspects of biology and physics. But the individual themselves? Was that something else? Was it conceivable that belief in something gave it power? Had Calvis so thoroughly believed in the wendigo that, in his own mind, he'd granted it life? If so, could that same belief be experienced by another, the consequence of which was akin to possession? Was this really the work of a serial killer, driven by some deep-seated and profound delusion that he was something other than human?

Looking at the graves, it didn't seem possible that each of these girls had been subject to random animal attacks. This environment, especially this climate, while its absence of life could motivate desperation on the part of any carnivore, also dictated that there was a very noticeable absence of animals. In the sixteen years that Jack had lived here, he couldn't recall more than two or three wolf sightings, and just one occasion of a bear. Even then, it had been a good distance away. They avoided humans. That was their instinct. Provoked, they didn't hesitate to strike and kill, but they were not naturally aggressive.

Eight girls, five of them from Jasperville, the others from Menihek, Fermont and Wabush. And those were just the ones that were known about. It was too much of a coincidence to credit their deaths to animals, if only from the viewpoint that they were all young women. Why no young men? Why no older women? Why no children?

After less than twenty-four hours in Jasperville, was he already beginning to think like Papi, like his mother, like Calvis? He believed he was being logical, realistic, seeing what was right there in front of him and doing everything possible to detach his own fears and emotions from it. He experienced grief when he thought of Thérèse. He had known her. He hadn't known the others in the same way. He could retain some objectivity. He had to, if only for his own state of mind.

Jack started to make his way back to the main drag. He needed to understand why Lefebvre had been the target of

Calvis's attack. Unless Calvis was utterly deluded, unless the entire thing began and ended in his own imagination, then there had to be reasons for his certainty that Lefebvre was a killer.

Back at the police station, Nadeau was preparing to lock up and leave.

'I wanted to ask you some questions,' Jack said.

Nadeau glanced up at the clock on the wall.

'It won't take long,' Jack said.

Nadeau sat down at his desk.

'How is Calvis?' Jack asked.

'Slept most of the day. Isn't saying much of anything. He's eating, so evidently he's planning on staying alive.'

Jack hadn't considered this. 'You think he might commit suicide?'

'You know, I don't know what to think, Monsieur Devereaux. It's my problem, but only because I'm here. Maybe that's because I don't have a family, or maybe it was just one of those bad hands you get dealt. I don't know anything about the place, except that it's pretty much as far away from Montréal as you could get. Five months in, and this is what I'm dealing with.'

Nadeau leaned back in the chair and looked at the ceiling. When he looked back at Jack, there was something so tired in his demeanour. That was the only way Jack could describe it.

'What do I think about your brother? I think he got it into his head that these deaths were all linked, that they were all perpetrated by the same man. He went through employment records, work schedules, vacation records, whatever he could find, and he concluded that Jean-Paul Lefebvre was the only man who could have been in those places at those times. But that's an assumption on my part. Granted, he's been more willing to talk to me than he has to you, but he still hasn't said a great deal.'

'How much do you know about the dead girls?'

'As much as it's possible to know with archived records, missing records, incomplete dossiers and everything else that seems routine when you put a man out here on his own for two or three years with no efficient report line back to Sept-Îles or Montréal. This is a . . . hell, I don't even know what you'd call it. A courtesy posting? Something that gives the impression that we have a presence out here, when in truth we really have no presence at all. Places like these, the rule of law exists solely because of what people think we can do, not because of what we can actually do.'

'You don't think these girls were killed by animals, do you?'

'I don't, no.'

'So?'

'A series of killings carried out by one man over all these years?' Nadeau shook his head. 'If Lisette Roy was the first, then we're talking – what? – eighteen years.'

'Yes,' Jack said. 'Lisette was February '72.'

'I guess it's as easy to believe such a thing as to doubt it.'

'And if Calvis got it into his mind that all those old stories were true, then it's not so hard to imagine him doing what he did.'

'You're saying it was justified?'

'I'm saying that he thought it was justified.'

'He believed that this man Lefebvre was – what? – possessed?'

'Wouldn't a man have to be possessed by something in order to—'

'Some*thing*, yes,' Nadeau interjected. 'An idea, an imagined wrong, some mental disorder, but you're saying that your brother believes Lefebvre was possessed by an identity. This wendigo thing.'

Jack understood that if he pursued this then he might be considered as crazy as his brother.

'All I'm saying is that we're dealing with what Calvis believes, not what you or I might believe.'

'No, absolutely,' Nadeau replied. 'And if he was genuinely convinced that Lefebvre was a murderer, then I can understand his actions.'

'Did he attack him in public?'

'No, it was in his home. He broke into his home at night.'

'And he just fought with him?'

'He fought with him, yes. But with the intention of stabbing him through the heart with a silver cross.'

Jack couldn't disguise his shock. 'A silver cross?'

'Yes. He took it from the church. That's what he used to attack Lefebvre.'

'This is how you kill a wendigo.'

'What?'

'The legend. The ways in which you can kill a wendigo. Silver, steel or iron. In some tribal legends, they believe that the wendigo has a heart made of ice. It has to be shattered with a silver spike, and then the body has to be hacked to pieces with a silver axe.'

'And you, Monsieur Devereaux? What do you believe?'

'I believe in the belief of others,' Jack said. 'Every culture has its demons. Demons are as old as Man. Perhaps it's nothing more than the way in which human beings explain their own duality, the unwanted urges, the violence, the madness. Possession, as far as I can see, is a way to assign responsibility to something other than yourself. If you're crazy, if there are evil spirits that drove you to do something, then you're not to blame. It's faith, right? If you can have faith in God, then why can't you have faith in the Devil and everything that such a concept represents?'

'Whichever way we look at this,' Nadeau said, 'I have a man in the medical centre with three or four deep wounds in his chest, another at the base of his throat. He has severe lacerations on his shoulders and upper arms, defensive wounds on his hands, a broken clavicle and three cracked ribs. From what I can piece together, your brother broke into the man's house while he was asleep. He straddled him and held him down with his full body weight. He then did everything he could to kill him with a cross that he'd stolen from the church. That's what I have, Monsieur Devereaux. It's not something that requires faith to see as a reality. Lefebvre is clinging onto life with the narrowest of threads, and when I ask your brother what happened, all he tells me is that he failed to do what he intended, that the wendigo will live, that there will be more killings. And yes, I see that Lefebvre was here before the death of Lisette Roy. I also see how you can convince yourself of something, and then everything you look at is viewed from the perspective of how it aligns with your basic assumption. You don't want to see the things that don't add up. You don't want to see the contradictions. And if you do, then you explain them away because you've already made up your mind.'

Nadeau leaned forward and put his hands flat on the desk as if to really emphasize his viewpoint.

'I've no doubt that with enough time and enough perseverance, you or I could take any number of men who've worked for Canada Iron as long as Lefebvre and present proof that they were also a suspect. But that's the point. It wouldn't be proof. It would be circumstantial. It would be one assumption clouded by numerous other assumptions, and all of that wrapped up very neatly in a package of possibilities, coincidences and hypothetical scenarios.'

Nadeau leaned back once more. 'Your brother acts crazy. He sounds crazy. He did something that in most peoples' eyes proves how crazy he actually is. And a man might very well die as a result. That's where we stand right now. If you bring me information that mitigates his actions, or show me something that isn't journals full of indecipherable ramblings, then I'll listen, of course. I'm not asking you to investigate this. However, if you decide to look into this to resolve your own questions, then I can't stop you. If you break the law I'll arrest you, and then you'll have more than enough time to get your brother to talk to you because you'll be in the adjoining cell.'

'I have no intention of breaking the law, Sergeant.'

'Then we won't have a problem, will we?'

'One more question.'

'Go ahead.'

'Why did you track me down? Why did you ask me to come out here?'

'Because you're next of kin. Your father's in a state mental institution. The rest of your family is dead. And even if your brother's crazy, I still don't think he should have to deal with this alone. This is what family is, Monsieur Devereaux. This is how family works. We don't get to choose who we're related to, but blood is blood. It ties us together, even when we don't want to be tied.'

36

Less than an hour later, Jack stood in the reception area of the medical centre. He asked the receptionist about Lefebvre.

'I'm sorry, I can't help you. I'll see if Dr Pelletier is available to speak to you.'

'Dr Pelletier?' Jack asked. 'Er, yes. That would be appreciated.'

It was hard to believe that Pelletier was still here after all these years. It was true that there were some who could never leave.

The woman put the call through. She asked Jack to take a seat, and he did so.

The centre was so very different from when he'd last been there. Modernized, spotlessly clean, informative notices about influenza, vaccines, animal bites, an array of magazines on a low table ahead of two wide sofas, a large clock on the wall that punctuated the silence with its metronomic tick. He had to think for a moment to remember the name of the doctor. It came to him without too much difficulty. Bayard Pelletier. Looking back, he must have been in his late forties even then. Now he had to be seventy years old or more. That led to thoughts of all the others he remembered. He imagined that a good few others might still be here, too accustomed to the environment, too fixed in their ways to even consider living somewhere else. Like men released from prison after countless years – only happy in the smallest room in the house, agitated

237

by the slightest variation in mealtimes. That kind of routine took years to establish; taking it apart took even longer.

Another woman came through the door behind the reception desk.

'Can I help you?' she asked.

'I was waiting to see Dr Pelletier.'

'And you are?'

'Calvis Devereaux's brother,' he said.

'Right. Yes. Sergeant Nadeau said he'd been trying to find you.'

'Well, he found me,' Jack said. 'Is the doctor available?'

'I am the doctor.'

'But ...'

'I'm Rosamond Pelletier.'

'You're Bayard Pelletier's daughter?'

'I am, yes.'

'I'm sorry. I remember Dr Pelletier from when I lived here. Is he—'

'He died, Monsieur Devereaux,' she said matter-of-factly. 'More than ten years ago.'

'I'm sorry to hear that.'

Pelletier indicated the sofa. Jack sat down once more. Pelletier sat on the adjacent sofa. Her manner was aloof, verging on dismissive.

'So, what can we do for you, Monsieur Devereaux?' she asked.

'I came to see about Monsieur Lefebvre.'

'To *see* about him?'

'To find out how he was doing. If he was improving. If there were any indications that—'

'You want to know if your brother will be charged with murder,' Pelletier said, interrupting Jack for the second time.

Jack felt angered by her tone. He paused before speaking.

'I'm sorry,' he said.

238

Pelletier frowned.

'Sorry for what, Monsieur Devereaux?'

'For whatever it is that I have done to offend you.'

'You've not offended me.'

'Then I've no idea why you're being so abrupt with me. I'm not my brother. I've not seen him for more than twenty-five years. Why we've been out of touch doesn't really have anything to do with what's happened. However, he's done this terrible thing, and I came to see if there was anything I could do to help.'

Pelletier seemed to relax a little. 'I must apologize, Monsieur Devereaux. You're completely right. You're not your brother, and there's nothing you've done that has offended me. I know a lot of the people here on a personal basis. I have been acquainted with Monsieur Lefebvre and his brother for a long time, and this has been a shock and a tragedy for all of us.'

'I understand completely. I'm here for one reason only, and that's to see whether there's any way to mitigate the damage that my brother has caused.'

Pelletier nodded agreeably. 'Then we shall begin again.'

Jack could still feel the tension in his chest, but he let it go. He'd said what he needed to say, and his viewpoint had been acknowledged.

'Jean-Paul Lefebvre is in a critical condition, Monsieur Devereaux,' Pelletier went on. 'Will he survive? That's not a question that is always easy to answer. A great deal has to do with the individual themselves, and whether they want to survive.'

'And my brother? Have you been asked to examine him?'

'Why would I be asked to do that?'

'To determine his mental state, perhaps?'

'I am a doctor of medicine, Monsieur Devereaux, not a psychiatrist. And besides, my experience with the psychiatric profession has demonstrated that a great deal of what they say is based purely on personal opinion, as opposed to any substantive scientific evidence or case study.'

'Is there anything I can do?' Jack asked.

'I'm not sure I understand.'

'My brother attacked this man, and he may very well die. He has a brother here in Jasperville, as far as I understand, and an ex-wife in Fort Mackenzie. Does he have children? Are there dependents that are relying on him being able to work?'

'He's fifty-seven years old. He and his wife didn't have children. His brother visits daily.' Pelletier glanced at her watch. 'In fact, he's due in the next thirty minutes or so. He comes here directly from work. As for his wife, I know nothing. I'm sure she's been told by Sergeant Nadeau, but she's not been here and no one's said anything to me that would suggest she's coming.'

'I guess I feel partly to blame,' Jack said. 'Actually, that's not true. I'm to blame.'

'You weren't here, Monsieur Devereaux. As you said, you haven't even seen your brother in over twenty-five years.'

'Exactly,' Jack said.

Pelletier leaned forward. Her bedside manner came to the fore.

'It's easy to look at it this way,' she said. 'It's human nature. But it's a redundant activity. It does no one any good, least of all your brother.'

'I know,' Jack said, 'but I left and he stayed out here, and we know very well what this much isolation can do to a human being.'

'It depends on the human being,' Pelletier replied. 'You speak to some people and it's almost as if they belong here. There's nowhere else they would even consider living. Take my father, for example. He got sick, very sick in fact, and he should've been hospitalized in Montréal. Would he go? Would he even talk about going? Not a hope in Hell.'

'And how long have you been the doctor here?'

'Since my father retired. I was away for a good many years. I studied in the US. I always planned to stay there, to raise a family, and then when my father got sick, I came back to take care of him and I just stayed.'

'And your mother?'

'She died a good five or six years before my father.' Pelletier smiled unexpectedly. 'Listen to me. You've got me telling you my life story.'

'I'm sorry. You must be very busy.' Jack started to get up.

'Not at all,' she said. 'Please. Sit. If I'm needed, they will come and get me.'

'Do you think—' Jack started, and then he checked himself.

'Do I think what, Monsieur Devereaux?'

'Do you think it would be inappropriate for me to see Monsieur Lefebvre?'

'On what basis?'

'I don't know, Dr Pelletier. I just feel I'm inescapably connected to this thing, and maybe the more I understand about what happened and the people involved, the more I might be able to do something to help.'

Pelletier was quiet for a moment, her expression pensive.

'I see no harm in it,' she eventually said. 'But I will draw the line at allowing you into his room. As I said, he's in a critical condition. I won't permit noise or disturbance around him. More to the point, I don't know you—'

'And my brother's the psycho who put him here in the first place.'

'Not how I would have put it, but that also needs to be taken into consideration, yes.'

Pelletier got up. 'Follow me,' she said.

*

The upper floor of the medical centre was centred by a dividing partition. On one side was a ward with six beds, none of which were occupied. The other half of the floor was taken up by four separate rooms, a corridor between two rooms on the right and two on the left. Again, the beds were empty, save that occupied by Jean-Paul Lefebvre.

After the initial shock of the quantity of dressing that enclosed the man's head, the drips, the saline, the ECG, all the machinery required to monitor his condition, Jack was struck by the size of the man.

From where he stood in the corridor, looking through the observation window, the foot of the bed was nearest to him. Despite the effect of foreshortening, Lefebvre couldn't have been more than five foot six or seven. Why it surprised him, he didn't know. It could only be that he'd anticipated a monster of some description.

He remembered the schoolteacher, Lapointe, and what he'd said of the wendigo.

Very tall and slender. Emaciated, their skin like parchment. The wendigo turns a man into a cannibal. Not only that, the wendigo spirit can drive a man to murder...

'He's so small,' Jack said, unaware that he was speaking out loud.

'Smaller than your brother,' Pelletier said. 'And your brother gave him no warning of the attack. The man had little opportunity to defend himself.'

'And he attacked him with a cross from the church.'

'He did, yes. In his house at night.'

'Nadeau told me.'

'It was a brutal assault, Monsieur Devereaux, vicious and unrelenting. There's no doubt in my mind that your brother very much intended to kill this man.'

242

'So what stopped him?'

'I don't know. I can only imagine that he thought Lefebvre was dead.'

'Yes, that's the only explanation I have.'

'But your brother had guns. There's not a man in Jasperville who doesn't own a gun. Most of them have several. If he'd been so hell-bent on killing Lefebvre, why didn't he just shoot him?'

'Nadeau didn't tell you?'

Pelletier frowned. 'Tell me what?'

'About the wendigo.'

Pelletier's intake of breath was slight, but sudden. It was audible even to Jack. She blanched, and then a sudden flush of colour reddened her upper cheeks.

'You know the stories, right?' Jack asked.

'My father used to scare me with them.'

'As did our grandfather. We thought he was crazy. Maybe he was. He was old, and most of the time he even forgot where he was, but he told us about these things, the power to possess a man, to drive him to acts of cannibalism and murder.'

'And your brother thought—'

'That Lefebvre was possessed by a wendigo, yes. He'd convinced himself that Lefebvre was the man responsible for the deaths of girls in Jasperville, Fermont and Wabush all the way back to 1972.'

'Oh my God,' Pelletier said. 'I had no idea.'

'I thought you knew,' Jack said. It suddenly dawned on him that if Nadeau had not told Lefebvre's doctor what had motivated the attack, then he'd more than likely told no one else either.

'Keep that to yourself, would you?' Jack said. 'God only knows what would happen if a rumour started that Lefebvre was responsible for these unsolved deaths.'

'You think that he is?'

243

'I've no idea, Dr Pelletier.'

'I don't envy your situation, Monsieur Devereaux.'

'Well, right now I don't think anyone's responsible for that but me.'

37

Even in the short walk from the medical centre back to the house, there was no escape from the brutal cold. It was even more invasive than he remembered. It cut through every layer of clothing, it found its way into his throat, his lungs, the very core of his body.

Once inside, Jack lit the kitchen stove, lit the fire in the parlour, made coffee, added whiskey, and sat as close to the heat as he could.

Beyond the walls and beneath the leaden charcoal sky, the atmosphere was disturbingly still. The silence was unlike anywhere else, as if the air itself was too thin to carry the slightest sound. He remembered all those frozen nights, peering out into the blackness, in his mind Papi's words about the creatures that waited beyond the walls. It was a terrible image to plant in the fertile imagination of a child. His departure had exorcized some of it, but Calvis, remaining here, had seen his mind overgrown and strangled by tendrils of fear and paranoia.

Tomorrow he would visit Lefebvre's brother, see if the man was willing to speak to him. If needed, he would go to Fort Mackenzie and see the ex-wife. According to Nadeau, she'd left him only five or six years before. That meant that they'd been together in Jasperville for all the years between 1971 and 2004. Could a man kill half a dozen or more girls and his wife and brother know nothing of these things? Anything was possible, of course. His experience in arson investigation had revealed instances of close family members harbouring cruel intentions that were utterly unknown and unexpected. This, however, was different. Burning a house down as a single act of rage or vengeance, even when it was considered with some forethought, was very different from a series of murders spanning nearly three decades. Transient impulses, no matter how intense, were not comparable to the methodical planning and preparation, the continued deception, the layer upon layer of deceit and misdirection required to cover up the actions of a serial killer.

Jack tried to focus his thoughts elsewhere. It was nearly eight. He was hungry and tired, but he knew he wouldn't sleep if he didn't take dinner. There was nothing in the house but a handful of crackers and some dry sausage. He'd have to go to one of the bars, and though he didn't want to travel out again, he had no choice. He put his boots back on, a jacket, a coat, his oilskin over that, tied a scarf around the lower half of his face, donned his gloves, and left the house.

Surprisingly, the crowded hubbub he found was more than welcome. He was anonymous, just another unknown face in a sea of faces as men came and went through this place. At the bar, he ordered a meat broth. While he waited he drank two whiskeys, and then carried his broth to a corner table. A jukebox played music he didn't recognize, much of it in French. Every once in a while, the unfamiliar was interspersed with a song from Merle Haggard or Willie Nelson. Jack put chunks of dark rye bread into the broth. By the time he was done, he felt as if he'd eaten enough for tomorrow. He returned the bowl to the bar, ordered another whiskey, resumed his corner table and took time to observe the men around him.

Everywhere he looked he saw his father. These people were hard-working, bullish, rowdy, blunt and uncompromising. Their lives appeared to be so very uncomplicated, but he knew such things were merely superficial. Had anyone seen Henri Devereaux, they would've thought him the same: a man's man, equipped for tough, dirty work, as much suited to drink as he was to an absence of conversation. A man like that didn't discuss his innermost thoughts, his feelings, his anxieties and aspirations. A man like that was the epitome of *what you see is what you get*, as obvious and predictable as the work he did. But that was a lie. Henri Devereaux was a man burdened by guilt and secrets. He had a father-in-law who had fled his home country, bringing with him a daughter who had abandoned her vocation to marry a man with few prospects. They had ventured into a white and hollow wilderness with the promise of wealth and security. The father-in-law lost his mind, his daughter took her own life, his wife went crazy and did the same. Then whatever moorings held Henri to his sanity slipped free. It was an unrelenting litany of tragedies and horror.

'I know who you are now.'

Jack looked up. Martin stood in front of him.

'Martin,' Jack said.

'My mother used to talk about you all the time,' he said. His expression was deadpan, as if he was delivering a message that bore no personal significance.

Jack's immediate and reflexive question was *And what did she say?* Instead, he said, 'Can I get you a drink?'

'Yes,' Martin said. 'Whatever you're having.'

'How old are you? Are you actually even allowed in here?'

'No one gives a fuck, man. How the hell would they know who the drinks are for?' He paused, looked at Jack with a smirk on his face. 'However, if you want me to leave and not tell you anything about my mom, then that's your decision.'

Jack hesitated for just a second, and then he got up and walked to the bar. He glanced back as Martin took a chair from an adjacent table and sat down.

When Jack resumed his seat, the two of them were facing one another.

Jack raised his glass. 'Salut,' he said.

Martin nodded in acknowledgement, but didn't respond.

'Do you think your mother would be okay with us talking?'

'My life, my business,' Martin said.

'And is there something in particular you wanted to say to me?'

'I guess I wanted to know if you were as much of an asshole as she said you were.'

'Maybe she tempered her opinion for you.'

'Maybe she exaggerated it because she was just as responsible for whatever happened between you.'

'And what do you think happened between us, Martin?'

Martin shrugged. There was something arrogant about his manner, but when he spoke Jack saw that it wasn't arrogance, but rather a lack of concern for what anyone might think about him.

'You were s'posed to spring her out of here, weren't you?'

'I was, yes.'

'Well, I don't know about you, but this place seems like the last place on earth anyone would want to live. I can understand why someone would want to leave as soon as they could.' Martin sipped his whiskey. 'You lived here. You had a family here, right?'

'I did, yes.'

'From what I've heard, it seems your family was as much of a fuck-up as mine. Far as I can work out, your sister and my aunt were sleeping together, and then my aunt got murdered or killed by an animal or something. After that, your sister committed suicide.'

'You don't pull any punches, do you, Martin?'

Martin shrugged. 'What's the point? It's true or it's not. If I've pissed you off, then you can tell me to fuck off. I don't want any hassle. I'm just trying to figure out the dynamics of all of this crap, and I see my mom right in the middle of it with the weight of the world on her shoulders. That's the way it seems to me, anyway.'

'Okay,' Jack said. 'You're right. It was pretty much as you said. My sister and your aunt were lovers. My mother and your grandmother tried to keep them apart. It all went downhill from there.'

'It's bullshit, man. That's what it is.'

'What is?'

'Keeping people apart. Trying to make people be different from who they are. What the living fuck is that all about, eh?'

'Different times. This all happened a good few years before you were born.'

'And then you promised to come back and get my mom but she never heard another word from you.'

'She's right. That's exactly what happened.'

'She said she waited and waited. She said she tried everything she could to find you, but it was like you just vanished off the face of the earth. Finally, she gave up. She figured that you just said whatever you had to say to get off with her, and then—'

'That's not true.'

'Ah fuck, man, I know it's not true. The way she is when she talks about it, you can tell that you guys were like soulmates and all that shit. But you fucked up, you know? Big time fucked up.'

'I know.'

'And hey, if you'd stayed together then maybe I'd have been your son instead of the son of another fuck-up who bailed out at the earliest available opportunity.'

'Who is your father?'

There was the characteristic shrug, and this time there was a shadow of bitterness in Martin's eyes. 'Who the fuck cares, eh?

Some guy from Montréal. He left when I was six or seven. I don't really remember him to be honest.'

'How long did your mother stay here in Jasperville?'

'She left about 1990. I was born in '93. Then after my folks split up, me and Mom stayed in the city until I was twelve or so. When Grandpa got sick, we came out here to help him, and we've been here ever since.'

'And you want to leave as soon as you can,' Jack said.

'Who the hell would wanna stay?'

'That was exactly how I felt when I was your age.'

'So what was the deal, then? Why didn't you come back and get her?'

Jack looked up at the ceiling, then out over the sea of faces in the bar. He shook his head. A weight came over him. He felt as if he was drowning in the past.

'Man, you look just like she does when I ask her why you left her behind.'

'Get me another one,' Martin said, 'and then I gotta go.'

Jack went to the bar and ordered more drinks, this time to escape the line of questioning.

When he got back, Martin seemed uninterested in discussing his mother any further.

'You think she'll ever give me the time of day?' Jack asked.

'Hell, I don't know. Women are crazy, and she's my mom so that makes her even crazier.'

Martin downed the shot in one.

'You gotta smoke?' he asked.

'Whiskey *and* cigarettes? Really?'

'Just give me a cigarette, man. I'm outta here.'

Jack gave Martin a cigarette. Martin got up.

'Tell you one thing, Jack Devereaux,' he said. 'Whatever is going on with your crazy brother is all my mom seems to talk about. And that was even before you showed up. Now I can't get away from it.' He looked round the bar. 'Fucked-up place, this is. Cold as anything all the goddamned time, and seems like everyone who stays here just loses the plot, right?'

'Loses the plot or loses their life,' Jack replied.

Martin smiled. 'Well, maybe you should take me the fuck with you when you leave, eh?'

38

The following morning, his head a little worse for wear, Jack headed over to the station to speak with Nadeau. He figured that would be the fastest way of finding out where Lefebvre's brother lived.

'Monsieur Devereaux,' Nadeau said as Jack entered the reception area. 'You have saved me a journey.'

'How so?'

'I was planning to come down and speak with you.'

Jack waited for Nadeau to explain.

'There has been a complaint from Madame Bergeron.'

Jack knew what Nadeau was going to say before he said it.

'Sixteen years old. Whiskey and cigarettes. She will deal with her son, but I have to deal with you.'

'Yes,' Jack said. 'Of course.'

'I'm not going to ask what you were thinking because I don't believe you were.'

'You're right,' Jack said. 'I wasn't thinking.'

Nadeau paused, and then said, 'But, then again, perhaps you were. I have no real understanding of the history between yourself and Madame Bergeron, but I do know that there was a history. You told me as much. I'm guessing you were trying to obtain information from her son because she won't speak to you.'

'Am I really that transparent?'

'This was your intention?'

'I don't know, Sergeant,' Jack said. 'I was tired, and I'd already had two or three whiskeys. The boy showed up, he seemed to want to say something. I had no reason to discourage him.'

'You broke the law. You do understand that, don't you?'

'Yes, I do.'

'Madame Bergeron hasn't filed a formal complaint, so you just get a caution. You can't come here and behave as you please, Monsieur Devereaux, especially under the current circumstances. What seems routine in Montréal is anything but routine out here, and you of all people should know this.'

'I'm sorry, Sergeant Nadeau. If you could pass on my apology to Madame Bergeron, that would be appreciated. Tell her that I didn't intend to cause any upset, and I won't give her any further reasons to complain.'

'Very well,' Nadeau said. 'Now, you're here for a different reason?'

'I am, yes. I wanted to know if I could go and speak with Lefebvre's brother.'

'Don't you think it would be more appropriate to speak with your own brother first?'

'Er ... yes. Yes, of course. He's awake?'

'He is awake. He asked if you were still here.'

'Seriously?'

'He ate some breakfast, and then he asked about you, yes. As I told you, he seems to change from one day to the next. Today he's communicative. He says he wants to tell you what happened.'

'With Lefebvre?'

'I imagine so, Monsieur Devereaux. That's all he said to me. That he wants to tell you what happened.'

*

Calvis had showered. His hair was combed back flat against his head. His beard, though thick, was no longer dishevelled and greasy. Jack could see more of his face, and there was no mistaking him for anyone but his younger brother.

Jack waited for Calvis to realize that he was there. When he did, he smiled. It was heartfelt and genuine. Jack felt a rush of emotion that seemed so utterly familiar, and yet so desperately absent. There was no one he'd ever loved as much as his brother. Carine, yes – he'd loved her, and loved her as much as it was possible to love someone, but that was different. Calvis was blood. Across the entire span of humankind, Calvis was the closest person to himself. They looked like one another, they sounded like one another, even their mannerisms and gaits were the same. See one, you saw the other, as if some spiritual force drove both bodies in unison.

'Calvis,' Jack said.

'Jacques,' Calvis replied, the Québécois inflection so clear in his pronunciation.

Calvis got up from the bed, and, just for a moment, he stood there with his arms down by his side, the palms of his hands facing outward. It was an invitation for Jack to come closer, to cross the room and stand where they could see one another clearly.

It seemed a long way. Jack's heart pounded, his pulse raced, his mouth was dry.

They were six feet apart, nothing between them but the bars of the holding cell.

Calvis moved forward until the toes of his shoes touched the steel rail that ran along the floor. Slowly, tentatively, he reached through the bars with his right hand. Jack glanced back. Nadeau had come down the stairs behind him.

Jack raised his eyebrows.

Nadeau put the heel of his hand on the butt of his revolver. He nodded.

Jack reached out. Their hands met. Calvis held on with such firm resolve, and as he did so, he closed his eyes and started to cry. He barely moved. His chest rose and fell. He breathed with difficulty as he choked up. Tears spilled over his lower lids and coursed down his cheeks.

Jack was overwhelmed. He wanted to let go of Calvis's hand, but he didn't dare. He wanted to turn and run from that basement, up and out through the door and into the hard, frozen light of day. He wanted to run, to keep on running, to run until he reached some place where he'd never be found. He knew it would be futile. What he was feeling was deep within the very core of himself. No matter how far he went, it would always be waiting for him.

'Brother,' Calvis said.

Jack couldn't speak.

Nadeau was behind him then. He had a fold-out chair. He set it down. Jack released Calvis's hand and backed up a few feet.

Calvis watched him. He smiled again, and with the sleeve of his shirt he wiped the tears from his face.

Both Calvis and Jack sat down simultaneously.

Nadeau backed up to the base of the stairs.

'You never came back,' Calvis said. 'I wanted you to come back, and you never came back.'

'I know,' Jack said, 'and I'm sorry. You have no idea how sorry I am for leaving you here.'

Calvis smiled understandingly. 'I think I do,' he said. 'I have imagined many times how it would have felt for me if I'd been the one who turned his back on you. I don't think I would have been able to live with myself.'

'I have lived with myself,' Jack replied, 'but it hasn't been much of a life.'

'I thought we were the same, but we're so very different,' Calvis said. 'Things were not good for a long time, Jacques, and Papa drank more and drank more, and he was distant and violent and he hurt me so much.'

Jack closed his eyes and lowered his head.

'Some nights he would come and wake me. He would make me get out of bed, and we would go from the front of the house with shovels and we would dig up snow and pile it up against the back door. We would pack it hard, and it was like a wall against the door, and he told me we had to do this to stop them getting in.'

Jack looked up.

'He told me they were out there. All of them. All the ones who went missing, the ones who died, the ones who got lost and never came home. He told me it was the wendigo that took them.'

'Calvis—'

'I know it's just a ghost story, Jacques. I know that. I'm not crazy, you know? Papa might be crazy, but I'm not.'

'Then what happened with this man? You attacked him and hurt him very badly. There's a strong possibility that he will die. You do know that, right?'

'All the things we ever feared were human things,' Calvis said. 'Even when a man is possessed by the spirit of evil, even when his heart is black with sin and he tells you that he was driven by the Devil, it's just superstition. There is no Devil. And there's no God. No matter how much praying you do, prayers ain't gonna put the skin back on the cat now, are they?'

Calvis leaned forward. He rested his elbows on his knees. He placed the palms of his hands together. He spoke with such clarity that it was hard not to be mesmerized. That was the only way Jack could describe what he was feeling. He was being told something by someone who understood what had happened here with so much more certainty and conviction than himself.

'There are things that hide in the shadows, Jacques, but the shadows are in the minds of men. We think, we imagine, we project, we convince ourselves that what we see and what we *think* we see are the same thing, but they're not. So very rarely are they the same thing. We give a man, even a wicked man, the benefit of the doubt because we know that we're not blameless, and we would want someone to give us the benefit of the doubt. We trust too much. We have too much faith in the basic nature of Man. But there are weak men, vulnerable men, and they can become possessed by an idea, a belief, and it's as if they're possessed. But they created that possession themselves. They want to believe it's something else that drives them to do terrible things, to commit atrocities against another human, and they want that explanation just as much as we do.'

'I don't understand what this has to do with—'

'Lefebvre?' Calvis asked.

Jack nodded.

'He's a weak man. Look. You will see. The circumstances, Jack. The circumstances and the coincidences. Too many threads tie this man to the things that have happened here. He's been possessed by the wendigo, but it's a possession that comes from his own imagination.'

'But you didn't hurt his imagination, Calvis. You hurt the man. The man is in hospital. I have seen him.'

'You've seen the body that's occupied by the idea, Jacques. The body holds the knife. The body strangles and rapes. The body digs the holes where the victims are buried. But the mind is the engine. The mind drives everything. The mind that created the wendigo created the need for blood, the need for killing, the need to inflict pain and violence on those poor girls.'

'And you believe that Lefebvre was such a man? That he was

driven by this idea that he was a wendigo, that he needed to kill?'

'I don't believe, Jacques. I *know*.'

Jack took a deep breath. Calvis appeared so calm, so clear in his rationale.

For a moment, he looked away. Nadeau stood no more than ten feet away. He hadn't moved, and he hadn't said a word.

The silence in that basement was suddenly punctuated by the sound of a telephone from upstairs.

'You okay?' Nadeau asked Jack.

'Yes. Yes, of course,' Jack replied.

Nadeau went back up to reception.

Jack watched him go. For just those few moments he felt more settled than he had since taking that phone call back in Montréal. Calvis was lucid, and what he said made sense. Yes, it was strange, even nightmarish, but he was not talking about some parchment-yellow creature with sunken eyes prowling the shadows of Jasperville and tearing young women apart. He was talking about a man – a dangerous, sick man – but a man all the same, and possessed by an idea, a belief, a superstition.

In that handful of seconds before he turned back toward Calvis, he could see Lefebvre surviving, and yes, Calvis would more than likely serve a few years in jail for the assault, and yes, he would have to find a way to visit, to spend time with him, to contribute to his recovery and rehabilitation, but it was hope. Faint, yes, but nevertheless it really was the first glimmer of hope in this whole nightmare.

Jack turned to his brother, knowing exactly what to say, knowing precisely how to deal with this.

Calvis – his hands gripping the bars, his face pressed between them with such force that the veins stood out on his forehead, his neck – hissed at Jack.

'You have to finish this. You have to finish this, Jacques. You have to go to the medical centre and kill this creature. You have to do it now, while it's weak.'

'Calvis—'

'Now, Jacques,' Calvis said. His voice was a strained and desperate whisper, with such fear, such terror, such urgency within every syllable. 'Don't waste a second. The creature is powerful. It will find a way back. It will kill...'

Jack was unable to speak. He opened his mouth, but there was no sound. He started to get up, took a step backward. The chair fell and hit the ground. Jack took another step. His foot caught the crossbeam, and he lost his balance. He staggered sideways, made it to the wall, and there he stood, looking back towards the cell where his brother urged him again and again to go to the medical centre and kill Lefebvre.

Every conceivable positive vanished in a heartbeat.

Calvis pulled back and forth on the bars. He was like some caged animal himself, desperate to get out, desperate to finish what he'd started.

Jack wasn't seeing his younger brother any more. He saw how the last twenty-five years of failure and abandonment had driven him crazy. The thing that scared him more than anything else was that he saw his father as well.

It was hard to breathe, hard to see as his eyes filled with tears. With one hand against the wall to steady himself, Jack made his way around the room to the stairwell. He reached the base just as Nadeau appeared at the top.

'What's going on?' Nadeau asked.

Jack said nothing. He grabbed the banister and raced up the stairs. He pushed past Nadeau, and made it out into the street.

The cold air hit him like a fist. He doubled over, retching dryly into the snow. Pain lanced through his chest and throat. He held onto the railing, oblivious to the fact that the metal immediately adhered to his skin.

Nadeau was behind him. He put his hand on Jack's shoulder.

'Are you okay, Monsieur Devereaux?'

'Just … just need some air,' Jack said. 'I'll be okay. Just need some air. A few moments.'

'Take these,' Nadeau said, handing Jack his gloves. Jack took them.

'Appreciated.'

'So what did he tell you?' Nadeau asked.

'That I should go to the medical centre and kill Lefebvre.'

Nadeau nodded. He didn't seem at all surprised.

'This is why I asked you to come, Monsieur Devereaux. I can't keep him here, but I can't take him to Sept-Îles or Montréal. When the spring comes, maybe they will send people who have experience in transporting prisoners. Until then, he's my responsibility.'

'And mine,' Jack said. 'My responsibility in many more ways than yours.'

'We can't go backward,' Nadeau said. 'This thing has happened. Why it happened is a secondary issue.'

'I know,' Jack said. 'I understand completely.'

'Do you believe your brother?'

'Believe him? About what, exactly?'

'Not the crazy wendigo stuff. Just the thing about Lefebvre. Do you think that Lefebvre could be the one who did these killings?'

Jack looked at Nadeau. Where had he come from? Traffic citations, some desk duty in a back office processing speeding tickets, maybe getting out every once in a while to marshal city processions or caution teenagers about playing music too loud? Nadeau was out of his depth, possessing neither protocol nor precedent for dealing with this, and yet he was duty-bound to fulfil his official obligation.

'I don't know,' Jack said. 'I don't have the faintest fucking clue. Do you?'

Nadeau didn't answer the question. He just looked at Jack for a good ten seconds, and then said, 'I'm gonna make some fresh coffee. Come back in when you're ready.'

39

Jack told Nadeau as much as he could remember of the things Calvis had said.

When they were done, Jack went back to the house. Ignoring the intense and unrelenting barrage of emotions that seemed set to bury him, he laboured through Calvis's journals, back-tracking to earlier pages, trying to cross-reference margin notes with dates marked on a calendar, struggling to decipher both Calvis's almost illegible handwriting and the cryptic nature of his monologues.

Calvis had devoted himself to solving this to the same degree that Jack had devoted himself to ignoring it. It was now clear – if only from his outburst in the cell – that Calvis had taken his obsession to an almost psychotic level. Jack couldn't even say he was crazy. In fact, how could you even define it? To consider that something the majority sees as real is not? And the reverse, too. To have created a 'reality' that is so far removed from accepted reality that it's classed as a delusion. But by whose standards? Jack had to ask himself whether he would be seen as any less crazy. He'd cut himself off from all family and personal connections; he'd lied about his past; he'd misled people about his siblings and parents; he'd created a life of small deceits and distractions, every one of them designed to divert attention away from who he was and where he'd come from. Even Caroline Vallat, a girl with whom he'd shared his life for over two years, had never even heard of Jasperville. She had no idea that Jack's father was locked up in an institution in Saguenay, nor that both his sister and mother had committed suicide.

It begged the question: if he'd invested all this time and energy in disguising who he was, then who was he? Did he even know himself?

So many things buried, so many things lost, so many hidden and disguised memories.

Jack put on his coat and gloves and dragged Papi's rocker onto the porch.

Looking out toward the horizon, he already knew that this was now under his skin. He *had* to know. He *had* to understand how Calvis had reached this conclusion about Lefebvre. If every element of the supernatural was taken out of it, was this man responsible for a series of murders spanning the better part of two decades, or had Calvis judged and then attempted to execute an entirely innocent man? That was the only question that really needed to be answered, and when it came right down to it, Jack was the only person who possessed a vested interest in finding that answer.

Nadeau would do his job as best he could. All that was required of him was to follow the letter of the law to the best of his ability. If Lefebvre died, then Canada Iron would have to take action. Both Calvis and Lefebvre were employees of this behemoth, and if anyone possessed the resources to get a man to Montréal, it was them.

The cold ate away at Jack. He smoked one more cigarette and went back inside. He stoked both the fire in the parlour and the stove in the kitchen. Before too long, the place was warm enough to take off his coat and gloves. When he'd lived here, he'd been much younger – stronger, fitter, a far better constitution and metabolism. The cold had been something he'd dealt with as a matter of course, trudging back and forth to school every day, out to the boarding house or down to the general store for his mother.

He looked at the material Calvis had collected over the years. There had to be a thread that tied it all together. Perhaps it was an imaginary thread, and everything was based on a fundamental assumption that was catastrophically wrong. Jack had to keep on looking until he saw something, or until he'd convinced himself beyond any shadow of a doubt that there was nothing to see.

Lefebvre's work days; the days when he reported in sick; the days he took as vacation. Every single instance when Lefebvre was not accounted for at Canada Iron was noted in Calvis's journals. Over twenty-five years there were dozens and dozens, each one circled in red in a diary, on a calendar, noted down and underlined three times in a separate entry somewhere at the back of a journal. There were detailed itineraries of Calvis's attempts to follow the man, no matter where he went, no matter what he did. In the back of one journal Jack found a reference to *Photo #71*. The fact that Calvis had pictures had never crossed Jack's mind. Where were they?

Upstairs in Papi's room there was little in the way of furniture. A single chair, a low table, beneath the window a narrow bookcase that held nothing but ancient copies of *National Geographic* that he and Juliette had managed to accumulate over the years. There were no boxes, no picture albums, no binders of negatives or prints. How many photos were there? And were they all of Lefebvre? Nadeau had mentioned Lefebvre's injunction against Calvis, but that had only been a year earlier. Had Calvis just hounded the man relentlessly for all those previous years?

Jack needed to know at what point Calvis had concluded that Lefebvre was his man. It didn't take long. The death of Madeleine Desjardins back in May of 1990 seemed to be the event that focused Calvis's mind in Lefebvre's direction. From that point, his recording of Lefebvre's work schedule had gone back eighteen years to the death of Lisette Roy. And after 1990? Had the deaths just stopped? That was all of twenty years prior, and there seemed to be no explanation for what had occurred during those two decades.

Jack returned to the small amount of information pertaining to Madeleine. Aside from a brief paragraph in the newspaper covering her disappearance and discovery there was a page and a half from Calvis. Madeleine was just sixteen. Her parents, Fabien and Valérie, were in their late thirties, and had been resident in Jasperville for a year. The father was an existing Canada Iron surveyor, dispatched by the Sept-Îles office on a short-range assignment to evaluate the commercial viability of extending a mine further to the north-west. Three months, perhaps even less, but still sufficient for him to want his wife and daughter with him. Twenty years on, and the regret wouldn't have diminished. The power and consequence of a single decision was all too familiar to Jack.

Valérie Desjardins took a part-time position at the school. According to Calvis's notes, she fulfilled minor administrative work. Evidently she'd had her daughter assist with some of those functions. On Monday, 15th August, Madeleine went down to the rail terminal to collect a package of examination papers. It was close to the end of the school day, and already dark. After two hours and no sign of her daughter, Valérie contacted her husband. He came down from the foundry and spoke with the sergeant, Emmanuel Gaillard. By then it was close to six. Facing the same challenges – the dark, the impracticality of searching any real distance beyond the immediate lots and known walkways – the party called it quits at about nine. Fabien and his wife, according to the journal entry, went on looking until close to midnight. Jack knew from experience that such a thing was beyond disheartening – looking with no hope of seeing, searching with no hope of finding.

They discovered the girl's body in the morning. Calvis had sketched the location. He'd marked precisely where she was found in relation to the discovery of Thérèse Bergeron's body. In the margin, he'd written *Approx. thirty feet.*

The last paragraph of the page was about Lefebvre.

J-P L worked the second early shift on Thursday, seventeenth. Left at 3.15 p.m. MD left the school for the rail terminal at about the same time. Almost impossible for them not to have seen one another if they both took the obvious routes, MD heading out, J-P L heading back in.

Jack turned the page. Calvis had added: *No newspaper report about manner of death, but spoke to Gaillard. MD was slashed numerous times with something jagged. Strangled. Extensive blood loss. No sexual assault. Rage. Fury. An intention to destroy. That's how it appears to me. J-P L has no children of his own. Impotent? Destroy all the reminders of his inadequacy? Some twisted rationale: if he can't have a child, then no one else can?*

Jack retraced his steps. Prior to Madeleine, Génèvieve Beaulieu was found dead in Fermont, and then Virginie Fortin here in Jasperville. She was the girl who'd been discovered face-down in the cemetery. Before that it was Estelle Poirier in Menihek, Fleur Dillard in Wabush at the end of 1979, and then Thérèse Bergeron.

Twenty missing years. Girls across four separate locations. Gaps between these killings of a little more than a year to as much as four years. But then there was always the possibility that those gaps were not gaps at all. There may very well have been other killings, unknown to Calvis, perhaps to the authorities. And the killings themselves seemed more opportunistic than meticulously premeditated. Strangulation, attempted rape, furious attempts to do as much damage to the body as possible. These were acts of brutal, unthinking savagery. This was not some methodical execution, but rather a kind of sacrificial slaughter. That was the concept that was forming in Jack's mind. A sacrificial thing. Calvis had used the word *ritual*, but that implied a specific sequence of events. These were very different, and yet somehow sufficiently similar to be attributable to the same perpetrator. And a sacrifice was enacted for a reason. It was *to* something, perhaps to prevent something.

Jack had intended to find Lefebvre's brother. Discussing the complaint from Carine, and then what had happened with Calvis, meant he'd left the station none the wiser. Perhaps his own reticence to ask Nadeau for this information had come into play. Nadeau, he felt sure, would advise him against it, but Jack needed to speak to someone who could help him make sense of what had happened. He considered returning to the medical centre and just waiting there until Lefebvre's brother showed up, but he really wanted to speak to him away from the eyes and ears of anyone else.

And then it came to him. There was a telephone in the general store.

Jack dressed quickly and walked up there. It was mere minutes before his plan was disappointed.

'Lines are down,' the storeowner told him.

'I was in the police station this afternoon and a call came through.'

The owner shrugged. 'Don't know what to say. If you're looking for reliable, this is not the place to be.'

Jack stood there, momentarily uncertain of what to do next.

'Urgent, was it?'

'I just needed to find out where someone lived,' Jack said.

'Here in town?'

'Yes.'

'Who is it?'

'Lefebvre.'

The storeowner frowned. 'Not the one in the med centre.'

'His brother, Guy.'

'Well, go over there and see him. He's no more than five hundred yards from here.'

'You know his address?' Jack asked.

'I know his house.'

Out on the front steps, Jack took directions.

'Three windows to the right of the front door, one on the left. You can't miss it.'

Jack expressed his thanks. He went back into the store and bought a fifth of whiskey and a couple more packs of cigarettes. He smoked two as he walked. His stomach turned in knots. He didn't know how he would be received, but he felt sure that any blood relative of Calvis Devereaux would be the last person in the world Guy Lefebvre would want to see.

40

Jack couldn't have been more wrong in his expectation.

As soon as Guy Lefebvre opened the door, he said, 'You're the brother, aren't you?'

'Of Calvis Devereaux. Yes, sir, I am.'

'And what's your name?'

'Jack.'

'Jack or Jacques?'

'It's actually Jacques, yes.'

Lefebvre looked Jack up and down for a few seconds, and then said, 'And are you as batshit crazy as that one in the police station?'

'A little crazy perhaps, but not in the same way.'

'Well, I guess I'll have to take your word for that. You better come on in.'

Jack went into the house. It was warm, and he recognized the distinctive smell of caribou stew.

'You're making dinner?' Jack asked. 'I don't want to disturb you if you're eating.'

'Did you eat?'

'Er ... no. No, I didn't.'

'Well, it would be discourteous of you to refuse a plate then, wouldn't it?'

'That's very kind of you,' Jack said. He produced the fifth from his coat pocket.

'We can drink that too,' Lefebvre said.

The kitchen was much the same size and layout as that in the Devereaux house. Lefebvre fetched down glasses. Jack poured.

Lefebvre raised the glass and said, 'To low friends in high places, high friends in low places.'

They drank. Jack refilled.

Lefebvre took a seat at the table. He motioned for Jack to do the same.

'If I'd have expected anyone, it'd have been the sergeant,' Lefebvre said. 'But then, I guess he knows well enough that my brother and I aren't on the best terms.' Lefebvre sipped his whiskey. 'He dead yet?'

'Not as far as I know,' Jack replied. 'Didn't you go and see him? The woman at the med centre said you're there every day.'

'Did she now?'

'I thought of waiting for you, but I wanted to see you somewhere that wasn't public.'

'And how did you find me?'

'The guy at the general store.'

Lefebvre smiled. 'Seems everyone's all set to minding everyone else's business.'

'How did you know it was me when you opened the door?'

'I seen your brother,' Lefebvre said. 'I knew your pa 'fore he lost his mind. Know enough about your kin to see you've had a great deal of bad news. But you've been away a long time, haven't you?'

'Twenty-six years.'

'Sept-Îles?'

'Montréal.'

'And what have you been doing out in Montréal for the past twenty-six years?'

'Finding reasons not to come back,' Jack replied.

Lefebvre looked at Jack intently for just a few seconds, and then he smiled knowingly. 'Yes, I can see how that would be. For folks like us, it gets to a point where we've been here so long we just wouldn't fit anyplace else.'

Lefebvre got up from the table and went to the stove. He took the lid off a pan and stirred the stew awhile.

Back at the table, he nudged his glass toward Jack. Jack poured once more for Lefebvre, again for himself.

'You shoulda brought a bigger bottle,' Lefebvre said.

'If I'd known you would let me in, I would've done.'

'You were scared I was gonna beat you senseless like your brother done to mine?'

'Maybe, yes.'

'Well, I don't know what to say, Jacques Devereaux. My brother and I had a falling out. We've been at different ends of the room for more years than I care to think, and I can't even remember what started it. Something to do with a girl, more than likely. And this...' He tapped his glass against the empty whiskey bottle.

'And what happens if he dies?' Jack asked.

'Well, then I'll get to see him buried, and you'll get to see your brother in a small cell at the end of a long corridor for the rest of his days. Unless, of course, it turns out that Jean-Paul *is* the one that's been choppin' these little girls up. Then they might give your boy a medal and a hunting cabin in the mountains.'

'Do you think that he...'

Lefebvre smiled wryly. 'Look, I don't even know what to try and make sense of here. I hear what I hear, and it seems none of it has any basis in reason.'

'Calvis seems to have decided that your brother is a killer. So much so that he went and did what he did.'

Lefebvre looked rueful. 'The decisions of a crazy man are crazy, and if what I hear is true, then Calvis is a special kind of crazy.'

'You've been here as long as your brother?'

'Longer. I turned up at the end of '69, not so long after your lot if I remember rightly. Jean-Paul is a handful of years younger 'an me. He came out towards the end of '71. Nineteen years old. Figured he'd make a fortune in half a dozen years, and then go back to the city, marry, get a family organized. Same idea most of us had.'

'But it holds you, doesn't it?' Jack said. 'This place.'

'Oh, I hear that kinda thing and I pay it no mind. One place is not a great deal different from any other place. If a man intends to move and doesn't, then it seems to me that it's the man, not the geography.'

'And you heard what my brother has been saying. The things about wendigos, men becoming cannibals?'

'I heard it. Indian stories. Legends.'

'Calvis believed it, and still does. He convinced himself that your brother was possessed by the wendigo, and that's what drove him to kill these girls.'

'If you're after compliments from me about my brother's nature, then you're in the wrong place. However, even I would have to stretch my low opinion of him a good deal to call him a cannibal.'

'You said you had a disagreement?'

'What I said was that we had a falling out. Each of us swore never to talk to the other, and we've kept our word.'

'But you both work for Canada Iron. How did you—'

'You can see and choose not to see, if you know what I mean,' Lefebvre said. 'Every once in a while, we'd find ourselves on the same shift. We just paid no mind to one another, and it went on as if nothing had happened. One time we did talk, but that was due to the circumstances. It was necessary for the good of others.'

'What was that?'

'You remember the mine collapse? The one they called the Second Collapse. Back at the end of '79.'

'Yes, I remember that. My father was a supervisor.'

'We lost a good few men. We spent two or three days tryin' to dig those bodies out. I talked to Jean-Paul plenty during that time. It was filthy, dangerous work, and the whole crew had to be coordinated. After that, he and I went back to the same silent routine.'

'But you didn't get on even before you had this falling out?'

'Hell, I don't know what to tell you. You don't choose your family, do you? He had a streak of temper the like of which I've never seen in another human being. Vicious, all full of rage and fury. He didn't seem like much, but he had a strength in him that was something powerful to witness. I've seen him put down a man twice his size. He's all bone and muscle. Not a scrap of fat on him. Fast, too. Get into a tussle with him and you're tussling with a corn thresher. I worked hard to like him, but it never took. Whatever finally split us up was just the tail-end of a long run of things.'

Evidently, there was no love lost between the brothers, but Jack knew this was just one side of the story. Jean-Paul was not here to present his version or defend himself against the criticisms. Nevertheless, it seemed clear that Jean-Paul was a strong man with a short and volatile temper. The murdered girls would have been no match for him.

Lefebvre got up and stirred the stew again.

The bottle was empty. Jack offered to fetch another.

'You come again, bring two,' Lefebvre said. 'Meanwhile, this'll do.' He reached down a bottle from a shelf beside the stove.

Lefebvre served the stew. It was rich and substantial. Aside from the caribou and root vegetables, there was a heap of fiddlehead ferns.

'Where the hell d'you get these?' Jack asked.

'I get 'em shipped in. They're the salted kind. They boil up good in a stew. I always had a taste for them, even since I was a kid.'

The men ate. They drank. When they were done, they smoked. Jack looked at his watch. It was close to ten. He'd been there a good three hours.

'You know, there's one thing that I'm really struggling to figure out in all of this,' Jack eventually said. 'You've always been here, right? Ever since you arrived?'

'Yes, I have,' Lefebvre replied.

'And your brother, too?'

'I'm sure he's gone walkabout every once in a while, but he ain't never moved away from town, no. Why'd you ask?'

'Because I've gone through my brother's journals and newspaper clippings and anything else I can find, and the last murder happened back in 1990. Doesn't make sense to me that someone would kill eight girls over eighteen years and then just stop.'

'Unless you were right about the wendigo, of course?'

'How so?' Jack asked.

'Man possessed can get himself un-possessed, I would say. Or maybe he found himself some Jesus or somethin'.'

Jack smiled. He liked Lefebvre – his humour, his way of speaking. He raised his glass. 'Let's drink to your brother's recovery, eh?'

'That for my benefit, or because you don't wanna see yours in jail for the rest of time?'

Jack was surprised. He didn't know how to respond.

Lefebvre set down his glass. 'I might not believe in old Indian legends and spooks and ghouls and whatever, but I do have a sense for some kind of universal justice. I like to think that folks get what's comin' to them, even if it takes a long time. Like karma could be the most patient killer of all, right? Your brother damaged Jean-Paul a good deal. Maybe he survives, maybe he don't. Maybe he gets brain damage or something. I don't know what's gonna happen, and I'm just gonna wait it out and see. But if he done killed those girls, then he deserves everything that's happened to him, and I think a great deal more people than me would be set to let your brother go with a slap on the shoulder and a good farewell.'

He paused to take a drink.

'Now, on the other hand, if Jean-Paul didn't do the killing, then maybe he did some other stuff and this was his punishment. Great many people say there's a God up there. Even though I ain't never been the prayin' kind, there's too many who are for me to argue with. And if there's a God, then you gotta have the other side of the coin, right? You have something that compels men to acts of virtue, then you're gonna have something that compels men to acts of wickedness and hate.'

Lefebvre shook his head. He rubbed his hand along his chin. The sound of calluses against stubble reminded Jack of his father.

'Those girls got hurt bad before they died,' Lefebvre went on. 'Lot of pain, lot of grief. Taking such a young life is a terrible thing, and the man who done that is gonna be a terrible human being. Why would someone do that? Damned if I know. If it was Jean-Paul, then he ain't gonna go blaming his childhood or some hardship or whatever. He and I was brung up the same, and the only darn thing I ever killed was what I planned to eat. So no, the thing that drives a man to do that ain't the fault of others, is it? It's something out there, or it's something so deep inside of him he more than likely brought it from before he was born.'

Lefebvre emptied his glass in one.

'And now,' he said, 'I've drank more than enough and I'm gonna throw you into the street. You mightn't have to get up and work, but some of us do.'

275

Jack finished his whiskey. He got up, and only then realized how unsteady he was on his feet.

'You gonna make it home?' Lefebvre asked.

'Sure I will,' Jack said, and wrestled his coat from the back of the chair.

41

Surfacing from sleep was hard work. Jack didn't make a habit of drinking, at least not to excess, and the previous night he and Lefebvre must have drunk half a bottle each.

Had he been in Montréal, he would've sat in the shower and let water run over him until he felt something closer to human. Here there was no shower. Here a bath took a good deal of fetching and carrying from the stove. Jack possessed neither the will nor the energy to do that. Back when he was a teenager, he would take a shower at the boarding house. Thoughts of the boarding house precipitated thoughts of Carine, then on to Thérèse and Juliette. Before he'd a chance to stop himself, he felt a wave of grief wash over him. He knew a good deal of how bad he felt was the whiskey, but he was also getting closer to the overwhelming emotions he'd left behind. He had to keep it together, if not for himself then for Calvis.

Sitting at the kitchen table, nursing his second cup of therapeutically strong coffee, he thought back to the previous evening's discussion with Guy Lefebvre.

It didn't seem possible that Jean-Paul Lefebvre had killed for nearly twenty years and then just stopped. It didn't seem possible that someone could change such a pattern so suddenly. Jack believed Calvis had committed himself to one idea and then persuaded himself that everything else was a confirmation of that fundamental premise. However, a man's temper didn't make him a serial killer. What was needed were method, motive and opportunity. Jean-Paul Lefebvre possessed no lack of opportunity, and there was some semblance of similarity in the ways in which the girls had been killed. As for motive, that was in the realm of criminal profiling, a subject about which Jack knew very little. What he did know, however, was that any attempt to rationalize the truly irrational went down a long, blind alley into nowhere. These weren't premeditated murders for personal profit, nor were they motivated by vengeance or vigilantism. A killer of this type was solving a problem that existed solely in their own mind, and no one but the killer themselves could explain it.

It was only after a walk to the store for bread and bacon that Jack managed to focus on something that he realized had been bothering him. At the time, he'd not paid any great attention to it, but it must've triggered something because it kept haunting the edges of his consciousness.

The Second Collapse. He remembered it clearly. He'd been fourteen years old. Nine men had lost their lives, some of them fathers to his schoolfriends. Henri had been the primary shift supervisor, and though he wasn't held responsible for what happened, he did bear a burden of responsibility and shame. In fact, the incident had been a significant factor in the escalation of Henri's drinking, and the drinking had exaggerated the distance and disconnection between him and his family.

So why was it nagging at him?

Guy was clear about what had happened. He and Jean-Paul had worked for a number of days recovering bodies. It was November of 1979. But when exactly?

Jack made a sandwich. He ate it hurriedly. He put on his coats and boots and walked up to the Canada Iron administrative office. It was here that his father must have first signed in for his shift rota and work detail, Calvis too, and when he stepped inside the brightly lit foyer of the one-storey building, he appreciated that he too would more than likely have wound up here had he not left back in 1984.

A young woman looked up from the desk and smiled cheerily.

'Good morning, sir,' she chimed. 'How can I help you?'

'Hi,' Jack said. 'I was actually after some historical information about a mine collapse back in the seventies.'

The woman frowned. 'A mine collapse?'

'Yes. Back in November '79.'

'I'm sorry, sir. I don't know anything about that.'

'You have an office in Sept-Îles, right? Maybe we could call someone.'

'We do have an office there, sir, but the phone lines are down right now. We've had no calls in or out for nearly two days.'

'Right. Sure.' Jack stood there in the reception area and didn't know what to say next.

'Was that all, sir?'

'Payroll,' Jack said.

'Sorry, sir?'

'Payroll. Accounts. That's who I need. You have a new guy here. Girard. Pierre... no, Paul Girard.'

The woman scrolled through her extension directory. 'Yes,' she said. 'Paul Girard. But his office is up at the foundry.'

'Okay. Thank you. I really appreciate your help.'

The last time Jack had walked that same route to the foundry was with Calvis at his side, both of them being marched towards the furnaces by their father.

It was nowhere near as far as he remembered it, and when he arrived he had no difficulty in finding the accounts office.

Girard himself seemed overly pleased to see Jack. Perhaps it was just a case of one familiar face in a sea of unknowns.

'We were planning on tracking you down,' he said. 'Vivi really wants you to come over for dinner.'

'That's really kind of you. I would like that,' Jack said. 'So, how are you getting on? Is your place okay?'

'Culture shock. And that's an understatement. However, I have to give it to Vivi. She seems in her element. How long her appreciation of quiet and isolation will last, I don't know, but for now she seems happy enough.'

'Some people just get it,' Jack said. 'There're people who've been here for thirty, forty years, and they have no wish to be elsewhere.'

'So, what can I do for you?'

'I'm trying to find out something. In November '79 there was a major incident here. A mine collapse. My father was one of the shift supervisors. Nine dead, three survivors.'

'And how can I help?'

'Payroll records. They must go back to the beginning. I guess there would be a way of finding out the date it happened and how long the recovery went on for.'

'Not payroll, I wouldn't think,' Girard said. 'Personnel yes, but not Accounts.'

'Can you ask someone, maybe?'

'Sure I can, but why d'you need to know?'

'My brother's in trouble. That's why I came back. I'm trying to help him, and it has something to do with things that happened when I was here.'

Girard seemed hesitant. 'Okay, so it's a personal matter, then?'

'I guess you could say so, yes.'

'I don't know if I can get information about employees ...'

'Look, all I need to know is the date of the Second Collapse in November '79. No names, no other information, nothing confidential. You don't even need to tell me where you got the information from. It's just the date I need, and that's all.'

'Wait here. I'll see what I can do.'

Girard headed toward the interior of the building. Jack went out and smoked a cigarette. He came back in and sat in the corner of the reception area. He wished to be as inconspicuous as possible.

Girard was gone for close to an hour by Jack's reckoning, but when he appeared he had the answer to Jack's question.

'The fifteenth,' he said. 'The incident itself happened on 15 November 1979.'

'That's really appreciated,' Jack said, already making his way back towards the door.

'And dinner?' Girard said.

'Yes, of course. Just give me a couple of days or so to get some of these things sorted out, and then we'll arrange it.'

Girard walked out of the building with Jack.

'Is everything okay?' he asked.

'Some things to handle,' Jack replied. 'I'm really grateful for your time, Paul, but I need to go. We'll speak soon, okay?'

'For sure,' Girard replied. 'And let me know if there's anything else I can do to help.'

It was right there. The connection that made no sense. A mine collapse in Jasperville on 15th November. The killing of Fleur Dillard in Wabush on the sixteenth.

Jack stared at the newspaper article. He then went back through Calvis's journals.

There was no denying the contradiction. Unless Guy was lying, and he seemingly had no motivation for doing so, then Jean-Paul was working like fury to recover bodies from beneath tons of dirt and rock. Sure, Wabush was little more than a hundred and fifty miles from Jasperville, but it was across some of the most hostile and unforgivable terrain. Given a snowmobile capable of making that journey, it couldn't have been done in less than two or three hours. Jean-Paul Lefebvre would've had to be absent from the rescue detail for at least eight hours to have been responsible for the girl's murder.

Jack re-read the Wabush newspaper article. He looked once more at the school photo of Fleur Dillard. He considered the fact that Jean-Paul Lefebvre had never left Jasperville for any length of time, and yet no more killings had been recorded in Calvis's journals beyond that of Madeleine Desjardins in May of 1990.

Psychosis didn't cure itself. Homicidal mania didn't just fade and disappear. Addictions – whether to drugs, alcohol, violence, even murder – were far stronger than any self-motivated force to the contrary. Killers stopped killing because they were locked up or because they themselves were killed. That was the simplicity of it.

If Lefebvre was not responsible, then the cessation of killings in Jasperville and the surrounding towns could be attributed to the actual perpetrator having left after the death of Madeleine Desjardins.

If not Lefebvre, then someone else. And if that someone was not themselves dead, then they were still out there, and still driven by the same violent and sadistic compulsion.

Right now, Nadeau was the only person Jack wanted to talk to, and perhaps the only person who could help him.

42

'So what do you want me to do?' Nadeau asked.

'Your job?' Jack replied, and knew immediately that it was the worst thing he could have said.

Nadeau sat down. He looked at Jack until Jack sat down, too.

'I'm trying to like you, Monsieur Devereaux, but I have to say it's hard work.'

'You're not the first person to tell me that.'

'Perhaps you could introduce us all to each other and we could start a club, eh?'

'I'm trying to figure this out, you know?' Jack said. 'Not just for my brother, but for the simple reason that you have a great many unsolved deaths.'

'*I* have a great many unsolved deaths?'

'You know what I'm saying.'

'You get angry with me, Monsieur Devereaux, then you just might lose the only ally you've got right now.'

Jack paused. He took a breath. 'Yes,' he said. 'Okay.'

'I understand your frustration. I get it. I am similarly frustrated.'

'But for you it's not personal.'

'Depends how personally I take it. This is my duty here. I'm expected to deal with this, and to a very clear and specific conclusion.'

'So let me help you,' Jack said. 'I'm not here in an official capacity.'

'You spoke to Lefebvre's brother, didn't you?'

'How do you know that?'

'Because I saw him this morning. He said you and he got very drunk and talked about a great many things.'

'We did, yes.'

'Tell me what you discussed.'

After Jack had given Nadeau the bare bones, Nadeau said, 'So if Jean-Paul was working here on digging bodies out from under a collapse, he couldn't have been murdering the Dillard girl in Wabush.'

'Exactly.'

'That's one girl of eight we know about. That he didn't kill Fleur doesn't mean he's innocent of the other killings. You're assuming they're all attributable to one man, but assumption isn't a good premise for an investigation.'

'The MOs are almost identical.'

'Which also says they're not completely identical.'

'You seriously think there's more than one person responsible for murdering young women out here, Sergeant Nadeau?'

'I don't seriously think anything at the moment,' Nadeau replied. 'I have doubts about whether or not some of these killings were murders. Perhaps they were accidental. Perhaps animal attacks.'

'You've seen the photographs.'

'The ones that are available to us, yes.'

'And you think an animal would have killed a girl and then not eaten her or dragged her away?'

'I'm not an expert in the feeding habits of animals in the north-east of Quebec. All I'm saying is that you now appear to have made your own decision about Lefebvre. Your brother made a decision about him, too, and that decision put the man in a coma.'

'Hey, like it or not, you're the official representative of the Sûreté out here, and—'

'I know who I am, Monsieur Devereaux, and I know exactly what I'm doing out here. What I actually do about this particular situation is another thing entirely.'

'Oh, for Christ's sake! Really? We're just gonna dance around this thing?'

'Tell me what you want me to do, Monsieur Devereaux. I'm willing to follow any legal suggestion. I can't ask Lefebvre because he's in a coma. Your brother talks mostly crazy. What now? Aside from waiting until they send some people to fetch him.'

'Okay, so is there any update on Lefebvre?'

'Last I checked, there was no change in his condition.'

Jack was relieved to hear that he hadn't worsened.

'You need to let the law do its job, Monsieur Devereaux. You are not a police officer.'

'And how exactly is the law going to do its job, Sergeant Nadeau?'

'As I said before, people will come from Sept-Îles or Montréal to collect your brother. He will be interviewed. They will decide if he's able to stand trial. If so, he'll be tried. If not, he'll be turned over to those who deal with such people.'

'And the murder investigation? What happens then? Do we all just continue to pretend to ourselves that eight girls were killed by fucking bears or wolves or whatever?'

Nadeau's expression was that of a man approaching the limit of his patience.

'No one's pretending anything,' he said. 'And no one but you and your brother are tying all these things together in such an orderly fashion. But even you're now saying that your brother

285

got it wrong, that the man in the medical centre is no killer. Seems to me that we're back where we started, talking about thirty- and forty-year-old cases. I don't have the resources, the administrative staff, the funds or the personnel to initiate a manhunt. I don't have the time to trawl back through faded paperwork that was already incomplete and insufficient.'

'Then let me,' Jack said. 'Let me go through the paperwork. Let me look at the files and see if I can make some sense of it.'

'That is not possible,' Nadeau said.

'They're closed, right? Cold cases. They're not ongoing invest-igations. If it's the same as the criminal investigations we—'

'You really want to look at these files?'

'I do, yes,' Jack replied. 'And if I find something that opens this thing up, then you can action it. I'm not looking for some sort of acknowledgement or recognition here, Sergeant. I'm simply trying to understand what happened to these girls and why my brother became so obsessed with finding out the truth.'

Nadeau remained silent. He was thinking, and Jack knew better than to interrupt him.

'If I say yes,' Nadeau eventually said, 'then you review them here. You don't take them from this office. You don't take copies of anything. You don't tell anyone that you're doing this. Anything you find that you think warrants a new investigation, you tell me. You don't go to any outside agency, and you don't contact the Sûreté offices in Sept-Îles or Montréal.'

'Absolutely,' Jack replied.

'I need to hear you say that you understand and agree to all these conditions, Monsieur Devereaux.'

'I understand and agree to all these conditions, Sergeant.'

Nadeau leaned forward. 'And if I agree, and then you violate this agreement, I will lose my job. Do you understand that?'

'Yes,' Jack said. 'In my work, I also have access to confidential material. I understand the implications of what we're doing here.'

Nadeau looked at Jack unerringly. Jack didn't look away.

'There's a room back there.' Nadeau indicated over his shoulder toward the rear of the building. 'You can work in there.'

The files, such that they were, related solely to the five girls from Jasperville: Lisette, Anne-Louise, Thérèse, Virginie Fortin and Madeleine Desjardins.

Jack laid out their pictures side by side across the table.

They looked back at him with innocence and youth and all the expectation of their age. Thérèse looked so much like Carine, and that tore his heart a second time. He studied the original missing person reports, the few facts that had been collated for each. There were names here – Gustave Levesque, Maurice Thibault, Émile Landry, Odile and Étienne Fournier, Baptiste and Violetta Roy – and with each one a flood of memories returned, some of them moments of quiet reflection, many of them replete with fear and the threat of violence. He'd been a frightened child. Out here in the wilderness, his papi going crazy and telling him stories of the wendigo, his father angry and hateful, convincing them that they'd be consigned to Hell for eternity. And then there was his mother, his port in every storm, the safe harbour where he could find some semblance of calm and comfort. Everything fell apart so horribly, so tragically, and he could no longer wait for Carine, or Calvis, and he fled. It was not cowardice. It was self-preservation.

The crime-scene images shocked Jack. They were monochrome and grainy, and that made them even more brutal. The images lent themselves to separation and disconnection. These are not your people. This didn't happen in your life. This was someone else's life, and now it's over and will be forgotten in less time than it takes to say their name.

There was a savagery to the way in which these girls had been killed, and the more Jack studied the photographs, the more he felt sure that this was the work of one man and one man alone. Perhaps explained by nothing more than his own revulsion at such acts, he could not imagine two people agreeing to do such things to another human being. The girls looked too alike, their ages were too close, and even their manner of dress and hair colour bore similarities. It gave Jack the impression that whoever was doing this was ridding the world of one person time and time again.

Jack kept going back to the picture of Thérèse. The bloody, shattered mess of her features, as if she'd been beaten viciously and relentlessly with a club, a bat, perhaps a rock. At twenty years old, she was the oldest of all of them by three years. The others – those he was aware of – were fifteen, sixteen and seventeen.

Jack spent a good two hours poring through every page, every margin note, every letter. The file with the most information was that of Anne-Louise Fournier, the bulk of that being exchanges between Sergeant Maurice Thibault and the girl's parents. Of all the sergeants, Thibault seemed the most intent and focused. He'd begged them to let him have an autopsy done, but they'd refused. From his own reports, he was in no doubt that the murder had been committed by an extraordinarily dangerous individual, and he seemed quite sure that it was the same man who had murdered Lisette Roy.

The one common denominator in every file was the absence of a suspect. Not a single person had been interviewed. There were a couple of shortlists of names, all of them transient workers who had passed through Jasperville at the time of two of the killings, but there was no recurring identity. Sergeant Emmanuel Gaillard, in the last three months of his tenure following the death of Madeleine Desjardins, had also considered there was a serial to investigate. He'd left a letter for his successor urging him to *pursue any and all lines of inquiry*, but there were no indications that anything had been done.

Jack went through everything again, and by the time he was done his thoughts were no clearer than when he'd started, save for the ever-increasing certainty that he was looking for one person. Given the fact that these killings took place in Jasperville, Menihek, Fermont and Wabush, then the assumption that this person hailed from Jasperville had only a one in four chance of being correct; Canada Iron sent people back and forth across the whole region.

Jack wanted to look at Jean-Paul Lefebvre's work record. It was this that had been the basis of Calvis's 'evidence'. According to Calvis's rationale, Lefebvre had the opportunity to commit each murder due to the fact that he'd not been present at work on the stated days. The fact that Lefebvre was directly involved in the recovery attempts after the Second Collapse undermined that theory, but Jack had to look into every aspect of this. What if Guy Lefebvre was lying? What if he was complicit and was doing whatever he could to protect his brother? What if Jean-Paul had left the recovery operation for much of a day, his absence unnoticed due to the sheer confusion of the situation? Jack had to operate with one of the guiding principles he'd been taught as a fire investigator: *Get a source, confirm it twice.*

As far as accessing Lefebvre's work records, there was only one way he could do that, and he would need help. He knew who to ask, and he knew it would take a little while. He also knew that to accomplish this he would have to share some of the details of why he was there and what he was trying to do.

But before even that, there was something he had to face and overcome. Looking at images of the battered corpse of Thérèse Bergeron had brought it home to him with such profound force that he knew he could avoid it no longer.

He had to speak to Carine. Twenty-six years earlier, he'd promised to come back and rescue her from Jasperville. She needed to know why he'd failed her, and he needed to ask for her forgiveness.

43

'She told me what happened,' Martin said.

'But only what she thought happened. We haven't spoken since.'

'Hey, I'm not getting involved. You have some fight with my ma and you can't sort it out after twenty-six years, then I guess she's got good reason. She said you were bad news, and that I shouldn't hang out with you.'

Jack knew Martin was right. He stood there in the foyer of the boarding house, and he felt a sense of frustrated despair.

'Can you at least go and tell her I'm here?' Jack asked.

'I don't think it's gonna do any good.'

'Go and tell her I'm here to find out the truth about Thérèse. Just tell her that for me, would you?'

Ten minutes later, Jack was standing in one of the rooms. His back to the door, he looked at Carine. She was at the window, her face turned away.

'The only reason I'm speaking to you is to tell you not to have anything to do with my son.'

'I don't believe you don't want to know what—'

Carine turned to face him. Anger flashed in her eyes. 'You don't believe what? That I don't want to revisit the past? That I don't want to stir up everything again? Twenty-six years. Twenty-six fucking years. I can't believe that after everything we went through, everything you told me, every promise you made—'

'I know, Carine, I know. There's no way to make you understand how sorry I am.'

She folded her arms defiantly. 'You need to leave. You need to leave now, and you shouldn't come back. I don't want you here, I don't want to talk to you, and I don't want you to speak to Martin ever again. You understand me?'

'I understand you,' Jack said, 'but I won't agree to that.'

'What?'

'What I said. I'm here to tell you what happened, to give you an explanation.'

Both Carine's tone and expression were dismissive. 'I don't want your apology. I don't want an explanation. You left. I waited for you. Do you have any idea what I went through? My sister was dead. Murdered. My parents were fucking heartbroken. Completely devastated. I was here alone waiting for you to do what you promised, and a year went by, then another, then another. I was here for nearly six years, Jack. Six fucking years. By the time I got out of here I was twenty-three years old. Do you have even the faintest clue what it was like to wait for someone for six years, all the while knowing that they lied to you?'

'I didn't lie to you, Carine.'

Carine looked at him in abject disbelief. 'You didn't lie? Of course you lied. You said something that wasn't true. That's what a lie is, Jacques. You said you would come back and you didn't. It's black and white. There are no shades of grey here. There are no mitigating circumstances. There's no excuse or reason or justification that buys you any grace with me, Jacques Devereaux. Whatever the hell you thought you were going through, I was going through the same thing a thousand times over. You were scared to come back? Was that it? Well, I was scared to stay. Scared out of my fucking wits. You thought that if you came back, you would never be able to leave again? Maybe that's what you believed. Well, I was here, and I thought I was going to have a chance to get away, and that chance was you. And what about Calvis, eh? We were trapped, just like you were. You do know that, right? You not only abandoned me here, you abandoned Calvis, and now Calvis has lost his fucking mind and he's probably gonna spend the rest of his life in jail.'

'Not if I have anything to do with it.'

'Oh well, I appreciate the noble sentiment, Jacques, but I think you're about two and half fucking decades too late.'

'You know your father wrote and told me to stay away.'

'Of course I know. I told him to write to you!'

'You told him?'

The revelation hit him like a North Shore train. His eyes widened, and somewhere within him he felt his entire reality twist and distort.

Carine frowned in disbelief. 'You're struggling to understand why I would do that? Really?'

Jack didn't speak for a moment. He steeled himself to say what he wanted to say. It was his last gamble, and if it didn't pay off then whatever might have been salvaged between himself and Carine was all done and finished.

'The man in the medical centre. The one that Calvis attacked. That is not the man that killed Thérèse.'

At first there was nothing. Carine didn't even flinch. There was nothing about her body language or expression that gave Jack any indication that he'd reached her.

'The person that killed Thérèse,' he said, his voice calm and measured, 'is still out there. I believe that, Carine. I believe that as much as I believe anything. He killed Thérèse and he killed Lisette and Anne-Louise. He even killed some other girls out in Fermont, Wabush and Menihek. I know of eight, and there might be more, because I think whoever did this left here at the same time as you, and they haven't been back. Calvis thought it was this man Lefebvre, but it wasn't. I don't believe that. I think—'

'Enough,' Carine said, raising her hands as if to block him. 'Enough, Jacques. That's enough. For Christ's sake, just stop talking. I don't want to hear it. I don't want any more crazy fucking theories from you or your brother. You're no different, you know? And your goddamned father is in some nuthouse in Saguenay, right? Whole goddamned family is crazy!'

'Someone killed your sister, Carine. She loved Juliette. Juliette loved her. They were going to have a life together, away from here, away from everyone's preconceptions and judgements and bullshit. And someone got her. Out there by the rail terminal while she waited for Juliette to buy the train tickets. Someone went out there and smashed her face in. I've seen the pictures. They're in the police station in a file. You want to see them? I can take you down there and you can see what this fucking animal did to your beautiful sister!'

'Stop!' Carine screamed. 'Stop, stop, stop!' She rushed forward then, faster than Jack could move, and she struck him hard across the face. Jack barely had time to register the blow before she struck him again. He lurched sideways, pain lancing through his face and neck. He was shocked and disorientated. He felt his balance going, and he reached sideways to find the wall. His hand slid along it, and he went down on one knee. Carine was over him then, her fists flailing, striking him again and again on the shoulder, the back of the head, the side of his face. She was completely out of control, and it was only when Martin burst through the door and managed to pull her away that she stopped swinging for Jack.

Carine was breathless, tears running down her face. She took two or three steps backward and sat down heavily on the bed.

'What the fuck is going on here?' Martin asked. 'Are you fucking crazy?'

Carine said nothing.

Martin turned to Jack. 'You need to leave.'

Jack shook his head. He sat down on the floor, his back against the wall.

'I'm serious,' Martin said, his voice hard-edged. 'You need to leave right the fuck now, mister.'

'I'm not going anywhere,' Jack said. 'Your mother and I haven't finished our conversation.'

Martin was flustered. He turned to Carine. 'Ma?'

'It's okay,' Carine said breathlessly. 'Go back downstairs. I'm okay.'

'But Ma...'

She looked up at her son. Her mascara was smudged. She looked simultaneously enraged and defeated. 'Go,' she said. 'I've been waiting a long time to hurt him, and now I've done it. I'll be okay.'

Martin hesitated, then looked at Jack, then back to his mother.

'Crazy fucking people,' he said. He walked back to the door and left the room.

Carine didn't speak until the sound of her son's footsteps had disappeared.

'I don't think I'll ever feel anything but betrayed by you,' she said. 'I tried so many times to put myself in your shoes, to try and understand why you didn't come back, but I never made sense of it. A few months yes, even a year, but twenty-six years?'

Jack said nothing.

'First place I went was Montréal. To look for you. That was my plan. I got there and I realized that I actually didn't want to speak to you, didn't even want to see you again. Then I met someone, Martin's father, and I got married. We were married for five years. It didn't work out and we got divorced. I stayed there for another six years, and then my papa died and I came back. I didn't even know that he'd bought this place. I wanted to clean it up, sell it, but after a while it seemed like there was no reason to go back to the city.'

Carine looked up. 'You got a cigarette?'

Jack took the packet from his jacket pocket. He slid it across the carpet toward her. Carine took one, slid the box back. He offered her his lighter, but she had one in her jeans.

She smoked for a while. Jack didn't speak.

'I've seen Calvis while I've been here,' she said. 'Not often, but I've seen him. In the general store, once or twice in the street. I don't think he saw me. I don't think he *wanted* to see me.'

Carine looked up. Her eyes were swollen and red.

'He looks like you, but he still looks like the little kid he was. After you left, we used to spend time together. He was a mess. Your dad used to bully the crap out of him. Fucking awful, actually.'

Jack took a cigarette himself. He just wanted her to keep talking. Perhaps if she said all the things she'd harboured over the years, then maybe there was a hope that they could talk about the present.

'And now you're here,' she said. 'Jacques fucking Devereaux.'

Jack tried to smile. It was a weak effort.

'You know what, don't look at me,' she said.

'Carine...'

'And don't talk to me. That's even worse.'

She shifted sideways and got up. She walked around the edge of the bed and inched open the window. 'Not s'posed to smoke in here but it's my fucking boarding house, right?' She flicked her cigarette butt out of the window and onto the roof of the porch. 'Give me another,' she said.

Jack tossed the packet over the bed and she caught it.

'So what's the deal here? You actually believe what you're saying, or are you here simply to get forgiveness for being a complete asshole?'

'Both,' Jack said.

'And you've seen your brother.'

'Yes.'

'He as crazy as I've been hearing?'

'He says that Lefebvre was possessed by the spirit of a wendigo. That's why he killed the girls.'

Carine's reaction was reflexive. Her laughter was hard and cold. It ended as soon as it had started. 'Oh fuck,' she said. 'Then he's even crazier than I thought.'

'He told me to go to the med centre and finish the job.'

Carine came back from the window and sat on the bed once more.

'Jesus Christ,' she said. 'What a fucking mess.'

'Him and Henri are all that's left of my family.'

'Martin is all that's left of mine.'

'What happened to your ma?'

'She left my pa years ago. She died back in '97.'

'I'm sorry to hear that. She was a good woman.'

'So was your ma and your sister and Thérèse. Calvis was a good person, too.'

'It's this place, Carine,' Jack said. 'It does something to people.'

'Places don't do things to people, Jacques. Not unless there's already something inside them that's set to go wrong.'

'Well, whoever did these things is about as wrong as you can get.'

'And you really believe that this guy, the one that Calvis attacked, is innocent?'

'Don't you?'

Carine shook her head. 'From what I hear, he wasn't a very

sociable guy. No friends. Lived alone. Didn't much speak to anyone, even his own brother. Bad temper.'

Jack smiled ruefully. 'That could describe me, and I haven't killed anyone.'

'So you have some notion about this?'

'That the guy is still out there.'

'And you think he was here until twenty years ago and then he left?'

'I don't know,' Jack replied, 'but I do know that bad people don't just stop doing bad things.'

'Unless they wind up dead themselves.'

'Right.'

Carine sighed. 'Fuck, you got me talking. I had decided not to talk to you. I mean, to not even say a word to you.'

'I'm sorry. You have no idea how—'

'So tell me, Jack. If you're so goddamned sorry that I couldn't possibly have an idea, then explain it to me. You tell me why you fucking left me here in this godforsaken nowhere.'

'For the reasons you said. Scared. Afraid if I came back that I wouldn't be able to get out again. I convinced myself that you were okay, that you'd found some way to get out and make a life for yourself. It was a gradual thing, you know? Little by little I thought about it less and less, and then there would be days when I somehow managed to not think of it once. That became a week, a month. I made myself believe that what I'd done wasn't so bad. And then the letter from your father was another reason not to come back.'

'And your pa? When he got really sick and they took him away? You didn't come back then?'

Jack shook his head.

'Man, you really are a piece of work. You are most definitely not the man I thought you were. You were supposed to be my knight in shining armour, right?'

'I was, yes.'

'And what did you have in Montréal? Wife, family, a great job?'

'None of the above.'

'Wow. Impressive. Ran away into precisely nothing, and the nothing was so rewarding that you couldn't come back for me or your own father.'

'Fuck you, Carine.'

Carine laughed harshly. 'No, fuck you, Jacques.'

'It happened. I screwed up. Truly, and in the most extraordinary way. Would I go back and do it all different? Yes, I would. And I think you could probably say the same. Thérèse, Juliette, my ma, your folks, even my pa would probably do things a whole lot different if they had the time again. We all fuck up, some of us worse than others. You know, it's not what people do that matters most. It's what they do next.'

'I'm not gonna fight with you any more. Just thinking about it is exhausting.'

'I'm not trying to fight with you, Carine. I'm trying to make up the damage.'

'Oh, right,' Carine replied, her tone sarcastic. 'And how in God's name could you ever hope to do that, Jacques?'

'By finding out who murdered your sister, Carine. By finding out who did it and bringing you their head.'

44

Early on Friday morning, Jack went back up the foundry and saw Paul Girard. He asked if it would be possible for them to speak that evening.

'We can speak now,' Girard said. 'I'm not so busy.'

'Privately,' Jack said. 'Away from here.'

Girard hesitated, a little baffled. 'Er... sure. Yeah. No problem. Come this evening. Come for dinner. I'll tell Vivi.'

Girard told Jack where they lived. Jack knew the street. They agreed he would be there by seven-thirty.

Back at the house, Jack went through everything that related to Jean-Paul Lefebvre's work schedule. Calvis had been painstakingly meticulous, appearing to have left nothing out. Lefebvre had been away from work on every date a girl had been killed, and in some cases he'd been away a day prior, sometimes two or three subsequent days as well. There were long and vicious diatribes following occasions when Calvis had seen Lefebvre at work. In these, he referred to Lefebvre as *the wendigo*.

I smell him, Calvis had written. *I can see the blood on his hands. There is no light in the eyes. The wendigo is soulless. There's nothing inside of it but hunger and pain and this craving for torture and violence.*

And later: *No one sees. The wendigo has to die, but they are all too afraid.*

Jack remembered Papi, and then the class at school when he'd learned about the old Indian legends. His mother had begun to believe the stories, too. It hurt Jack so much to think of her. She died at forty-seven, just a couple of years older than Jack was now. It had been no life to speak of, and the life she'd had was one of personal sacrifice for the well-being of her father, her husband and her children. Their whole history was buried beneath grief and heartbreak. It was a tragic horror story. It was the story of the Devereauxs.

He put everything in order. He carried it back up to Papi's room, and then he went to the police station.

On the way he paused outside the boarding house. He looked up at the windows, hoping perhaps to see some sign of Carine. She'd said little after he'd told her what he intended to do. She didn't question it, but that was more to do with her complete unwillingness to trust him. Perhaps she never would again. He understood that his words would always be nothing but hollow and meaningless. The only thing that could possibly change her mind was action.

Jack's primary interest was confirmation of Calvis's theory. Everything hinged on opportunity, planned or otherwise, and that had been fundamentally undermined by the fact that Lefebvre couldn't have killed Fleur Dillard unless someone had covered his tracks. As Nadeau had said, that was no alibi for the other seven deaths. But then there was the sudden and un-explained cessation of murders.

Jack couldn't appeal to Nadeau for assistance. Nadeau was required to follow the letter of the law, and from what he'd seen, Nadeau didn't seem the kind to suddenly change his mind about how he was going to do his job. Though he was smart, he was still a company man. Jack was also resistant to asking Calvis for further information. Calvis was utterly certain of Lefebvre's culpability, and Jack – determined to remain as uninfluenced as possible – knew that his own sense of guilt for leaving Calvis behind would compromise his objectivity regarding anything his brother told him.

Arriving at the police station, he greeted Nadeau and asked if it would be okay for him to visit Calvis.

'Someone else came to see him a while back,' Nadeau said.

'Who?'

'Madame Bergeron.'

'Really?'

'Yep. She was here, not for long. Left maybe an hour ago. She looked distressed when she arrived. I figured that might have been your doing.'

'I don't know whether to resent that assumption,' Jack said. 'But yes, it was my doing. We shared words.'

'Well, she went on down there. Asked to see him alone. I couldn't allow that, of course, but I gave them some privacy. She said a bunch of things to him. Don't know what, but he didn't seem to even acknowledge that she was there.'

'How was she when she left?' Jack asked.

'I'd say she was even more distressed.'

'Has he been saying anything to you?'

'Nothing of significance.'

'Can you take me down there?'

Nadeau got up from his desk. 'You've got fifteen minutes,' he said. 'I have to make a house call.'

'Fifteen minutes is fine,' Jack said.

Nadeau went down first, Jack just seconds behind him, and as Nadeau reached the basement, Jack heard him voice a sudden exclamation.

Nadeau moved quickly, and was already at the bars of Calvis's cell by the time Jack reached the bottom of the stairs.

Calvis lay on the ground. There was no sign of movement. His face was red, his eyes shut tight, and the sound of his lungs fighting for air was thin and desperate. Nadeau had the cell open, and he was down on his knees trying to loosen something from around Calvis's throat.

'Help me!' Nadeau said. 'Get him up. Lift him up!'

Jack struggled to get his hands beneath Calvis's shoulders. It then became clear what he'd done. He'd torn his blanket into strips, wound them together to fashion a rope, tied one end to the foot of the bed, the other to one of the bars. Lying down, he'd wrapped it around his neck, and then rotated his entire body beneath. In this way he'd created a tourniquet with which to strangle himself. As soon as Nadeau had untied one end of the rope and loosened it, Calvis's body responded instinctively. His entire frame seemed to heave as air filled his lungs. Jack was behind him, trying to hold Calvis in a sitting position. Calvis was deadweight, barely conscious, and both Nadeau and Jack knew that they had to get him to the med centre as quickly as possible.

Jack held him up while Nadeau fetched another blanket. They laid Calvis down on it, and then carried him stretcher-like up the stairs and out of the door. Another couple of men saw what was happening and lent a hand. They skidded here and there on the rough ice, but they made rapid progress.

Jack went backward through the front door of the med centre. The receptionist was out of her chair and hollering for the doctor.

Rosamond Pelletier took immediate control. The speed and efficiency with which she acted was remarkable. Within ten minutes of their arrival, she had Calvis on a stretcher in an examination room, an oxygen mask over his face, cold packs around his throat to reduce the swelling, and was checking all vital signs. She had given him two injections, one in his right forearm, the other in his thigh.

'His pulse is weak,' she said. 'His heart, too, but he will survive. He attempted suicide, yes?'

'He did, yes,' Nadeau replied.

Jack stood with his back against the wall. He was in shock. His body was trembling with the after-effects of such a huge rush of adrenalin.

'Once he's stable, I will put detention straps on him, but right now I need him treatable. Can you stay with him, Sergeant Nadeau?'

'Yes, of course. I just need to lock the office. I will be a few minutes. Monsieur Devereaux will remain until I get back.'

Once Nadeau was gone, Pelletier turned to Jack. 'Are you feeling faint?' she asked.

Jack nodded.

'Breathe slowly and deeply,' she said. 'Stand upright, shoulders against the wall.'

Jack did as she instructed.

'Shock,' she said. 'Adrenalin. It will pass soon enough. If it doesn't, I can give you something to calm you down.'

'I'll be okay,' Jack said. He started to settle.

'Neither the Sûreté nor us are equipped to deal with what's happening here,' Pelletier said. 'Outside assistance is needed. Someone needs to come from Sept-Îles or Montréal to get this thing under control.'

'I wouldn't bank on anyone coming, Doctor,' Jack said. 'Not until the thaw.'

'I don't understand.'

'Right now you have an injured man. If he dies then it's a different issue, but the Sûreté has enough going on without having to deal with one incident of assault out here in the wilderness.'

Jack stepped away from the wall and looked down at his brother.

'Is that all it was?' Pelletier asked. 'An incident of assault? Your brother tried to kill that man. And all because of some horror story that we were told as children.'

'A story that a great many people have taken very seriously, Doctor.'

She shook her head. 'It defies belief. It really does.'

'He will be okay?'

'Yes,' she said. 'He will be okay. It's very difficult to strangle yourself. Usually the person passes out, and then they cease to lend their own physicality to the process. Human beings are designed to survive, and it goes against our own nature to defy that.'

'How long will he be unconscious for?'

'That depends on how long oxygen was denied. I'll do everything I can, but sometimes the person can slip into a coma. Regardless, he's now a danger to himself, and I need Sergeant Nadeau to help me deal with that.'

Nadeau arrived moments later. He had Jack's hat and gloves with him.

'He should come through this,' Pelletier said, 'but there's always the possibility of brain hypoxia when oxygen has been denied for any extended period. Whatever happens, I need you here. This man is now a danger to himself as well as others, and that falls within your remit, not mine.'

'I know,' Nadeau said.

'Is there anything I can do?' Jack asked.

'Medically, no,' Pelletier replied. 'I don't know if the sergeant can use your help.'

'You cannot be involved in this,' Nadeau said. 'Not here. I can't have you near your brother right now, not until he's secure again.'

'What? You think I'm going to wake him up and let him go?'

'It's not what I think, Monsieur Devereaux,' Nadeau replied, 'it's what is right. It's protocol. I know you understand what I mean, so don't make me explain this any further.'

Jack understood. Nadeau didn't know him, and had no reason to trust him. Who's to say that he wouldn't try and spring his crazy, suicidal brother out of the hospital? How they would get away, where they would go, God only knew, but if anything untoward happened, it was Nadeau who would take the fall.

Paramount in Jack's mind was finding out what Carine had said to Calvis. He also had to meet with the Girards.

He stepped closer to the bed. He reached for Calvis's hand, and then hesitated. He glanced at Nadeau.

'It's okay,' Nadeau said.

Jack took his brother's hand. His chest heaved. He went to his knees, and there was nothing he could do to stop the flood of pent-up emotion that broke over him like a wave.

45

Despite his fragile state, Jack refused any medication from Rosamond Pelletier. Once he'd gathered himself together, he just wanted to get out of there. He felt torn up, emotionally shattered, but he needed to focus for his meeting that evening.

En route back to the house, he stopped at the general store and bought a bottle of good red and a bottle of whiskey. He couldn't go to the Girards' empty-handed.

By the time he'd washed and changed, it was close to seven. He smoked one last cigarette as he looked over his notes about Jean-Paul Lefebvre. He had to know with absolute certainty that not only had Lefebvre had been present in Jasperville during the Second Collapse recovery operation, but that he'd also been absent on every occasion when each of the girls had been murdered.

As he walked through the dark streets to the Girards' house, Jack knew that there was no way he could ever go back to Montréal without dealing with every aspect of this nightmare. Passing the darkened façade of the police station, he thought of Nadeau – consigned to watch over Calvis until this was all set to rights. Five months into his posting, and this was his life. He felt for the man, perhaps knew he should've felt more, but he was emotionally exhausted. Whatever life he'd had was that of a different person. In four days, everything had come apart at the seams and there was no hope it would ever go back together again.

At the end of the street he paused. He looked back towards the black horizon, the impenetrable barrier of the Torngat Mountains, the way earth and sky just seemed to fold into one another without any visible join. The effect was simple: there was no way out. Once you were here, that was it. Reconcile yourself to it, because even if you left, it would bring you back.

Paul answered when Jack knocked on the door. Vivi appeared, and she looked so pleased to see him, greeting him effusively, thanking him for the wine and the whiskey.

The house was warm, and though there was very little furniture or personal items, it was still homely. Jack remembered something his mother once said: *A building makes a house, but people make a home.*

The food was good. Vivi had roasted a chicken, and there was rice with dried peppers and onion. They drank the wine, and once the plates were cleared back to the sink, they sat and talked of inconsequential things.

He'd been there a good two hours before Vivi looked at him with an expression of concern and said, 'You came back here because your brother's in trouble, right?'

'Vivi,' Paul interjected.

'It's okay,' Jack said. 'I want to talk about it.'

'Is he all right?' Vivi asked.

'No,' Jack said. 'He's very far from all right. In fact, he's in the medical centre right now under the watchful eye of Bastien Nadeau.'

'He's in trouble with the police?' she asked, her concern quite genuine.

Jack lit a cigarette and leaned back in the chair. In his left hand he held a glass of whiskey, a thin fragment of ice floating on the top, and he downed it before he spoke again.

'My family has a long history here,' he started, 'and my brother, Calvis, is the only one that stayed. My father is in an institution in Saguenay. I haven't seen him since I took off back in '84. My mother and my older sister both committed suicide.'

'Oh my God,' Vivi said, her eyes wide. Reflexively, her hand went to her mouth.

'Some people say that it has something to do with this place, but that's not true. There are thousands of people who have come and gone through Jasperville over the last fifty or sixty years, and some of them have been so happy here that they would never live anywhere else.'

Jack looked at Vivi, then at Paul. Their expressions were intent, expectant, and he knew he had to tell them more than he'd told anyone else.

'My brother was in a cell under the police station because he tried to kill a man. I don't know if that man will live. If he dies, my brother will be charged with murder. If he survives, then it'll be attempted. And now he's in the med centre because he tried to choke himself to death.'

'Why?' Paul asked.

'Because he's completely fucking crazy, Paul. He's completely out of his mind. He believes that the man he attacked was possessed by a wendigo.'

Paul frowned. 'A what?'

'The Indian myth, right?' Vivi said. 'What I was going to ask you about on the train.'

'Kind of, yes. It's a myth, and it comes from this part of the country.'

Jack went back to the early seventies and the death of Lisette Roy. He told them about his grandfather and the stories he used to tell, about how he and Calvis were scared out of their wits at the idea of some cannibalistic creature lurking in the darkness. He told them about the killings that had taken place, both here and elsewhere, and then he explained what had happened with his brother, how he'd become obsessed with Lefebvre, convincing himself not only that the man was possessed, but that he was single-handedly responsible for these terrible atrocities.

When he was done, both Paul and Vivi Girard were speechless.

'And so I've come to ask for your help,' Jack said.

'Our help?' Vivi asked. 'How could we possibly help you?'

'Not you,' Paul said. 'Me. You want me to get information for you, don't you?'

'I do, yes,' Jack said.

'Lefebvre's employment history back to 1972.'

'Exactly,' Jack said.

'Which is property of Canada Iron. And confidential.'

Jack said nothing. He looked back at Paul and held his gaze.

Vivi reached out and took her husband's hand. 'What would happen if you got this information and they found out?'

Paul shrugged. 'I guess I wouldn't have a job.'

Vivi said nothing.

'You can refuse,' Jack said. 'You can absolutely refuse, and there'll be no need for you to explain your refusal. I'm asking a lot of you, I know, but this is my family. This is my situation. It's got nothing to do with you, and I'm only asking you because you're the one person I know who works for Canada Iron and could get this information for me.'

'Of course I can find it,' Paul said. 'Accounts, finance, wages, settlements, dismissals, even compensation payments. I know exactly where to find what you're looking for.'

Paul took a drink. Vivi did the same.

For a good twenty or thirty seconds, the only sounds were the hiss and crackle of the fire in the grate and the wind beyond the walls.

Eventually Paul leaned forward. 'I'm not going to get it for you,' he said.

Jack's heart sank.

Vivi sat forward. 'But, Paul—' she started.

'However, I can tell you where it is.'

'You can tell me where it is?' Jack asked.

'Vivi is pregnant,' Paul said. 'I can't risk losing my job. I can't go back to Montréal and start all over again with a dismissal hanging over my head. Not with a family to support.'

'I understand completely,' Jack said.

'There are thousands of records up there,' Paul said. 'And ninety per cent of the difficulty is knowing where to look. I know exactly where they are and I can tell you. I can also give you the keys to the building and to the storage area. If you were careful, you could get in there and find what you were looking for and no one would be any the wiser. The foundry is running tomorrow and Sunday, but the administrative areas are all closed for the weekend. Something happens, you say you stole the keys when you came here for dinner. I have plausible deniability. I get a caution for being inadequately secure, but I won't lose my job.'

'That works for me,' Jack said. 'And I really appreciate it.'

They drank more, all three of them, and Paul drew out a floorplan of the administrative offices of Canada Iron. He explained where the banks of filing cabinets were, which of those contained the archive employment records that went back to the very first employees who signed up, and how Jack could locate the files relating to a specific individual.

'Everything you need should be there,' he said. 'Canada Iron is very organized when it comes to paperwork. I guess all of it will be computerized one day, but right now it's all hard copy.'

Jack stared at the plan that Paul had drawn until he knew it cold. The diagram went into the fire. Paul gave him two keys.

'No alarm, no security guard,' Paul said. 'It's just paperwork, no money, nothing of any actual value to steal. Only way you can screw this up is to be seen entering or leaving.'

'I won't be seen,' Jack said. 'I can assure you of that.'

It was near midnight when Jack left. Had he not drunk so much he would have gone up to the foundry site there and then. He would do it tomorrow, and as soon as he was done, he would come by the Girards' place and return the keys.

Back in the house, he took off his coat. It was mind-numbingly cold, but too late to be lighting fires. He tugged blankets out and buried himself beneath them. Even though the events of the day turned over and over in his mind, he was drunk enough to sleep without dreams.

46

A little after eleven on Saturday morning, Jack went to check on Calvis at the med centre. Nadeau had slept there, but had left a couple of hours earlier to get a change of clothes and make arrangements for Calvis to be brought back to the police station.

'Your brother will be okay,' Dr Pelletier said. 'To be honest, I have never seen someone do that. Hang themselves yes, but that...' She shook her head, seemingly still in disbelief. 'That was quite extraordinary.'

'And Lefebvre?'

'No real improvement, but no deterioration, either. I think this situation will have to force some changes here, both at the police station and as far as our medical facilities are concerned.'

'I always thought that there should've been at least two Sûreté officers out here,' Jack said. 'If that'd been the case, then maybe things wouldn't have gone unresolved for so long.'

'Perhaps,' Pelletier said. 'And you? You are okay?'

'As good as can be expected,' Jack said. 'Actually, I have no real idea how I'm doing. The whole of my life has caught up with me in a matter of four or five days, and I don't know what to think about so much of it. All these years keeping it at arm's length, pretending that it had nothing to do with me, and now it's like I've driven into a brick wall.'

'You've not had an easy life.'

'Is there such a thing as an easy life?'

'Easier than yours, for sure. So, what are you going to do?'

'The best I can,' Jack said. 'Do some things differently. Be a better brother, for starters.'

'You want to see him?'

'Is he unconscious?'

'Yes, he is. I've kept him sedated. I want the internal swelling in his neck to go down.'

'Then I'll let him rest,' Jack said. 'I'll see him another time.'

From the med centre, Jack went back down to the boarding house. He found Carine there at the reception desk.

Her expression said everything. She knew Jack had come to ask what she'd said to Calvis. She looked as if she hadn't slept.

Jack felt a sense of protest. That was the only way he could describe it. As if the blame for all that had happened was directed toward him, and it was unwarranted.

'I heard about Calvis,' she said. 'Is he okay?'

'He tried to kill himself, Carine. He constructed a fucking tourniquet between the base of his bed and the cell bars. He almost choked himself to death.'

'Oh my God. And it happened just after I saw him, didn't it?'

'What did he say to you, Carine? Did he say anything that made any sense?'

'Not a great deal, no. I think he thought I was Thérèse. He kept saying sorry for what happened to me. Then I think he realized that I couldn't be Thérèse, and then he started crying and telling me that he didn't mean it.'

'He didn't mean what?'

'I don't know, Jack. I don't know what he was talking about. He said he was only trying to help and he didn't mean it to happen. He got kind of hysterical, and the sergeant told me to leave.'

'And you have no idea what he was talking about?'

'Not a clue.'

'Okay.' He turned to leave.

'Jack?'

Jack looked back toward Carine.

'What the hell is happening here? In this place? To us?'

Jack had no words for her.

'You think it's just going to get worse? Do you think I should just run now, while I have the chance?'

'I ran,' Jack said, 'and yet here I am, right back where I started, and it still doesn't make any sense to me.'

'But what if—'

'Carine, I have to go. I'm sorry, but I really need to handle some things. I'm doing my best to fix this, and it's better if you're not involved.'

Jack opened the inner door and was in the vestibule before she had a chance to say another word. He was halfway down the street before he acknowledged what he'd known from the first moment he'd seen her: that his feelings for her had never changed.

The trepidation he felt as he left the house and started up towards the foundry was unlike anything he'd experienced in his adult years.

The lights of the boarding house cast a yellow halo across the street. Jack walked to the left and stayed in the shadows, doing his best to avoid the slick black runnels of ice that would remain unchanged until the spring. The police station was in darkness, as was the general store. The vast majority of Jasperville's inhabitants would be inside, doors and windows closed, fires raging, or in the bars finding warmth some other way.

But for the keys that Girard had given him, Jack had a small torch and his cellphone. Though there was no signal out here, he could still use it as a camera.

He took the same route as always. He thought of every time he'd been sent up here by his mother with his father's lunch pail or a message or to get some money for groceries. He remembered standing there in the yard outside the foreman's cabin, the thundering machinery in the background, the roar of the furnaces, the monolithic smokestacks belching black filth into the sky. And then his father would appear, and there would be a moment of trepidation as he tried to judge whether he would be greeted noncommittally, perhaps with a few words, or whether his father would rage at him for disturbing him yet again when he was at work.

Now, in hindsight, it seemed that his entire childhood had been unpredictable. He'd walked on eggshells for years, and that feeling of uncertainty and instability came back with such familiarity.

Jack stopped when he reached the lee of the outer building. Scaling the low fence was not a problem, but he stood there for some minutes to ensure there was no movement within the compound or anyone down in the street who was interested in what he was doing.

He followed the route that Paul had explained to him, and within a few minutes he was at the main door of the administrative complex. The offices were obscured from the street by the truck bays. Even if someone looked in through the outer fence, they wouldn't see him.

Once inside, Jack closed the door and locked it behind him. Ahead of him was a vast network of corridors and offices. Without Paul's diagram, he would have been utterly lost. The complex was on one level, a design stipulation due to the proximity of the furnaces. Jack walked, and kept on walking. It seemed some small eternity before he found the room he was looking for, and when he opened it and shone his torch inside, he realized just how impossible this task would have been without help. The file cabinets went back a good fifty feet to the rear wall, a further thirty or forty to his left and right. There were hundreds of cabinets, all of them arranged back-to-back with a narrow walkway between. Archives were arranged by decade. The first three dates – February 1972, November 1974 and July 1978 – were all in the same area. The files were kept by month, and every single month's work rota had been completed by the shift supervisor. Three daily shifts, three different crews, three supervisors. Around ninety pages per month. Jack pulled out a lower drawer and set the opened file on it. For Sunday, 13 February 1972, Lefebvre was not listed at all. He was also absent from Monday 18th to Wednesday 20th in 1974. Anne-Louise Fournier had been killed on the 19th. Jack took a picture of it with his phone.

Thérèse had been killed in the thirty-minute window while Juliette had gone to buy tickets on the morning of 10 July 1978. Lefebvre had been at work. He'd run a shift from 4.00 a.m. until noon that day. Jack double-checked. His name was right there: 10 July 1978, third shift for the eight hours until midday. Jack took another picture.

November of 1979, the week of the collapse, and Lefebvre was recorded as absent. According to the documentation right there in front of Jack, the man had not been working on the recovery operation as his brother had said. Jack read it again. There was no doubt. If the document was correct – and he had no reason to doubt it – then Guy Lefebvre had lied to protect his brother.

Jack sat on the floor with his back against the cabinet. Simultaneously, he experienced disquiet and relief. If Jean-Paul was guilty of these things, his brother complicit in the cover-up, then how would Nadeau and the Sûreté deal with it? Would Lefebvre's guilt mitigate the penalty that his brother would receive?

Jack stopped thinking about it. He had to finish what he was doing and get out of there.

The 1980s were in a different bank of cabinets. Estelle Poirier, murdered in June 1981, and for that day and the following Saturday, Lefebvre was not on shift. Tuesday, 16 August 1983, and once again Lefebvre was absent from work when Virginie Fortin was murdered. In fact, he was recorded as absent for the entirety of that week. March 1986, and for three days in March – the 5th to the 7th – Lefebvre was listed as off-site, though there was no indication of why he was away. Génèvieve Beaulieu was found dead in Fermont on Thursday 6th. Lastly, and from another aisle of cabinets, Jack found the file for the week of 14–18 May 1990. This was the last recorded killing in Calvis's journals. Lefebvre was on vacation from Wednesday 15th until Tuesday of the following week. Madeleine Desjardins's body was discovered on Friday 18th.

Jack took pictures of every relevant document. Every file went back exactly where he'd found it, and he checked that every drawer was firmly closed.

Locking the door of the office behind him, he retraced his steps to the foyer. He stood there in the silence and the darkness for a good three or four minutes before he slowly and carefully opened the door. He closed it, locked it, and then made his way down to the perimeter fence.

By the time Jack reached the house, he was out of breath. He had no idea how cold it was – minus fifteen, perhaps – but every joint in his body ached with a kind of sharp nagging sensation.

He lit the fire, took a good three inches of whiskey, and stood ahead of the fireplace to warm through before removing his coat.

At the kitchen table he tabulated every piece of relevant information – days, dates, shift hours – and alongside these, the name, date and location of each of the girls.

Jean-Paul Lefebvre was absent from work for every one of the relevant dates except the day when Thérèse was killed. How Calvis had resolved that question, he didn't know. Jack, however, couldn't afford to accept it. There was the possibility that a mistake had been made. Every document was typed up by hand. People made errors. Every completed shift had to be recorded precisely for wage calculations.

He needed to cross-check these dates against the salary records. Find a source, confirm it twice. If Jean-Paul Lefebvre had been paid for an early shift on Monday, 10 July 1978, then someone else had killed Thérèse. Confronting Lefebvre's brother would be premature until he'd reconciled this fully. Jack would have to ask Paul Girard for his help once again. He would see him first thing.

Jack poured another whiskey. He lit another cigarette. He stood with his back to the fire and he closed his eyes. He focused on Calvis, on Carine, on all that had happened since his arrival in Jasperville. He saw a light at the end of a very long and a very dark tunnel, and he hoped – for all their sakes – that there was now a way to find respite from this nightmare.

Outside, the wind picked up. Jack could hear it howling through the narrow gullies between the houses. Stand in the face of that and you would be dead in an hour. It was with that thought that Jack understood that Jasperville itself had been complicit in these deaths. Jasperville had served to hide the truth, to give another explanation, to reconcile people's fears. Perhaps Papi had been right all along. The place was cursed, and the curse was contagious. Leave, and you took it with you. Leave, and it possessed the power to pull you back.

47

Just after seven, Jack met with Paul a little way down the street from his house. Jack explained precisely what he was trying to verify. Girard agreed in principle, but insisted that any further conversations about what was happening take place away from his home.

'Vivi doesn't sleep great at the best of times, and she was up half the night after you came over.'

'I'm really sorry.'

'It's fine,' Girard said. 'It's not you. She's just keyed up anyway, what with the move, the complete change of circumstances, everything that has to be done to get ready for the baby. I want to help, within limits, but I don't want her to get stressed about it.'

'I understand,' Jack said, 'and I really appreciate your help.'

Jack gave him the list of dates that he wanted to cross-check.

'So you just need to know if he was paid for an early shift on this date in July '78, right?'

'If you can, double-check all of them,' Jack said. 'I just really want to make sure that the shift rota and the wage records tally.'

'It really looks like this guy killed these girls, doesn't it? And that would make your brother a hero in some people's eyes.'

'But not in the eyes of the law. It would still be murder, attempted or otherwise. If Lefebvre did these things, then my brother's nothing more than a vigilante. The courts err towards making an example of people who take the law into their own hands.'

'Yes, of course,' Girard said. 'Well, I can do this for you, but like I said before, you didn't get this information from me.'

'Absolutely,' Jack replied. 'And thank you.'

They agreed to meet at the bar nearest to Girard's house around eight that evening.

Jack arrived early. Girard was on time, almost to the minute.

Girard accepted Jack's offer of a drink, and then said it would be better if they spoke where they couldn't be overheard. His expression seemed grave, and Jack wondered what he'd found out. Perhaps he'd not been able to find anything, and was coming to explain how he could offer no further assistance. If that was the case, Jack knew he would have to accept it. He was already a liability, and he really didn't want to jeopardise the man's job.

Once seated, Girard seemed hesitant to speak.

'What is it?' Jack asked.

'These dates,' Girard replied. 'You're absolutely sure they're right?'

'The dates I listed, yes. Absolutely positive.'

'Then there's a lot that doesn't make sense.'

'Meaning what?'

'I checked, and then I checked again. This man has a brother who also worked up there, doesn't he?'

'Yes,' Jack said. 'Guy Lefebvre.'

'I made sure that there was no confusion between this man and his brother. I even went through both their records to see if the dates correlated in any way, and they did.'

'What did you find out?'

'This first one. July of 1978. He was definitely working the early shift. You already knew that, right?'

'Yes,' Jack said.

'It's the others. There are seven other dates on this list and I checked all of them. He was only absent from work on three occasions. Every other date he was paid for.'

'What?' Jack said. 'What are you talking about?'

'Four of the dates he's marked as absent on the shift rota, he was actually working. The only dates he was away from work were Tuesday, 19 November 1974; Friday to Monday, 19 to 22 June in 1981, and then for a full week, Monday 15 to Friday 19 in August '83. His brother was absent on the same dates in '81 and '83.'

'And November '74?'

'Just Jean-Paul as far as I can see.'

Jack stared at Girard, his mind struggling to grasp what he was being told.

'If there's a mistake, then it's going to be on the shift rota. I know Canada Iron well enough to know that they wouldn't be paying for shifts that haven't been worked.'

'But I saw the rotas,' Jack said. 'Last night. Right there in the files. I even have pictures of them. The dates and shifts were right there on the page. Those dates tallied up with the dates these girls were killed.'

'Apart from July '78.'

'Yes, apart from that one. But the other seven—'

'I'm only telling you what I can see right there in the wage records. Four of those seven dates, your man Lefebvre was paid for a full week's work. He wasn't absent, Jack. That tells me that there's a possibility someone changed the shift rotas after the fact. One error I can understand, but four for the same man. That goes far beyond coincidence.'

Jack went on staring at Girard. He was not seeing him; he was looking right through him, his mind turning back and forth as he took on board what had happened here. If this was true, then someone had selected Jean-Paul Lefebvre. Someone had created their own fall guy. Aside from one single day, a weekend and then a full week away, someone had altered the records to make it appear that Lefebvre was absent when he was not.

'Who would've been able to change the shift rotas?' Jack asked.

'Anyone in a senior administrative position could have accessed those files. But that would mean someone not only committing these murders, but also creating the apparency that someone else did it.'

'I'm a fire insurance investigator,' Jack said. 'You wouldn't believe some of the things people are capable of when it comes to misleading us, making things appear to be something else entirely. The ease with which some people can lie never ceases to amaze me, and I've been doing this for a long time.'

'Jesus Christ,' Girard said. He leaned back in his chair.

'I need to see Lefebvre's brother,' Jack said.

'Now?'

'Yes, now.'

'You want to know about the times they were absent together.'

'Yes, I do.'

'Christ, Jack, this is nearly twenty years ago we're talking.'

'I have to ask,' Jack said. He drained his glass, told Girard once again how grateful he was for his help.

'Let me know what happens,' Girard said.

'I will,' Jack said. He put on his coat and headed for the door.

Guy Lefebvre was home. After his initial surprise, he invited Jack into the house. Jack declined a drink, and then explained that he needed to ask him about a couple of things that had happened back in the early 1980s.

'And you expect me to remember this?' Lefebvre asked.

'There were two occasions when you and your brother were away from work at the same time.'

Lefebvre walked through to the kitchen. Jack followed, and they sat at the table facing one another.

'Can you be any more specific?' Lefebvre asked.

'The first time was from Friday 19 to Monday 22 June 1981, and then another occasion when you were both gone for a week in—'

'August '83,' Lefebvre interjected.

'Yes, that's right,' Jack said.

'Our mother died,' Lefebvre said. 'We went home for a week.'

'Can I ask where you went?'

'Back to Edmonton.'

'Alberta?'

'Only one I know,' Lefebvre replied.

'That's a hell of a way.'

'It is, yes.' Lefebvre leaned forward. 'Why are you asking me about this?'

'There are some things that don't make sense as far as shifts recorded and wages paid. Of the dates I'm interested in, there are only two occasions when Jean-Paul wasn't paid. One was the week you just said, and the other was those three days in June.'

'If it was June and we were both gone, then more than likely we were up fishing at Lac Chantale. May, June, July we used to rent a cabin up there and spend a couple of days here and there. That was before things went bad between us, of course.'

Jack had no reason to doubt Guy. There was bad blood between the brothers, and thus no obvious reason for Guy to provide Jean-Paul with an alibi. If this was true, then Jean-Paul couldn't have been responsible for the deaths of Estelle Poirier or Virginie Fortin.

'Monsieur Lefebvre, do you think someone might have wanted to make your brother a suspect in these killings?'

Lefebvre smiled sardonically. 'You mean someone other than me?'

'Surely you can't have had that much animosity between you?'

'Seems to me the closer you are to someone, the worse it can be when you fall apart. That's the nature of things, I guess. Bitterness and hatred between members of the same family is really hard to understand, but these are people you're stuck with and you never did make that choice. When it goes wrong, it goes wrong hard.'

'But there's no one you can think of who might want to make it look like he murdered these girls?'

'Is that what you're saying has happened here? That someone set him up for these things, and your brother got all fired up and done what he did to Jean-Paul because of that?'

'All I know is that a man can't be in two places at the same time.'

Guy Lefebvre was a tough man, but he couldn't conceal his emotion. He closed his eyes and leaned forward. He pressed his open hand over his eyes and his chest rose and fell as he tried to quell his reaction.

'I'm sorry,' he said after a while.

'Please, don't be sorry,' Jack said. 'I've been dealing with more in the past few days than I have in the last twenty-five years. I have some idea how you must feel.'

Lefebvre's hand came down. He breathed deeply, his eyes still closed, and then he got up.

'I'm having a drink,' he said. 'You should take one with me.'

Once he was seated again, Lefebvre said, 'So what do you do now? You take this information to the sergeant?'

'I don't know. I'm running blind on this. I'm a fire insurance investigator, not a cop. I don't know how these things are supposed to be handled.'

'What else do you need to find out?'

'If I go with what's here, then someone falsified the shift rotas. It was just a few pages. It wouldn't have been a great deal of work. Whoever it was must have hated your brother something terrible, or maybe it was just opportunistic. I don't know.'

Lefebvre poured whiskey into each glass.

'If Jean-Paul didn't kill these girls, then your brother has no motive or defence for his actions.'

'Two days ago my brother tried to kill himself.'

'What?'

'Calvis is crazy. This is something else I've had to come to terms with. He's living in some delusion where...' Jack paused, dismayed. 'Where I don't know what. He convinced himself that Jean-Paul killed these girls. He found enough evidence to justify his belief, and he didn't go any further. Or maybe he'd already made up his mind and that was that. When people are certain of something, they stop asking questions.'

'And these killings ended twenty years ago, you say?'

'Well, 1990 is the last one I know about, and the last one that my brother was looking at. Either they ended, or there were subsequent ones that were never discovered.'

'Or the person responsible moved away.'

'Or died,' Jack said.

Lefebvre drank his whiskey. He refilled his glass and drank that, too.

'Seems to me you need the law on your side now. Don't see how you can get much further than this without some sort of official intervention. You have a man who might die and another who wants to die, and it appears that neither one of them is to blame for what's happened here.'

Lefebvre was right. The more Jack considered his position, the less he knew what to do. He didn't want to tell Nadeau – not because he didn't trust the man, but because Nadeau would tell him to back off. That was something he wasn't prepared to do, and yet he was smart enough to appreciate that he was out of his depth. Between a rock and a hard place, for sure.

'Can I do something to help?' Lefebvre asked.

'I don't know whether to try and find out if there were further murders, or look for who had access to those records and could've changed them. There must have been dozens of people over the years. I'm also thinking about people who left twenty years ago, maybe someone who wanted to cover their tracks, maybe someone who was in an official position here and knew your brother and—'

'There's a man here,' Lefebvre said. 'He's the supervisor of everything to do with hiring people, their housing, their work rotas. He deals with everything like that.'

'His name?'

'Edouard Rondel. You should speak to him. He's been here a long time. He knows everyone, has access to everything, and he might remember people from back then.'

'Rondel,' Jack said. 'Okay. I will try and see him tomorrow. It will either come to something or it won't.'

Lefebvre leaned forward and placed his hand over Jack's.

'You feel guilty for your brother,' he said. 'For what he's done.'

'I feel guilty for leaving him behind, Monsieur Lefebvre. I know it's futile, but I keep asking myself how things would have been different if I'd stayed.'

'Regret is worthless,' Lefebvre said. 'It changes nothing.'

'I know that,' Jack said, 'but we still spend our time wondering what would have happened if we'd made different decisions.'

'True,' Lefebvre said ruefully. 'So very true.'

48

Canada Iron's Director of Administration, Edouard Rondel, was a narrow-faced, intense man. He looked at Jack suspiciously before Jack had even said a word.

'Devereaux,' Rondel said. 'Like the one in jail.'

'My brother.'

'Is that so?'

'Yes, Monsieur Rondel. Calvis is my brother. And Henri Devereaux was my father.'

'I knew your father,' Rondel said. 'He was a hard worker and a good man. I thought the same of your brother.' He looked around the small office, toward the door, then through the window. The light was dull and flat from the condensation. A feeble electric heater did little to elevate the temperature beyond tolerable.

'But then, what we think of people and what we know of people are not the same thing are they, Monsieur Devereaux?'

Jack sensed animosity. Perhaps Rondel thought he was here to apportion blame for what had happened to Canada Iron.

'I wanted to ask for your help, Monsieur Rondel,' Jack said. 'I've been looking into everything that happened, talking to people, following up on some things that don't make sense.'

'You've been looking into everything that happened? In what capacity, Monsieur Devereaux?'

'As a brother, Monsieur Rondel. A concerned brother. That's all.'

'And you believe that we're somehow complicit in this most recent situation?'

'Not at all. Quite the contrary. As far as I'm concerned, Canada Iron has supported my family through some very difficult times. Other people, too. People who lost their children all those years ago.'

Rondel seemed unmoved by Jack's public relations effort.

'All I'm trying to do is understand how this thing happened, and I appreciate that you've been here a long time and might be able to help me.'

'With what, exactly?' Rondel asked.

'Well, I'm trying to find out if someone who used to work here might have had a grudge against Jean-Paul Lefebvre.'

'A grudge against the man? I don't see what this has to do with me or Canada Iron or anyone I might know, Monsieur Devereaux.'

'There's a possibility...' Jack hesitated. The conversation would go no further until he was more specific about what he knew, and yet he couldn't say anything that would create problems for Paul Girard.

'A possibility of what?' Rondel prompted.

'I want to speak to you as a person, Monsieur Rondel, not as an official of Canada Iron.'

Rondel didn't respond.

'Do you understand what I'm saying?' Jack asked.

'Continue.'

'A man may die. I think that man is innocent. I think my brother thought he was responsible for things that happened twenty and thirty years ago. If Lefebvre is not guilty, then whoever was responsible continues to evade justice for what he did.'

Rondel leaned forward and took a cigarette from a packet on

the desk. He lit it, leaned back, all of this without a word or a shift in his expression.

'I know something,' Jack said, 'but I cannot say how I know it.'

'Because someone here has given you information,' Rondel said matter-of-factly.

'I'm not saying it's someone here, Monsieur Rondel, but I do have some information that contradicts other information.'

'Monsieur Devereaux, I am neither stupid nor insensitive. If you want something from me, then you should ask me. If I'm able to answer your question, I'll answer it. However, you want assurance that I won't pursue an investigation if the information you have suggests a breach of company confidentiality.'

'Yes,' Jack said.

Rondel smoked. He said nothing for a few moments. He looked at Jack unerringly.

'Then we make a deal, Monsieur Devereaux. I give you my word that I won't pursue this matter, and you give me your word that you won't use what you find to damage the reputation of this office or this company.'

'I give you my word,' Jack said.

'You answer too quickly. Think about what I'm saying. I am the administrative supervisor here. The welfare of every worker and their families is my responsibility. I oversee their wages, their vacations, their housing, everything. I deal with the families when men are killed in the mines. I address matters of damages and compensation for injuries and accidents. This is a vast collaboration of people, Monsieur Devereaux, and every single person relies on every other person to do their job, to fulfil their duties, to consider not only their own good, but the good of everyone else whose livelihood and welfare is supported by Canada Iron. You're talking of murder, of a number of murders. I'm not unaware of these things. Even though these things happened many years ago, memories are long and forgiveness is short. If it's somehow considered that we were negligent or remiss…' Rondel waved his hand to indicate that no further explanation was required.

'I can't see how the company itself could be held responsible for what happened here,' Jack said.

'Perhaps you cannot see it, but you're not the one who will be required to make statements for the press or to deal with the police.'

Jack appreciated that Rondel was in the business of self-preservation, as all men were. He had a job. It was more than likely very well paid. He didn't want to lose it, but more than that, he didn't want to be held responsible for exposing Canada Iron to a barrage of press interest. This was a closed community. Jasperville had been created by the company, and thus anything that happened here was their concern, directly or indirectly. The world didn't know about Lisette Roy and Anne-Louise Fournier. They didn't know about eight girls brutalized and murdered in the far north-east of Canada, all of it under the nose of a vast industrial giant, a giant that had the wherewithal and influence to fly in as many company and Sûreté officials as it wanted in order to find out what had happened. The fact that they weren't responsible and couldn't have done anything to prevent it was not the point. The court of public opinion was influenced by the press, and the press was in the business of finding controversy and apportioning blame even when there was none.

'How long have you been here, Monsieur Rondel?'

'In Jasperville, or in this position?'

'Both.'

'I have worked for the company since 1976. I have been in this job since I took over from my predecessor in 1992.'

'And who was that?'

'His name was Gaines. Wilson Gaines. He was an American.'

'I remember that name,' Jack said. 'And he did this exact same job before you?'

'He did, Monsieur Devereaux.'

'And where is he now?'

'He left the company due to ill health, as far as I know. He was not a young man. I don't know what happened to him. Perhaps he's dead.'

'So anything that related to shift records, wage records, anything at all that was documented about Canada Iron employees for that period of time would have been dealt with by this man Gaines?'

'Yes, but not alone, Monsieur Devereaux. I have a staff of more than twenty people, and I'm sure Gaines had the same. Perhaps he had more. Company production during that period was far greater than it is now.'

'I will see if he's still alive, Monsieur Rondel. If he's dead, or if he can't help me with what I'm trying to find out, then I'll come back and speak to you again.'

'And you're now reporting this conversation to Sergeant Nadeau?'

'I have nothing to report, Monsieur Rondel.'

Rondel nodded approvingly and stood up.

'See the personnel clerk. I will call him and tell him to expect you. Perhaps we have some information on file about Monsieur Gaines. Maybe there's a record of where he went.'

'Thank you, Monsieur Rondel. I really appreciate your help.'

49

Though the personnel clerk was helpful, it was to no avail.

The employment records for Wilson Gaines had been closed after his retirement in March 1992. Gaines had been hired in July 1964. At the time he was thirty-three years old. He came in as an administrative assistant, and fulfilled the role of Housing Supervisor until 1973. He would have been the one to make arrangements for the Devereaux family when they'd arrived back in April 1969. After that, Gaines had fulfilled numerous bureaucratic functions, finally assuming the position of Director of Administration in 1978. He kept that job for fourteen years, and was then succeeded by Rondel. The file gave no specifics as to the nature of his medical retirement.

Wilson Gaines would now be seventy-nine years old. Jack's suspicion was that he was either dead or had returned to the United States.

The personnel clerk had made one suggestion that sounded promising. There was another file under the same name – that of Wilson's son, Robert. Jack vaguely remembered him from the boarding house. Robert Gaines had begun employment in May 1971, aged just eighteen. Robert's employment had also been terminated in early 1992.

'Perhaps he went with his father,' the clerk said. 'To look after him perhaps? There's no record of a wife for the older Gaines, either when he arrived in '64 or when he left.'

Looking through Robert Gaines's file, it appeared that he'd also worked in administration, though not such a senior position. He would now be fifty-seven years old, so the likelihood of his being still alive was greater. Jack made a mental note of the dates of birth for both of them.

Leaving the foundry offices, Jack knew he was chasing ghosts. Even if he did find Wilson Gaines, what was he going to ask him? Of all the thousands of people he must have dealt with in his years of service, was there even the slightest chance that he might remember Jean-Paul Lefebvre? It was a ludicrous expectation, and yet Jack felt compelled to pursue any and all possibilities. It really was a case of following this thread because there was nothing else to follow.

The most efficient way to make enquiries about both Wilson and Robert Gaines was through Nadeau and the Sûreté, but once again Jack was reluctant to let it be known that he was pursuing this. There was a telephone at the general store, but it was in a public area and he could be very easily overheard. His other option was the boarding house, and he knew he'd have to tell Carine something of what was going on.

It was a little before noon when he arrived. That she'd been the last person to speak with Calvis before he tried to kill himself had unsettled her greatly.

'I haven't slept,' she said. 'Not really. Three nights now. What he said to me just keeps going round and round in my mind. I've tried to work out what he meant, and I can only think of the very worst things.'

'I don't think he even knows what he's saying, Carine.'

'That's not the way it seemed to me,' she replied. 'As soon as he realized who I was, he was a different person.' She paused, looked away. When she looked back there were tears in her eyes. 'Like the boy I remembered.'

'And he said he was sorry for what happened to you.'

'Yes, but only because he thought I was Thérèse.'

'I don't think you should read a great deal into it,' Jack said. 'The fact he thought you were Thérèse tells you where he's at.'

'Maybe,' she said, 'but it's got me thinking about everything that happened back then, what happened to her, to Juliette, to your mother.'

'And that's why I'm here. I'm trying to track someone down who worked up at Canada Iron during that time. He got sick. I don't know the details, but he left back in 1992. I don't know what will come of it, but I need to find him.'

'Can't Sergeant Nadeau help you?'

'Maybe he could, but I don't want the police involved in this. He'll just tell me to back off.'

'What do you need?'

'Just a telephone. A computer would be good, but I don't think you get internet out here, do you?'

'Not a prayer. You can use the phone here, or there's another one in the back office.'

'Is the line up?'

'Seems to be,' Carine said. 'But you never know.'

'Give me the number for the desk here. I'm gonna call someone who'll need to call me back.'

Carine gave him the boarding house number, and then showed him to the office. He remembered it as a storage room where Marguerite kept the towels and linen. Jack commented on how much time they'd both spent making up beds back then. Carine just looked at him and shook her head.

'I'm not gonna do this with you, Jack,' she said. 'Use the phone, sure, but whatever's going on here and whatever you're trying to do doesn't change what happened between us. All those years of being angry and hurt doesn't go away in a weekend.'

'I'm sorry,' he said.

'Don't be sorry,' Carine replied. 'There's no point. The time we spent together is the history of two very different people.'

Carine closed the door behind her.

Jack sat for a few moments. His perception had been wrong. What he'd done would perhaps never be forgiven, and he had to come to terms with that.

Jack picked up the receiver and dialled Ludo's Montréal office extension. It rang out. He called the main desk and asked if Ludo was in.

'Not today. Off tomorrow, too. Back on Wednesday.'

Jack hung up and then dialled the home number. Florence answered.

'Hey, Florence. It's Jack. I'm after Ludo.'

'He's not here. Should be back any moment. He was just dropping the girls off at skating. He's been trying to get hold of you, actually. They've been asking after you at the office. I guess they want to know when you're coming back.'

'They've only got my cell number, and there's no signal out here.'

'Ludo said you were up in the north-east sorting something out for your brother.'

Jack heard the bemused smile in her voice.

'I didn't even know you had a brother.'

'Different story for a different day,' Jack said. 'I'm still dealing with some things out here. I just called work, in fact.'

'Hang on,' Florence said. 'He's just got back.'

Jack waited a few moments, and then heard the sound of footsteps.

'Jack,' Ludo said.

'Hey, Ludo. How goes it?'

'Good enough. How about you?'

'Still wrestling with a few things, you know?'

'You gonna be out there a while longer?'

'I don't know exactly,' Jack said. 'I know I got a week's grace. However much longer will have to be vacation time.'

'Sure, sure. You need me to tell them anything?'

'Just say that I'm taking another week, and if it runs longer than that, I'll be in touch.'

'No problem.'

'But that's not why I called,' Jack said. 'I need your help with something.'

'Sure thing. What do you need?'

'I need to find someone. You got a pen and paper?'

'Hang on,' Ludo said. 'Okay, shoot.'

'Gaines,' Jack said. 'G-A-I-N-E-S. First name Wilson. Born 7 January 1931. Worked for Canada Iron from 1964, and then retired on medical grounds in 1992. He's American, but might have stayed in Canada. There's also another Gaines. Robert. Date of birth is 15 March 1953. Father and son.'

'But this Wilson Gaines is the important one?'

'Yes.'

'Any idea where he was originally from?'

'I don't, no,' Jack said.

'Okay, I'll see what I can do.'

'And if you find out that he's dead, then I need to track down the son.'

'I'll get on it now,' Ludo said. 'I'm guessing you don't have internet up there.'

'Lucky to have a phone line.'

'Give me a number to call you back on.'

Jack did so.

'Shouldn't take long,' Ludo said. 'If needed, I can get into the work system from home and get access to no end of databases.'

'I'm not asking you to break the law, Ludo,' Jack said. 'This is on me, not you.'

Ludo laughed. 'Hey, I'm gonna do what I do, man. Give me half an hour or so, and I'll come back to you.'

'I really appreciate it,' Jack said, and hung up.

He left the office and went back to reception.

'Someone's gonna call me back,' he told Carine. 'Maybe half an hour or so. Is it okay if I wait?'

'Sure,' Carine said. 'You want some winter coffee?'

'That would be great,' he said.

Jack followed her to the back kitchen. He took a seat at the wide table that centred the room. It was where Carine and her mother had prepared food for the guests. Jack had sat there more times than he remembered – doing homework, talking to Philippe Bergeron, watching Carine and hoping that she didn't realize she was being watched.

'No wife,' Carine said as she put a cup in front of him. 'No kids either.' Carine fetched down a bottle of rye, another of maple syrup. 'So what the hell have you been doing with your life?'

'Working, sleeping, eating, going to hockey games. Existing, basically.'

Jack added an inch of rye and a good tablespoon of syrup to his coffee.

Carine sat down. 'You just disconnected from everything and went into hiding?'

'As good as,' he said.

'If you ask me, it's pretty fucking sad.'

'Remind me not to ask you then.'

'I guess you weren't the man I thought you were.'

The statement went through him like a knife. He knew she was right. 'I deserve that,' he said.

'It's not whether you deserve it or not,' Carine said. 'You know, after a while it wasn't even that you didn't come back, it was that you never made an effort to tell me that you weren't coming back. That's why I told my father to write to you. It was the only way I could think of to hurt you in return.'

Jack sighed and shook his head. 'What purpose does it serve for us to do this?' he asked. 'I mean, really. This is more than two decades ago. We were teenagers. We said things, we did things, we made promises—'

'You were the only one of us who broke a promise, Jack.'

Jack felt awkward and small. He was a child again, waiting in this very kitchen as long as possible so he didn't have to go home and deal with his crazy, unpredictable father.

'That was unnecessary,' Carine said.

'But not incorrect,' Jack replied.

'Perhaps, but as you said, it serves no purpose.'

They sat in silence for a little while, and for the first time it didn't feel so stilted and awkward. Jack knew what she thought, and he'd accepted it. That was the way it was, and he doubted it would ever change.

The phone rang. Jack was snapped out of his reverie. Carine, still standing, went to reception to answer it. Jack followed her.

'Your call,' Carine said, and Jack took the receiver.

'Easy enough,' Ludo said. 'Your Wilson Gaines is in a residential facility in Labrador City. It's one of those places people go when they're dying. I couldn't find out what's wrong with him, but he's been there for about a year. Prior to that he was co-habiting at an address with Robert Gaines. As far as I can tell, that address is still rented under the same name.'

'What are the addresses?'

Jack asked Carine for a pen and paper. He wrote them down.

'You gonna go out there?' Ludo asked.

'I am, yes.'

'You need any help, Jack? You want me to come out there?'

'No, it's okay,' Jack said.

'Well, you know where I am if you need to cause some trouble for someone, right?'

'You'll be the first one I call, Ludo.'

'Take care,' Ludo said, and hung up.

Jack looked at the address of the residential home. Labrador City was somewhere around a hundred and fifty miles by road. If he had the right vehicle, he could be there in a couple of hours.

'Do you have a truck?' he asked Carine.

'How did I know you were gonna ask me that?' she said.

50

By the time Jack reached the St Peregrine Nursing Home in Labrador City, it was close to four o'clock. Once beyond the Jasperville limits and closer to the highway, the roads were passable. Carine's GMC Yukon, though a good ten or twelve years old, had no great difficulty with the frozen mud ruts and ice ridges that would have made the journey impossible for a smaller vehicle.

Though Carine had been all too willing to loan him the car, he knew that her willingness was born out of a wish to better understand what had happened when they were children, and, above all, perhaps find some closure regarding the death of her sister. She owed Jack nothing, and yet he felt a tremendous sense of debt to her. He hoped the truth – if he found it – would go some way toward making amends.

Jack pulled up outside the nursing home and took the brightly lit walkway to the front of the building. It was an expansive facility, and from what he could see there were numerous wings and additional buildings that went in both directions.

He kicked the snow and mud off his boots in the vestibule. The automatic doors opened. He was drowned in dry, warm air.

The receptionist smiled in a practised and disconnected manner. 'How may I help you, sir?'

'I came to see someone,' Jack said.

The woman glanced at her watch. 'Visiting hours finish at five, sir.'

'Yes, I know. I hit some traffic. However, since I made it all the way here, I didn't want to turn around and go back without at least checking in on him, you know?'

'And who is it that you're visiting today, sir?'

'Gaines,' Jack said. 'Wilson Gaines.' He paused for a second. 'Uncle Wilson.'

The receptionist went to her computer. 'And your name, sir?'

'Devereaux. Jack Devereaux.'

The overlong nails rattled away on the keyboard. She frowned, looked up. 'I don't have you on our system as a registered visitor, sir.'

'First time,' Jack said. 'I've been working abroad. I'm back now so I'll be visiting as regularly as I can.'

The woman smiled. 'Okay. That won't be a problem. I'll just need you to fill out the visitor registration form, provide some ID, and then we can get you a visitor card.'

'Will it take long?'

'Fill out the form,' she said. 'You have your driver's licence?'

'Yes,' Jack said, and took out his wallet.

The woman handed him a slip of paper.

'Name, address, telephone number, relationship to the client ... then sign here ... and initial here.'

Jack did as he was asked.

'Okay, so you go out of here, turn right. Follow the walkway until you see a sign that says Palliative Units. Take the first door on the right. There's another reception area there.' The woman glanced at something on her desk. 'Lacey is on the desk. Tell her Ruth sent you, and that you're here to see Mr Gaines. She'll direct you from there. When your visit is finished, come back here and I'll have your card for you.'

'That's really kind of you, Ruth,' Jack said.

'Not at all,' she said. She returned Jack's licence. 'You go on and have a nice visit now.'

Jack followed the directions he'd been given. Lacey was just as helpful as Ruth. She told him that Wilson Gaines was in Suite 7, and that he would find an orderly at the end of the corridor who would show him precisely where to go.

Jack was surprised that no effort had been made to determine whether or not he was in fact the nephew of Wilson Gaines. These people took it on trust.

The orderly asked why Jack had no visitor card.

'First time,' Jack said. 'I'm later than I intended. Traffic was bad. Ruth sent me down to Lacey. Lacey told me to speak to you.'

The orderly nodded. 'Bear with me,' he said. From his belt he took a walkie-talkie. He buzzed reception, pressed his fingers against the earpiece.

'Ruth. Marcus here. Got a visitor for 7.'

He listened, nodded. 'Okay.'

Marcus smiled. 'Suite 7 is fourth on the left.'

'Thank you, Marcus,' Jack said, and he headed down the corridor.

Wilson Gaines was not going to live much longer. Emaciated and pallid, his skin like creased tissue paper, he was nevertheless awake and sitting up in bed. As the door opened, he turned. He squinted as if trying to determine who was there. A radio played light classical music from the corner of the room.

'Robert?' he asked. 'Is that you, Robert?'

Jack neared the bed.

'Mr Gaines,' Jack said.

'Who are you?' Gaines asked.

343

'I'm from Jasperville,' Jack said.

Jack didn't think it would've been possible for Gaines to lose any more colour from his face, but he did. Jack felt the very air between himself and this frail old man become cooler.

'Jasperville,' Gaines said. It left his lips as a forced whisper, as if the word itself tasted bad.

'I wanted to ask you about a man called Jean-Paul Lefebvre,' Jack said. He took a chair from against the wall and brought it closer to the bed.

Gaines was still squinting at him, as if he could barely make out who it was. It was then that Jack realized the man was close to blind.

'Who are you?' Gaines repeated. 'And what are you doing here?'

Jack sensed panic in the man's voice. He knew to remain calm, that pressuring the man to speak would only generate an instinctive defensiveness. He'd been caught off-guard. Questions about Jasperville, perhaps Lefebvre, were unsettling for him.

'I'm here to help,' Jack said calmly.

'Help? Help with what?'

'The truth, Mr Gaines.'

'The truth? The truth about what?'

'Do you remember your time in Jasperville, Mr Gaines? Do you remember a man called Jean-Paul Lefebvre?'

'I don't remember anything!' Gaines snapped. 'I'm sick. I'm dying. Leave me alone!'

Gaines reached for the alarm cord that hung by his bed, but Jack was quicker. He leaned up and held it out of reach.

Gaines continued to grope for it, but his hand closed on nothing.

Jack knew he was onto something. Gaines had not denied knowing the name, and his agitated response was of someone who had something to conceal.

'Jean-Paul Lefebvre is dying, too,' Jack said. 'He had a terrible accident. It's very likely that he won't live.'

Gaines didn't say a thing. He sat there looking at Jack. Though Jack appreciated that Gaines could perhaps see only a vague outline, the feeling was one of being fixed by a searching beam of light.

Jack's skin crawled. It was the strangest sensation.

'Then he got what he deserved,' Gaines said. 'And he will burn in Hell for what he did.'

'What did he do, Mr Gaines? What did Lefebvre do?'

Gaines remained motionless for a few seconds, and then it was as if every ounce of life remaining in that frail body was emptied out. He pressed his hands to his face and he started to sob. His chest heaved. A sound of anguish escaped from his throat that was both terrifying and heartrending.

Jack leaned forward. 'Did he hurt those girls, Mr Gaines? Did he hurt those girls in Jasperville?'

Gaines gasped for air. He struggled to speak. His body shook.

'He hurt my boy,' he said. 'He hurt my little boy. He poisoned him and made him bad. Oh God, I can't bear to even think about what they did. But it was Lefebvre. He was the one who made him do it. He tricked him. He corrupted him. He was such a good boy. A gentle boy, a kind boy, and he was so frightened. It was a mistake. It was an accident. He loved her. He never meant to hurt her. It was a terrible, terrible mistake ...'

'Loved who, Mr Gaines? Who did he love?'

Gaines breathed heavily, desperately trying to calm the raging torrent of emotion he was experiencing.

'Who did your boy love, Mr Gaines? Who was it that got hurt?'

'The one from the boarding house,' Gaines said. 'Such a beautiful girl. Such a beautiful, beautiful girl. And he loved her so, and then ...'

Gaines broke down again.

Jack realized his breath had stopped dead in his chest even as Gaines said that name. Lisette Roy. The first girl. The first of eight. February 1972. And with this connection, Jack began to piece it together. He could be wrong, of course, and if he was wrong then he wouldn't even know how to make sense of it, but in that moment he saw how Lefebvre could have been guilty of so very much of this, even though there was evidence that he was innocent.

Jack closed his eyes. Some things began to fall into place; other things began to unravel. 'Your boy, Robert,' he said. 'Your boy was good, wasn't he?'

'Such a good boy,' Gaines said. 'Until that happened, he was so kind and quiet and gentle.'

'And he worked with you, didn't he? He worked with you at the company, didn't he, Mr Gaines?'

'He worked with me, yes. And he left to care for me. He's cared for me all this time. Such a kind boy, such a gentle boy.'

'What did he do at Canada Iron, Mr Gaines?' Jack asked.

'What? What do you mean?'

'His job. What was Robert's job?'

Gaines frowned. 'He was the shift administrator. He was responsible for the shift rotas at Canada Iron.'

51

Jack didn't go back through reception, nor did he collect his visitor pass. He had no intention of visiting Wilson Gaines again. If the man lived to see this house of cards fall down, then the police could deal with him. The only person Jack wanted to see was the son.

It was a jigsaw puzzle with missing pieces. There were elements of this that fitted together but still he couldn't see the entire picture. He didn't believe for a moment that Robert Gaines was the person his father professed him to be. The same could be said for his own opinion of Lefebvre. The two of them had been involved. Which one had been the driving force behind this, he didn't know. Nor did he have any understanding of how it had all started, but Gaines spoke of Lisette Roy, how there had been an accident, a terrible mistake. Lefebvre couldn't give him any answers, and might never be able to, but Robert Gaines was right there in Labrador City.

Back in the car, Jack checked his phone. The signal was good. He called Ludo. Ludo picked up immediately.

'I need something else,' Jack said. 'Can you do a police records check from your computer at home, or do you need to be in the office?'

'I can do it from here,' Ludo said.

'Check this Robert Gaines for me, would you?'

'Now?'

'If you can, yes.'

'Sure. You wanna stay on the line?'

'Yes.'

It was a routine activity in their line of work. They couldn't access information regarding ongoing criminal prosecutions, but past history – already available in the public domain – was collated and stored for their own investigatory procedure. When it came to insurance claims, the first thing verified was whether or not the person had prior claims, a history of arrests, criminal charges or custodial sentences. Some people were bright enough to attempt fraud, and yet unaware that the vast majority of their past could be accessed in a matter of minutes.

'He's got a record,' Ludo said. 'He's been pretty busy over the last twenty years.'

'Attempted rape. Charges were dropped. Four assaults. Harassment. Seven of those. Three of them were for the same person. Court order issued back in September 2004. It goes on. He did the best part of a year in Labrador Correctional for possession with intent to sell. Looks like he's been dragged in and questioned at least half a dozen times, but it doesn't say what for. No charges filed for any of them.' Ludo paused. 'What's your interest in this guy, Jack?'

'I think he was involved in a series of killings back when I lived in Jasperville.'

'Involved? How do you mean, involved?'

'Him and another guy. I don't know. I'm still trying to make sense of this.'

'Well, it's a hell of a thing to suspect someone of, Jack. Is this to do with your brother?'

'Yes,' Jack replied. 'The guy my brother attacked is the other one who was involved.'

Ludo was silent at the other end of the line.

'I gotta go,' Jack said. 'Thanks, Ludo. Again.'

'Hey, hang on a minute. Are you going to the cops about this, or are you gonna go see this guy yourself?'

'Probably best you don't know what I'm doing, Ludo, nor what I'm going to do.'

'Jack, seriously—'

'Ludo, I gotta go. I'll call you.'

Jack hung up. Within ten seconds the phone rang. Ludo was calling back. Jack didn't take it.

Jack started the car and headed toward Robert Gaines' house. He needed to see the man. He needed to look him in the eye and hear him speak. He had to steer him in the direction of those years in Jasperville and see what response it provoked.

By the time he reached the address it was gone six o'clock. He parked up a good twenty yards from the house. He lit a cigarette, and then cracked the window open. Biting cold snatched every ounce of warmth from within the car. He closed the window and turned the heater to its maximum output.

It was a nondescript suburban street. The houses were set back from the pavement by featureless yards. Snow was banked here and there, much of it dirty. Where tyre tracks had made impressions, those impressions were deep and hard.

Lights burned on both floors of the Gaines house. He knew nothing of Robert Gaines, but assumed – based on his yellow sheet – that he was neither married nor lived with anyone.

At quarter to seven, Jack got out of the car and crossed the street. He stood on the opposite side and just watched the house for a few minutes. At one point, he thought he saw movement behind a curtain on the upper floor, but it so easily could have been his imagination.

Jack couldn't think of any plausible means of getting into Gaines' house. If that was the reality, then so be it. He would have to get into the house regardless, and deal with the consequences as they arose.

From the collar of his overcoat, he unzipped the hood and pulled it over his head. He crossed to the facing pavement and slipped down the side of the house. At the end of the path was a low wire fence. Jack stepped over it and was in Gaines' yard. Looking up, he saw that none of the lights were on in the rear of the house. His assumption changed. Perhaps the house was empty.

For someone unfamiliar with the numerous ways in which door and window locks could be sprung, it would perhaps have been challenging. Jack's comprehensive experience with seemingly solid barriers – usually for escaping a building rather than illegally entering it – meant that it didn't take long for him to find the most accessible means of getting inside.

The back door was a standard design with two heavy frosted glass panels. With the tip of a key, Jack began the process of working the beading loose. Once started, it came away easily and silently. With the beading gone, the outer pane was held in place by a rubberized sealant. Again, with no great difficulty, the sealant came away with a little work. With one hand against the upper part of the pane to prevent it from falling out, Jack eased a coin under the edge of the pane and twisted it slowly. The frosted glass was heavy, but the weight of it was more help than hindrance once it came away at the lower edge. Jack lifted the pane out and leaned it against the wall beside the door.

Jack took stock of what he was doing. He'd done nothing but damage the door, but once he got the second pane out and entered the property, then it would be a far more serious offence.

The question of pursuing some other approach to this didn't occupy Jack's mind for long. He wanted to get inside, to confront Gaines if he was there, to find out more about what had happened to Lisette Roy back in 1972. There was no doubt that Gaines had been involved, and Jack had to get some answers.

The second pane of glass was harder work. Secured to the inner beading, it took twice as much time as the first. Nevertheless, sheer determination on Jack's part won through. Ensuring he didn't apply too much pressure, Jack eased the upper part of the pane forward, the lower part still being retained by sealant, until he got his fingers through the narrow gaps on each side. He was then able to lift the pane free and bring it back through the aperture.

From within the house, there had been no sound, no movement, no lights coming on.

Jack went in head-first. He stood there in the darkness of the kitchen. His breathing slowed down, as did his heart rate, and after a minute or two he felt remarkably calm. He'd made the decision and followed through. There was no going back now, and thus there was no point wasting energy on what else he could've done, or what might happen as a result.

Jack stood in the front hallway. Aside from the lights, there was nothing to suggest that Gaines was home. Conscious that he'd be visible as a silhouette through the curtained windows, Jack stayed low as he moved from room to room. There was nothing out of the ordinary as far as Jack could see, but what had he expected? Shelves with preserved body parts, a large leatherbound volume detailing the comings and goings of some present-day Jack the Ripper? It was ludicrous to think that a man would keep mementoes of criminal activities in plain view.

Upstairs, it was much the same. It was obvious which bedroom belonged to Robert and which to his father. The father's room had not been used for some considerable time. In a small ensuite bathroom, runnels of soap had dried hard on the edge of the ceramic sink. The floor of the bath had a thin layer of dust.

Robert's room was different. It was untidy, and yet the untidiness was not the primary feature. The bed was unmade, and the sheets had not been washed for a long time. There was a collection of pill bottles on the bedside table, and on the lower shelf a stack of pornographic magazines. Beneath the bed was yet another two or three dozen magazines, and they all possessed the same sado-masochistic theme: women bound, women gagged, women striking provocative poses who yet appeared genuinely fearful.

At the foot of the bed and beneath the window were a TV and a DVD player. A collection of unboxed DVDs bore titles like *Torture Girls* and *Carnival of Pain*.

Jack surveyed the room. Unwashed plates and cups, dirty clothes, empty wine bottles. It was a degraded and filthy hovel. Back at the bedside table, Jack checked the pills. Antidepressants, an anti-psychotic, sleeping tablets and Sildenafil. The last was the chemical name for Viagra, but this was an unbranded product. Jack couldn't imagine that someone would come here voluntarily to have sex with a man like Gaines, but then Gaines was perhaps the kind of man who didn't look for agreement from his sexual partners.

Jack knew he was jumping to conclusions. Nothing in the room was illegal, save perhaps a black-market medication. Whatever might be on the DVDs could also be of interest to the police, but the police were far too busy to investigate and charge voyeurs. They were after producers and distributors, and only then if it violated the law.

Jack checked for an attic. If there was one, then its access was not immediately visible.

Back downstairs, Jack opened a door in the side of the stairwell and saw a short flight of wooden steps running down to the basement. A pull cord at the head of the stairs switched the light on. He closed the door behind him and went down, now in no doubt that he was alone in the house.

It was only after a couple of minutes rooting around in boxes of old shoes and looking behind rusted paint cans that Jack was aware of something about the basement that didn't make sense. This was a standard two-storey design, the kind of house found right across the length and breadth of Canada, and yet the dimensions barely spanned half the footprint of the building above. Jack picked up a short length of timber and used it to check the walls. Three of them gave back nothing, but the fourth returned the hollow sound of a cavity. Half the wall was taken up by a floor-to-ceiling shelving unit. Stacked with tools, old telephone directories, metal tins full of nails and screws, it took some effort to inch it away from the wall. Once Jack had it moving, it became easier, and before he even created a gap of twelve inches, he could see a low hatch. Knowing that there was something back there gave Jack even greater incentive, and within moments he'd managed to pull the unit away from the wall and get behind it.

The room that he crawled into was on the same electrical circuit. Gaines, or someone in Gaines' employ, had constructed a stud and drywall partition with an entranceway low enough to be hidden by the shelving unit.

But how the room had been created was not important. The reason for its creation was the only matter of interest to Jack. The right-hand wall was – once again – a floor-to-ceiling shelf unit, but the contents of the shelves was uniform from top to bottom. Photo albums, the same brand, all the same size, and each of them with a label on the spine that bore a *From* and *To* date. Jack took one down and opened it. Page after page of photographs of young women on train platforms, on street benches, in stores, in shopping malls, even crowds of girls coming out of school gates. Jack took another album. It was the same thing, but this time some of the women were looking at the camera with expressions of surprise, annoyance, even anxiety. In one album, a single silver hoop earring was taped beneath a photo of a brunette in her late teens or early twenties. Had it belonged to her? Had Gaines stolen it, or had she perhaps dropped it and he had retrieved it?

On a narrow table against the opposite wall was a laptop. It was switched off. Jack could only imagine what might be retrieved from its hard drive and search history.

Turning back toward the hatch, Jack saw a metal box beneath yet another pile of magazines. He kicked it sideways with the toe of his boot and the magazines spilled sideways across the floor. The box was locked, but the lock was of no significant complexity or strength. Holding it by one corner, Jack struck the raised keyhole hard against the concrete floor until the metal buckled. From the shelves of tools on the other side of the hatch he fetched a screwdriver and pried the box open.

What he found inside suggested only one thing to Jack. There were earrings, a charm bracelet, items of underwear, a driver's licence in the name of *Amanda Webb*, a key chain from Labrador West Campus, three false fingernails, a St. Patrick's Middle School lanyard, a collection of bus tickets, an elasticated hairband with strands of hair still tangled in it, a number of keys, one of which had a tag which read *Lucy*. Jack sat back on his haunches. This was Gaines. This was who he was and what he did, and it explained why everything had stopped in Jasperville after the death of Madeleine Desjardins. Those eight girls died across a span of eighteen years. If there were no others, then whatever motivation this man had to kill surfaced every two years, sometimes even three or four. Madeleine was dead in May of 1990. Gaines left with his father in 1992. If he was the killer, then he was in Labrador City by the time he killed again.

Jack exited the room with the box. He left the shelving

precisely where it was. He went back upstairs and put the box on Robert Gaines' bed. From the bathroom he took three towels, wet them beneath the tap, and then wrung them out. On his way back down to the basement he took the rug from the hallway.

From the shelf unit he took a power drill with a long electrical cord. He used his car key to fray the fabric casing, running it back and forth until the wires were exposed. He laid the cable along the floor, its exposed wiring right against the rug. Once he'd plugged in the drill, he used his lighter to ignite the frayed edge. It caught quickly and started to smoulder. Once it was burning, Jack laid one of the damp towels over it, allowing a small gap for oxygen to feed the fire. He laid the other two towels over the rug and waited until thick smoke started to fill the room. The rug would burn, but the towels would prevent a too-rapid escalation of the fire. What he would get was a great deal of smoke.

Jack backed out of the hatch. He went up the basement steps, and left the door open behind him. He opened the rear kitchen door, and within a handful of minutes had replaced the glass panes and the beading. Smoke had filled the basement, the stairwell, and was already finding its way along the hallway and up towards the second floor. Jack opened one of the windows in the kitchen, another in the downstairs toilet. By the time he'd made his way back along the side of the house, walked a good thirty yards, crossed the street and returned to his car, he could see a ghostly pall of smoke shrouding the entire lower floor of the building. He couldn't call it in himself. His number would be recorded, and a follow-up would place him at the scene. He had to pray that someone would see it.

Jack didn't have to pray long. A dog walker saw what was going on and raised the alarm. It was less than minutes before

355

neighbours were gathering on the sidewalk and the sound of sirens could be heard growing ever nearer.

Jack waited until firefighters began playing water over the smouldering building before he started his truck and pulled away.

52

Jack had been back for four days before he heard word of Robert Gaines.

On the night of the fire he'd left Labrador City and driven straight back to Jasperville. He'd returned Carine's truck to the rear parking lot of the boarding house and walked home. After that he kept himself to himself as best he could. He visited Calvis in the med centre, and again when Calvis was transferred back to the police station. He and Nadeau shared little but pleasantries. Calvis, though out of any physical danger, still behaved as though Jack was a stranger to him.

A little after eleven on Friday morning, Bastien Nadeau came to the Devereaux house.

Jack welcomed him in, asked if he wanted coffee. There was fresh-brewed on the stove.

'Please, yes,' Nadeau said.

They sat at the table. Nadeau seemed intense.

'What is it?' Jack asked.

'A man has been arrested,' Nadeau began. 'In Labrador City.'

Jack said nothing.

'There was a fire in his home. It wasn't serious. Nevertheless, the officers attending the scene entered the premises to ensure that it was safe and they found evidence that crimes had been committed. The police were called, the owner of the property was arrested and remains in custody.'

Nadeau looked at Jack unerringly.

'And you're telling me this because?' Jack asked.

'There's a possibility, Monsieur Devereaux, that this man was responsible for the killings that took place here all those years ago.'

Jack was no actor, but his feigning of shock seemed sufficient to convince Nadeau.

'I know what this means to you,' Nadeau said. 'That your brother attacked an innocent man, but it's not that straight-forward. The man being held is saying that Lefebvre was responsible for these killings.'

Jack frowned. 'What? I don't understand...'

'There's a great deal that doesn't make sense at this time, but there's something more important that I have to tell you.'

Nadeau leaned forward. 'Your brother is being moved to Québec City. Lefebvre is also being transferred to a hospital there. This whole situation has now become something far beyond the responsibility of myself and the Jasperville Sûreté office.'

'This man,' Jack said. 'The one they have arrested. He's someone from here?'

'Not for a long time, Monsieur Devereaux. He moved out to Labrador City in 1992.'

'His name?'

'Robert Gaines. He worked for Canada Iron, as did his father.'

'And he claims that Lefebvre was guilty of the killings in Jasperville?'

'Like I said, it's not that simple. There are other matters being investigated. It will go to the Superior Court. It's no longer a provincial matter. I can't tell you what I don't know.'

'When is Calvis being moved?' Jack asked. 'And where's he being moved to?'

'As far as I understand, he will be remanded to Quebec

Detention Centre on Monday. There are people on the way to take Lefebvre, too.'

'All of a sudden you get the help you need,' Jack said.

'All of a sudden it's a case of national interest.'

Jack leaned back and shook his head. 'I don't know what to say.'

Nadeau looked at Jack for an inordinately long time, and then he said, 'If you want my advice, Monsieur Devereaux, it would be better if you said nothing at all.'

Late that evening, a medical team flew into Wabush Airport from the *Centre hospitalier universitaire de Québec*. Accompanied by two officers from the *Service de police de la Ville*, they drove to Jasperville and made the necessary preparations for Jean-Paul Lefebvre to be taken back to Québec City on Saturday afternoon. Jack was in the street when a convoy of three SUVs made its way along the main drag and headed back toward Labrador City. They would take the very same route he'd taken just days before.

Once they'd left, Jack went to the boarding house.

He told Carine that Calvis would be moved on Monday, and that he would be leaving with him.

'Of course,' she said.

'From what I understand, it's far more than what happened here,' Jack replied. 'Apparently, there were killings in Labrador City and Wabush.'

'How did they find this guy?'

'There was a fire at his home last Monday. There wasn't a great deal of damage, and when they got inside they found evidence relating to a girl who had been murdered out there a few years ago.' Jack paused. 'I don't know too much, to be honest.'

'There was a fire at this guy's home,' Carine said. 'In Labrador

City. Last Monday. And that would be the same Monday you borrowed my truck.'

Jack didn't reply.

'What was his name?' Carine asked.

'Gaines.'

She frowned. 'There was a man called Gaines who used to come and do work for my father at the boarding house,' she said.

'That was Robert. His father was also here. Wilson Gaines. He was a senior administrative official at Canada Iron.'

'And the son worked for Canada Iron, too?'

'He did, yes. Some administrative function. There was some connection between Robert and the guy that Calvis attacked, but I don't know what.'

'And Robert Gaines is the man who murdered my sister?'

'It looks that way, yes. I've been trying to get updates, seeing if I could get some information from Nadeau, but most of it's supposition right now.'

'So this is it,' Carine said matter-of-factly. 'You're leaving. Again.'

'Not the same scenario, Carine. I need to go with Calvis. I need to find out exactly what happened. And you need to know, too.'

'I guess I'll find out from the newspapers.'

'You want to find out what happened, don't you? I mean, the truth of what really happened to Thérèse.'

'My sister has been dead for over twenty years, Jacques. I stayed here for another twelve, left, got married, had a kid. I had a life, Jacques. A complete life for a long time. It hasn't been the same for me.' She stepped out from behind the desk. 'Yes, of course I want to find out what happened. I'd like to understand why, sure. But if this guy killed all those girls, and then he went on and killed a whole lot more, then he's a psychopath. There won't be a reason why, will there? At least no reason that fits into any context ordinary people can comprehend. People like that are driven by impulses we don't understand. The problems they're solving exist only in their own minds.'

'You're absolutely right,' Jack said. 'It's not something you can rationalize.'

'So go,' Carine said. She smiled. 'Who knows, eh? We might collide one of these days in a situation that doesn't involve dead girls and crazy people.'

53

Calvis Devereaux was remanded into custody at the Quebec Correctional Centre late on Monday, 1st November. He was charged with attempted murder of Jean-Paul Lefebvre. He was permitted no visitors, and was scheduled for a full psychiatric evaluation.

On Friday, 5th November, shortly after 8.00 p.m., Jean-Paul Lefebvre died of his injuries. The University Hospital Critical Care Unit had isolated a brain aneurysm within hours of Lefebvre's admission, yet despite their best efforts they couldn't prevent it from rupturing.

By 11.00 p.m., the charge against Calvis became first-degree murder.

Jack didn't find out until late afternoon on Sunday the 7th.

The case against Robert Gaines began to build momentum once it was established beyond all doubt that he was responsible for the death of a Labrador City girl called Melanie Perrin.

Melanie's bracelet was one of the items discovered in Gaines' house. Unsolved for four years, her death had made province-wide headlines, and though countless hours had been devoted to its resolution, it had remained an open investigation.

Just sixteen, Melanie had last been seen leaving school. The walk home was no more than twenty-five minutes, a route she'd repeatedly take when the weather was sufficiently forgiving. Her body was found that same evening in a copse of trees about three-quarters of a mile from her home. She'd been raped, strangled, and then an attempt had been made to burn the body. The perpetrator had used inadequate accelerant, and appeared to have fled before the fire took hold. Whatever physical evidence might have been recovered from the body was lost.

Gaines was charged with her first-degree murder on 23rd November.

It was then that the Office of the Prosecutor made a proposal to Gaines that appeared favourable to Gaines' defence. The Canadian Criminal Code possessed something known as the faint hope clause. Murder carried a twenty-five-year term, but the clause allowed for a convicted murderer to apply for parole after serving only fifteen years. Gaines' interrogation officer, a veteran detective by the name of Yvan Fauth, told Gaines that he had to cooperate in every aspect of the investigation. If he told them everything – precise details of every single abduction, sexual molestation, rape, assault, every instance of stalking and harassment – then his cooperation would hold sway with the court. If he then received concurrent sentences for the crimes he'd committed, he would fall within the remit of the faint hope clause. It was entirely misleading. For the Perrin murder conviction, Gaines would more than likely die in prison. He was fifty-seven years of age. The influence of public opinion alone would see him serve the full twenty-five. But Fauth knew there were other murders, and he was committed to closing as many open cases as possible.

Gaines, smart enough to get away with murder for the better part of four decades, yet insufficiently bright to see the trap that had been sprung, refused his right to public defence representation at interrogation. Why he made that decision was something that he didn't explain, and no one could ever fathom. It seemed that once he'd decided to confess, he wished to make his confession to Fauth. Over the weeks that they'd been together, Fauth had become his counsellor, his confidante, his psychoanalyst and his priest. Perhaps he believed that Fauth was capable of forgiving him, and thus there was the possibility he would walk free once he'd told the truth.

At 9.30 a.m. on Friday, 26 November 2010, Robert Gaines began talking. He didn't stop for five days. For close to eight hours a day, Gaines backtracked to Jasperville and spoke of the first girl he ever killed.

'I didn't kill her alone,' he told Fauth. 'Lefebvre. He killed her. He was guilty of that poor girl's death.'

'How so, Robert? What happened?'

Gaines spoke of his devotion to this Lisette Roy, a seventeen-year-old who worked in a boarding house that was managed by her parents. At the time, she was romantically involved with Jean-Paul Lefebvre. Lefebvre was nineteen, just as he was. They both worked for Canada Iron.

'But he was an ignorant brute,' Gaines explained. 'He wanted her for sex. He just wanted to do those things to her. He didn't love her. Not at all. He just wanted to fuck her.'

Driven perhaps by jealousy and an obsession for a girl who seemed unaware of his existence, Gaines had followed her one afternoon when she went to see Lefebvre at his house. Lefebvre lived with his brother, Guy, but the brother was away. The girl had gone into the house. Gaines had waited for fifteen minutes, and then entered the house through the unlocked back door.

Gaines had found Lefebvre wrestling with the girl. The girl was resisting him, but Lefebvre was overpowering her without any difficulty.

Gaines struck Lefebvre. Lefebvre, falling back, took the girl with him. She landed heavily, striking her head against the lower edge of the fireplace. She was killed instantly.

In the panic that followed, he and Lefebvre had agreed to take her body out beyond the town limits. They wouldn't take it too far, maybe a hundred yards or so, and they would do whatever was necessary to make it appear that she'd been savaged and killed by an animal. Lefebvre had taken a poker from the fireplace. He had with him a heavy knife, serrated on one edge. Using these and rocks that were to hand, they cut off the girl's fingers, her nose, her ears too. They cut deep gashes in her belly and her thighs. Lefebvre also used his knife to cut out one of Lisette's eyes.

'A bird,' Gaines said. 'He wanted to make it look as if a bird had taken her eye. There was something else. Lefebvre didn't cry. He seemed to feel nothing. He didn't love her as I did.'

The second girl was also the daughter of people who ran the boarding house in Jasperville. Fauth had to look at a map of the very north-eastern part of the province. He'd never heard of the place, but there it was.

According to Gaines, Anne-Louise Fournier had spurned Lefebvre's advances. Lefebvre wanted to hurt her. He wanted to rape her and hurt her.

Gaines had tried to stop him. He'd done everything he could to persuade Lefebvre to leave the girl alone, but Lefebvre was obsessed. He said that if Gaines didn't help him, he would tell Sergeant Thibault about the killing of Lisette Roy.

What could Gaines do? He was trapped. So they did as Lefebvre asked. They took Anne-Louise and Lefebvre tried to rape her but he couldn't. Then he killed her and he made Gaines help him as they tore her stomach open and threw her innards out across the snow.

Fauth listened. He recorded everything. He didn't interrupt Gaines, save to encourage him to give further and more specific details. It wasn't long before Fauth knew that Gaines was the prime mover, that Lefebvre had been nothing more than an unfortunate victim of Gaines' powers of manipulation. Perhaps Lefebvre had only been involved in those first two killings, or perhaps he'd been involved in every murder that happened in this town called Jasperville.

Robert Gaines knew that Jean-Paul Lefebvre was dead. Lefebvre would never be able to counter Gaines' testimony or present his own explanation of what had occurred. Gaines believed he had the advantage, but the precision with which he detailed each event, each girl, their names, their physical appearance, the circumstances of their death, was something that could only come from someone who had been directly responsible.

The final detail that gave Fauth complete certainty that Gaines was the dominant player was something that Gaines mentioned in passing. He had fulfilled an administrative function for Canada Iron, something to do with the production of shift records. Fauth didn't understand it completely, but Gaines boasted about how easy it had been to change shift documents so Lefebvre appeared to be absent from work on the days when the girls were murdered. Fauth let it slide. He didn't draw Gaines' attention to it. Ego took over. Gaines was intent on demonstrating his own remarkable intellect and cunning, meanwhile digging a hole deep enough to bury himself for ever.

Only Robert Gaines would know how significant a part Jean-Paul Lefebvre had played, and that was something Lefebvre had taken to the grave.

Beyond Jasperville, Gaines became more reluctant to speak. After the move to Labrador City in 1992, he'd been alone. Here there was no one to offset the culpability. Fauth already had him bang to rights for the murder of Melanie Perrin. It took another two days of coaxing, persuading, unrelated conversation, misdirection, even presenting Gaines with tokens he'd kept

– hairbands, Amanda Webb's driver's licence, the key chain from Campus West, a dried and crumpled cigarette butt in a plastic baggie, a train ticket from Labrador to Fermont – to break apart the stoic façade that he'd thus far maintained.

On Saturday, 11 December, *Le Voix de Québec* ran a four-person byline feature regarding the Gaines murders. Spanning seven pages, it was as detailed as it was lurid. Gaines had been christened by the media. He was now known as the *Wabush Wendigo*.

Jack saw it, and realized that this was the first time he'd ever seen a photograph of Robert Gaines. The resemblance to his father was striking, and yet Gaines the younger wore the haggard, haunted demeanour of a man unused to sunlight. What struck Jack was the man's utterly inconspicuous banality. There was nothing memorable about him, and perhaps that was the very reason he'd gone undetected for so long.

Beginning with a total of nine murders that had taken place while Gaines was living in Labrador City, the editorial regaled the reader with the blunt and horrific nature of the perpetrator's depravity and craven homicidal thirst. Unsolved murders across five separate locations and two provinces were finally closed, and the grieving families could at least gain some small comfort in the closure afforded by Gaines' confessions.

Before Labrador City, the article explained – in the period from 1972 to 1990 – Gaines had committed a further seven murders in a far north-eastern industrial town called Jasperville.

Jack stopped reading. His heart stopped, too.

He turned to the final pages of the editorial to find photographs of each of Gaines' victims displayed in date sequence.

Lisette was there, as was Anne-Louise, also Fleur Dillard, Estelle Poirier, Virginie Fortin, Génèvieve Beaulieu and Madeleine Desjardins.

Thérèse Bergeron was not listed.

A vast chasm opened beneath Jack, and he could do nothing to stop himself falling.

54

It had taken another eight days for Jack's visitation request to be approved. It was Sunday, 19 December. On the walls of the waiting area, a thin paper banner announcing *Merry Christmas* had been hung. It was the only decoration. The faded colour of the paper and the yellowing tape that held it suggested that it had been there since the previous year.

Already it had been determined that Calvis was mentally unfit to stand trial for the murder of Jean-Paul Lefebvre. In fact, it was true to say that the world knew very little of Calvis Devereaux, nor was there any great interest or concern for his fate. He was to be absorbed into the national mental healthcare programme for the criminally insane. His ramblings and non-sequitur monologues were inadequate grist for the tabloid mill. They wanted abductions, rape and teenage sex murders, and Robert Gaines was giving them more than enough to satiate their immediate requirements.

Where Calvis would go had yet to be decided. There were numerous facilities with the resources to keep him detained. What would become of him – more to the point, *who* he would become – once they'd buckled him into a chemical straitjacket and taken him apart with opinionated evaluations, Jack didn't know. He would visit him, of course, and he would do his very best to be the brother Calvis needed. Nevertheless, he knew that Calvis would be pretty much alone from here on out. It broke his heart, as if it needed breaking again, but he was up against the machinery of the state.

Jack knew that was his one chance to get through to Calvis, to ask him the question that needed asking. The fact that he already knew the answer mattered not at all. He needed to hear it from Calvis's lips. He needed to know, and know without doubt. Only then could he go back to Carine and tell her the complete story.

Jack had called her many times during his time away from Jasperville. Their conversations had been brief and noncommittal. At one point Carine had asked him why he kept calling.

'Because you're the only person who has the slightest understanding of what this means. You're the only person in the world who I can talk to about what happened back there and what's happening now.'

'You've never asked me if I wanted to know, Jacques.'

'If you want me to stop—'

'No,' she interjected. 'I want to know.'

Jack had stayed a further week in Québec City, and then returned to Montréal. Work had granted him unpaid leave, the arrangement to be reviewed in February. He'd seen Ludo and Florence. He'd even seen Caroline Vallat. Their exchange had been pleasant but insignificant. She was in a new relationship. She seemed happy. She wished Jack well, and he expressed the same sentiment in return.

Jack knew, even before that final trip to see Calvis, that he wouldn't be returning to the same house, the same job, the same life. It was not that recent events had changed him, but rather that they'd allowed him to see – perhaps for the first time in his adult life – the person he could still become if he let go of the past.

It was a long shot, and he knew it, but it seemed to be the only shot he had.

55

Jack sat across from Calvis. Nothing but three feet of plain wooden table separated them. Nevertheless, he felt as if he was looking down at his younger brother from a very great height.

A guard stood with his back to the door. A second guard was stationed in the corridor beyond. Calvis was in handcuffs, a chain securing them through a hole in the table to a hasp embedded in the concrete floor beneath. He had been seated there when Jack arrived, and Jack would leave before they unlocked the cuffs and returned him to his cell.

There was to be no physical contact, no exchange of any object or item, nothing but twenty minutes of conversation.

Jack didn't know what drugs Calvis had been given, but he seemed to be drifting back and forth between where he was and wherever he believed himself to be.

Ten minutes had already passed.

Despite Jack's best efforts, Calvis had yet to say a word.

It was another five before Jack decided that the only way he might get through to his brother was by reaching way back into the past they'd shared.

'Hey, Kiddo,' he said. 'What's happening with you? What's going on with you, Little Man?'

Calvis half smiled. His expression changed ever so slightly, and he started turning towards Jack.

'You wanna go up the merc and thieve some chocolate?'

371

Calvis smiled, and then he laughed, and for the very first time there was something in his eyes that suggested he might actually be hearing what Jack was saying.

'You wanna go with me, Shortie?'

'Don't call me Shortie,' Calvis slurred. It was as if he was waking up, his words still submerged in a dream, everything in slow-motion.

'Why not, Shortie?'

Calvis laughed. 'Because I said so, Rabbit.'

Jack smiled. He leaned forward ever so slightly.

'You see Pa, Calvis?'

Calvis frowned. 'No. Why? Is he lookin' for me?'

'He said he wants you to go find Juliette. He says she's gone someplace and he can't find her.'

Calvis closed his eyes. 'I told him.'

'You told him already?'

'I told him already.'

'Where d'you say she was?'

'Up at the rail terminal.'

Jack's mouth was dry. He could feel his heart hammering furiously in his chest.

'You told him she was up at the terminal with Thérèse? Is that what you did, Cal?'

'That's what I did. Didn't know, okay? I didn't know what would happen? I just did what I was asked. I found her. I said where she was. It don't make me a bad person.'

Jack heard the words, saw the expression. It was like watching a frightened little boy.

'Did he go on up there to bring her back, Cal?' Jack asked.

'I don't know what he did, Rabbit. I don't know what he did.'

'Did he hurt her, Cal? Was Pa the one who hurt Thérèse?'

Cal stopped moving. He lowered his head. He started to sob,

and before long he was struggling to breathe as his whole body was wracked with grief.

'Did he go out there, Cal? To the rail terminal?'

Cal's sobbing slowed up. He turned his head away from Jack.

'You didn't do anything wrong,' Jack said. 'It wasn't you that hurt her, Cal.'

'But I told him, Rabbit. I told him where she was.'

'I know, Kiddo, but it wasn't your fault. You didn't know. You couldn't have known.'

Calvis didn't move for a long time. Jack could hear every breath he took. His eyes were bloodshot, his face streaked with tears. Everything about him was so very wretched and pathetic.

Jack wanted nothing more than to put his arms around his little brother and take him to safety – away from all of this, away from the past, away from the violence and madness that had punctuated every aspect of their life together.

But he couldn't. He had to let him go.

The guard at the door took a step forward. 'Time,' he said.

'A little longer,' Jack said. 'Could we just have a few more minutes?'

'No, monsieur. That won't be possible.'

Jack took a breath. He started to get up.

He looked down at Calvis.

Calvis didn't move, didn't look up, didn't say a word.

'I have to go now,' Jack said. 'I will come and see you, I promise.'

Calvis half smiled. 'You said that last time.'

'I know,' Jack said, 'but this time I won't break my promise.'

Jack started around the table in the direction of the door. As he passed Calvis, he moved suddenly, reaching down to put his arms around his younger brother's shoulders.

'No contact!' the guard barked.

'It wasn't your fault, Calvis. Don't ever forget that.'

373

Jack let go. He stood back. He raised his hands apologetically.

The guard knocked on the door. The second guard looked through the porthole, and then the door was unlocked.

Jack made it to the threshold. He glanced back.

Calvis was looking directly at him.

'See you after school, Rabbit,' he said, and then he smiled like a child.

56

Friday, 24 December

Jack stood at the side of the rail track for a good fifteen minutes. The snow was banked high on either side. The ice sat in between the sleepers, hard like stone. The cold was beyond bitter. It wound its way through layers of wool and fleece, and then beneath skin and muscle to find the bones inside. It was every winter he'd ever spent in this godforsaken place. It was his past, and the past would never change, but the future – perhaps – might offer something different.

The rail terminal. Thérèse. Juliette. All of it a thousand years ago, yet still like yesterday.

Jack smoked one more cigarette, and then he turned back towards Jasperville and started walking.

By the time he reached the boarding house he was out of breath. He kicked the snow off his boots in the vestibule, waited for the outer door to close firmly, and then opened the door into the reception area.

Martin was at the desk. 'Hey, Jack.'

'How goes it, Martin?'

'Dead as it could get. Christmas, you know? I mean, given any choice at all, who the hell would spend Christmas out here, right?'

'Crazy people, that's who. Your ma in?'

'She is. I'll get her.'

Jack had been away close to eight weeks. He'd last spoken to

Carine after his visit with Calvis. He'd told her the truth, that Robert Gaines was not responsible for Thérèse's death. She'd taken it stoically, but what had happened after the call he didn't know.

He turned to see Carine coming down the stairs.

'Why didn't you say you were coming? What are you doing here?'

'Keeping my word,' Jack said.

'Keeping your word?'

He looked down at his boots, then across toward the window. He felt like a foolish teenager.

'I said I'd come back and rescue you.'

Carine paused, raised her eyebrows. 'And if I don't need rescuing?'

'Then maybe you need someone who remembers how to paint walls and make beds.'

Jack thought she smiled, but he couldn't be sure.

He waited for her to say something, his fragile heart like a bird in his chest.

'I'm not looking for anyone,' she said. 'Then again, the spring might get busy for us.'

'So a second pair of hands…'

'Leave your boots there, Jacques,' she said. 'And there's some fresh coffee in the back kitchen.'

Credits

R.J. Ellory and Orion Fiction would like to thank everyone at Orion who worked on the publication of *The Darkest Season* in the UK.

Editorial
Emad Akhtar
Celia Killen

Copy editor
Clare Wallis

Proof reader
Linda Joyce

Contracts
Anne Goddard

Design
Debbie Holmes
Joanna Ridley
Nick May

Marketing
Lucy Cameron

Editorial Management
Charlie Panayiotou
Jane Hughes
Alice Davis

Finance
Jasdip Nandra
Afeera Ahmed
Elizabeth Beaumont
Sue Baker

Audio
Paul Stark
Jake Alderson

Production
Ruth Sharvell

Publicity
Patricia Deveer

Rights
Susan Howe
Krystyna Kujawinska
Jessica Purdue
Richard King
Louise Henderson

Operations
Jo Jacobs
Sharon Willis
Lisa Pryde

Sales
Jen Wilson
Esther Waters
Victoria Laws
Rachael Hum
Frances Doyle
Georgina Cutler
Anna Egelstaff